Moon Lake

Other Novels by Wayne Tefs
Figures on a Wharf
The Cartier Street Contract
The Canasta Players
Dickie
Home Free
Red Rock

MOON LAKE

a novel by

WAYNE TEFS

TURNSTONE PRESS

Moon Lake
copyright © 2000 Wayne Tefs

published by
Turnstone Press
607–100 Arthur Street
Artspace Building
Winnipeg, Manitoba
Canada R3B 1H3
www.TurnstonePress.com

All rights reserved. No part of this book may be reproduced by any means without the prior written permission of the publisher. Permission to photocopy shall be directed to the Canadian Copyright Licensing Agency, Toronto.

Turnstone Press gratefully acknowledges the assistance of The Canada Council for the Arts, the Manitoba Arts Council and the Book Publishing Industry Development Program, Government of Canada, for our publishing activities.

Canada

Cover photograph: Karen Barry

Design: Manuela Dias

This book was printed and bound in Canada by Friesens for Turnstone Press.

Canadian Cataloguing in Publication Data

Tefs, Wayne, 1947–

Moon Lake

ISBN 0-88801-251-9

I. Title.

PS8589.E37 M66 2000   C813'.54   C00-920186-6
PR9199.3.T4 M66 2000

*to the memory of my father, Armin Alexander,
and to my son, Andrew Armin*

Acknowledgements

Thanks to Bob Stewart, for his useful information regarding the flora and fauna of the Whiteshell and surround; to Kelly Bekeris for lengthy chats about the landscape we both cherish; to Birk Sproxton, for his shared enthusiasm for the rocks and waters of the Shield; to Sharon Tefs, for remembering history long-buried; to Mark Golden, Professor of Classics at the University of Winnipeg; to Ralph Friesen, for listening to rambles over coffee; to Kristen and Andrew, for all the good reasons; to Manuela Dias for support and enthusiasm; to Pat Sanders, for a great eye; to Geoffrey Ursell, for the gentle push into the crime zone; to Edmond Beaudry, for his knowledge of the terrain; to Lori Janower, at the Mines Library, for digging out the maps; to Phil Hansen, trivialist; to Liisa Tella, student of languages; to Armin Tefs, who preserved the story.

For fictional purposes two areas of eastern Manitoba have been collapsed and melded into one, and some place names altered or adapted, for all of which I apologize.

PART ONE

the croaking raven doth bellow for revenge
—Hamlet

THE SOUND OF LAFLAMME'S VOICE made her start. "Get the boxes I set aside." A bark. A command waiting to be contradicted. "And be damn quick about it, boy." She lifted her head but only a fraction of an inch and peered into the gloom of the long, low, and overcrowded room to the shelves along the far wall where they were stood side by side, father and son, restocking shelves.

LaFlamme's massive head under the hat, Roger's dark hair.

She had thought things were going well.

It was the Saturday of the Labour Day weekend, 1967, the Centennial year. Though the flag outside Moon Lake Trading Post was not the bright, new, red and white Maple Leaf but the British Ensign. Day was approaching dusk. Shadows from the dry goods display in the front window fell all the way to the back of the store, fingering the counter where she was sitting and reading, since no one had come into the store for over an hour. Motes of dust danced in the air. Besides her and them, no one else was in the room. The clock behind her ticked. She heard the jangle of cutlery from the adjoining kitchen.

Roger flinched, looking up at LaFlamme. "Get," LaFlamme barked.

He meant boxes of tinned goods. Archie could have done it, or the Finn, both within calling distance, or even LaFlamme himself. They were heavy and bulky, wax-coated cardboard boxes containing twenty-four tins of tomatoes, peaches, whatever was running low on the shelves. When he had carried one up from the crawl space earlier LaFlamme had rested with the box propped on the counter for a moment while he breathed heavily, red in the cheeks, and he had stared at her until she looked away. So he knew the boxes were heavy and awkward. But it was to Roger he said, "Get," and when the boy blinked the way he did, LaFlamme glanced about, anticipating contradiction with a dark look, but Cassie was in the kitchen, rattling plates in preparation for supper, and the girl had her eyes fixed on the book she was reading. Not that he would have noticed her—or cared what she thought.

"Get," LaFlamme hissed. Reflexively, he pushed the hat up his forehead.

Roger's boots scraped across the floor. She heard the squeak of the swinging door as he left the room, then the sounds of distant clambering as he lowered himself down the wooden ladder to the crawl space. LaFlamme stood with his hands on his hips, surveying the prospect out of the window. In his line of vision: the field that Mortimer Mann had been harrowing all afternoon with the Fordson tractor, twenty bushels the acre of oats they had got in from that field less than a month ago; and beyond that field, the clearing field where Mann and the Finn hauled out tree stumps and picked stones when not busy doing whatever else LaFlamme had in mind on a given day.

She watched him shift his gaze farther out, eyeing the path that ran along the clearing field out toward the deer meadow. Cassie had told her he meant to put that into cultivation too. He was a man of plans, a man of ambitions, who was always thinking ahead, calculating. He was still now, though: the broad back, the bull neck, the meaty hands that clamped on your shoulder and squeezed until you cried out in pain but dare not because he would hit you. Or worse. He was absently running his fingers over the tops of the tins on the top shelf. She prayed he would not scrape up dust.

She took in a shallow breath. Must of damp wood, the pong of new rubber boots from the nearby shelves filled her nostrils. LaFlamme's thoughts were far away. She could tell by the way he drummed his fingers on the tins without looking at them.

The swinging door creaked on its hinges and Roger stumbled into the room. His face was red from exertion. The lock of black hair that curled across his forehead had fallen forward into his eyes. He glanced at her, smiling: see, he had done it, his blinking eyes were telling her, and at that moment, just as he passed the counter, the box he was carrying tilted sideways. He stumbled and lost his balance. She heard him gasp. Then half way along the aisle he dropped to his knees, cradling the box, trying to prevent its awkward and askew bulk from going down; she could almost hear him praying, but one corner of the waxed box struck the floor, and then came the nearly inaudible crunch of cardboard on hardwood, the rattle of tins.

He's for it now, the girl thought, not just for this but for the other, mostly for the other. LaFlamme had just been waiting for an excuse. She shrank into herself, tried not to peer over the top of the cash register. She licked her lips. She could feel her heart in her throat. It was like an animal running loose inside her.

"Fuck," LaFlamme said, addressing no one in particular. "Other men have sons who do what they ask, but what do I have?—a spastic, an idiot." The boy had been told many times about how easily the tins dented. Whatever was inside went bad, some chemical reaction or other when the coated tin cracked. Lost profits for LaFlamme. They all had heard it many times; they had had it screamed in their faces.

There was a broom leaning against the shelves. LaFlamme grabbed it. The boy looked up wide-eyed from the floor, still on his knees, still cradling the waxy cardboard box. LaFlamme struck out at his head as if he was hitting a baseball, a clean swing, one dull sound. Thunk. When the head of the broom stuck the boy's skull, the wooden shaft snapped and the head fell to the floor. The boy grunted. LaFlamme looked at the broken shaft in his hands, splintered and sharp at one end. The girl looked away, trying not to cry out. "Fuck," LaFlamme said again, a kind of wonder in his voice but rage too, as if he could not believe anything in the world, animate or not, could defy him that way. He had meant to beat the boy using the mass of bundled broom bristles to teach him, but now all he had was a spindly, broken stick.

"God damn," LaFlamme said, touching the hat again.

She did not see the blows. She heard them, felt them. She did not count, but when he flung the shattered shaft aside with a clatter, she saw LaFlamme's shadow pass and heard his boots strike the wood, and then she heard the hinges creak and the door to the mud room farther along slam shut and then the room was silent. Only her heart, only her raspy breathing.

She waited for a few moments. From her angle she could not see to where Roger had fallen at the end of aisle. If he was not hurt badly he would stagger to his feet soon. But it was silent along the shelves. She glanced toward the door where LaFlamme had gone. What if he came back and found she was not at her post behind the cash register? She waited, counting ten. Inhaling deeply. She could smell the smoked leather of the moccasins Archie Cloud had brought in earlier, the shiny red Mac apples on the counter to her right.

She licked her lips and eased down from the stool, and then came around from behind the counter into the store proper on tiptoe.

Roger lay stretched out on the floor, head thrown back, that lock of hair trailing on the hardwood. The backs of his hands, she saw as she neared, were criss-crossed in bruises, he must have locked them on his skull for protection. There was a pool of blood on the floor. She groaned. It was as if a wound were tearing open inside her. She kneeled beside him and lifted his head into her lap. His eyes were glassy. Blood oozed out from the collar of his shirt. She had not witnessed the beating. Had he been stabbed in the throat? There were flat, ugly marks on his face, and his thick hair was matted with blood. He groaned and one arm twitched the way hers did just before she dropped into sleep. She looked around. The splintered broom handle rolled under a shelf when LaFlamme had flung it aside. Streaks of blood on its gleaming, polished wood.

The girl refused to cry out. She rocked forward, emitting a high-pitched sound, a wild animal about to die. She wasn't sure whether she was weeping or vomiting. This was Cassie's fault, this was Cassie's failure.

When Cassie finished sponging the cuts on Roger's face, she dabbed at them with gauze, wiping away the dried blood. She had bandaged the wound on his neck and cleaned the cuts in his hair. For a few frightening moments he had gurgled and lost his breath, but that was before Cassie sponged his face and neck with cold water. He was breathing easier now.

Cassie looked from one daughter to the other. Virginia licked her lips. Ruth's dark eyes flashed from face to face but the set of her mouth betrayed nothing. She had been cleaning in the bunkhouse when Virginia came to get her. Her fingers were red from soap, her apron spotted with cleaning powders, her long dark hair tied in back with a red ribbon that matched the gash of lipstick around her mouth.

Cassie said flatly, "He'll be all right."

When Cassie touched the wounds on his face, Roger flinched and opened his eyes. "Head hurts," he whispered. "Neck." Flecks of blood had caked in the corners of his mouth. Cassie picked up the sponge when she saw them.

"I'll get aspirin," Virginia said.

Roger closed his eyes but in a moment opened them again. There was pain in his squint. His eyelids flickered as he searched for Ruth's gaze, inquiring.

"Gone," Ruth said, holding his hazel eyes with a dark look. She glanced in the direction of the door where LaFlamme had disappeared.

Roger glanced that way too, then closed his eyes again.

He sighed. His breathing was not normal.

Virginia's shoes clumped over the hardwood.

Ruth said, "We should call the doctor."

"He'll be all right," Cassie said. She had been kneeling on the floor over Roger, his neck propped against one of her thighs. She made to stand up now, shifting her bulk backward from Roger as she released his head, and he was forced to roll sideways to support himself. There were streaks of blood on Cassie's fingers, a large smear running up one wrist under the cuff of her white blouse. Her face was flushed and her brow was slick with sweat.

"That's all you ever tell us," Ruth said, stamping one foot. "It'll be all right. Shit."

"Don't start," Cassie said.

"Well, it isn't," Ruth said. "It is not all bloody right."

"It's all right," Cassie repeated but not with conviction.

Ruth snorted. She said, "Some day...." But her voice trailed off.

Roger was resting on one elbow. Virginia had come up with a glass of water and aspirins. He blinked once and then threw them back into his mouth; he closed his eyes and swallowed the water. He muttered, "Bastard, I'm going to kill him."

"Don't ever say that," Cassie hissed, leaning over. "He's your father."

"And you're our mother," Ruth hissed back. "You should protect him, not be...."

"Us," Virginia said in a shaking voice. She was standing between Ruth and Cassie and looked quickly at Ruth and then dropped her gaze to the floor.

"One of these days," Roger said, emphasizing each word. "You'll see, the bastard, I'll lay for him and I'll fix him." His eyes closed and he looked as if he were going to pass out again, but in a moment they flickered open. "Bastard," he whispered.

Ruth's dark eyes flashed from Cassie's face to Roger's before settling on something out of the window. The last of the sun was peeking through the pines to the west; golden beams dispersed by the dusty glass of the window formed a spectrum of blues and pinks. A hawk swooped low over the trees and drifted toward Moon Lake, screeching.

"Hush," Cassie said, "you do something, they'll take you away." She wiped her hands on her apron but kept her eyes fixed on the floor. "You're talking crazy."

"He's the crazy one," Roger said, growing bolder. "I'll lay for him."

"Stop now," Cassie said, "just stop that talk. He's your father."

Ruth stood in front of Cassie, breathing through her nose, waiting for her gaze to lift, waiting for Cassie, but Cassie dare not look at either of her daughters. Cassie wiped her hands on her apron again and said to Virginia, "Go set the table." She placed one hand lightly on the girl's shoulder and gave her a nudge in the direction of the kitchen.

"He's not my father," Virginia whispered. She was hanging back, the fingers of one hand pinching a fold of Ruth's apron.

"Nor mine," Ruth whispered.

But Cassie pretended not to hear them.

When Virginia came back into the store they were standing at the door wiping tins, two shadows with the blue-black haze of dusk behind them. Ruth was talking quietly. Roger's head was tilted down and bobbing, as if he were agreeing silently to what Ruth was saying. Virginia had something to tell them but she stopped before coming out from behind the counter. An inner voice told her to do this. One hand rested on the wooden countertop, fingers caressing the thin steel yardstick kept there to measure bolts of cloth.

They were speaking in subdued voices. Roger said, *mines*, but the rest of what he said was lost in the sounds coming in the screen door. Someone had opened it. A breeze was blowing from the deer meadow toward the lake, tossing the branches of the trees, tugging the first leaves free, and carrying the earth smells of the breaking into the store. A loose piece of tin rattled somewhere. A loon called on the lake.

Barker was behind the counter, curled up on the throw rug. She was eleven and had white hairs on her muzzle and dragged one foot when she walked. She thumped her tail once and looked up at the girl.

Ruth stopped wiping the tins and placed her hand on Roger's shoulder. He looked up and into her face: for a moment they were silhouettes like the paper cut-outs Virginia had played with as a child. Ruth said something but all she could make out was *better dead*. She strained forward but heard no more words. Only the whistle of wind in the trees, the rattle of leaves, only the thudding of blood in her temples.

They were always doing this, conferring together, leaving her out. Ruth was eighteen and Roger sixteen. She was fourteen. Virginia did not think the not quite two years between him and her made such a big difference. But he shut her out, even though Ruth sometimes talked to her about grown-up stuff: how to dance with boys you did not like, periods, protecting yourself, if it came to that. But this was different.

Still, they did not know what she had seen. Heard.

She made to step forward. Cassie wanted them to supper. LaFlamme had not come in, but if he did and they were not in their seats he would pound the table with his fist until the cutlery rattled, and maybe hit someone. They all three should be at the table. That's when she heard her name: Ginny.

She felt her heart in her throat again. She eased forward.

That was Ruth, whispering. And then Roger said *the city*.

He ran his free hand back through his hair and then touched the bandage Cassie had applied to the gash on his throat.

Ruth said *no*, and then after a pause, *maybe, maybe*.

They both looked out the screen, nodding. The horizon was a series of purple and orange bands running from north to south, the kind of sky Virginia sometimes sat and looked at for hours. There would be a harvest moon that night. If you stood at the twin rocks it would paint Moon Lake golden, like a plate. The fish would surface and the herons flap past on their way to the narrows, and then your heart would go still.

They were not thinking about that.

Virginia watched them a moment longer. Her fingers moved along the yardstick, feeling the markings etched in the steel. If you snapped it with your wrist, it made a sound: *boing*. She had imagined hurting him with that yardstick, swinging it at his bull-like head and making the blood flow from the fat creases at the bottom of his thick neck. Sometimes when no one was in the store she picked the yardstick up and smacked it down hard on the countertop. It made a hollow sound and vibrated in her hand so her palm tingled.

She listened to their whisperings, straining to hear.

Behind her Virginia heard a door squeak on its hinges. LaFlamme. She could sense his brutish body moving through the building. She coughed into her hand, as if she had just come into the room.

They turned as one, startled, guilty.

Ruth said something to him. It may have been *soon*. Then they both came through the shadows of the room towards her.

Alexander Mann was staring absently out of the train window. The boy had fallen asleep again, with his mouth open. His head was twisted back on the seat opposite Alexander. Tufts of his red hair stuck straight up. It had been a long day for a boy of ten, a day of meaningless stops at places so small the conductor had to throw a wooden stool off at the door before he could climb down with the bag of mail or bundle of newspapers. It had been a day of sandwiches and coffee from a thermos, a day passed in an empty, stuffy compartment while the slow train poked through scrub bush and granite hills and swampy lake after swampy lake. They had seen little except stunted spruces, bulrushes, blackbirds, ripples from fish jumping in the water. Peter was impressed by that. He wanted his father to teach him about pike and walleye: which were easy to catch, which tasted best. Could he have a rod and line of his own?

Now they were nearly at the end of the line: Moon Lake. The Shield.

It was a foreign country to them. Alexander had been raised on a farm on the prairie and Peter in Winnipeg where Alexander had managed a small hardware store. They were used to open spaces, a big sky. Here the land closed in. The railroad tracks ran through the humped grey rocks of the Shield, disappearing around bends of sheared granite. Pines towered overhead, stunted swamp spruce were packed one on top of another against a backdrop of tangled underbrush. Occasionally there was an opening in the bush for one of the tiny lakes; the eye saw something more than a blur of tree trunks rushing past the windows; then miles more of scrub and grey granite rocks sheared into slabs where the narrow rail track bed had been blasted through the Precambrian Shield.

Moon Lake was a small lake that flowed into a larger one. He had seen it on a map. There was a narrows, it looked like. Then the big lake to the east.

Alexander's older brother, Mortimer, had said over the phone that there was work at Moon Lake, outdoor labour: painting buildings, picking stones, clearing fields, and then when the ground froze, cutting wood. Hard work, but the kind a man who had just lost a business to bankruptcy could use. The kind of work to take the mind off things, especially the mind of a man who had buried a wife and was raising a son alone.

Alexander had often relied on Mortimer. He had wanted to hear something good and Mortimer's voice had been reassuring. There was a lake where he and Peter could fish. It was quiet and beautiful in a rugged way. A cheap place to live, the boy could have the run of the fields and forest and learn to hunt. There were manly arts to master in a locale far removed from the places where they had endured so much pain together. It was clear on the telephone that Mortimer was talking the place up, but it sounded okay.

There was something about the man he worked for, though, LaFlamme, or maybe the woman, his wife—something Mortimer was not saying that made Alexander uneasy. He had wanted to ask about that but Mort had cut their conversation short. Maybe because long-distance calls cost money, maybe because the phone was in the store and LaFlamme had been hovering nearby.

Maybe something else. It had always been that way with Mort.

Probably the man, LaFlamme, who sounded to be a hard case.

Alexander had worked for hard men: a farmer at Carman, and later at the coal yard in the north end of the city. These were dirty jobs involving long hours and danger. One harvest time at the farm, the boy he was working with lost an arm in a power take-off. Alexander was only twenty at the time, the boy on vacation from school. It was because of the farmer, who yelled at them and made the boy nervous at his work. The coal yard was another thing. The load at the coal yard had tipped onto a guy one morning and when the yard manager bundled him into the back of his car to take him to the hospital he had said *keep shovelling*. And Alexander had. He did not shy away from hard work but he was not afraid of any man, either.

He worried sometimes about his boy, though, who tossed in his sleep, called out his mother's name. He was too young to be without a woman in his life; he had not been raised hard like his father. The fingers of one hand were twitching in his sleep. Such delicate skin. His mouth was open, emitting faint popping noises. He was wearing a white T-shirt and there were goosebumps on his arms. Alexander wondered if he should throw the thin jacket over him but that might wake him, and they were almost at Moon Lake.

Alexander stared out the window. The sun was about to set. They were passing another of the tiny swampy lakes and the fish were jumping, making ripples on the surface of the water. The water looked cold. The sky was nearly clear. There were a few streaky clouds above the tops of the pines. A heron stood in the reeds. A pair of mallards scudded low over the bulrushes. It seemed peaceful but lonely and sad at the same time. Or maybe that was just his mood.

He could have used a smoke but in closed spaces it bothered the boy.

Alexander closed his eyes and rested his head back against the seat. For as long as he could remember he had always loved the sounds of trains: the rattling of steel wheels, the huff of engines, the long lonesome call in the still night air. When he was a boy it had meant the dawn was coming. He did not know what it meant for them now. Was there such a thing as a new life? He looked at the tuft of Peter's red hair and felt something big and wild in his chest he had not felt for a long time.

Alexander studied his reflection in the window. He looked older than his thirty years but he still had all his hair, and the fresh air, the sun would take the lines and pallor from his skin. He was still a young man. Mort had made that point again and again. Fresh start. This would be good for him. It would be good for the boy too. Maybe in the winter they could clear a spot on the lake and play hockey. Mort too.

Mort said he would meet them at the train but if he could not it was a short walk down the path to the trading post. The bunkhouse was in back, there was a bed for each of them. It would be good to see Mort again, to work together as they had when they left home, hardly older than Peter, boys, really, but that was how the world was in the fifties, you had to take the bull by the horns, as Mort said. It was a different world now.

The train was late. It was almost dark when they pulled up beside the ramshackle station with the blistered and peeling sign: Moon Lake. The train was always late and Alexander had expected that. He had not expected the mosquitoes, though. They were larger than in the city and moved slower, but there were many more, forming clouds around their heads. He put the bags down on the ground and swatted at them with his hands. He told Peter to do the same.

The train had chugged back down the track almost before the conductor had thrown off the bundle of papers and they had descended onto the platform in the cool of the evening. It was silent at the edge of the forest, and eerie.

Where was Mortimer?

The boy looked behind them at the building, hands on hips. In the half-light of dusk it seemed ghostly, this station house that had been abandoned for a long time, with birds nesting in the eaves troughing and shingles creaking in the wind. Windows were cracked, the red paint was peeling, the screen had been ripped out of the front door. Mort was not there. He had said he would meet them. But the train was late.

Alexander looked at the boy. He had put on the light jacket and was swatting at the mosquitoes with both hands. His hair was tousled. He was probably hungry but they had eaten the sandwiches and drunk the last of the coffee hours ago. There was no point in waiting around while the mosquitoes bit at them. Now the sun had set, it was getting darker by the moment. Mort might have been detained. He had hinted as much.

Alexander needed a smoke but the mosquitoes were landing on them in swarms, stinging their exposed flesh.

"Pick up the bags," he told the boy. "We'll walk." Mort had said it was just a short distance from the station to the store.

The small clearing they were in formed a half moon around one side of the station. There was a narrow path running into the forest ahead of them, single file. He picked up his bags and started down the path. Peter followed behind him.

The ground was soft and spongy. He had expected the granite of the Shield underfoot but then he remembered the low spots, the muskeg. Mort had told him once you could track deer for miles. He listened to Peter's laboured breathing and called back to him, "All right?" The boy grunted. The path wound through the woods and dense scrub, making sudden sharp turns to avoid trees. Roots crisscrossed the trail. The heels of his shoes struck the roots or slipped suddenly on a surface worn to slippery. Behind him Peter stumbled and cursed.

He wanted to call back to him, *it's an adventure*, but he did not.

In the pale light coming from above Alexander could make out dogwood between the stunted spruces and snarls of hemlock growing further back in the poplars. There was deadfall everywhere: rotten stumps, uprooted trees, brown tendrils of fern. Near the path the grass grew waist high. That must have been where the crickets hid, whistling until they approached, then suddenly silent. Scotch thistles stood to shoulder height, reaching out their barbs and snagging on Alexander's clothing. Everywhere the smell of vegetation dying and rotting. Or maybe a stagnant pool of water. Alexander shifted the duffel bag to an easier place on his shoulder and found a better grip for the cardboard suitcase in his other hand. The walk was longer than he had anticipated.

The mosquitoes were not as bad in the forest as they had been in the clearing near the derelict station. That was odd; he thought they'd be worse in the woods. Maybe they had gone to ground for the night.

There were other sounds above their occasional buzzings: the chatter of night birds, skitterings in the leaves of the bushes, in the far distance what sounded like voices shouting or calling, strange in the quiet night. They trudged over rocks and uneven terrain, silent and grimly determined. Just off the path there was a sudden brief crashing of tree limbs and a ruckus in the undergrowth.

Behind him Peter said, "What is it?"

Alexander stopped and peered into the trees. "A deer?"

"It sounded more like a bear. They kill people, Dad."

"More likely a deer or a raccoon. Something small anyway. Sounds are amplified in the bush."

"Dad, I'm scared. These woods, you can't see up to the sky because the treetops reach so high. It's dark tonight, you can't see three feet off the path, things are crashing in the trees. I have the crazy feeling something's watching us or following us. It's spooky. I don't like it." Peter said it all in one breathless rush and then let out a puff of air. In the dusky light Alexander saw the boy's eyes were misted over, but whether from sweat or tears he could not tell.

Alexander had been thinking the same things himself. The woods were vast and tangled with more fallen trees and snarled roots than he had imagined. Impenetrable to the eye. Sinister. His heart had been pumping with adrenaline ever since he'd realized he'd lost his bearings. He didn't have a compass. If they were really lost, they might have to shelter under a tree for the night. Where was Mort? He drew a deep breath. "You'll like it better in the morning," he said. "The bush won't seem so on top of you." They plunged on.

"Bobcats," Peter said behind him. "They lurk in the branches and drop onto people walking below."

"That's jaguars. There are no jaguars in North America. And bobcats are notoriously shy. They even hear a human, they run." He knew that half of what he said was true but he stole glances up between the spruces whenever there was a patch of sky above. Bright stars blinked overhead, the dippers and the bear casting a thin silver light. The moon was down near the horizon behind the trees, but casting its own uncanny glow. He knew they had to stay on the path. People who wandered off the path circled around in the woods and ended up miles from where others were expecting them, dead from exposure. He said, "It can't be far now."

Peter grunted again. Lately he was doing that instead of speaking. He was only a few years away from being a teenager. A few pimples had come out on his chin; he watched Alexander shaving with obvious interest. There were subjects he did not talk about with his father. He had a secret life.

There were things Alexander wanted to say to the boy but had not been able to for a long time. That pained him. Maybe it would happen now. The new circumstances might bring them together. He didn't know about feelings and sensitivities the way Maria had and it was something he would have to learn.

They came around a sharp bend where the path rose suddenly and Alexander could see something through the stunted trees and the undergrowth, a golden light flickering in the distance through the woods far below them.

"Hey," Peter said when he spotted it. It was the first hopeful sound he had made in some time.

"Not far," Alexander said. He had paused when the boy spoke. Voices were coming from the direction of the light. Maybe a hundred yards separated them, it was difficult to gauge the distance in the dark of the forest. They started off again. The path dropped almost immediately into the muskeg and the light disappeared from sight. The voices were not as distinct but Alexander could tell from the occasional clear note that the path swung sharply left. He had thought the trading post and the bunkhouse were to the right, but that was probably a mistaken impression. If only he had a compass. Mort hadn't said much more than that they wouldn't have trouble finding the buildings.

They must have descended a fair distance because the ground underfoot was wetter than before. Their shoes made squishing sounds in the muskeg. Or maybe they were skirting one of those swampy little lakes they had spotted all afternoon from the train windows. Then they crossed a dip in the terrain, what might be a creek when the water ran in spring. There was a singular odour on the air, rotting, only worse, but he could not place it. Alexander listened for Peter's breathing and paused to let the boy catch up. Despite the cool of the evening, he was getting hot. The back of his shirt was sticking to his skin and his throat felt clammy.

"I'm okay," Peter said. "Stop stopping." There was an irritation in his tone that made him seem adult.

"Shh," Alexander said. He was listening intently and could hear an irregular noise and a thumping from the woods near the path. It was coming closer and he realized something was moving toward them. He put his hand out and found Peter's arm and tugged him back off the path, in between two stunted spruces. The boy lost his footing in the soft ground and almost toppled over. Uttered a short cry, a curse. Then Alexander realized the noise in the forest was heavy breathing, panting. It was coming towards them. He could not tell if it was a person or an animal. He tried to recall what Mortimer had said about bears. Did you try to run away when they attacked, or were you supposed to play dead? He held the boy's elbow and strained his eyes into the forest. *Don't say anything*, he was thinking, *don't breathe*, but he could not utter the words for fear they would be heard. He was counting on the boy to have that much savvy.

The panting was suddenly on top of them and then receding.

All he caught was a glimpse of a head from behind and a quickly receding back. Apparently they were at the junction of two paths, where the one twisted off at an oblique angle from the other, because the figure had come suddenly into a clearing to the right of them and they were staring at the path directly in front of them, expecting to see whatever was coming there. So all he saw was a blur, a man—maybe a boy—running away from them, a short person, in any case, with dark hair. His laboured breathing had come in short, sharp gasps, his arms had been pumping. Then he was gone.

Peter was standing beside him, mouth open. It was clear he was frightened.

"It was only a boy," Alexander said, hoping to dispel the terror in Peter's eyes.

"He had something in his hand," Peter said. "A knife."

"No," Alexander said. "That was the moonlight on his clothes."

"A glint," Peter insisted. "Clothes do not glint."

They had regained the path and taken a few steps forward. To the left, in the direction the boy had disappeared, the path seemed to curve into the woods toward the light they had seen earlier, the voices they had heard. To the right, in the direction he had come from, there was a straight narrow track between the spruces, running toward an opening in the distance, what could be a lake, what Alexander hoped was Moon Lake and the trading post. He remembered now that there were a number of bays coming off the main lake, the Lake of the Woods: Snowshoe Bay, Crowduck Bay.

"When I first heard it," Peter said, "I thought it was a bear."

Alexander was studying the sky through the opening in the trees. Mort had mentioned that the bunkhouse was within a few yards of the Moon Lake Trading Post.

"I think we go right," Alexander said—though he was tempted to follow after the running figure who had gone past them a moment earlier. He stepped forward, ears cocked to the forest, then glanced back at Peter. What if whoever was running on the path was to come back down the path? It would be Peter he encountered first. What if he really had been carrying a knife?

"We must hurry," he said over his shoulder. "It's getting late."

The going was easier with the moon shining straight down through the opening between the trees onto the path in front of them. The footing was firmer and the track seemed wider, with fewer roots to trip them up. Their shoes thudded along at a good pace. From time to time Alexander caught snatches of voices coming from behind them and deeper in the woods, but they faded as he and Peter travelled down the path. He wondered again if they had headed in the wrong direction. He did not relish the idea of retracing their steps. He heard an owl hoot in the distance and rustlings in the undergrowth near at hand. Again he thought about bears. Were they nocturnal hunters?

In less than five minutes they came to the end of the track they had been following and into what seemed to be another junction. The lake was visible through the trees and bush directly in front of them: moonlight dancing on dark water, the calling of frogs. But there were no buildings, there was no evidence of civilization, though the path skirting the lake went in both directions back into the woods, left and right, circling the water in long loops. Mort was wrong. There were many false turnings possible: and ditches and dried-out creeks, and dips in the terrain that jolted the knees and confused the brain. They seemed to be lost.

He hated the idea of sheltering under the trees for the night. They were both hungry. The mosquitoes would drive you insane. The woods were filled with predators.

Peter was breathing beside him in that way that said he was exasperated.

Alexander swatted at a mosquito on his neck. His mouth was dry. The boy's forehead glistened with sweat. In the pale moonlight his face was white. He looked sick. He did not say anything about being tired and Alexander did not dare ask. He wiped his own brow. He realized that the humidity was high; it was a close evening, chilly but clammy.

"Come on," he said, trying to sound decisive, "this way." They took the path to the right. The store and bunkhouse had to be that way, what Alexander figured was west, the direction they had come from generally, having made a kind of rough sweeping loop from left to right since leaving the station. The other way meant going deeper into the woods. They trudged along, keeping the lake to their left, watching the moonlight on the still water. There was a breeze up in the treetops but it did not cause the lake to ripple.

They heard a loon calling and frogs croaking.

After a few moments the path went up onto some rocks and the woods to their left disappeared entirely. The lake opened up beside them, vast and dark. The air seemed warmer. Water sloshed noisily somewhere below their feet. They were walking along the lake's edge, though the water was down from them some ten feet or more, walking along giant rocks with lichen and moss growing on them. Hummocks of granite. Tiny spruces hardly knee high clung with their stunted roots in the cracks between rocks. The moon they had sensed earlier behind the trees had been golden, a harvest moon, but overhead now it was a shimmering globe of silver that formed a giant reflecting plate on the lake's surface. Alexander pointed at it. "Nice," he said. But Peter only grunted.

Then they saw lights in front of them, a row. "Aha," Alexander said.

Quite suddenly the underbrush thinned and they could see through the pines the outline of buildings standing back from the lake in a large clearing.

"Finally," Peter said behind him, a gasp filled with relief.

"First thing we get a drink," Alexander said. He put one hand over his chest.

"Maybe," Peter said, "they have Pepsi."

"Sure," Alexander said with a sigh. "Sandwiches." He patted his trouser pocket. Not long until he could have a smoke.

They had come through the trees and were approaching the biggest of the buildings, a long, low structure with a line of windows looking out toward the lake. There was a door near the end closest to them with a raised landing and three steps to the ground: a clothesline with towels and sheets pegged to it. Garbage cans. A number of empty cardboard boxes were piled neatly to one side of the steps. An old gas-driven lawn mower with a tin bucket over its engine to keep off the rain. They had come up, Alexander realized, on the back of the store, though he had the clear impression from his conversation with Mort that they would be arriving at the front, which faced back toward the abandoned station. It was obvious then why it had taken them so long. They had taken the wrong route, had become turned around on the paths in the forest. In a moment they were looking in on what appeared to be the kitchen window, the glow of light from a bulb overhead, a table with food and utensils on it, a domestic scene that might have been, but for one anomalous note, warm and inviting.

When she had put the last of the dishes in the sink and submerged them in the soapy water, Cassie said to her, "Let's go now before it's too dark." She meant to the deer meadow, where they fed the yearlings and the does.

Virginia wiped her hands on a tea towel and located the tin pail under the sink where Cassie kept packets of pectin for the canning season.

Moon Lake was located on the edge of the Shield, just past the transition between the scrub brush and the eastern prairie. Winters were long and harsh, November to April, and the snow built up along the escarpments to more than twenty feet. But the woods provided shelter from the icy winds that swept down from the Arctic or the western plains. Springs were short and mucky, summers hot but bug-infested. The fall was often the best season. During the day, at least, the bugs tapered off, and then the hot prairie winds of summer died, the evenings were long and warm. In town people sat out on their stoops, listening to the birds and the leaves rattling in the breezes. The sun set over a period of hours and then the dusk extended for a few more, thin light from the fallen sun that eventually gave way to starlight and moonlight, and then the black of night, which increased until midnight.

Cassie and Virginia stepped off the wooden stairs at the front of the trading post into an evening of shifting shadows and darkening silhouettes. Each was carrying something, Cassie a woven rattan basket and Virginia the tin pail. At the foot of the stairs Virginia hesitated a moment, but Cassie put one hand on the girl's shoulder and nudged her forward.

Virginia said, "There will be mosquitoes."

"No. By now they've settled in the grass to sleep. But there will be blooms still," Cassie said, "on the pumpkins."

"Pumpkin flowers, big deal," Virginia said.

"What talk," Cassie said. "They look gorgeous in your brown hair," she went on. "Just like mine was years ago." She touched the braid on the nape of her neck: a fading brown knot of hair, streaked with a few strands of grey.

Up until this year Barker had come with them. But her hips and legs were bad. Virginia employed ruses so the dog would not know they were going out walking without her. They had crossed the grassy clearing in front of the store and paused a moment by the well. "No," Cassie said, looking at the bucket on the ground, "that they can manage on their own." Virginia shrugged. She was leading the way but she glanced back over her shoulder toward the long, low building with the fading sign reading Moon Lake Trading Post, the store proper on the far side, their bedrooms on the other. The light was on in Ruth's room and the blind was up.

Cassie had her hand on her shoulder. "Someone's coming," she said.

They were on the path that ran along the edge of the oats field almost to the place where Mortimer and the Finn were doing the clearing. Beyond that lay the deer meadow. Someone was coming down the path toward them, not yet identifiable in the dusk. *Please*, Virginia caught herself wishing. It was the Finn. He was wearing the flat cap he seemed never to take off, and he was swinging an empty galvanized bucket in one hand.

When he came up to them he stepped off the path. He wiped his mouth with his free hand. He had a name, Virginia knew, Sauli something or other, a lot of peculiar-sounding syllables, but everyone called him the Finn. He was a slightly built young man of twenty, with sharp blue eyes and pale skin made more so whenever he removed his cap for a moment to reveal a shock of hair so blond it was almost white. He touched his hand to his mouth. "Good," he said, "oats for the deers."

Cassie asked, "They've been?"

"Will be back," the Finn said. He looked at Virginia, smiling. "No need worry."

Virginia looked at the ground.

There was a silence and then the Finn said, "I give them water."

Cassie said, "They can get that themselves."

Ya," the Finn said. "But I like to watch them drink." He smiled, revealing one silver tooth in an otherwise bright white smile. Even in the bad light Virginia saw he was blushing. He glanced at the tractor standing idle in the field, then at his shoes, and then he stepped on to the path behind them and was moving away.

"Odd fellow," Cassie said.

"Cute," Virginia said.

"Poor as a church mouse. An immigrant."

"Nice eyes."

"Ginny," Cassie said, "don't you start getting ideas."

The girl grunted. They had been over the lipstick thing. She had to wait until sixteen. And LaFlamme insisted she put on a dress when working in the store, though tonight she was wearing jeans and a sweater. She'd considered the yellow ribbon Ruth had given her for her birthday but her heart wasn't in it.

The deer meadow was on slightly higher ground than the two fields they had just passed. The path curved gently away from the woods to their left as it rose. They came into the open space on the side of the hill where the grass grew long and the moss flourished around the base of the rocks jutting through. The ground was uneven but clear of trees. A heady aroma wafted up from the meadow flowers and grasses. They paused. The crickets had stopped buzzing. Their arrival had prompted four deer to dart into the woods, white tails flashing as their rumps bounced into the undergrowth. They would reappear in a few minutes, she knew, fifty to a hundred yards from where they had melted into the bush, having made in the interim a loop through the woods. Roger had told her this.

She stepped into the clearing a distance and tipped over the pail of oats, then kicked the oats with the flat of her foot, spreading it out somewhat. Cassie had gone over to the plot of garden on the edge of the meadow. She was stooped over the plants. The crickets had resumed buzzing. The smells of the meadow flowers and mosses tickled Virginia's nose.

Virginia had gone to stand near Cassie. She stared blankly at the moon and then to the north. The roof of the abandoned station house at the end of the rail line from the city was just visible that way in daylight. She rotated her shoulders away from it and toward the store. The lights were on near the back counter, and in Ruth's bedroom. Virginia licked her lips. Behind the store to one side and nearly hidden by the woods in the far distance she could just make out the big smoky bonfire near Cuthand's tent, where the Indians met to drink and buy stuff they couldn't get at the trading post. LaFlamme himself went there to get drunk. He came home smelling of liquor, cigarettes, and wood smoke; Indian smells, Cassie called them. When he came home like that, he would hit them. Sometimes the other. Which was what Roger had yelled at him about; which was why he was always laying for Roger.

To her side Cassie whispered, "Look."

Two does and two yearlings had come back into the clearing and were nuzzling the oats in the grass. One watched while three ate but the other three looked up from time to time, the moonlight from above glittering in their eyes as their tongues scoured the grass. It took them only a minute and then they suddenly wheeled as one, following the doe who had not eaten back into the woods. They made barely a sound, a flick of tails.

"Hard to believe they were here," Virginia whispered. "Like ghosts."

"What always amazes me," Cassie said, "is how small they are."

"When the men talk about them at hunting season, they make them seem big and threatening. *Bucks.*"

"Delicate is what they are. Delicate as a deer."

"I wonder if they know we're not the same ones who come after them with guns when the snow falls," Virginia said.

After a silence Cassie said, "I got two cucumbers and three zucchini."

Virginia looked into the basket. She asked, "Do you think he's that way?"

"Who? Is who what way?"

"The Finn, I mean. Not a real man, like. That way."

Cassie cleared her throat. "I wish he were. He looks sometimes at your sister. You too, I think." She snorted.

Virginia laughed. She thought of Archie Cloud, who'd offered her a bite out of an apple he'd bought and hung around the store sometimes kitbitzing with her. She said to Cassie, "That's a good one. Ruth and the Finn, that is a joke."

"Maybe not to him." Cassie laughed. "He connives to come into the store when only Ruth is there. Pretends to be interested in the stuff in the glass case—compasses, knives. It's her he's interested in."

Virginia said, "But he's harmless."

"There's anger flares up in him sometimes," Cassie said. "You know what they say about still waters running deep."

"Nonsense."

Cassie said, "Men. They feel things but say nothing and then suddenly they're on top of you." She put her free hand on Virginia's shoulder, a gesture the girl felt was supposed to take them across some gap. But it could not, not now. "Come on," Cassie said, "there's chocolate chip cookies."

Cassie was standing on the top step looking down at her. In the shadow made by the light from the store her eyes were dark and sunken, and her nose long. Cassie had put the basket down on the step. Her hands were on her hips. "It's just the drink," she was saying, "some men can take it and it doesn't seem to matter but some it gets the better of. They give in to the drink, see, the demon whiskey. It's a matter of willpower and he doesn't have much. It gets the better of him."

Virginia looked up at her from the foot of the steps. It sounded like a rehearsed speech. She wondered if Cassie believed what she was saying. It struck her that Cassie knew her far better than she knew Cassie. She was her mother, and the things she did around the store were predictable, but Virginia knew nothing of the important things about Cassie. What she actually thought of LaFlamme, what had drawn her to him in the first place. If Cassie suspected that she gave herself away around Mort the Sport sometimes. Virginia drew her toe along the gravel at the base of the stairs. Did Cassie suspect that she and Ruth hated her—parts of them, anyway? Letting LaFlamme touch them and beat Roger? If I'm fourteen, she thought, and you can legally leave home at eighteen. Or was it sixteen? She screwed up her eyes.

Cassie had been talking all the way back from the fields, idle chatter to distract them from what they both feared was going on. The plans LaFlamme had for the fields, what they needed for the store before the snow flew, the quality of furs the Indians had been bringing in, how things looked for the coming winter. She had plans for rearranging the shelving in the store to display the goods better. She was keen on a potted fig tree she'd seen in the city. There was a time not long ago when Virginia might have been interested in all that stuff, improvements to the store and so on. Now she watched Cassie's lips moving and she thought: what a pile of crap. She glanced at Ruth's window. The blind was drawn but the light was still on. Cassie said, "He's not a bad man."

Virginia looked up at her. She spat in the grass. *Fuck you.*

"Ginny," Cassie said. "That's no way for a lady to behave."

Virginia looked directly into her mother's face. Yes, it was hate that she felt—but also fear. How could you feel so much and be able to say so little?

"All right," Cassie said. "We both know what he is."

Virginia wondered: do we? Did Cassie know that LaFlamme had punched out Young Beaudry at the Lakeland Hotel in town over money that was owed him? That LaFlamme had gone to Carl Cuthand's tent when he heard Cuthand was selling boxes of potato chips and grabbed him by the throat until Cuthand had passed out? That more than once he had gone after Archie Cloud and only the intervention of Mortimer Mann had kept that from coming to violence? The Finn was not afraid of him and he wouldn't raise his voice to Mortimer Mann. But violence hung in the air always.

Had Cassie known when she married LaFlamme? Maybe there was another side to the Cassie who liked flipping through Eaton's catalogues and writing flowing ink letters to her aunts on the west coast a side that also liked the violence. The stuff in the night? Virginia licked her lips. Her stomach was in a knot. It was not right to think such things. But then Cassie deserved it, she always took his side, which was weak and stupid and low.

She glanced at Ruth's window. It would be over now. She would not have to pull the pillow over her head, she would not hear the thumping of boots on the floor and the suppressed weeping. She said to Cassie, "You believe what you want to."

"There's a moon," Cassie said, "out at the twin rocks…."

"Oh, yes," she said, "real romantic, that."

Cassie said, "Chocolate chip cookies?"

"Not tonight," she said, but she was thinking *I could kill you both*.

When she pushed through the swinging doors and made the sharp turn toward the bedrooms, head down, lost in thought, she saw him and started to back up but then in his stumbling he saw her. Those smells emanated from his body, those Indian smells, and something else too. A kind of sour sweat. Sex smell. His eyes were glassy. He was wearing a tank-top undershirt and was pulling up his pants with one hand.

"Aha," he said, seeing her. "The princess." He laughed, revealing stained teeth.

She pressed herself against the wall.

"I won't bite," he said. He pushed back a lock of his greasy black hair with one hand. He laughed, shoulders shaking, and added, "Then again, maybe I will."

She was trembling, teeth tight together, sweat on her lip. She waited until he was past, had nearly taken his repugnant smells through the swinging door. *You bastard*, she was thinking, but the words would not come out. Her jaw was locked, her vocal chords refused to work. What came out was a sputter.

He stopped and turned his head slowly toward her. "Say it," he challenged her. When she said nothing, he grunted and then said, "No spunk, eh? I've always enjoyed that, a little spunk in my women."

She was thinking: *Ruth*. Ruth had spunk.

She kept her eyes fixed on his. She had the same hazel irises as his and hated it. That was the only thing she would acknowledge they had in common. When she didn't say anything, he said, guessing what she was thinking and laughing, "I am that, a bastard, and you'd better count on it, girlie." He stumbled toward her.

The knob of her bedroom door was in her hand. She knew better, she should have kept her mouth shut. *You're disgusting*, she wanted to say. *A pig.*

He took one fast step toward her and raised his hand. But then he laughed and said, "Plenty of time for that, eh? You and me."

She had eased the door open and was sliding backwards into the room. She thought she saw exhaustion in his eyes. He was drunk, he was at the end of the day, and no longer a threat. But he lurched forward suddenly and gripped her head in one of his massive hands, fingers cupped around the back of her skull, his thumb pressing into her cheek so that her teeth hurt. Tears started in her eyes.

"I could crush you," he whispered, and he squeezed once to let her see that he meant it. His breath was sour, but she smelled too the cheap aftershave he splashed under his arms. There were flecks of saliva drying in the corners of his mouth.

"Don't touch me," she managed to whisper, barely a sound.

He laughed. "That's good," he said. He pushed her back with one flip of his elbow, releasing her head from his grip and sending her reeling backwards like a dancer who'd stumbled in mid-performance. The back of her head struck the wall. Both knees buckled. She slid down the wall until her legs splayed out flat on the floor out front of her body like a collapsed doll. He laughed again and then said, "Sweet dreams, princess, sweet dreams."

He left the door open and she heard his shoes thudding across the floor of the store, not through the kitchen on the way to the back bedroom as she had expected, but out the mud door near the trap door to the cellar. He was heading outside.

T HEY WERE LOOKING in on what appeared to be the kitchen window, the golden glow of light from a bulb overhead, a table with food and utensils on it, a man standing with his hand on the shoulder of a woman. She was wearing a white blouse with a flower print, he had on a checked shirt. They were talking intently into each other's faces, not arguing, it seemed, but going over something important. Alexander had been intending to go up the steps and knock on the door, but the air of familiarity in that kitchen made him pause.

He looked at Peter. The boy had put his canvas bag down on the grass and was shuffling slowly from one foot to the other, like an athlete before the big game. He thought it was the end of the journey. At least there were no bugs.

Alexander said, "Maybe we should check out the bunkhouse."

"He's got a gun," Peter said. He tipped his head toward the window.

Alexander focused intently on the glass. "No," he said, "a broom."

"It glints," Peter said. "Wood doesn't glint."

An owl hooted in the trees behind them and they both started. The boy laughed, a snort really. Alexander felt his pulse throbbing in his throat. They moved back from the steps into the shadows of the trees. Alexander reached down and picked up the cardboard case, feeling relief to have finally arrived but also uneasy about what he had seen at the window. Peter lifted his canvas bag.

They did not go back as far as the path that skirted the lake, but dodged through the pine trees beside the building, away from the light coming from the kitchen window and along the length of the building. Through the trees they could see the lake, a slab of black water reflecting moonlight. The ground here was soft, and pine needles scrunched underfoot, the scent of them so intense it was nearly choking.

Peter was breathing heavily but not complaining. They were near the end of the journey. It wouldn't be long now before he got something to drink and eat and could stretch out on a bed. He was a good boy, Alexander realized. He wanted to please.

He paused and Peter came up beside him and asked, "What is it?"

"Something on the path," Alexander said. They peered through the trees toward the lake.

"Nothing there," Peter said.

"Heard something," Alexander said. "Feet. Running."

"He had something in his hand," Peter insisted. "A knife or a gun."

They peered intently through the trees. Alexander shrugged and moved on. It was a night of false impressions and wrong turnings. He felt he could not trust his reactions. And he did not want to frighten the boy any more. "I'm just jumpy," he muttered.

The trees thinned into a clearing. They passed another doorway coming out of the back of the trading post, a set of rough plank steps, and then arrived at the far end of the building. They paused. In front of them an open space led out into what appeared to be a field, where moonlight flooded down from the sky, highlighting the dim outlines of yard tools and small machines in the distance. A little in front of them and off to their left stood another low building, Spartan and simple.

"Bingo," Alexander said.

They circled round to the side of this new building, which faced onto the field. It had rough wood siding that appeared never to have been painted, but two windows from which thin light shone out and three wooden steps that climbed to a landing and a door. He pulled on the handle and the door swung open on squeaky hinges. Inside were four beds in a row along the back wall, a wooden cupboard beside each. There was a window in that wall too, that looked out toward the lake from which they'd just come. A small bulb hung down from the ceiling on a cord. The beds were steel-framed cots with thin mattresses and one pillow per bed. The two to the right of the window had clothes strewn about on the grey blankets, the rumpled look of having been recently sat on. The two to the left were unused: on the top of the cupboard between them sat a bottled soft drink and food wrapped in wax paper. Underneath the bottle was a slip of paper with one word scrawled in pencil: *Dick.*

Alexander sighed. The tension was draining out of his body. He looked at his watch, though moments later he found himself doing it again, as if the information had not sunk in. He put his bags down at the end of one bed and signalled Peter to do the same. The boy grunted, then sighed. In a moment he had the bottle of Coke in his hand. With the other he was poking at the wax paper.

Alexander studied the face of his watch. Almost ten. They had left the city at noon. His mouth was dry, his underarms clammy. He wondered if there was a bathtub or a shower in the other building. He looked about the room, taking in a square table in one corner with an enamel basin on top and a simple, straight-backed wooden chair on the side of the door near the light switch. In the far corner sat a wood stove, squat to the floor, beside it a box with bits of kindling sticking out at erratic angles. The flooring was rough plank and no curtains hung on the windows. Everything about the room shouted one word: bachelors.

Peter was examining the wax paper package. "Go ahead," Alexander said.

"There's no opener," the boy said, a hint of a whine in his voice now that they had put the frightening part of the journey behind them.

"Here," Alexander said. He took the bottle from Peter. He lifted the edge of the mattress on one bed and struck the cap off on the sharp steel slat of the frame. It rolled under the bed. Alexander looked at Peter and smiled. "We could take losing that as a bad sign," he added, "but we won't."

Peter looked at him oddly, then took a long swig of the drink. He passed the bottle to Alexander.

"Let's go outside," Alexander said after drinking. "I need a smoke."

They sat on the stoop, facing out toward an open field. After a minute his eyes adjusted to the light from the night sky and Alexander saw a well in the distance not far along the edge of the field. The building they had passed earlier was a shadow to their right. Alexander guessed it was the living quarters of the LaFlamme family as well as the trading post. They had looked into the kitchen. That was probably the wife they had seen.

It was good to rest the back and stretch the legs. It was good to get past the panic he had felt in the woods.

He found his pouch of loose tobacco in his back pocket and his pipe in the front. Then he tamped the loose strands into the bowl and struck a match. When he was a child Peter had liked to blow out the match: *bwow*. He was sitting near at hand, chewing on one of the cheese sandwiches and taking sips of Coke. Alexander could smell him as well as hear his chewing. Alexander puffed on the pipe, feeling the narcotic brown of the tobacco seeping into his blood. Crickets were going at it in the long grass. After he blew away the smoke, he could smell the boy's body again, a not unpleasant tang he associated with locker rooms. Alexander sighed.

Sometimes you just wanted to forget what you had seen.

He looked over at the boy again, munching absently on the sandwich. He had not recognized the massive form of his uncle.

Alexander tried to reconstruct the look on the faces in the kitchen, the man looking down, puzzled perhaps, the woman's hand poised in the air only an inch from his chest, as if she meant to touch him or had just done so. *Intimate* was the word that came to mind. But after a moment he gave up trying to read what he had seen and puffed on his pipe. They had had a long day. Who knew what tomorrow held for them?

"It's quiet here," he said.

"I like the city," Peter said between swallows. "Lights and action."

"It's a different kind of action out here," he said. He puffed on his pipe. "You get to like the croaking of frogs and the starlight and the quiet."

Peter grunted.

They sat for a moment thinking their private thoughts.

Someone came around the corner of the bunkhouse from the opposite direction they had come. It was a man and he was looking down at one leg. Then he slowed when he glanced up and saw them. He was a slight man wearing a soft cap and shoes that made squelching sounds as he came up to them. Sneakers that had seen a better day.

He asked, "You Alex?"

"Alexander Mann. This here is Peter."

"Sauli Affenimi," the man with the cap said.

Alexander said, "I can manage Sauli." He laughed.

"Everyone here calls me the Finn," the man said, laughing too.

"They called me Dick when I was kid," Alexander said. "I was fat, and in German *dick* means *fat*."

The Finn noticed Alexander staring at his leg. The bottom of his trouser was wet and muddy. "Slipping," he said. "I done it near the well." He tipped his head in the direction of the open area immediately in front of them.

Peter said, "You live here?"

"Ya," the Finn said. "You?"

"I guess," Alexander said. "I'm Mortimer Mann's brother."

"He say something," the Finn said, "about a brother coming to work here. Ya."

Peter said, "He was supposed to meet us at the train."

The Finn opened his mouth but instead of speaking, he looked over their heads at the door behind them. In the light coming from inside, his eyes were blue and his cheeks pale, like a girl's, Alexander thought. He wasn't as old as Alexander had at first guessed. Barely a man. Twenty-five at most. "He is say something," the Finn repeated finally.

"You took quite a tumble," Alexander said. "You all right?"

"Is all right," the Finn said. "A little bumps."

There was a silence for a few moments. Alexander puffed his pipe, the boy took another bite of sandwich. Behind them a loon cackled. Alexander said, "Mortimer was supposed to meet us at the train."

"He's a good man," the Finn said. But he offered no more.

"Dad," Peter said, "I'm tired. I'm hitting the sack."

"In a minute," Alexander said. "I came to work for LaFlamme," he told the Finn. He didn't want there to be any misunderstanding or hard feelings.

The Finn nodded. "Not such a good man," he said, smiling.

Alexander puffed on his pipe. "I gather," he said.

"Has got," the Finn said, "how you say here, a steam head."

"Hot-headed," Alexander said.

"Ya," the Finn said. "Hot-headed. Bad manners, him." He butted his fists together suddenly and spat into the grass.

There seemed nothing more to say. Alexander turned to Peter. "You go on in," he said. "Turn in. I'm just going to smoke down this pipe."

The Finn eased past him on the steps but did not say anything else.

Alexander puffed on his pipe and studied the sky. The moon was bright and round but thin clouds obscured it from time to time. A bird called every minute or so, an odd tocking cackle. Was it a signal? A breeze shook the tops of the trees. In the woods behind the bunkhouse where the Finn had come, from something crashed and thumped, but then it stopped just as abruptly as it had begun. He peered into the darkness. Maybe it wasn't a person. He was not used to the sounds of nature. His heart pounded. Another building twenty yards further on had emerged from the gloom, he saw now, a granary, ten feet square with a small door for shoveling in the grain, and maybe the dim shadow of another similar building behind it. Alexander realized he was very tired. He should get up and go to bed proper. His eyes were smarting; he was drifting off.

When he woke up he felt a hand on his arm. *Dick*, a voice was saying, *Dick*.

He looked into his brother's big face. "Mort," he said, "Mort, my God."

His brother smiled. "By gum, Dick," he said, "you were right out there."

Alexander shook his head to clear the sleep away. The pipe was still clenched in his fingers but his hand felt stiff. He worked the joints. Mortimer had been standing right over him but he stepped back. He was taller and heavier than Alexander, beefy, whereas Alexander considered himself wiry. Mortimer had to have his size fourteen shoes made special at a factory in the city. He always wore the collars of his shirts loose. At a fair years ago he had got hold of the front bumper of a car and lifted the front tires off the ground. His face looked a little drawn, dark lines under the eyes. He was working hard, maybe, and keeping late hours. Alexander had never lived as hard as his older brother.

"I was gone there," he said, ruffling the back of his head with his free hand. "Dead to the world."

"You were twitching," Mortimer said. He paused, and then added, "Remember Mom used to say *twitch in your sleep, out for a week*?"

Alexander smiled wanly. He was still shaking the cobwebs out of his brain. "Pete's inside," he offered. "He missed seeing you."

Mortimer shrugged. "I walked down there but the train was late. The mosquitoes over there are terrible. There's an old cistern where they breed. Smells like hell now. I made tracks and came back here to wait for you."

Mortimer had stepped back and the two brothers were appraising each other. It had been almost a year since they had sat together over glasses of rye at a bar in the city. Mortimer had gained weight. He was breathing heavily and looked more solid than ever, but his eyes shifted away from Alexander's.

Alexander said, "We took the first path but we got lost."

Mortimer grunted. "I should have given you better directions."

"My fault. I got us tangled up. It's no matter."

"Just out of the station you must have taken the left fork up toward Cuthand's place. He's got a tent just inside the reservation."

"A big fire? Voices?"

"Drunks sitting on logs," Mortimer said. "He pointed you the way?"

"We never got there. We ended up on a path that joined another near the lake. Then another."

Mortimer laughed. "You did get tangled up. But now that I think about it there's a series of criss-crossing paths up there that no one really uses except the Indians and the animals. An old logging road that comes down from Beausejour. The main path runs straight here from the station, if you get on it, and then up and around the lake on both sides where there are fishing spots and open places that look out onto the lake. Farther up to the east is the narrows and the big lake that flows into this one, which is really a bay, though everyone calls it Moon Lake. The Finn likes to fish at night. LaFlamme says that's where he goes too."

Alexander cleared his throat. "I think I would have recognized a logging road." He paused and then added, "You said there was good honest work."

"Lots of that, Dick," Mortimer said, "if you can stomach the man."

"I've worked for hard men."

"This one's a bastard plain and simple. Mean and cruel. He likes to throw his weight around."

"A barroom brawler?"

"That too."

"A wife beater?"

Mortimer gave him a look. "Yes," he said. He lowered his voice. "His own kids. The Indians too, there's some won't come in the store."

"He sells them stuff, is that the deal with the trading post?"

"Yes. He and Cassie have this ninety-nine-year lease to do business with the Indians. Canned goods, clothing, utensils, and bits of this and that, skunk-and-junk is what it amounts to. They bring in furs and handiwork and in the winter birch wood and they do a kind of barter. Robs them blind and if anyone so much as opens their mouth to complain he beats them up. So they go to Cuthand's place. He's got even worse junk. But he goes there, LaFlamme, gets drunk on Cuthand's cheap whiskey and beats up whoever he can lay hands on. There's no rhyme or reason to it. He just grabs someone he doesn't like the look of at the time."

"You're scaring me."

"Won't touch you or me. Or the boy. He's basically a coward who needs to be taught a lesson." Mortimer butted his fists together the same way the Finn had earlier. He'd stepped back even farther and glanced around, as if expecting someone to emerge out of the shadows.

Alexander looked at his watch, twisting it to catch the pale light coming from the window behind them. Just past ten. "I'm bushed," he said.

"Think I'll take a late stroll along the lake," Mortimer said. "Join me?"

"I'm turning in," Alexander said.

"Suit yourself. There's a great moon this time of year. The lake water shimmers. The Finn likes to angle for pike from the rocks further down where the willows start. He's got a knack for it. They make a great breakfast."

"Another time," Alexander said. "Anyway, I should check on the boy."

"You bet, Dick. Get some sleep. You'll find that when he's put in a day's work up here a man drops off like the stone."

"One thing I'll say, I'm looking forward to seeing the place in the day light."

"I'll give you the full tour tomorrow," Mortimer said. He turned and went around the far end of the bunkhouse, where the Finn had come from earlier. Alexander guessed there must be a path to the lake there, away from the trading post. He stood up and stretched his legs. His back ached but in a good way. He could taste the sheets. Maybe this was going to work out. That bird was still cackling every minute or so. Alexander looked around but could not tell where the sound was coming from. He put his hand on the door handle. Just as he went in he heard rustling from the bush in the direction Mort had gone. Then sudden silence.

THE MUD ROOM DOOR banged behind her and she jumped off the landing and onto the grass below, twisting one ankle, but paying no heed. The cool air of the night struck her face. She was running, dodging the trunks and brushing away the low boughs of the pines in her way. They stung her fingers. The ground was soft underfoot, spongy and dense with pungent odours. She stumbled once or twice as she crossed in behind the bunkhouse where the pines were thickest, lurched forward, crashing in the undergrowth, and nearly fell. But she kept her balance. She ran to the path that circled the lake and turned right without thinking. Her mouth was dry, the back of her head throbbing, so that stars danced in her eyes. There had been blood, and when she had run her hand up the back of her skull, her fingers had encountered crust in her hair, the line of a jagged cut in her skin. How long had she been out? She had read in a magazine that brain cells died by the millions if people who had been knocked unconscious fell asleep. Your thinking was no good any more. You became simple.

Virginia felt that way. Hot. Muddled up.

The path around the lake was hard-packed. It hadn't rained for weeks. She ran blindly. Some instinct guided her because she did not fall or stumble into a tree. The bunkhouse was behind her. She passed the granaries and then she was into the woods, where the air cooled suddenly. The lake was to her left, the water glimmering through the trees. They passed in a blur, the poplars, spruces, willows. The insects had all gone down for the night. She couldn't hear anything except her thumping shoes and pounding heart. Had Ruth even come this way?

She had a plan, that was the important thing, a solution.

Cassie wouldn't care; she hated him and she wanted to do something that would cause things to change. You could see it in her eyes, the way she stared absently out the kitchen window when she didn't think she was being watched. She had told Roger in so many words. She kept a shotgun in the broom closet, a place he never looked. Cassie was preparing for something, something violent or terminal, or both. But she did not have the strength to make the first move.

Ruth did. Maybe Roger.

That's probably what they were talking about when Virginia came in on them earlier. Why they had started like that. Guilty. But there was no reason for guilt. He deserved whatever happened to him, even if it was the worst thing.

Her breathing was laboured. Her throat ached. The pounding at the back of her head was worse. Bright stars jumped in her eyes. Maybe she was about to vomit. She remembered suddenly that there had been spots of vomit on her legs when she came to. That was what had made her jump to her feet and bolt out of the room, wanting to get away. He had that effect on everyone he encountered. You wanted to vomit him up, to run away from his stinking presence. But she should slow down now, she should walk. It was dangerous to run pell-mell through the woods, especially in the dark. People fell in the woods and broke limbs and died. But something inside her no longer cared.

She had to find Ruth. That was all.

Ruth would have gone to Penny and Lucy. There was a rowboat tied in the willows past Moose Point. Ruth rowed across the wild rice field sometimes and spent the night with the Cloud girls. They sat outside and smoked cigarettes and talked and watched the sun come up. They shared things, like opinions about boys at school. They made plans about leaving Moon Lake, about escaping to a place where they would never have to worry about LaFlamme again.

It was all too much. She was going to run away and she wanted Ruth to go with her. That was the plan. Not much of a plan, she realized, but a plan.

She came to a place where the path curved sharply away from the lake; it was marshy there, and in her haste she stumbled on a tree root, staggered two or three paces off the path and then headlong through the bush, where she fell face first into the waist-high grass and tangled undergrowth. Nettles. If she hadn't been running it wouldn't have happened. Stupid. The heels of both hands struck the ground which rushed up to meet her face. Brambles and thorns cut into the soft flesh of her palms. Instantly she felt pain in her wrists, pain shooting up both her elbows. She lay there for a moment. Stupid, stupid. The earth smelled close and dank; already things were rotting. Her wrists ached, especially the one, and she feared she had broken it. Her nose hurt too. She had landed maybe fifteen feet off the path. She rolled onto her back, feeling her heart pounding in her rib cage. She was breathing deeply, trying to compose herself. The stars were bright. A few wispy clouds scudded across the sky, which was a dark purple. Rocks and nettles were digging through her clothes and into her skin. But she was not injured, not badly.

It was stupid to have lost her way on the path, like she had blanked out for a moment. She held her arms up and studied her hands in the moonlight: scraped but not bloody. Slowly she revolved her wrists: nothing broken anyway. The backs of her wrists hurt. Muscles had been jammed or torn in the fall. She was lucky she had not broken bones. Roger had slipped on the wet rocks near the shore the summer before and fractured his ankle and LaFlamme had beat him for that too.

She needed to think, she realized that now. Despite the pain she would lie there until her heart slowed down and she could catch her breath. She knew she had hurt one leg, though not badly. And she felt that sickness in the pit of her stomach, vomit sickness. She would hardly be able to walk. So she knew it was no use trying to get across the lake to Penny and Lucy now. She would go back to the room and collect her things, collect her thoughts.

Her mind was buzzing. Try counting to a hundred, that was it. Remember the afternoon at the fair in the city: hot dogs, Kewpie dolls. Now things were coming into focus. She could make a move. She studied the sky: stars, moon, not a cloud now.

She had just made up her mind to get moving when she heard someone coming along the path, the thumping of feet. She raised her head slightly and peered through the tangle of underbrush and trees. She was maybe twenty feet off the path, hidden from view by the grasses, but she could see out. A man—a big man—passed in a hurry. It might have been him. She thought she recognized the smell. Was he heading back to the store? So he had gone that way, past Moose Point. Had he been to the place where he kept the canoe? She had not considered that a possibility: Penny and Lucy. That was not the pattern. She got slowly to her feet. Something did not make sense: why was he coming back so soon? She pushed aside the tangle of underbrush and picked her way over to the path and when she got there she unaccountably turned back into the woods, in the direction the man had come from, not to the trading post, where moments earlier she had intended to go.

She stood on the path, brushing at her clothes. There was just enough light to see her hands. Dried leaves hooked on her sweater, nettles, a few sticks. Her skin itched. Her shoes were muddy. How had that happened? The earth off the path must have been wet. That happened in the autumn when the muskeg seemed to retain moisture. Her palms stung. The throbbing in the back of her skull was like the insistent beat of a sharp drum. The air was cooler now: the bite of winter was in the breeze that swayed the treetops. She stared directly up at the moon and puffed her breath in the air. Just testing. She knew she would not see her breath in ghosts, not yet. That wouldn't happen until October when the moon would be brighter and more distinct in the night sky. Still, she was getting cold. She hugged her arms for warmth. The chilly air was paralyzing her thoughts as well as her movements. She should have worn a jacket.

Standing there silently she heard the water lapping at the shore. She was at Moose Point, then, where the lakeshore was marshy, and bulrushes and long grass grew in the water, and a shallow creek ran down to the water's edge. In the spring she picked the pussy willows that grew higher up, making a bouquet of their sticky buds and putting them in a vase in her room. The animals came to this low spot to drink, moose, deer. Roger had pointed out to her the tracks of porcupine and skunk. Once he had spotted a bobcat. They would never attack a human, he said. He shot the rabbits up at the deer meadow with his twenty-two and skinned them with his sharp knife. She did not like to think of that.

The Indian boys had taught him things, Sammy Crowduck and Archie Cloud, the brother of Lucy and Penny. Even if Ruth was not there, they would be happy to see her. Ginny. Teach her to smoke cigarettes. Make a hot drink and sit on the stoop together and talk until the sun came up and burned away the terrors of the night.

She shuddered with cold. Move, keep warm. Her feet thudded over the uneven terrain. Now she was awake in every nerve of her body. Aching, sore, distracted. But clear of purpose too.

She was walking on the path beside the lake, making the loop towards the narrows where there was a rowboat that would take her across to the Cloud place and away from him. Even though she wanted to run, she was forcing herself to walk now, deliberate, forcing calm on herself. He wouldn't come back. She knew that. She wished there was someone there with her, to talk to: Ruth, the Finn. His bright eyes followed yours when you spoke to him; he did not interrupt, and he nodded as if listening to every word you spoke, lips smiling, blue eyes alert. He was not attractive exactly, yet she was attracted to him. He made no secret of his interest in Ruth. But she was getting out, getting shut of LaFlamme with the black wiry hairs on his hands and that cheap aftershave stink. She'd wanted to think but not like this. Not in images and in random pictures flashing through her mind. Difficult to sort and impossible to make sense out of.

LaFlamme coming toward her, the tuft of black hairs sticking out of the top of his undershirt, awful wiry stuff, his broken teeth, his rotten-cheese breath. The accumulated dirt and grease under his fingernails. She was trying to push these images away but they kept coming to her mind. LaFlamme bent over the kitchen sink and Cassie washing his back with soap and water. Brown spots on his skin, hair where the crack of his back ran into his pants above the belt. Cassie stroking the soap into his hair where it covered the nape of his neck, scooping warm water with her cupped hands and rinsing his back, LaFlamme grunting like a pig. Why did this picture insist itself on her thoughts?

She was no longer his daughter. Theirs. That was a trap she was escaping: their store, their house, their food. She could not choke down another mouthful. She would not stay there another night. He had brought in the money. It was his. It was all his and it was tainted because of it. But every cell of her body, she realized, was a product of their doing, everything she was capable of doing and even thinking. And now her brain was overheated with anger and exhaustion, a jumble of images and thoughts about his violence and Cassie's vile deceit that she could not shut off.

Home. What a joke!

She had been walking hurriedly and was unaware of how far she had gone. Past Moose Point for sure. She came around a bend in the path and almost tripped over it. At first she did not know what she was looking at. Her thoughts had been far away, and her brain was overwrought. Part of her was already with Penny and Lucy and Ruth on the far side of Moon Lake, looking back at the pines along the shoreline of this side, *their* side of the lake. So. A series of impressions. Articles of clothing, skin glimmering blue in the moonlight, an arm, a leg, bare mottled flesh at the throat, a hand crooked like a claw, a twisted torso reflecting light from above so it seemed blue.

Her first thought wa to dodge, but no, you couldn't dodge past this.

What did she actually see? She would go over it in her mind

many times in the years following. But it was never clear, never the way she wanted it to be. Later she heard others describing it, and she could never be sure that it was what they said, or what she read in the papers that she remembered, and not what she herself had seen.

Her hands though. Wiping the palms on her thighs, they were sticky and did not slide smoothly along the denim of her jeans. Then they were frightened birds on the ends of her arms, trying to flap away, not part of her body, but things which she desperately wished to control. For a long time that was the major impression. But how could you tell that to the people who wanted to know what she had seen—birds?

She wanted to get away but she hadn't. Had come closer. A few steps and then she realized what it was. She dropped to her knees. Did she vomit? She had felt the need. There was that taste in her throat. But everything else was a blur. What she remembered was the way she had puffed her breath into the air toward the moon and not seen ghosts rise from the exhalations. But that was much earlier. Then she was on her feet and rubbing her hands on her jeans. Panic. She remembered staggering back along the path until she came to Moose Point, where she stumbled along the creek and into the marshy water and tried to wash her hands, get off the sticky stuff. So she must have touched it. The water ran into her shoes, soaking her jeans almost to the knees. She held her hands up in the moonlight. That she remembered. It was no use. There was not enough light, not enough water. Her fingers stuck together with it and she plunged them in the cold water again and again. *Off, off.*

When she regained the path she put one foot down after the other. *Do not panic*, she said to herself. *Not far to go.* The moonlight from above splashed on the path. A kind of clarity had come into her mind, even though the path under her feet was rough and she lurched as she walked, so things were jumbled in her vision. But she had no difficulty finding her way.

Later when she could face walking over the ground again, she could not find the place where it had happened. The trees around all looked the same; the path wound through the undergrowth, twisting and turning; there was no particular spot that seemed to call out to her: *here*.

WHEN HE WOKE HE DIDN'T KNOW what had caused it to happen. Maybe the boy had done something. Since Maria had died Peter called out in his sleep and tossed and turned with such violence sometimes it was difficult to imagine he could remain asleep. In any case, Alexander was a light sleeper. Worse now, he thought. He was in an unfamiliar bed, a room that creaked and groaned in the darkness. He was subject to the frenzied thoughts that buzzed through his head day and night like a pop song you couldn't help humming. Maria on the hospital bed squeezing his hand in hers, the business lost to mortgages and creditors, the look of his own face in the mirror, the lawyer's panelled oak offices and bitter coffee. He needed a smoke.

He lifted the blanket off carefully so he wouldn't wake the boy, who had taken the bed close to the wall, leaving Alexander the bed closer to the other two. The one next over was the Finn's, empty, but with a dent in the pillow where someone had rested his head. Had he gone fishing? The bed on the far wall was Mort's, and it was untouched. There were things about his brother Alexander preferred not to think on too deeply.

It was enough that he had found them a place to land. Enough for now.

Alexander's pants were folded on top of his shoes at the foot of the bed, and he slipped the shoes on without tying the laces. He located his shirt, folded on top of the cupboard. Above it there was the tiny square window looking out toward the lake, which was a dull metallic gleam, just visible in the moonlight beyond the path and through the trees.

What time was it? He might have been sleeping for hours or only fifteen minutes. The new surroundings were disorienting. He turned his watch toward the window, but there was not quite enough light to make out the hands of the watch. He thought he heard someone moving outside, the crunch of shoes moving swiftly over hard ground. Didn't anyone sleep around here? But then despite the fact that he was exhausted, it was probably no later than midnight on a Saturday night, the Labour Day weekend, so people would still be out.

Alexander slipped his shirt over his head and tiptoed out of the room. It was silent out of doors. No bugs. The birds had ceased their rattling in the woods. He smelled wood smoke in the air—coming from the bonfire Cuthand made every night just inside the reservation? They had almost stumbled into the place by accident: Indians and white trash drinking by a campfire. Though it sounded okay: warm and companionable.

The thought of cheap whiskey was tempting. There was likely a party in full glow there and he could use something to take the edge off his nerves.

He walked around the side of the bunkhouse, keeping to the grass. Was there really someone down by the lake, or was his fevered imagination playing tricks on him, as he had thought on the path earlier? No. When he stepped to the path he saw a figure down by the rocks near the lake. He stepped closer. A man was standing on the rocks near the shore, stooped over the water. It was the Finn. Alexander recognized the flat cap. He was bent over, fiddling with a line running into the water. So. He really was keen on fishing. Out at night, angling for a big pike. Alexander moved closer, intending to exchange a few words, but the Finn made a gesture and Alexander suddenly felt he should leave the other man alone. He was not fishing, it appeared on closer examination, but fastening a line to the base of a tree near the water. Fish he had already caught on a metal stringer? The morning's breakfast? In any case, when he had dropped the line into the water, the Finn stood up and crossed himself. Then he stared at the moon, chin tilted up, legs wide apart. That's what made Alexander stop and then sidle backwards toward the shadows of the bunkhouse, the privacy of that ancient gesture. A man did not cross himself for no reason; a man did not cross himself for taking the life of a fish. Alexander could not help wondering what was attached to the stringer. Maybe he'd have a look for himself tomorrow.

He moved quietly through the grass and the pines and made his way around the bunkhouse to the stoop. He located his pipe and tamped in the tobacco. He struck a match and it flared in the darkness. He wondered if the Finn was a religious man or if the gesture had some private meaning unconnected to churches and rituals. The gesture had not seemed automatic but studied, the gesture of an earnest man, or a passionate one. Though not a believer, Alexander had offered up prayers himself in the past year. The memory of those unanswered appeals to the deities left him hollow inside. You were alone in this world, you had no one to lean on in the final analysis. Whatever unfolded was up to what you did yourself. Throughout the day he'd been forcing black thoughts from his mind but here they were again. They were poor, he and Peter; they'd been knocked down by fate and were barely clinging to the bottom rung of the ladder. He would have to work every day with his hands. He did not mind that. Then he would have to give the boy lessons at night. He had arranged that with the officials at the education department in the city. There would be exams. The boy had to keep up.

Yes, here they were living in a barren bunkhouse with a chipped enamel basin to wash in and mattresses an inch thin to sleep on. Not a picture on the walls, not a flower stalk in sight. Desperate bachelors. The place could use a woman's touch.

That was the hard part. Maria. Not that she was gone. But that she was never coming back. The hard part was that she was gone forever.

At first she thought she was going home to think, but on the path she realized that was no good: Cassie would be hanging around in her nightdress, fixing cups of cocoa, fiddling with the television in the little sitting room. It brought in snowy pictures only but Cassie liked watching the late movie. She kept up a running commentary, which Virginia found so annoying she had to leave most nights.

And if Virginia went to her bedroom and nested under the blankets, she would start weeping, she just knew it. Cassie would hear and then she would have to explain, and that would bring on tears followed by bursts of anger, leading to recriminations and soggy embraces. She wasn't ready for that. Not yet.

Then she thought of the hideaway. That was the place to go.

It was the second granary, the one Ruth called theirs, the back one, the one he did not yet use because there was not enough grain, and that he had put a padlock on. But Ruth had broken it open with a crowbar. *Our place.* She had helped Ruth move in the mattress and the blanket. A secret even from Roger, she thought.

She ducked through the pines and found the door. It was absolute pitch black in the granary. And after she'd pushed her way in, wary of mice, she left the door open a crack, and in a few minutes her eyes adjusted to the darkness and she could make out the mattress and blanket near the far wall. Ruth had put them there. Our retreat, she called it, our hideaway. There was a candle and matches too, in one corner, but Virginia did not care about that. She smelled the must of closed-in space and the stink of mice droppings. She did not care about that, either.

She found the mattress and wrapped the blanket around her shoulders. Her teeth were chattering and not just from the cold. Her feet were wet, she realized, and ached with pins and needles. She squirmed around on the mattress until her back rested against the wall and she could close her eyes to think. That was what she needed; then she would be able to fall asleep.

The buzzing in her head was still there but not as sharp as earlier. She could use one of the aspirins she had given Roger before. Where was he? She had not seen him since after supper when he had gone out of the mud room door carrying a small metal object in his hands. Probably something to do with Archie Cloud and hunting or fishing or something Virginia did not understand but liked to get Roger talking about. That was the only time he stopped blinking and looking like he'd rather be somewhere else. But maybe that was him on the path earlier. No. Not those thoughts.

She froze, listening intently for a moment. A rustling sound outside the door.

A bear could be wandering down to the lake to get water. They struck out at you with their sharp claws. Skunks sprayed you and you had to throw away your clothes. And there was a killer in the woods. She knew that much. *Not Roger, not Roger.* She sat dead still, listening intently. A crow was squawking continuously down near the lake. At Cuthand's tent a party would be underway; there would be bottles of cheap liquor and music played on a violin. In a minute she recognized what the sound was. Outside the wind had picked up. A tree branch was being tossed about so that it scratched on the wall of the granary, like fingernails scraping on wood. The night birds had ceased their calling. What time was it? Late, she guessed. She tipped her wrist this way and that but not enough light was coming in at the door to see the hands of her watch. It was of no importance, time.

Her wrists hurt, though. She rubbed one and then the other. Bird wrists, Roger called them. She was not a big girl like Ruth. She had narrow hips and tiny feet. The Finn had told her once that she had better be careful, the wind could pick her up and whisk her over the lake to the spirit world. He was always making jokes like that. And he had a thing for Ruth, she had been right about that, she had tricked it out of Cassie with that silly remark on the path on the way back from the deer meadow. He did look at her, often, eyeing her breasts in a way that made Virginia's heart race and her stomach hurt at the same time. Ruth. There were dark corners in her sister's life, places she did not let Roger or anyone else see, places where anger and violence lurked in the shadows. Maybe she did not know they were there herself. She possessed a fury that flashed in her eyes sometimes. Spunk. She had thrown a cut-glass decanter Cassie had received as a wedding gift against the kitchen wall, smashing it to a heap of rubble, and then she had told Cassie she had dropped it while looking for something in the cupboard and laughed about it later.

Ruth had told Virginia, *he is not my father.* That's where Virginia got the idea. She had noted the look in Cassie's eyes when she had said it and known then that she could use that to deliver pain. Cassie had told her once that she worried that if something happened to

LaFlamme she'd be forced to go back to working in a truck stop to support them. That pained Cassie.

Right now it was she who was in pain. There was a lump on one knee where she had fallen and it throbbed but not as badly as the one wrist. How stupid to lose the path like that, stumble and fall. But she closed her mind to the images that came after that.

She heard scrapings and rustlings on the far side of the wall, mice probably, but they did not bother her. She sat dead still and listened to the beating of her heart. There were black corners in Roger too, in all three of them, it was true. When he was her age he had killed things with his gun and once had captured a squirrel and then plunged the blade of his sharp little pocket knife into its stomach while it was still alive; it was a female with tiny, pink squirming babies. They had both thrown up in the bushes down near the lake's edge, but he had made her swear never to tell anyone.

It was silly to think this way.

She wondered: *could I be the killer on the loose?* She was capable of it, and there was all that missing time she could not recall now, like she'd gone blank and out of her head. But no. She twiddled her toes inside her shoes to warm them. Sensible shoes, Cassie called them, black lace-ups with soft rubber heels and soles. They were good for around the trading post but she preferred loafers, the kind you put pennies in and then went to the school dance. Cassie wore them too, the sensible shoes, and Ruth, though she preferred moccasins around the store and heels to the school dances.

It was then that the thought came to her, abruptly and with no warning: dead. Actually dead. She had been suppressing the images, the whiteness of flesh in the moonlight, the rigidity of the fingers clawing the earth, one eye glinting upwards, like dead squirrels she had seen in the forest. She remembered then the stillness of the woods, holding its breath along with her. And she felt the sickness come again as it had at Moose Point, her stomach heaving suddenly under her skin. Dead.

She would not vomit again. She closed her eyes. Part of her was alive with a thousand thoughts and part of her was exhausted. Quite a long time must have passed while she was out in the woods. She was warm now under the blanket and with the mattress underneath. Her toes no longer felt like pins and needles. She wanted to be with Ruth, but it was comfy under the blanket and she did not have the energy or the will to move. Maybe in a few minutes. The warmth seemed to be rising from her stomach and spreading into her trembling limbs. She dozed off with the back of her head resting on the rough plank wall.

She woke with her heart beating fiercely, thinking someone was tugging her arm, but it was only numb from the angle at which she had fallen in her sleep. She was slumped awkwardly against the wall and sweating, though the air in the granary was cool on her face. Her arm, after a moment passed, ached with pain from a pinched nerve.

She had been dreaming. A man was chasing her across water, not a lake but bigger, he was swimming and she was paddling the canoe frantically, and then the man's hand had shot up out of the water at her, gigantic, and she had screamed. Ridiculous. But her heart was racing and it seemed real enough in that way.

She was thirsty, she realized. Her tongue was stuck to her palate. A terrible cold fear had come over her. When she tried to stand up she found her joints were stiff. She rubbed the backs of her knees. The pain from the lump was not as bad as before. She stood and dropped the blanket on to the mattress, feeling instantly chilled. And now she was frightened too, not in the way she had been in the woods, of that one specific thing, but in a far deeper way, thinking of all the bad things that could happen, the worst things imaginable.

Slipping on the rocks at night and drowning in the lake because there was no one else around. That had happened to one of the Indian girls from the reservation, someone Penny and Lucy had known. Joyce something. She'd struck her head and then drowned in two feet of water. Cassie had warned her about that. *Careful.*

She had heard too about the oil stove that tipped over and burned down a shack with a family of five inside, reducing them to cinders in less than an hour. Bits of clothes and bodies floated in the air. You could smell the flesh for miles. There was no way to identify the bodies.

Things just happened sometimes, bad things.

A mother screwed up and they took away the trading post she'd built up with her hard work and forced her to go back to waitressing in a truck stop.

She had to get out of the granary. Find Ruth. Get under the quilt in her own room and away from these thoughts.

She crossed to the door, carefully keeping her eye on the light coming in at the crack. Stepped outside and pulled the door shut behind her. It was quiet outside, the breeze giving the night a spooky Hallowe'en feeling, things moving about in the dark, presences within an overall stillness: feet moving along the gravel, eyes watching from the trees. She could feel her heart in her throat. It was childish but it was also real. She hugged both arms around herself. Winter was coming, snow. She knew where the path was but stood silently in the trees for a moment before screwing up the resolve to turn her feet toward home. Uttered a silent prayer that Ruth would be there when she arrived. But what could she say to her?

When Cassie came in to her room Virginia was under the quilt weeping. She knew Cassie would find her that way but she could not help it. "Go away," she told Cassie, "hate you." And she did. He touched them and she did nothing. She was unfit to be a mother. And yet Virginia needed her too. Stupid.

Cassie said, "Where have you been? Your jeans are filthy."

"I hate it," she said to Cassie, "your snivelling and mine." She realized she was rubbing her sore wrist and she forced herself to stop.

"You're fourteen trying to be forty-one," Cassie was saying. "Give yourself a chance." Cassie was sitting on the edge of the bed: cloying smells of powder and cream.

"I'm weak," she said from under the quilt, "a piece of human crap."

"Your sister," Cassie said, "tells me you're the strong one."

"You're a piece of human crap too. Worse."

"Your sister tells me you want to attend college in the city." She always said that, your sister. Never Ruth.

"Get lost," she said. "You stink. You stink of him."

Cassie said, "Come out from under the quilt now. I'll give you a hug."

But she tightened herself farther into a ball. Cassie tugged on the quilt but gently. She had thickish hands and Virginia could feel them through the quilt, trying to contact her. She hated Cassie's mannish hands, her simpering voice, her hair curlers and Avon stinky creams. "College," she sneered through the quilt. "What will that help?"

"You'll have a future," Cassie said. "You'll be a big success."

"You don't know anything," she said. "Shit."

"You're like your sister. Full of bile."

"Moon Lake. It's a pile of shit."

"You're slippery. I know you don't mean the things you say."

"I do. I mean every goddamn word."

"You have so much anger inside, for one. You go running around in the woods in the middle of the night like a mad person. You chastise me as if I'm your enemy and won't answer a civil question. You talk tough. You're up and down like a yo-yo. You lash out and hurt people's feelings. You mean well but your emotions get the best of you and you hurt the people who love you. Your own mother."

She sat up suddenly. Pushed the quilt away, pain shooting up her elbow from the wrist. Cassie's moon face was staring into hers, the light from the bedside lamp throwing shadows on her cheeks, making her flesh look white and lumpy. "It's down by the lake," she blurted out. "Moose Point."

That shut Cassie up. She smoothed the quilt with her fingers. Her eyes were bloodshot. Had she been crying? "Come again?"

"Don't be stupid," she said. "There's something down by the lake that you should see, something that will wipe that cow look off your stupid face."

"See," Cassie said. "Such talk from a girl." She put out one hand and placed it on Virginia's arm but Virginia shook it off roughly.

"See, you don't know for shit," she said. "For shit."

"Whatever it is," Cassie said, "it will keep until tomorrow."

Virginia snorted. It was always that way with Cassie. "A body," she said, almost shouting, a tone of triumph in her voice. She was watching Cassie's face. The cow eyes hardly flickered.

"I see," Cassie said, measuring each word, refusing to be provoked. Her self-possession made Virginia hot with rage.

"A body," she screeched, "and the law is going to get you and your boyfriend for it."

The truck was bouncing in the ruts and Victor was having a difficult time keeping the steering wheel straight but that was not his main concern. Whenever there was a pothole, the beams from the headlights jumped from the road to the lower tree branches and he momentarily lost sight of where they were going. His feet moved reflexively to the brake. Metal pieces in the truck's undercarriage crunched loudly. Swatches of brilliantly illuminated leaves loomed and thick black branches appeared to be about to pierce the windshield and then as suddenly he was looking at the rutted track again. It was hazardous making the trip on the old logging road to Moon Lake in the full light of day. In the half-light of dawn it was outright suicidal.

But the call had come in and he had buzzed Max McNair and now they were jostling around on the bench seat of the pickup as the first glow of light came over the horizon. It was a good thing the call hadn't come earlier. He had been up watching television well past midnight, drinking a beer and eating sandwiches. It was not good for the local RCMP corporal to show up at a scene with booze on his breath, but if you thought that way all the time you could never kick back. You'd spend your life in fear of what the locals would say in the Lakeland Hotel. But the call had found him asleep on the couch with the set still humming. After calling Max he'd brushed his teeth and put his uniform pants and jacket back on, glanced in the bedroom—but not to stop—and that was perfect timing, because when he pulled up at the McNairs' house, Max was waving goodbye to his wife, Yvette, and coming down the steps with his black bag in hand.

Victor pinched his eyes shut briefly. His gut was acting up again. He wanted to burp, but when he did, the burning sensation did not go away, it got worse. He should not have eaten meat sandwiches. Noodles, that was the key; and for breakfast, porridge. Soon the headache would start. And now this lurching around on a logging road. You could expect one bad thing every long weekend, a suicide or a highway accident.

A body for them to poke and examine, he and Max McNair both.

McNair grunted. They had come over the roughest section of the road and were on the low, soft ground that skirted the reservation. The logging road had once been the principal transportation artery between the reservation and the town of Beausejour but the wood cutting had fallen off in the past decade and now the road was hardly ever used. If you had reason to travel there you took the train into Moon Lake, but that was only twice weekly and this was an emergency. So, the road it was. In most places it was little more than a pair of ruts through the woods. Overhanging branches, high grass, deadfall. Near Moon Lake it narrowed to a meter or so, not much more than a track or path. The branches of trees whipped the windows of the pickup as it brushed past. The wheels bounced in the grass verges. From time to time they struck deadwood and Victor held his breath a moment each time.

It was possible they would get a puncture. He said so to the doc. McNair grunted again. "We could walk," he muttered.

Victor glanced over at him: a tall, thin man with a sharp hawk face and hair that stuck out at odd angles on his hatchet head, he was not the image people usually had of a doctor. McNair was relatively new to the area; he had never been to Moon Lake before. They went fishing together, he and Max. They were both men who liked to sit still for long periods when they had finished working, listening to the singing of fishing lines being cast, the plop in the still water. Max read books too. Not Victor's style.

"Just a bit farther," he said. He was not overweight but he was stocky and he had no enthusiasm for walking, though in his job he was called on often enough to do it. He preferred cruising around in the squad car with the insignia on the door. Even the old pickup would do. Let the internal combustion engine do the work.

They came to the junction where the logging road crossed the path up from the rail station. If you did not know the logging road ran through there, you would miss it. He had once. The headlights of the pickup splashed this way and that. Victor braked and geared down. The track they were following slashed through the woods at a sharp angle as it went past Cuthand's. Victor glanced over. The bonfire was no longer going, the party was over for the night. He was glad he'd developed the be-and-let-be attitude with Cuthand. He hated shouting and shoving matches with drunks. The trading post would come in sight in a few hundred yards.

He had both hands on the wheel. The pickup had a mind of its own. In the spring it had veered sharply on a country road and landed him in the ditch just outside of town, not a good thing to happen to the local corporal, either. That occasioned snickering in the beer parlor of the Lakeland. At least the pickup had not rolled, the scene had not turned into a three-ring circus, the whole town gathered on the side of the ditch, pointing and whispering. Though there was plenty enough to snicker about. His domestic failures.

They bounced into the clearing, the trading post on their left, and he relaxed both hands on the wheel. For a moment he caught a glimpse of the lake behind it: flat water, gunmetal grey. He was expecting someone to be waiting on the steps outside the store but the windows all were dark. He shut off the engine and glanced at McNair.

McNair grunted and picked his bag up off the seat. It was an old bag, black cracked leather. Had McNair's father been a doctor too?

Victor opened the door of the pickup. The engine was ticking and thin steam rose off of the hood. It was the coolest part of the day, the hour or so while night was no longer in predominance but the sun had not risen, either. He zipped up his leather jacket. Beside him McNair coughed into his hand.

The original trading post had been built, he recalled hearing, in the early part of the century. It was a low, flat, wood-frame structure, one major squarish section forming the centre block, and several boxy add-ons that had come a decade or so ago, making it a sizable building. In the dawn it looked ghostly, a misshapen object thrown up against the trees that stood between it and the water, as foreign as the flotsam that drifted up on the shores of a big lake. The flag hanging from the pole near the steps hung limp. It was the old flag, not the red and white Maple Leaf. That would be LaFlamme's doing. As the state's representative would Victor be required to say something about it officially?

A light came on in the depths of the building and a shadowy figure moved toward the front door. The outside light went on, a yard light that illuminated the area in front of the building with a powerful beam. They had come around to the front of the pickup. McNair turned his head sharply away from the bright beam. Victor shaded his eyes with one hand.

It was Cassie LaFlamme. She opened the door. "I didn't know when to expect you," she called out loudly. She was wearing a nightdress with a quilted robe over the top. Her voice was gravelly and she cleared her throat.

Victor said, "The girl should come too."

"One minute," Cassie said, "give us just a minute."

They leaned against the hood of the pickup.

"That's the wife," Victor said. "She made the call after the girl told her about finding the body. It was her folks, Cassie's aunt and uncle, that first got the lease on the trading post from a federal department, ninety-nine years to trade with the Indians. The Indians liked them, they were easygoing and fair. They did not look down their noses. They retired to the city where the uncle died shortly after, but they left the lease to Cassie and the husband, who folks think pushed the old folks out. He's not from around here. He's a loudmouth and a bully. Gets in people's faces. I've had to arrest him twice in town where he comes just often enough to be a pain in the ass. Punches people out in the Lakeland Hotel."

Victor hesitated. He'd been on the receiving end of a punch or two from drunk LaFlamme himself not so long ago when he'd been called to the Lakeland to break up a fight between LaFlamme and Young Beaudry. He had had to use his quickness of foot and his nightstick to get the better of the bigger man, and had been lucky to get the shot in and luckier that no one had seen it. One quick jab to the throat. That had shut the bigmouth up. He'd turned purple in the face, almost puked. It had been satisfying to Victor to see LaFlamme go down, but in a way he was not yet prepared to share with anyone.

McNair was listening with his head bowed and eyes half closed. He looked as if he might drop off at any moment. But they were both used to the hours, the urgent banging on the door, and the phone calls in the middle of the night. Victor had learned to sleep when he could and so had the doctor.

When they were out together in the summer, Max McNair had slept in the pickup while Victor drove, Victor recalled. They had been called to a drowning up north. A canoe had tipped in the water while a boy and his father were out fishing. Somehow the old man had become tangled in weeds near the shore. The boy was fifteen; he was not strong enough to get the man's legs free. The boy had only just escaped a watery death himself. Both legs were lacerated from weeds where he had torn free. His feet were bleeding. The whole time they were examining the body the boy had stood on the shore near them, a blanket that Victor kept in the back of the pickup wrapped around his thin shoulders, a stream of blood oozing from between his blue toes. Later they had taken him home to the mother and two smaller children. She had made them coffee and offered cinnamon buns. McNair had to use the bathroom. It had been almost too much to bear.

They had got to know each other on that long drive back home.

"There's an older daughter too," Victor continued. "And a boy. They all seem a little wild but who wouldn't get that way, living out here at the end of civilization."

"It's nice in a way. Rugged. Majestic."

"Crap. It's spooky."

"I've seen the daughter at the clinic," McNair said. "A looker."

Victor glanced at him quickly. McNair's back was propped against the hood of the pickup, the steam from the engine scarving his face. He was staring straight ahead at the building in front of them and was rubbing the end of his long nose with one finger. The bunkhouse was emerging from the shadows. Victor felt the burp coming and put his hand on his gut, preparing to swallow back. He should ask McNair about it but that would be admitting weakness, and weakness was not acceptable for a guy angling for Sergeant in the RCMP.

Victor said, "Things are not good here. He's a mean and cruel bastard. The kids hate him and the wife spends her time acting as a buffer zone between them. A punching bag, more like. He beats them all. Cuthand has seen it. But no one complains, so what can I do?"

McNair turned his gaze to Victor's. He said, "The law can't do anything?"

"Cassie's afraid that Health and Welfare will come after the kids."

"So she lets him beat them. Interesting logic."

"Cuthand says other things. There's two Indian girls live across the lake on the reservation, the Cloud girls, their brother, Archie, helps out around here, and the father is a trapper who brings his furs here to trade. Cuthand says LaFlamme goes after them sometimes. He says the father of the girls and his brothers are laying for him."

"He goes after them," McNair repeated. "You mean…?"

"Assault, rape. Again no actual complaint has been lodged. Cuthand's afraid of him and no one else will say anything, either."

"And you, what do you say?"

"Officially I say it's a lot of talk." Victor drew the toe of his shoe in a line through the dew-wet grass. The headache was starting in the usual place, the corners of his eyes. He added, "Personally I think it's true. But I have to deal in facts."

"His own girls?" McNair asked.

"The younger girl is smart, they say. The mother has plans to send her to the city after high school. There's something a little wrong with the brother. He's dark and secretive. He has learned from the Indians how to melt into the woods. He's a friend of Archie Cloud. He keeps to the shadows but that doesn't mean he's not thinking—or doing—things. Something happened at school a year or more ago. Something violent. But I cannot recall the details."

"Not exactly what I meant," McNair said.

Victor looked at him, waiting for an explanation. But before Max could clarify, the door banged open again and the mother and the girl were coming down the steps, looking dishevelled and pale and frightened.

SHE WAS BLEARY-EYED and somewhat disoriented from being woken from a restless sleep. Woozy. Her legs felt like rubber. She and Cassie walked in front. They knew where the paths were, so they would be able to find the one that angled into the woods past the bunkhouse and the one leading off it that ran in a curve around the lake. The two men walked behind. They were the Mountie and the doctor from Beausejour. She had seen the Mountie driving around in the blue squad car in town but the doctor was new and she hadn't seen him before. Months ago Ruth had gone into town to ask him about periods and things. That's what she said, anyway.

Right away she liked the doctor. He was tall and skinny and his hands and wrists stuck out of his jacket like a cartoon character's, thin white wrists and long fingers with close-clipped nails. He had hooded eyes that gave him the appearance of being half asleep when he was wide awake. He had yawned, though, when the Mountie was introducing him to Cassie and then to her. The doctor didn't seem to care about social niceties. That's why she liked him; he did not put on airs. The doctor in Beausejour before this one wore a shirt with a tie and called her Miss LaFlamme when Cassie took her in for a checkup.

The Mountie she wasn't sure of. His eyes looked into you, not at your eyes. He was looking for something, a deception he could trip you up on, or a weakness he could use against you. His watery blue eyes reminded her of the husky dog Roger had had as a boy and that LaFlamme had shot for barking in the night. She had heard LaFlamme curse the Mountie, and say he was going to get him. The Mountie had thrown LaFlamme in jail when he was in Beausejour on one of his drunk-ups. Too bad he hadn't been able to keep him there. But he was like most men, the Mountie, he looked right past women, which Virginia hated.

The Mountie had spoken to her first. "Just show us where," he said. He had placed his hand on her arm and she had felt the strength of his grip through her jacket. He was staring into her face but she had had the feeling that he was looking at her hands, searching for something on her clothing. That made her fidgety. Up close there was an odour about him, clothes that had been slept in. No, she did not like him.

"She's a little shaken," Cassie had offered.

That's when the doctor said, "I've got some relaxants. Something to take away a headache, maybe." He had looked at Virginia and smiled. He had brown eyes; she trusted them the way she trusted half-breed dogs; they were not that pure thing that went out of control when you least expected it.

But she had refused the pills. People took too many pills.

She was not feeling good. Her stomach was in a knot. Her wrist hurt, the one she had fallen on earlier. If she had had her choice she would have stayed in bed under the quilt. Though that would have meant being subject to those terrible images.

They passed the bunkhouse and found the trail that cut down to the main path around the lake. Light was coming into the sky. She looked up. At this point in the dawn the moon was a pale disc against the blue-grey of the sky. The hawk was circling over the trees, diving down toward the water and then swooping suddenly up again. The air was heavy with damp. She was wearing a jacket but felt cold. If Cassie had known better when the Mountie was arriving, she could have made them cocoa. Then Virginia's insides would have felt warm, instead of like cold porridge.

They turned on to the main path. She had not worn the same jeans as earlier. Cassie had taken them and thrown them in the laundry hamper. Had she noticed the blood? She had not said anything. She had told Virginia to wash her hands and face and put a jacket on over her sweater. It was all said in the mother tone, firm and sharp, as if she were still eight years old and had broken a plate doing the washing up. Cassie bustled around. While Cassie was in the bathroom she must have cleaned Virginia's shoes because when she came back to the bedroom, they were beside her bed, scrubbed and freshly polished. Likely Cassie had washed the blood out of the jeans.

So Cassie was afraid too.

Virginia touched the back of her head. She had combed over the spot where the skin had broken when LaFlamme had knocked her against the wall. Not much more than a scratch. There was still a bit of a headache, though, a burning sensation in her eyes that she could only get rid of by squinting. The doctor had noticed that probably, and had wanted to ease her pain, which made the idea of leaning on his skinny arm attractive.

He was breathing easily behind her as they snaked through the woods. It was the Mountie who was puffing. Cassie ahead of her too. She had told Virginia, "Say as little as possible." Like she was a kid. The way she had said *stay here* when she had gone to telephone earlier, when Virginia had called her a cow. After she had hung up, she had gone into Ruth's room and spoken low for a few minutes.

Then Virginia had heard her checking in the back room where Roger had a cot, though he often slept out in the woods with Archie Cloud. Virginia had a feeling from the sounds Cassie had made in the back room that Roger was not there. She wondered if that indicated anything. She was having a difficult time deciding what things meant.

The path wound past Moose Point. She looked over at the lake. Mist was rising from the water, like ghost breaths from her own lips in winter. It was as if the earth had a mouth and were breathing. The path ahead was clear and the walking easy. It was a totally different world than at night, when shadows loomed up from the dark woods and the noises of night animals sounded everywhere. She smelled the mist from the water and the pine needles. In the dawn red-winged blackbirds called from the bulrushes and squirrels chattered in the trees. Insects buzzed in the grass. These sounds would have comforted her if she did not have that knot in her stomach, that taste of bile in her throat.

When they came near the place she felt dizzy suddenly. She stumbled and lost her footing. The doctor must have been expecting this. He was right there to catch her, both his hands under her armpits. She felt his body warmth and smelled aftershave. She did not want to go any farther. She did not want to see.

"All right," the Mountie said. He had gone ahead, carrying his knapsack in one hand. "You stay here with her," he said to the doctor. He motioned to Cassie to walk with him. They went around the sharp bend in the path, Cassie's quilted robe flapping and trailing in the dirt.

The doctor said, "Breathe deep through your nose." He was standing in front of Virginia, looking into her face. "The giddiness will pass in a minute."

He was right. The little stars that floated in her eyes cleared away suddenly. There was a green tinge to everything she looked at, though. She wanted to tell him that, but he told her to keep still and continue breathing.

She said, "I better sit down." A big tree had fallen near the path a little to the rear and they went back there. The outer bark had rotted and when she sat down on it, strips broke away and fell to the ground. Bugs rushed this way and that. She put her head down and closed her eyes and tried to breathe the way the doctor had said. She smelled the sourness of the rotting tree. It was him, she knew that now. She had been trying to push away the thought but now there was no denying it. Cassie would come back and say it. She had better get used to the idea.

THE WIFE HAD SAID, "YES, THAT'S HIM," and then turned and walked away. Not *oh my god*, but then not *I knew it*, either. She had looked once quickly at the body and then at Victor, her lips pursed tightly, and then turned and gone back down the path. The skirts of her purple robe trailed on the grass near the path, stirring up the new-fallen leaves. Victor watched her until her solid form disappeared around the bend. Standing on the steps earlier she had seemed small, but now he saw that substantial flesh was packed on her short frame. She was not going to break down and fall into someone's arms in tears. She had hardened herself against that sort of weakness, and against the husband too, it appeared. Victor had asked her to send the doctor back down.

In a moment McNair appeared, bag in hand.

He knelt over the body, fingers to the throat, as form required, though they could both see clearly what the case was. Then he slipped one hand under the closest shoulder, preparing to roll the body over. He didn't bother looking up.

"Wait," Victor said. He had put his knapsack down on the path and he reached to pick it up. He pulled out the camera and glanced at the sky. The sun was about to rise. Light was stealing in from the east. He removed the lens cap and fiddled with the settings. McNair had moved back, away from the body, and was standing motionless. Victor snapped six quick shots of the body face down as they had found it. It looked as if he had died crawling, and Victor reminded himself to check the path farther along for evidence that this was the case. There were grass stains on the clothes, and mud. He had dragged himself—or been dragged?—along the path. He said, "Okay."

McNair grunted, then slid his hands under again and eased the body over on to its back. The wife had identified LaFlamme when his face was down in the earth, one cheek visible, but now it was completely exposed: pencil moustache, lips drawn back, the eyelid that had been against the ground, closed. McNair leaned over and pushed shut the other, holding it down for a few seconds. Rigor mortis had set in. The knees were bent in crawling position, one hand had stiffened into a claw. Victor would want to take a sample of the dirt under the fingernails as well as the mud caked on the tops of the shoes: light work boots, he noted, black.

McNair was examining the throat area, then ran his hands down to the wrists, moving his fingers deftly and professionally over the skin and thick blue veins. LaFlamme had a beer belly, Victor noticed. His checked shirt sagged over the belt of the trousers. A tuft of wiry black hair stuck out of the collar of his shirt. Grass and mud stains marked the knees and thighs, a rip in one elbow of the shirt. McNair looked up at Victor. "Take your shots," he said. "Then I want to flip him over again and examine the wounds more closely."

He took six more shots of the full body on its back, two of the head only. The upper lip had dried and stuck to the gums above the teeth. The skin of the face had sagged and was grey in pallor. Death moved in quickly. Already flies were buzzing about and landing on the hardened cakes of blood on the clothes.

McNair eased the body over. He ran his hands over the rips in the shirt fabric and then tugged the shirt-tail gently out of the trousers before running his hands along the skin. He grunted. "Five," he said. "Five wounds altogether."

Victor had put away the camera and taken out his notepad. "I thought I saw only three," he said. It hurt his head to concentrate on the white paper and he tried to blink away the pain. The walk along the rough path had made his headache flare. He took a deep breath, trying to wish away the wooziness he felt coming up from his guts. It came in waves and he could sometimes hold it off with deep draughts of oxygen. But damn it anyway.

"There's a lot of hardened blood on the shirt," McNair said, "so it has bunched up somewhat and makes it difficult to tell. But I can feel five knife wounds distinctly."

Victor was making notes in his pad. "You're sure," he said. "A knife?"

"A one-sided blade of some length, it appears. A good-sized knife."

"Like a kitchen knife, or a butchering knife?"

"Exactly. Or a hunting knife. The interesting thing," McNair said, " is location." He cleared his throat. "Iliac, plexus, diaphragm. He got them all."

Victor said, "He?"

"A manner of speaking," McNair said.

Victor asked, "What's interesting about those places?"

"Like he was working his way up the torso—or down. Here and

here and then there. Methodical, you could say." His eyes held Victor's for a moment, then dropped again to the body. He seemed about to say something more, but then he shrugged and muttered, "Something doesn't make sense." He stood up from the body.

"Whatever does make sense in a murder? That girl in the gravel pit down south last year was stabbed eighteen times in the chest."

"With a screwdriver, ugh."

Victor grunted and said, "There's matted blood above one ear."

"From falling, likely, and striking the ground." McNair gave the hardened mud of the path a kick with the toe of his shoe. "We'll know in the lab."

Victor asked, "When did it happen, would you say?"

"It's pretty chilly these nights," McNair said. He looked at the sky as if to confirm it. "So it's hard to tell. But not before six and not much after midnight."

Victor said, "That's not much help. Six hours to account for."

McNair shrugged. "Best I can do," he said. "When we get the body on the table I may be able to tell something more from the stomach contents."

Victor said, "I have to take a lot of samples. It's the only hard evidence we'll get." He had put the notepad back in the knapsack with the camera and had in one hand a wad of small manila envelopes held together with a red elastic band. Mentally he reviewed a checklist of items to get. "You can go back with the wife and the girl," he added.

McNair squatted down on his haunches. He asked, "You're not afraid?"

Victor snorted.

"A killer on the loose and all that?"

"This was an act of blind fury, a sudden impulse. Whoever did this is long gone." Victor patted the holster on his side. "Anyway," he added, "there's Lucille."

McNair smiled wryly. "I'll stay," he said. "Help with the dirt under the nails and blood samples."

"First, then, I'll walk up the path," Victor said. "He's wearing a shirt, but it was cool last night. Maybe there's a jacket or a sweater or something."

"The knife, maybe."

"Fat chance."

McNair grunted. He was already digging samples of dirt from under the nails to put into an envelope.

Victor started down the path, at first fixing his gaze on the hard-packed earth. There were signs LaFlamme had crawled over the ground. He glanced farther along to gauge the distance he'd travelled. Victor heard a hawk screeching over the lake, as if it were angry. A squirrel up in the trees was chittering at something. Insects buzzed in the grass. The sky was blue now. It would be a warm fall day, the kind he should spend in the yard with Sheila. But he did not even know where Sheila was.

V︎IRGINIA WAS SITTING at the kitchen table with Cassie and the doctor. Cassie had made coffee and put out some muffins. The Mountie was standing with his back against the counter, seemingly relaxed with a coffee mug in one hand, but those washed-out blue eyes were alert.

"So," he said, "you just decided to take a walk in the dark of night." He was letting her know by his tone that he was unlikely to believe a word she said.

She could not remember making a decision about that. So *decided* was out of line. But how could she say she just found herself outside? Stumbling around with no idea of where she was going? She guessed he was the kind of man who made judgements about girls, and now she was on the point of proving him correct.

"Not so unusual," Cassie said, sensing that Virginia was not going to respond. "We go for walks all the time around here."

"The Finn fishes," Virginia said. "Just outside here or farther along the lake, past Moose Point, where we were this morning." She cleared her throat and took a sip of the water she had poured for herself. Her wrist throbbed with pain. In the past few minutes the headache had come back again. She felt dizzy. She must not rattle on like that or she would give stuff away about Roger, about herself, give them too much information and put herself in a position where she could not retract.

The Mountie looked at the doctor. "Don't fish sleep?"

"LaFlamme did too," Cassie said. "Fish, I mean. A year or two ago he dragged an old wooden chest down the trail and put his fishing gear in there, wrapped up in a rubber sheet to keep off the elements. Hidden just off the path, like. I'll show you if you care to see."

The Mountie said, "You're saying that's what he was doing last night, fishing?"

Cassie did not answer. Virginia could tell by the way Cassie's lips curled up that she did not like the question. How was all this going to look to Health and Welfare? It scared Virginia too. You shouldn't take kids away from their mother. And what if it was Roger? Cassie lifted her coffee cup.

The Mountie looked at Virginia. "And you have no idea what time?"

"I looked," she said, "but it was too dark." She felt foolish. When it happened it had not mattered, so she had not put any effort into making out the watch hands, but now it seemed foolish that she had no idea. He was cornering her on things like this and making her more nervous. What if they thought she had done it—what if she had? She knew that was impossible, but there was all that time she could not account for. And blood on her jeans. She shifted in the chair. Barker was sitting under the table at her feet and when she moved Barker thumped her tail.

The Mountie asked, "Is there any point earlier in the evening, say, when you could specify the time precisely?"

Cassie said, "We came in from feeding the deer at nine, quarter after."

"And was he here then?"

Again Cassie did not answer. She sipped her coffee. Virginia said, "I saw him after that. Not long after. He was going out the back door."

"No fishing gear, though?"

"I told you," Cassie said, "he kept that down by the lake."

"So," the Mountie said to Virginia, "he heads out sometime around nine-thirty, and then you head out in the same direction after that. But you say that you were not looking for him, your intent was not to go after him?"

Intent! Virginia looked down. "No, no." That's the last thing I would have been doing, she thought. She'd resolved earlier to answer his questions as briefly as possible so as not to get trapped. She must try to remember.

Cassie reached her hand across the table and covered hers. Virginia felt the fatty flesh of her mother's fingers and the cool of her wedding band against the hot skin of her own throbbing wrist. Virginia looked at the Mountie. "No more questions," Cassie said. "Look at her."

"Just a few," the Mountie said to Cassie. "We're almost done." He was looking at Cassie and he said, "I wonder if you could do something for us. Check to see if all the knives are here."

The doctor said to Virginia, "I have aspirin in my bag. It's not a crime to take an aspirin." He was trying to laugh them through it. He took a big bite of a muffin and then placed the stump back on the edge of the plate. Crumbs were stuck on his lower lip. He looked comical but not ludicrous. She felt the urge to reach over and brush them away.

The Mountie said, "Did you see anyone on the path?"

"No."

"There seemed a lot of foot marks out there." When she said nothing in response, she felt he did not believe her. "When you came to the—the place," he continued, "then, did you touch anything or do anything?"

She had lied a moment ago but it was better, she thought, to tell as much of it straight as possible. Less likely to be tripped up. She inhaled deeply and said in a firm tone, "I was walking fast and sort of stumbled across it in the dark. I didn't know what it was. At first. The moon shone through the trees and you could just tell. I felt sick to the stomach. Then I was running down the path home. That's all I remember."

"There are scratches and scrapes on your hands."

She looked at them, curled around the water glass. That was it, then. And dirt under the nails. She had not washed up as well as she should have. "I tripped on the path and fell."

"After? Before?"

The doctor was suddenly at her side, one hand on the throbbing wrist. Flashes of pain shot through her elbow straight to her temples. "Contusion," he muttered, revolving her wrist slowly and carefully. He looked at the Mountie.

"Broken?"

"Not broken. Swollen. Consistent with a fall."

"Was this after?" the Mountie repeated. "Or before you found the body?"

"After," she said. "No, before. It's all so confused."

Cassie said, "Stop, already." She was standing, lining up the knives on the counter beside the Mountie. She was making noises with the metal that rang in Virginia's ears. She said loudly, "They are all here. Every single one."

The Mountie turned his head toward her slowly, as if he was in pain. The doctor had released her wrist and stepped away. Maybe he was going to get an aspirin out of his bag.

Virginia had composed herself and said nothing. She was looking at the plaque on the wall to one side of the sink. Cassie had put a number of them up around the kitchen years ago. Home Sweet Home, Bless This House. She went in for sentimental stuff. Pious sayings burnt into polished wood. Their comforting messages seemed out of place that morning. As did the avocado-coloured refrigerator Cassie had been so proud to acquire in the summer, and the yellow print curtains around the window over the sink. Cassie usually had the radio on loud. It was peculiar not to hear its babble in the kitchen. Virginia noticed a smell too—onion—a smell she was never able to tolerate after that morning.

The Mountie was saying something to Cassie. She missed it. She had not slept well and her head hurt. She wanted to touch the back of her skull but she imagined her fingers might come away bloody. Then she would have to explain more. She'd already messed up the answers about what happened in the woods, and she would have to remember that lie. She closed her eyes to relieve the gritty pain in them and said nothing.

"You came back down the path, and what did you do then?"

"She went to her room," Cassie said.

It hurt Virginia to open her eyes. She wanted to sleep, to slide away from it all.

But they were taking their time with the questions, going over it all with care. The Mountie had crossed his short legs at the ankles. He looked very much in control, standing there in his jeans and blue shirt with the patches and his official leather jacket. She could see the place on his hip where the holster and gun bulged out, making him seem fat around the waist. But there was strain in his eyes: anger or exhaustion or both. He cut those eyes toward Cassie. "I wonder," he said to Cassie, "if you could itemize the knives on a piece of paper. Make a list."

Virginia hadn't realized it when he asked Cassie about the knives earlier, but he was trying to keep Cassie occupied, out of the conversation. The Mountie and the doctor looked at each other. Some sort of silent communication was taking place between them.

Virginia took another sip of water. She was beginning to think she had made a mistake about the doctor. He was in league with the Mountie. She had to go careful or she might dump them all in it.

"You came straight back here, then?"

"Yes."

"You were wearing these clothes?"

"Yes." Her cheeks were hot. She licked her lips. "No, wait. Mom, are these the jeans I had on last night?"

Cassie's answer came too quickly, she thought. "Of course."

The doctor stood up from the table suddenly. "You know," he

said, "now I think *I'm* getting a little bit of a headache. Could you point me the way to the bathroom?"

The Mountie was staring at her shoes. "So," he said, "you left here at, say, nine-thirty, ran down the path, fell and hurt your arm, kept on going down the path, came across the body just past Moose Point, then turned around and ran back here and went straight to your room. Is that correct? Is that your statement?"

Statement. It sounded so formal. Virginia momentarily pictured a judge and a courtroom. *Do you swear?* She swallowed hard, feeling tears welling in her eyes. The questions were not fair. And she was confused from lack of sleep.

Cassie said, "You're badgering her. She's just a girl. She's had an awful scare and she hasn't done anything wrong." She had her hands on her hips and now her lips were set tight. To Virginia she said, "Why don't you let Barker out?"

They were twisting what she said. They knew she hadn't slept well and that she was feeling sick, and they were trying to trap her. The waves of wooziness that were like a moment-long faint were still coming, and when they passed she felt she was about to vomit.

"That would put you back here by, what? eleven at the latest. But your mother only called in with this information early this morning. Five o'clock."

Virginia blinked her eyes. She saw what he was getting at. Yes. What he said was logical but so was what she had done and the way she had explained it. Neither of them was wrong. The Mountie was thinking in one set of steps and she another. The two ran in parallel lines but they did not cross and she did not want them to cross. She said, "I was under the quilt."

"She was upset," Cassie said. "Her father, for heaven's sake, she'd just seen him like that. She's just a girl. She was in shock. She was crying."

"For six hours?"

Cassie sighed dramatically and said, "The problem with you policemen is you want everything to add up neatly. Lists, times. Little boxes to check off with your sharp pencils. But life is not like that. Sometimes things do not add up and do not make perfect sense."

The Mountie said sharply, "After we have a list of those knives we'll want to examine each carefully. Maybe take some scrapings. They're evidence."

She felt her head tipping forward. His voice was going in and out, the way the radio did some nights. She held the water glass against her forehead. She heard the toilet flush and in a moment the doctor came back into the kitchen, rubbing his hands together. She may have lost consciousness for a moment because when she was able to focus, he was sitting across the table again, taking another bite of the muffin. She saw his long thin fingers holding the stump as his mouth moved toward the cap. *That coffee will be cold*, she thought. She hated cold coffee.

"Then," the Mountie was saying, "we'll need a list of anyone in the area last night. We'll have to talk to each of them."

"Separately," the doctor said.

Virginia saw him look at the Mountie meaningfully. She was aware of the refrigerator humming. She heard voices from out on the stoop. She was aware of Cassie in the background. Everything took on a green tinge suddenly, like the water in those large aquariums in California that she'd seen pictures of in school textbooks. The next thing she knew she was on her back on the floor, the doctor's thin face staring down into hers.

Victor said, "The whole statement is a tangle of lies, of half-truths."

"Untruths," McNair said.

They were standing by the pickup. Victor was making notes in the pad, holding it on the hood of the truck. Because of the waves of headache assaulting him, the characters he made with the blue ink jumped and blurred together. He bit his lower lip and forced his hand to keep moving across the page.

McNair had helped him carry the girl to her bed. He sniffed and rubbed the end of his nose. "The mother is right about one thing. Human beings are unpredictable."

"Crap. That's a dodge she's using because she's scared."

"Things don't always add up."

"Here," Victor said, "nothing adds up." The headache seemed to be subsiding a little. He shouldn't have taken the coffee, though. Already he could feel his guts gurgling. He looked up from his notes. The sun had risen over the treetops. Golden light streamed down on the lake. It glittered and hurt his eyes. Sparrows were making a racket in the bushes near the building, fluttering up in a flock from the gravel, then landing in the bushes near the steps. Victor sighed.

"She's scared," he said, "that she'll lose the place. Or lose the boy."

"And where," McNair asked, "did he get to exactly?"

"Hiding with his Indian pals. My bet is he knows what happened out there."

"And the older girl?"

"Says she took a walk by the lake. Says she went to bed early."

"Nothing about a knife, though?"

They had taken scrapings from two of the kitchen knives, but more as a formality than anything else. The murder weapon was long gone. Victor had written down precisely what the girl and mother had said. Would it make any difference? He was meticulous, that was the way it had to be, but he often thought his need to follow procedure to the letter was a peculiarity, given the circumstances in which he worked: hundreds of miles from the nearest city, patching evidence together long after the fact, interviewing dodgy witnesses who covered for each other or sometimes just lied to the police on principle. And they had their own way of doing things in this district. They settled their own scores. Rough justice. So maybe he was just covering his ass by following procedure. There were times when the interviews and note-taking seemed pointless. Or maybe it was just that he was tired and at the end of his rope these days. He was getting a testy gut, he did not sleep well, he had to eat noodles and porridge instead of steak and bacon.

"The girl's jeans," McNair said, "were in the laundry hamper. Still damp. Blood on the thighs, mud on the cuffs. Someone tried to clean them."

"And her shoes had been cleaned," Victor said. "Whatever that means."

"Whatever that means." McNair scratched his chin. "Yes, damp to the knee."

Victor tapped the pen on the hood of the pickup. "She's covering for the mother. She knows more than she's saying."

"Or the father."

"Why would she cover for the father? He's dead."

"Did you notice the cut on the back of her head?"

"You're saying he hit her?"

"And marks on her throat. Like someone had grabbed her hard."

"Like in a struggle."

"There were no signs of a struggle out there. The attacker came from behind."

"So who hit her on the back of the head?"

"He did. But not then. Earlier, I'd guess. Remember she said she saw him? She was edgy when she told us. Like she was covering for him."

"For him? Would she cover for someone who had choked her?"

McNair grunted. "You're going to have to do some reading, my friend." He puffed out his cheeks. "It's a common pattern. Lash out at him in private, but protect your attacker in public."

"But she has nothing to fear from him any longer."

"That's not the point. Not in these cases. Especially if it's a father or a brother or an uncle. Someone close. You pretend they never hurt you."

"If you don't admit it aloud, then it didn't happen?"

"Something like that. That way, see, you can go on."

Victor said sharply, "Where do you get this stuff?"

McNair caught his breath just as sharply and looked at him, and

Victor had to glance away. He had almost laughed in McNair's face and now he was ashamed and could not meet the doctor's eye. It was the pain in his gut. He became short-tempered without being aware of it. The sickness was spreading from his gut to his mind. He glanced down. "What I mean," he said, "is it makes more sense that she be the one to go after him. That the girl would be the one with the knife. He had hurt her, so she was angry at him, and then she ran after him and attacked him. It's a clean explanation."

"Yes. It has the appearance of logic."

"She was out there, after all. No denying that. She admits it."

"The wounds were deep. I doubt a slip of a girl could stick a knife into someone that way. Did you see those wrists?"

"My point exactly. Her wrist was damaged."

"The left, yes. And she's right-handed. It would take some feat for her to stab him so brutally with her weak hand."

"What about anger? Adrenaline and all that?"

"It's not impossible, just unlikely."

Victor looked off across the open space fronting the building. In the distance there was a well and farther still a small grey tractor in a field. He was thirsty. Coffee, McNair told him, dehydrated a person. Talking did too. And walking around in the woods when he should have been sleeping. McNair had a point about the girl, though. There were quite a few footprints out there on the path. When he had explored farther along the track he had noted the girl's were not among them, so she had not been past the place where they found the body. So it was not all lies. They had found LaFlamme's distinctive shoe mark, though, and at least one other. But then it had not rained for days, so the prints could have been made anytime in the last while.

So why had she cleaned her shoes, if not out of guilt? Panic?

McNair was yawning again. Best to get on with the interviews, press the family on the whereabouts of the boy and his Indian pal. It was going to be a long day. At least he would not have to worry about Sheila being upset at him for coming home late. No, but soon would come the desperate phone call.

H E WAS A LITTLE SURPRISED that Mortimer assumed a position of authority so quickly, a fact he registered at the time but which assumed more importance as the days went by. He was pulling on his socks and shoes and Mortimer was standing at the foot of his bed. Peter was still sleeping. The Finn was gone. Mortimer said, "There's been some goings on over at the store this morning. LaFlamme is dead. There's a cop and he wants to talk to everybody. The local Mountie."

Alexander was rubbing the sleep out of his eyes. Once he'd pulled the blanket up, he'd slept pretty well. Better than in a long while. He put it down to the country air, the walking they'd done the night previous. His legs ached in that good tired way, though, and he was having a difficult time taking in everything that Mort was saying. LaFlamme, the Mountie, something else that was not being said. But Mort seemed in a hurry, so Alexander took in what he was told without comment, but he was watching his brother's round face with interest. There was a downward curl to his lip that Alexander had known as a boy, as if Mort knew more than he was saying. Was he hiding something?

"The deal is," Mort continued, "we take breakfast in the kitchen up at the store after the family is finished. She makes lunch for us too."

He noted that *she* and was waiting to hear it again.

"Sundays," Mort said, "we usually linger a bit, yakkity-yak sort of thing, ease our way into the day of rest, but today we'll grab some toast and coffee and make ourselves scarce. She's busy up there."

Alexander looked over at Peter: a shock of red hair was visible above the blanket, one foot stuck out at the end of the bed. The boy slept on his stomach and sometimes ground his teeth. Alexander pulled on his shoes and walked over to his bed. He put one hand on his shoulder and called his name softly; looked back at Mort.

Mort was staring out of the window that looked toward the field. He had not shaved. The stubble near his ear was pepper and salt. He had a welt on one cheek where he had been kicked by a horse when he was a boy. He was aware that he was being watched. His eyes moved from the window to Alexander. Slowly. He was not a bright man, he was not clever at school the way Alexander had been, but he was a hard worker and determined. There was a cunning in the way he did things that did not show up in his flat brown eyes and halting speech. He was a force, a physical force. He was used to getting what he wanted. And he could not be trusted, not entirely.

Alexander shook Peter's shoulder again, smelling as he did the close and piquant odours of the boy's body.

"They're talking to the Finn now," Mort said. "Questioning him."

Alexander had the shirt he had worn the day before in his hand, a steel grey work shirt. He folded it carefully and put it on one of the shelves of the cupboard near his bed. Then he selected the only white shirt from the pile and pulled it on. It was the weekend, after all.

"You'd be well advised," Mort was continuing, "to say as little as possible."

Alexander gave Peter's shoulder one more tug. "Come on," he said.

"Not my thinking, only," Mort went on, "but what she wants."

There it was again. She. That's how the old man had referred to their mother when she was not present: the pronoun indicated more than familiarity.

Mort cleared his throat self-consciously and stepped outside after saying this.

Peter had pushed aside the blanket and was dressing. Body odours wafted over from him. Alexander would have to make a point of seeing that the boy took regular baths. He watched him for a moment: thinnish arms and long legs and square shoulders. He would be a good-looking man some day. He was yawning and stretching. Alexander found Peter's sweatshirt and threw it on the edge of the bed. Then he pulled on his own shirt and fastened the buttons.

"I'm awake," Peter was saying in a testy voice, "I'm coming already." He didn't know that something serious was going on, an adult thing that might affect their lives. Would there be time to tell him before the cops started the questions?

Alexander joined Mort on the stoop outside. The open space in front of the buildings was really quite large when viewed in the light of day. A pickup was parked in front of the store. Fields to the left of the bunkhouse stretched for two or three hundred yards in that direction before the bush and rocks started. To the right and directly in front of the store there was a kind of rough lawn area, more a meadow: various grasses, daisies. Pines and maples stood off in the background further to the right, where the woods proper began. But there was plenty of room in the foreground for the eye to roam. During their train journey the day before and the walk the night previous he had felt claustrophobic in the woods, with the trees looming overhead and the dense undergrowth pressing in on all sides, but in the light of day there seemed to be more space. He didn't feel as if killers were going to leap out of the woods at him at every moment. There were ornamental bushes near the steps leading into the store, dogwood, and what maybe was lilac growing as a border hedge on one flank of the building, and a lovely squat bush with red branches and striking purple leaves that he would ask someone to identify: the colours of a maple leaf, but too squat and bushy to be one.

A cat was sunning itself on the top step of the store.

His eyes focussed there on the old pickup: dull army green with oversize tires front and back. Like a jeep, only not a jeep. He guessed it belonged to the cop Mort had mentioned and that he was conducting his interviews inside. Alexander would have to steel himself for that and be prepared to evade.

A mosquito landed on his arm and he squashed it with a smack.

Beside him Mort turned, and looked at him and smiled before saying, "They're almost done for the year."

They made to sit. Mort took a tin of chewing tobacco out of his back pocket and poked a wad under his tongue. Alexander settled on the step beside him and took out his pipe. The sun was over the treetops. The sky was bright blue from horizon to horizon. Sparrows were twittering in the bushes near the store. A woodpecker was knocking on something noisily. Alexander was listening for sounds in the bunkhouse: to hear if Peter had finished dressing and was washing up at the enamel basin.

"Things are going to change," Mort said. "She wants me to help in the store. Help her and the girls out, like. The Finn will complete the work in the clearing field on his own. You will paint the store and then the bunkhouse. They sure need it. Also, you can turn over the oats in the granary and give me a hand from time to time. Then we'll see."

Alexander wanted to ask about the boy, Roger, but he was the newcomer, it was not his place. He glanced at his watch. Half past seven. He wondered when all this had been settled. He nodded and said, "Whatever is good for you, is all right by me."

"I know, Dick. I know I can count on you."

Alexander hoped so. He hoped he did not have to choose between Mort and Peter.

Peter came out of the door, yawning and groaning, and they stood up. "Let's get you some toast and coffee," Mort said. He put one large hand on the boy's shoulder and the other on Alexander's, like two people who needed guiding, and walked them toward the store.

She was sitting up in bed with a magazine on her lap, the sun streaming in through the window onto the quilt. She could not recall how she got to the room but she knew she had slept. It was ten o'clock. About a half hour earlier Cassie had come in with a hard-boiled egg and toast, and she had eaten them almost before Cassie was out of the room, and now she felt as good as if she had slept through the night. The headache was gone. The wrist hurt a bit but it was nothing really.

From the direction of the store she heard the thumping of feet on the floor from time to time and the rumble of voices. The Mountie was asking his questions. She closed her eyes and exhaled slowly. The window was open and she heard blue jays squawking in the trees, and the generator that produced the electricity thrumming. What had happened the night before and the walk back to the scene in the early morning seemed part of a dream world, something that had happened to someone else, like in a movie.

Only it was clear. LaFlamme was dead. Stabbed, it appeared. There had been talk of knives and of wounds but she could not recall details clearly. There were blank spots. It had all been a jumble, anyway—her, him, the paths in the woods. She did not want to recall details. It had happened to someone else. Then there had been the doctor and the Mountie with their questions. Buzzings had developed in her head. She closed her mind to what she had seen on the path. He was gone and all that was behind them.

Ruth came in. She had combed her hair out and was wearing the bright red lipstick. Jeans and a light sweater that flattered her breasts. She looked as good as the models in the magazine on Virginia's lap. Ruth sat on the end of the bed. The gold chain around her neck winked in the sunlight.

"We're going over to see Lucy and Penny," Ruth announced. She had the bright look in her eyes that she had sometimes after she had been out with boys: a spark, but not of anger. "An adventure, like." She twiddled her fingers a moment, waiting for Virginia to say something. Virginia wanted to ask Ruth where she'd been the night before; she wanted her to be in the clear, but there was no point in asking. Ruth only told her what she was ready to.

Virginia pushed away the quilt. She was surprised to discover she was still in her jeans and the sweater she had put on in the dawn. A maple leaf was snagged on one arm. She brushed it away and then stood in front of the mirror on her dresser and ran the comb through her hair. Ruth said, "That's good, you look great." It was her brusque voice—let's get on with it, keep your inane questions to yourself.

Virginia pulled on her shoes, which were still damp but okay for walking.

They were in a hurry, it seemed. Ruth stooped at the mud room door as they went out. She picked up a knapsack like the one the Mountie had carried earlier, khaki-coloured and square, with two shoulder straps. She led the way out and in a moment they were on the path that looped around the lake in the opposite direction Virginia had travelled in the morning with the Mountie and the others. It was farther that way to where Lucy and Penny lived, they could have taken the rowboat across the narrows, but she knew why they were not going past Moose Point that day.

The mosquitoes were not bad. They brushed them away.

The path was wide enough to walk side by side until they came to the rocks. Ruth said, "It was a game. He was trying to get me to say things and I was doing my best not to tell him anything." To protect Roger, Virginia was thinking—or herself. Ruth was breathing hard, walking fast, a brightness to her body movements that matched her face.

Virginia said, "The Mountie scares me."

Ruth said, "Those eyes. He's used to bullying things out of people."

"He could take us away from Mother. Break up the family."

"No," Ruth said, "they don't do that any more."

"If she's involved?"

"Cassie? You're out of your mind."

"She's scared out of her wits. They've been after Roger since he broke that kid's arm at school."

Instead of answering, Ruth said, "That doctor needs to eat. A skinny doctor."

"The Mountie wanted me to say I did it."

"He wants someone to say it. That makes his job easy. Then he can go home to the wife."

"His wife left him. Runs around, I mean."

Ruth slowed. She was slightly in front and she turned to Virginia. "You know all these things about people. How do you do it?" What she did not say was what the girls in Ruth's grade threw up in her face: the cop's wife and *him*.

They came to the rocks and Ruth went ahead. Sunlight was dancing on the surface of Moon Lake. Fish jumped near the shore and left rippling pools in the water. Virginia stopped. Was that a moose down in the bulrushes? She stood still but could not detect any motion in that direction. A pair of binoculars hung on a peg at the store but she had not thought to bring them.

When she caught up with her, Ruth said, "Feet hurt?"

"The lake looks so peaceful. Do you think we'll ever leave here?"

"Soon as possible, as far as I'm concerned."

"I love the lake, the quiet of the woods."

"Crap. Get out if you can."

Once they passed the junction past Cuthand's where the trail intersected the path they were following around the lake, the going became a bit difficult. Ruth had slipped the knapsack over one shoulder but she stopped for a moment to slide the other arm through its strap. Beads of sweat stood out on her lower lip. A few mosquitoes buzzed about their heads. She smiled at Virginia. "This is good," she said. "Out here."

"Clears the mind. Washes it clean."

"Putting distance between us and that lot."

Virginia said, "Get away from all that back there."

"Cops. Bullshit."

They did not mention him by name or by reference. They had been wishing him out of their lives for a long time. He had become nothing to them, a dark hole where there should have been good feelings. And now he was gone and they were relieved and prepared never to mention him again.

They walked along the path silently. The scent of pine needles rose up from the woods. Somewhere in the dark recesses of the trees a crow was croaking.

She had thought they were going to the Clouds' house but Penny and Lucy were sitting on a rock near the road that ran north and then looped east into the reservation, the road the men went down to cut wood in the winter. She had been down that road on walks before but never very far. She was afraid of bears. And Cassie was always going on about poison ivy.

Lucy and Penny stood up when they came abreast and they

walked into the woods without speaking. It was warm in the trees away from the lake; the sun beat down on the narrow opening. She had noticed before how many wild plants grew in the woods but she was seized by a sudden impulse to count just how many. She picked two brown fern leaves, then a columbine, then a plant Roger called stinkweed. She dare not go far off the path. The other three were ahead and making good progress. The Cloud girls both had ponytails and they bobbed ahead of Ruth in rhythm as they walked. Virginia picked more plants: hyssop and brown-eyed Susans that had hung on past the season. Bergamot and gentian. Many with names she did not know. Foxtail with its velvety leaves. She added stalks of long grass and a red maple leaf that had fallen on the path, a crowning touch.

Ruth dropped back for a moment. "Keep up," she said sharply.

Virginia looked at her bouquet. Twenty plants at least. It was a shame now that she had picked them. She wasn't sure what she was going to do with them. Fix up a vase in her bedroom, maybe. Give them to Cassie as a peace offering?

They had entered a dense section of the woods. Closer to the store they had heard squirrels in the trees and small birds but here the woods were silent. It was spooky. She looked up: blue sky, bright sun overhead. In the summer at this time of day the sun would be blazing hot, but on the Labour Day weekend it was just beginning to feel less than comfortable. The path wound through the trees. The undergrowth was thick with fallen branches and trunks; occasionally a branch blocked the path. The Cloud girls hopped over them. Ruth held the branches down for Virginia. The bouquet was an encumbrance. And the mosquitoes buzzed in thick clouds in the close and dense woods whenever they stopped. She slapped at them with her free hand.

Where the ruts of the road curved off to the north, they came to a massive hump of rock. Penny and Lucy stopped. In the other direction a narrow path went along the side of the rocky hump and seemed to rise through the scrub spruces as it went parallel to and then up the side of the rock. Apparently they were going that way. Penny took a pack of cigarettes out of her shirt pocket. She was the older of the two Cloud girls, older than Ruth. She struck a paper match to the end of a cigarette and after she puffed on it, passed it to her sister. That was the way they smoked: from Penny to Ruth and then to her. She coughed and waved the cigarette away when Ruth offered it the next time. Penny laughed. One of her front teeth was chipped at an sharp angle. There was a large mole on her nose. Lucy finished the cigarette. She stubbed it out on the ground with her sneaker and then found a rock and placed it over the stub.

"Thirsty," Penny said.

Ruth nodded. "Should have remembered water."

Lucy said, "Let's move. The mosquitoes are biting."

Ruth slipped the knapsack off her shoulders and took out an aerosol can of bug repellent which they sprayed about their ankles. "Won't do a damn bit of good," Penny said as she circled the bottom of her jeans with the spray.

"But I'll feel better," Ruth said. "And that's something."

"Bear fat," Lucy said, "that's the trick." She smiled at Virginia and then looked down. She and Penny were wearing moccasins, soiled and tatty.

They took the narrow path to the right and began climbing. The going was not easy. Stones jutted out of the path. The footing was treacherous. In places the passage between the rock face and the trees was very narrow, almost too tight to pass. Virginia had never ventured this far into the woods. She had not realized the Shield was as rugged as this. They lived by the lake where the terrain was relatively flat. But the rock face they were slowly climbing rose hundreds of feet toward the sky, maybe more, because she could not tell where it crested.

The path climbed slowly at an angle. At first they went south, with the sun in their faces, but then the path hairpinned back on itself. Then again. In a while they came to a ridge and could look down. Now the sun was off to one side. The treetops were below them. Moon Lake was a sparkle of light in the distance. It was not as large as she had thought, quite narrow, really, near the wild rice field that separated their side of the lake from where the Clouds lived on the opposite side. Beyond that the much larger lake.

Virginia said, "Wow!" She put the bouquet down to survey the scene.

The Cloud girls looked at each other and laughed. They were wearing short-sleeved tops. Virginia had wondered about that. She understood why now. The climbing was hard. They were all sweating. When they stopped, the mosquitoes had zeroed in on them and were landing on their necks and biting. But she had to keep her focus on the narrow ridge path; she did not want to slip on the stones and tumble down the escarpment of rock.

"Not far now," Penny said. "Then the breeze will blow them away."

The path ran along a rock ridge. Tiny, stunted spruces grew wherever there was a seam of earth. Red-veined vines of some kind too. Then the path doubled back on itself. The vegetation was thicker and the rocks more round. They were coming out on the crest. They stopped to catch their breath. They were standing on the flat rock surface of what appeared to be a giant hummock open to the sky. Trees grew along the margins but the open area was flattish and large, an acre or more. You could look down in all four directions. It was almost as if they were standing in the clouds.

Virginia said, "This is unbelievable. Beautiful." She wiped sweat off her brow and stared at the treetops below them: tall jack pines, poplars, oaks, stunted swamp spruce. A few openings where marsh grass grew. Above, the sun was near its zenith. A few fluffy white clouds had come into the sky.

"It's a sacred place," Penny said. "The men bring the boys here so they can have a dream. So they can pass from being boys to men. Change their lives."

Virginia was thinking of Archie, Penny's brother. His round brown eyes followed her when he came into the store. He laughed at her jokes; she envied his cheekbones.

Penny was continuing, "We have come here to get rid of him. To ward evil away. He is a badness in our spirits, an evil presence that we must—we must—"

"Purge," she offered.

"We are going to lie on our backs," Penny continued, "and stare at the sky and our minds will empty, and then the badness will fly up to the sky and be gone. We may have a vision. Something from the spirit world. Then he will be gone forever."

Ruth said, "Can the change happen that fast, after years of hate and fear, he will just be gone and we will just be cleansed?" There were furrows in her brow. She was snapping one thumb and forefinger together.

"You must relax first," Penny said, "for it to be a good moment for the spirits."

Lucy said, "It will be better if we don't talk much now."

"And we must not leave anything behind when we go," Penny said. "The men must never know we have been here."

Ruth said, "That's a pile of hokey-pokey. It's public land."

Lucy scowled and muttered something about dreams and spirits.

"It's a sacred place," Penny repeated.

There was a momentary silence. Lucy ran one toe over the rock, making a squeaking sound. She was shorter than Penny. She did not smile as much. And Penny was right. The breeze blowing across the rocks drove the mosquitoes away. There were insects, though, buzzing in the warm air and gulls way up high floating in the blue toward the lake.

Ruth had put down the knapsack. "All right," she said, making a face by drawing her lips back. "I won't tell." She laughed.

They all laughed. Ruth opened the knapsack and brought out a wineskin. She passed it to Penny. They sat on the ground in a circle, their toes almost touching. When Penny had drunk, she passed the wineskin to Ruth. It was the same routine as with the cigarette. She was getting better at holding down the smoke. Then Penny took a small plastic bag out of the pocket of her jeans. It contained two roll-your-own cigarettes. This time when she lit up she coughed a little herself. She passed the cigarette to Lucy and then took a sip of wine. She let out an audible sigh.

Then Ruth passed the cigarette to Virginia. She wanted to refuse but she knew it was special. This was what they had come to do. The wine and the dope. The smoke was hot in her throat but she choked it back and tried to inhale as much into her lungs as possible before reaching for the wineskin. It was white wine and it tasted sweet and warm but she smacked her lips.

They smoked two of the cigarettes and drank most of the wine.

They were lying flat on their backs in a circle looking up at the sky. The sun had passed its zenith. The clouds above seemed a long way off and then suddenly quite close. She blinked her eyes. It was warm on the rock. Sweat had formed behind her knees and on her belly. Her breasts felt itchy. The wine had made her drowsy but the dope had enlivened her senses. Each note the birds in the nearby trees struck sounded like a clarinet solo. She could not identify the bird. She must try not to think, she must empty her mind. She thought the marijuana would drift her into a sweet trance, but instead her mind went back to the previous night, and though she tried to shake it off, the first image she had was of his hand rising from the surface of the lake, fingers crooked, the black hairs on the back of his wrists wiry as those on his chest. She jerked to consciousness. That was just like him. She took several deep breaths and composed herself, wishing he would soon fade from her thoughts. *Try not to think. Empty the mind.*

She closed her eyes and when she opened them she found she had lifted her arms so that her hands were folded a foot or more in front of her face, as if in prayer. Why had she done that? Slowly she opened her hands, which were sweaty and sticky. The palms were still raw from the fall the night before but they did not sting any longer, and the swelling had nearly gone out of her wrist. The pain had gone entirely out of the knee. She felt at peace and filled with energy, both at once. She wanted to laugh but feared that would break the mood.

Beside her Ruth was breathing heavily and regularly. She could sense Penny and Lucy near her feet but she did not know what they were doing. She watched the clouds drift apart and form ragged shapes. She thought of a song she had sung as a girl at school. So peaceful. In a few moments it was just the thumping of her heart in her chest and Ruth's breathing at her side. She either dozed off or went into some kind of trance.

She heard Penny's voice saying from far away, "We must go now."

Virginia sighed and wished the feeling she was experiencing could go on forever. During the brief trance she felt she had transmuted into another being, an Indian girl from centuries ago. It was a vague sensation, like a half-remembered dream, a suffusion of warm sensations as much as a recollection of images. She had read about transmutation and wondered what it would be like to come back in another life as an animal, a hawk, maybe, or one of the half animal-half human creatures the Indians favoured in drawings.

She lifted her head. The Cloud girls were sitting up, stretching their legs and rubbing them. Ruth was asleep, her bottom lip twitching.

Lucy said, "I feel clean."

Penny said, "The badness has passed like rotten breath. I have breathed him out and now he is gone. That part of my life is over."

Her eyes when she looked at Virginia were glassy. She had taken the rubber ring out of her thick black hair to lie down but she was fixing it back into a ponytail.

Lucy asked Virginia, "Do you feel better? Did you have a vision?"

She said, "I saw a rose in the clouds."

Lucy grunted. She looked at Penny.

Ruth's eyes blinked open and then closed again. She folded her hands over her belly and sighed.

Virginia said, "Two roses, actually, but the one broke up fast. The clouds, I mean. The other stayed a long time. It seemed to be my friend."

Lucy said, "It's not quite a vision but it might do."

"Hush," Penny said. She was listening intently. She stood up. "We must go now," she whispered. "The men might come."

Lucy looked up at her. "They will not come today," she said. "They only come at night and then it must be a full moon."

"No," Penny said. "There are other times. When an old one dies."

"But no one has died," Lucy protested.

Virginia said, "Yes, exactly no one has died. Mister bloody Nobody."

They were silent for a moment. Lucy asked, "What do you hear?"

Penny whispered, "Maybe just the wind in the trees." She studied the spruces that formed a border on one side of the rock platform. "Still," she said, "we should get a move on. I don't want to have this feeling spoiled. I feel too clean inside now."

Lucy and Virginia stood. She felt the breeze on her face.

Ruth had raised herself onto one elbow. Penny looked from Ruth to Virginia. "It's their sacred place," she said. "They bring the boys here on a night when the moon is in a special place and they make a fire, and then they smoke but they do not eat until the boys have a dream. Then they give the boys a name. They become men."

"Our kind of name," Lucy added. "A name you never hear."

"At least that's what I understand happens. They don't say much about it."

Ruth was rubbing her eyes with the backs of her hands. She grunted and stood up. She picked up the wineskin and took a sip.

"We could call you Rose," Lucy said to Virginia, "or Little

Flower in the Cloud." She and Penny laughed. They both had broken lower teeth but their brown eyes danced when they found something amusing. They were treating her like a sister. She suddenly wanted to hug them. She thought again of Archie's skin and full lips. They had shared an apple the last time he'd come into the store and stood talking on either side of the counter until Cassie had come in and put Archie to work shifting some boxes.

Ruth said, "I'm starving." She put the wineskin back in the knapsack.

The Cloud girls looked around the site and then scuffed the places where they had been lying with the toes of their shoes so the little sweat marks they had made on the rock disappeared. Before they left Penny said to them, "You must not come back here."

It felt cooler on the way down, though the path was no less tricky. She had to watch every step. It was easy to lose your footing. From time to time one of them kicked a stone loose and it made loud noises as it ricocheted down the slopes. She imagined tumbling over the rocks that way and landing on the sharp tops of the trees projecting at them from below. Skewered. You could die. They all stood silently to listen, afraid now that they had been to the sacred place and not been discovered. They hurried on.

At the bottom of the rock face they paused. The sun had moved over on the horizon. Their faces were in shadow. A few mosquitoes found them but when they brushed at them half-heartedly, they flew away. It was the end of their season. Penny took out one of the Exports and they passed it around, the same as before. Lucy put her hand on Virginia's shoulder. "It's a time of grief," she said, "but we cannot grieve."

"I know," she said, sadly. But she was actually more sorry that she had left the bouquet of wild plants up on a ledge of rock where they had first stopped to look at Moon Lake.

Penny exhaled smoke through her nostrils. "We are not sorry."

"He was a bad man," Virginia offered.

Ruth took the cigarette from her and after she had exhaled, she said, "He was a bastard and an asshole and a creep and a monster and a plain vile human being who deserved to die. May he rot in hell."

Penny chuckled. "That about sums it up, yes."

"I never want to talk about him again," Virginia said. "Or think about him."

"I would have killed him," Ruth added, growing bolder, "if someone had not done it for me." She put her hand to her throat and fingered the gold chain.

Penny grunted. She was twiddling her fingers on her belly.

Lucy was stroking Virginia's shoulder. "I know how rotten I would feel if something bad happened to our father."

"He was not our father," Virginia said. "I refuse to accept it."

"Only in name," Ruth said. "A name I am not proud of."

She thought then that she would change her name and take the one that the Cloud girls had given her. It would signal a fresh start and put that life behind forever.

When they had smoked the cigarette down Lucy squashed it out with the same rock she had used before and placed it over both stubs. Virginia was to remember that all her life: the care with which Lucy Cloud extinguished the cigarette stubs and centred them under the rock with her short brown fingers.

T HE MOUNTIE WAS SITTING ACROSS from Alexander at the kitchen table, writing in his notebook. He was left-handed, Alexander noted. Same as Peter. Same as his own old man. They had to twist the paper around in front of them at an angle to accommodate the slant of their wrists. The old man found power tools tricky to operate, and certain types of door catches scraped his knuckles. The Mountie stared at his coffee cup but did not drink. Alexander exhaled and then lifted his cup to his mouth.

"Alexander Mann," the Mountie said, "brother of Mortimer Mann. You have something to identify you?"

"In my wallet," he answered. And fished it out of his back pocket.

The Mountie scrutinized his driver's licence and then made a note of the numbers on the white sticker. "1937," he said. "Same year as me." He passed the licence and the wallet back to Alexander. "You and your boy arriving on the night of a murder, that's not good, is it?"

"We were hoping for a fresh start, me and Peter," he said.

The Mountie nodded. "He told me," he said. Without looking up from the notepad he asked, "You came in on last night's train?"

"It was supposed to get here for seven-thirty but was delayed."

"Yeah. Surprise. Delayed until?"

"I don't know. Eight-thirty? Nine?"

"No one met you?"

"Mortimer was supposed to, but then the train was late and we ended up making our way here by ourselves."

"And you got here when?"

"Maybe nine-thirty. Maybe ten."

"It's a ten-minute walk."

He pushed the chair back, wondering if it would be all right to smoke. He had the coffee cup in one hand and he glanced into it before taking a sip. Grey more than brown in colour. That must have been the milk. It was tasty coffee, though. "We got lost," he muttered, and then checked the Mountie's gaze for a response. At the time it had not seemed a big deal, but now it was embarrassing, that getting lost on the way up from the station. And difficult to explain. He was glad they had told Peter to go back to the bunkhouse.

"Huh." The Mountie's eyes focussed directly on yours, uncomfortably so, but a smile played about the corners of his mouth, a smile he had seen on the old man's face. He was amused by what was happening as well as intrigued by it, smarter than you, ahead of you. A look that told you he could pounce.

There was a silence, then the Mountie said, "Lots of paths."

"It was dark. We had no idea." He was tempted to add that they were from the city, unused to the Shield, but that sounded like it might be admitting weakness.

The Mountie grunted. He had his pen poised above the lined paper. His fingers were stubby, like his body in general. He had a pug nose. Alexander guessed he'd been in a few scraps in his time. From the look in his eyes he did not discourage them. The Mountie was watching Alexander watch him. He said, "In his statement your son said you saw someone on the paths."

Alexander had not realized the boy had given a statement. It sounded such a formal proceeding for the impressions Peter might have formed in the woods in the darkness. "A fleeting glance," he said. "Someone short, with dark hair. I couldn't even say for sure if it was a man or woman."

"Or boy."

The Mountie was not really trying to trap him but it sounded like it. The voice came so sharply, and the statements were so brief. Like jabs in the boxing ring. "Or boy," he admitted, "or girl."

"Your son seemed quite certain."

"He's young, the young are always certain."

The Mountie smiled back at him. There were thin lines at the corners of his mouth and a heaviness to his gaze as well as dark pouches below his eyes. And similar to the doctor whom Alexander had encountered outside earlier, he was tired. They had been up half the night, it appeared. And now this questioning. The cup of coffee that Cassie LaFlamme had poured him sat at his elbow untouched. "Your son said the boy in the woods ran away from you."

"He was running. He may not have been running away."

It sounded too pat an answer to him, but the Mountie smiled again and went on scratching in his notepad. In other circumstances, Alexander would enjoy conversing with him. Prior to this he had met only two kinds of cops: some were bullies, most were fidgety. This one seemed to think a lot for a cop. He had a faraway look in his eyes, as if he was pondering other things. "Your son said he had a weapon, this boy on the path."

"He saw something glinting in the moonlight. I did not. It may have been a buckle or a rivet on the person's clothing. Or an optical illusion. He's a kid and we were a little wrought up." That was stupid, giving a cop an entry like that, but the Mountie was too busy writing to note it. Alexander thought a few words of caution to himself.

The Mountie said, "When you were waiting outside while I talked with your brother, the doc said you cleaned the bowl of your pipe out with a pen knife. Would you mind showing it to me?"

Alexander put his hand in the front pocket of his trousers. "Not a pen knife, exactly. A clasp knife." He placed it on the table.

The Mountie had a paper towel to hand. He lifted the knife up, turned it over, extricated the two blades from the knife with a practiced flick of a thumb nail. "This the only one?"

"Fits in my pocket. Small but handy."

"You keep it sharp," he said.

Mort had said that LaFlamme was dead but not much more than that. He had suspected foul play since the Mountie and the doctor were there. It was beginning to be clear to him what had happened. A messy death. "An old habit," he said. "A habit I picked up from the old man. Keep the tools in good repair." It was a banal enough comment. It fit in with the kitchen, he realized, with its off-white Arborite countertop, grey checked tiles, chrome chairs. In front of him he had the remains of the toast Cassie LaFlamme had given him earlier and he studied the pattern on the Melmac: swirls that suggested dandelion seeds blowing in the wind.

The Mountie grunted. He put the knife on the table. "Then you came through the woods and up to the bunkhouse. Did you see anyone else?"

This was the sticky part. He must not answer too quickly or too slowly. "No," he said, as if thinking it through as he was saying it, reliving that portion of the walk in his mind. He did not look at the Mountie.

"You walked past the kitchen right out there. I assume the lights were on. Did you look in the window?"

"Glanced. There was no one about so we kept on moving."

"You were lost, you came to the first lit room in the first building since you had left the railroad station and you did not stop to investigate where you were? Didn't knock on the door to see if you had the right place?"

"It had to be the right place." He looked the Mountie in the eye. "Anyway, we were turned around but not lost exactly."

"Not in danger, then, or afraid?"

"We kind of knew we had to have the right building. Mortimer had told me the bunkhouse was separate from this building so I was sort of looking for it."

"Sort of, kind of." The Mountie smiled again. "And it was dark by this time."

"You see outlines of buildings and light flickering through trees. Just."

"But no one, say, coming out of this building?"

"We were that tired. We made our way to the bunkhouse and located the beds. We turned in."

Alexander heard crows calling outside. The Mountie had noticed them too, and seemed momentarily distracted before going on with his interview. Plodding through the questions.

"Okay, one more thing."

He was expecting that. He had his answer ready. But he was caught off guard by the question the Mountie put to him: "Why did you come here?"

"To work." He did not want to explain but the Mountie looked directly into his eyes so he felt compelled to go on. "I owned a business in the city. Things did not go so well and we gave it up." Not quite a lie. "We came here to get away from it all. It gets you down when something like that happens." The way he said it made the loss sound casual, as if he had misplaced something. It had torn a hole in his heart: lawyers, bankers, the phone ringing with bad news.

The Mountie asked, "Wife?"

"Passed away. Last year. Maria." It still made his mouth dry to say her name, and he was instantly sorry he had uttered it. The Mountie, he noticed, looked down, at the floor. He thought for a moment he had dropped something but then realized that the Mountie was being tactful: the strong silent type who preferred to dodge around death.

The Mountie was going to ask something else but just then Cassie came back into the room. She stopped when she spotted the knife on the table. She said, "Is that his?"

"No," the Mountie said, glancing at Alexander. It was clear he knew something that he did not want revealed.

For the second time in less than twenty-four hours Alexander felt as if he was walking blind in a dark and unfamiliar place, about to trip over objects on the floor or crack his head on a door frame. He had no idea where he stood. It seemed the Mountie had already spoken to Peter. But had he talked with the older girl—or Roger? What did he know? What did he want to know? The Mountie asked questions that were simple-minded and then skipped over areas that seemed obvious. The method threw Alexander off balance. That was the point, he realized: the Mountie had already made up his mind about certain things but needed confirmation of others. Alexander sensed that the Mountie put some questions to him with the sole purpose of determining whether he was trustworthy.

Cassie was saying, "He had one just like that. Never went anywhere without the damn thing." She paused and tapped her fingers on the counter. "Just like the hat," she said. "Did you find the hat?"

The Mountie said, "The knife was in his back pocket. No hat."

"It was khaki-coloured, one of those Australian ones with the sides up."

"Outback hat," the Mountie offered.

"He bought it at the Army and Navy in the city at the same time as he bought the knapsacks. Old army issue, he told me. He loved that, getting a bargain."

"There was no hat," the Mountie said. "He left it here?"

"That hat went everywhere he did. He only took it off to eat and sleep."

The Mountie said, "You have another look around here. And we'll have another look out there." To Alexander he said, "The heels of your shoes might match up with what we found out at the scene."

Alexander resisted looking down but felt blood pulsing in his ankles. "We were not lost in that direction," he said. "We found the bunkhouse, like I said earlier."

"But you could have stumbled into LaFlamme."

"Could have." He was just mechanically repeating what the Mountie said, not admitting anything, so he added, "I didn't know the man, much less have a reason to hurt him."

"You may have had no reason. But your brother may have."

He felt his ears turning red. His blood was pumping with caffeine the same way it had beat with adrenaline the night before. He did not respond. It was idiotic to have lost their way out in the woods. So much now rested on a random series of blunders and misturnings, things that happen to everyone all the time and do not lead to embarrassment, things that are immediately forgotten and put behind you. The thought crossed his mind that they might be sent away. Maybe they would take Peter. Put him in a home.

"Anyway," the Mountie said, "I think we're done here for now. If you think of anything, anything at all, let me know." He sighed in a way that was supposed to suggest he was weary of the proceedings, but Alexander knew better.

For lunch Cassie LaFlamme cooked them pickerel and fried potatoes. The Finn was there. He had caught the fish the night before, he said. He was shaken up by the exchange with the Mountie. His interview had occurred before Alexander's, but the Finn was still agitated when they sat down at the table. He was tapping his fingers together and shifting around in his chair.

"I got no likes," he told Alexander, "of men in uniforms."

Alexander nodded. There was something about a leather jacket and patches on the shoulders of a shirt that distanced a man from the people he was talking to and the events they were talking about. An uncle had been in Europe during the war and he always talked about it in a loudmouth way that made Alexander think he was covering up for the awful things he had done. That was the way with war vets: stony silence followed by strident bravado. He suspected it was the same with cops. He said, "Bullies."

"Exactly," the Finn said, raising his voice suddenly. "Born bloody bullies." He banged one hand on the table and the plates rattled.

Cassie cut her eyes at him. "Easy, buster."

"Is always pushing at people," the Finn said by way of explanation. Blood had surged into his cheeks. His hands shook.

Alexander said softly, "He'll be gone soon enough."

"Not soon enough," the Finn muttered, but he'd said his piece.

Mortimer was telling Peter about fishing. "It's best early in the morning, just as the sun is coming up."

Peter said, "I know. They're feeding." He had washed up in the crude shower area off the mud room after breakfast and his red hair shone in the sunlight coming in through the kitchen window. He had inherited peaches-and-cream skin from his mother, who had also been a redhead, and whose skin also marked easily. Whenever he thought about it, Alexander felt protective toward the boy, who seemed feminine in some ways.

It was just the four of them at the table and Cassie puttering about with plates of food. Cassie's girls had disappeared early in the morning. The boy was still nowhere to be seen. The Mountie and the doctor were outside. They had said something about going back to Moose Point, the place where LaFlamme's body had been discovered. The doctor had been stomping around out there while the Mountie was conducting the interviews, checking details, securing the body. Alexander suspected that soon he and Mort would be asked to help carry it back.

The Finn said to Peter, "You got to jig for them. Lower the line with the little yellow jig down to the bottom and make it dance gentle." He lifted one hand off the table and flipped his wrist to demonstrate the proper motion.

"Or if you row in the boat," Mort said, "you can troll." He did not like being shown up in front of his nephew.

"Jigging," the Finn insisted, "that's the trick." The colour was still up in his face and he looked angry.

They ate silently for a while. The cat Alexander had seen earlier, grey and white, was walking through their legs, purring and rubbing its neck against their shins. He had noticed a dog too, old and infirm.

The Finn said, "We show you. You catch more fish than you can eat."

"Big pikes," Mort said.

"Pickerel, " the Finn said. "Perches that make delicious breakfast."

"Pikes are best," Mort insisted. There was a tension between them that must have come from working on the edge of the world, side by side, day after day. Each of them wanted to be the man in charge.

"We'll go for a stomp later," Mort said, "around the lake. Show you the rowboat and get you some fishing tackle." His eyes held Alexander's for a moment and he pursed his lips together. There were things he wanted to tell him, apparently. Alexander wondered what they might be. There were things he did not want to know.

Cassie was standing behind Mortimer with her hand on the back of his chair. She said, "You can show Peter the deer meadow."

"Or the horseshoe pit." The Finn laughed. "There's lots to do."

"Right," Mort said. "Roger can show him how to set up a tent the way the Indians do." He winked at the boy, then smiled at Alexander, who could not help wondering when Roger would make an appearance.

"A tipi," Peter said.

"Maybe," the Finn said, bolder, "teach him to make chokeberry wine."

"Chokecherry," Mort said. "The Finn makes a mean chokecherry wine."

"Only," the Finn said, "someone was stealing it all the time."

Peter wanted to ask who but Alexander placed his hand on the boy's arm.

The silence extended past the eating to the drinking of tea, the muffins.

When they had finished eating they went out on the front stoop. Alexander took out his pipe and had a smoke. The sun was pouring down past the treetops into their faces. A few mosquitoes buzzed around but they did not seem very interested. He smelled the grass being heated by the sun. Alexander felt suddenly tired. The prospect of a walk around the lake was much less appealing than a long snooze, but he could tell by the way Mortimer shuffled his feet on the steps that he was anxious about something. He had never been the one to keep secrets.

Peter had sat on the steps with them at first but now he was out in the grassy meadow area in front of the store. He had found a dead branch and was swinging it in one hand around his feet like a sword, decapitating thistles and knocking down brown-eyed Susans that had hung on into the fall. He was a city boy. He would have to learn to make his own games. And Alexander would have to watch out for him: make sure he did not tumble into the lake, make sure he did the lessons.

It was not possible, was it, that he was a suspect? It was not possible that they would take Peter away?

He watched the boy for a while longer as he smoked. He was grunting with each sweeping blow of the thin branch. When he came up near the steps Alexander looked in his face, sweaty and intense, but abstracted too, as if the entire point of his existence was to demolish the plants in the field. There was a determination in the boy's slim frame, an intensity that frightened Alexander. With that grim fierceness driving him, the boy could hurt another child on the playing fields, or climb over someone else to get to the top. It might have been tempered by his mother. All of that was up to him alone now: the boy's education, his progress into manhood. He could not help thinking: what is going to happen to us?

McNair had said they should move the body soon but there was time for one more quick look round. It was early afternoon. A few clouds had come into the sky, and he sensed them as a kind of thickness in the head. He was becoming annoyed with going up and down the path. His gut was upset and he felt waves of wooziness pass through him, but he was at the point where he gritted his teeth and just held on until he could get to the Tums, so he carried his knapsack and McNair carried his black bag into the woods once more.

They had eaten fish and fried potatoes with Cassie LaFlamme. Pickerel did not agree with him. He had been burping since he finished, a sour taste in the back of his mouth like vinegar or lemon that was slightly off. The fish had not seemed to bother McNair. He had had two helpings of potatoes.

Victor had completed all the interviews and had a full pad of notes that he would have to get Helen in the office to transcribe so he could read them through with care one night soon. That was a minor irritation. He wondered if he should track down Carl Cuthand, whose involvement, if any, seemed peripheral, but then you never knew. How long had it been since LaFlamme and Young Beaudry had punched each other out in the Lakeland? That was probably a cold fire. There were more pressing issues. Roger had disappeared and Archie Cloud too. He might have to bring in a team from the city to scour the woods if they did not show soon. Either one might be out there somewhere dead. Or hiding. From what Victor had heard of the goings-on at Moon Lake, it was more likely the latter.

When they came to the place where the ground sloped downward to the lake, he saw that it functioned as a watering hole for the animals. A number of their narrow trails led through the undergrowth to the muddy shore: tracks, footprints, droppings. If he was not mistaken the girl's shoe prints would be there too. The jeans McNair had found in the laundry hamper were wet at the cuffs and had stains on the thighs, he had reported. This would be the place where she had washed off the blood. Unlike the doctor, he thought the girl was easily capable of doing the deed. He reminded himself again not to be sidetracked by McNair's softness of heart and woolly thinking.

The older girl, of course, had more reason.

The Finn had let it slip that the boy had once said he was going to kill LaFlamme.

They came to the body. Only the bottoms of the shoes stuck out; flies buzzed around and sat flicking their wings and mating on the blanket covering the body. He and the doc paused beside it and looked around. McNair coughed. Victor should photograph the footprints in the area, also the marks on the trail that looked as if they might have been made by fingernails clawing the ground. Fifty yards LaFlamme had dragged his knees over the mud and tree roots before dying. Did Victor need more samples of coagulated blood? He put his knapsack down in the grass. Was that poison ivy growing just a little off the path? He'd contracted a bad rash as a child and had to be careful not to get infected again.

"She claimed there was a hat," Victor said to McNair. "Australian outback."

The doc was rubbing the end of his nose. He said, "The hair at the crown of his skull had an indent that is consistent with the frequent wearing of a hat."

"So what happened to it?"

"We'll look. Whoever did it would be foolish to take it away, no?"

"Killers do stupid things."

They stepped over the body. There was a slight over-ripe odour rising from the blanket. (Must be moved soon.) They walked slowly down the path, looking intently into the grass on the sides of the trail: a broken stick here, a gum wrapper there. Victor picked them both up and put the gum wrapper in one of the envelopes in the knapsack. When they had walked a distance they saw where the knifing had occurred: the earth on the path was packed down and the grasses just off the trail had been disturbed too. Some scuff marks remained in the earth. Victor had taken photos of them earlier, noting they were smaller shoe prints than LaFlamme's. Then came the striations in the ground where his hands had clawed the ground as he crawled forward.

Victor pictured that in his mind's eye, going over his mental checklist. It seemed an awful way to die. Did anyone deserve that? He burped up fish again and leaned over and spat in the grass. Was the fish that making him feel so out of sorts—dizzy and muzzy in the brain and short-tempered? Fish was good for you, but it was a fatty food. "The wife," he said to McNair, "told us there was a wood crate of some kind hidden off the path."

"For storing fishing gear," McNair said.

They went a little farther. McNair stopped suddenly, stooped over, and came up with a tiny object pinched between thumb and forefinger.

He held it up in the sunlight for Victor to see.

"You shouldn't have touched it," Victor said. He was always having to remind the doc about messing up the evidence. McNair's brown eyes blinked, and he flushed, a schoolboy being reprimanded for losing a mitten.

Victor had him drop the object into an envelope. A metal piece, highly polished and with the bluish sheen of gun oil on it. Brass, it was the size of the pin that might fit in a rifle stock or the works of a pistol. He had seen this exact kind of pin before but he could not recall when or where. He was having trouble keeping focus. The headache and then that bloody fish.

McNair shrugged. "It looks to me like a piece from a tool, the piece that goes between metal parts with holes in them to hold them together. A fastening device." He shrugged. "But then what do I know?"

Victor slipped the envelope in with the others in the knapsack. "A key," he said, "or a pin. It can function as a fastener or a pivot." He had spotted a wooden box pushed under a bush just off the path up ahead, like an apple crate, only bigger. When they came up to it he saw they would have to drag it on to the path to open it. He looked for marks in the grass and on the trail. It had been dragged in and out of the storage place recently. The shoe prints were those of LaFlamme, the distinctive cross-hatch of his soles.

There was something here to investigate further but he could not put his finger on it. He closed his eyes to think and saw the silhouette of the trees and the lake on the inside of his eyelids. But no, whatever had tweaked his mind would not come clear. He wondered for a moment if he was beginning to lose his knack for police work. It had happened to men younger than him. Burnout.

He opened his eyes and turned to the box. The lid swung open on rusty hinges. Inside there were three bundles: a rubber jacket with a hood and two black rubber ground sheets, one wrapped around two fishing rods, the other around a spin reel and a plastic box containing hooks and lures. Victor ran his hands through the pockets of the jacket: a safety pin, oddments of paper, two coins, a stick of gum. He spread the rods and other things out on the ground sheets and examined each in turn. He had to work hard to keep his mind clear: dropping and lifting his head to examine the oddments on the ground sheets brought on headrushes. Everything seemed to be in order, though: no bits missing from the tackle; all the working parts clean and functional. Victor was rewrapping them up in the ground sheets when McNair said, "This is interesting."

McNair had flipped the crate on end and was examining its bottom. A small metal box was attached to the underside of the crate with plastic clips. McNair unclipped it, then opened it and passed it to Victor. Inside was a carefully folded plastic package containing two condoms in their slippery sealed packages. The doc looked at Victor and raised his eyebrows.

Victor said, "This is no lover's lane." He was standing again. He looked around. Nowhere in the immediate surround seemed suitable for what the condoms suggested.

McNair said, "And why not in the pocket of the jacket?"

He passed the plastic package over to Victor, who placed them in yet another envelope and put it in the knapsack. They pushed the crate back under the bush and then began a scrutiny of the area, walking in concentric circles outward around the box until the undergrowth was too dense to penetrate. It was slow going and hot. The terrain was uneven and vines and brambles snagged on his shoes. He was looking for the weapon, anything, really, but also watching for the shiny leaves of poison ivy. His eyes stung with pain. He lost his balance when he stepped in a hole beside a spruce tree. Stars danced in his eyes. He righted himself and waited for the headrush to pass. He saw McNair slip and fall once. Victor was feeling as if he might vomit. Then he called out, "All right. Enough already."

They met back on the path. McNair was picking thorns out of the palm of one hand, wincing each time one tore free from the bleeding flesh. "It happened right there," McNair announced. "Someone came along the path and surprised him, maybe while he was messing with the fishing gear. End of story."

"Or messing with the other," Victor said.

McNair looked up from his palm. There were tiny pinpricks of blood on his skin, seven or eight. "Or that," he said, as if his pronouncement settled the matter. McNair lifted his bag off the ground and Victor shouldered the knapsack. They walked back to the body in silence. They would have to move the body soon, get Mortimer and Alexander Mann to help. Now it was time for the doc to do his thing in the lab.

Victor needed to get back to the truck. He had Tums in the glove compartment. Cold water would help too.

When they were past Moose Point he suddenly cried out, "No bloody hat!"

They had been in the yard only a minute when the wife came and called through the screen door, "The phone is for you." That tone. And she had that look on her face he had grown used to over the years. The downcast eye that betrayed a pity that was more than half sneer. He knew who it was and what it was. Not the thing the area corporal wants to encourage if he also wants to maintain respect. Still, this was part of his life too. She had probably been calling for an hour, once every ten minutes. For a woman who had attended college, she did not understand some simple principles: if the person was not there when you called on the telephone, they probably would not be there for the following half hour.

She was breathless. He heard traffic in the background. Pay phone?

He asked, "Where?" He'd learned not to sound exasperated. It was a matter of listening at this stage, not talking, of breathing slowly and hesitating before speaking. It was not advice she wanted. He had to remind himself. She wanted to talk, to blubber. She wanted him to come get her.

This was his job. Rescuer. Once a few years back she had called him her knight in tin armor. That was better than many things she'd called him.

Cassie was lingering near at hand, feigning concern but eavesdropping, actually, so he raised his eyes to hers and she shuffled off to the kitchen. He was standing at the counter at the rear of the store. His hand rested on the glass counter below which were stored the packages of cigarettes and tins of chewing tobacco and the chocolate bars. On shelves behind the counter various kinds of tape were piled up haphazardly: friction, electrical, masking. Along the counter nearer to the cash register were packets of candy crowded next to displays of seed packets. What principle of organization brought these items cheek to jowl—convenience, haste?

"Who?" he said, raising his voice, though the problem was on her end of the line. It was not traffic. It was a daytime TV program, a movie with a car chase. She raised her voice: the guy from the insurance agency, the young guy with the moustache who drove the yellow Camaro. Last of him they would be seeing in Beausejour. That was one advantage to being a cop: they cleared off quickly enough, the weekend Don Juans she found in the bars.

She was somewhere past Portage la Prairie, it appeared, at a run-down motel and had no money to pay the bill. It was a hole, she said, nothing but dusty wind blowing papers around the parking lot—and the suspicious glares of the desk clerk. Victor was familiar with the scene. A part of him he did not want to acknowledge considered leaving her there, punishing her, but that was petty and pointless. He looked at his watch. "Two hours," he said into the receiver, "three at most."

He had been rubbing his abdomen, he realized. He had neglected to get the Tums out of the truck. The taste in his mouth was more bitter than before. He needed to spit. But this time he would not vomit.

He said, "Why don't you put him on, then. I'll sort it with him."

There were these silences when he asked questions. They had started at the time of the bicycle. That was two years ago. Why did she have to ride the roads around the town with the pet rabbit in the wire carrier basket? He asked her that. Why bicycle clips? Why at night? He had fixed a lamp to the front handlebars and reflectors on the rear fender. She went out wearing a red toque and red rubber boots and made a circuit of the gravel roads that formed a rough rectangle around the town. He could imagine the snickering in the Lakeland.

The rabbit she called Sushi. It had come after the miscarriage.

He had wandered along the counter, pulling out the long coiled cord on the receiver, and was staring absently at the wall in front of him. Past the shelves of tapes hung a calendar with each day stroked off in red marker. Someone was particular about it; the diagonal lines had been made with a ruler. Above that hung a stuffed and mounted pike on a wooden plaque, below it a rifle hanging on two brass hooks, the old Lee Enfield. The stock was polished, the barrel gleamed in the thin autumn light coming in from the window.

"Three hours," he repeated. "You'll be back home tonight, sweetie."

She had seen the previous doctor but she did not like him. Now it was time to make an appointment with McNair, get her to a specialist in the city. It was her opinion that all she needed was to get out of the town, *this hole,* she called it. She claimed the water in town had something in it that upset her system, a chemical that had caused the miscarriage. She bled into her bowel movements. When he came home nights she showed him the red in the toilet bowl. *See.*

He said, "If the café is attached to the motel, just tell him to put whatever you eat on the bill. Whatever you want. Fried chicken, cutlets."

(It was a psychiatrist she needed. They had anti-depressant drugs now too.)

"Right away," he said, sounding as if he meant he was stepping out the door the moment he put down the receiver. "Won't be long."

McNair came over to him. He was holding something pinched between the tongs of a pair of tweezers, a folded piece of brown wrapping paper, the edges torn and ragged. It had been ripped from a larger hunk of paper. "I went through the contents of the pockets again," McNair said by way explanation, "while I was waiting. We didn't spot this at first because it was tucked between some of those five-dollar notes."

The corpse was under the grey blanket in the box of the pickup. While he had been on the telephone, Mortimer and Alexander Mann had carried the body in on the canvas stretcher he kept there. They were sitting on the stoop of the bunkhouse, smoking and talking. It was a pleasant day for that, or for a snooze on a hammock in the warm sun. At this time of year the first frosts had killed off enough mosquitoes for that to be possible. It was a day for cold beer, warm sun, crickets chirping. Country life. A night for a big steak, if you could eat steak.

The opposite to rushing down the highway to rescue your ditzy wife.

He took the tweezers from McNair and placed the folded paper on the hood of the pickup. With the end of a pen he opened the paper. It was a map, drawn crudely in pencil. Words were smudged on the crinkled surface. With the palm of one hand he smoothed the paper to make it flat.

"It depicts the immediate vicinity," McNair offered.

Victor pointed at the outline of the lake, amateurish sketches of trees, the buildings they were standing in front of. "That's a canoe," he said. It was on the same side of the lake as the body but farther up the path than they had gone. He realized they should have explored there, all the way up to the wild rice fields. He glanced at his watch again. Almost three-thirty. It would take an hour. Another hour. He felt the tug of duty pulling him one way and the tug of responsibility pulling him the other.

McNair said, "Why would he have a map of the area in his pocket?"

Victor held the paper up to the sunlight. "What's that there bit?"

McNair looked over his shoulder. "A smudge," he said.

"Looks like an arrow."

"It's in the crease of the paper," McNair said. "The graphite's smudged."

"It's pointing to the canoe." They should have gone there. It was one mistake to have missed going out there in the first place, but not going at all was a dereliction of duty. Up to that moment he'd been following procedures systematically and with a kind of bright confidence, but he suddenly felt the case was beginning to slip away between Sheila's needs and his superior, Sergeant Black's, injunctions.

Victor put the map back down on the hood of the pickup. It was impossible to be certain, really, because of the crease. But he knew what he should do.

McNair said, "He lived here for years and would have known the area like his own backyard. Why would he have needed a map?" In the shadows thrown by the sunlight his eyes were chocolate brown. Set in his narrow face they looked crossed as he glanced from the paper to Victor's face, inquiring.

"Unless," Victor said, "the map was given to him by someone else. Unless it was sent to him, for an assignation, like."

The trees on the side of the road looked entirely different in the light of day. The grass was a dull green still. He could make out the worst stretches of soft ground twenty yards before they got to them and manoeuvre the pickup around most of the deadfall. Not far from the trading post a pair of grey grouse flew up from the path, their wings beating loudly before they disappeared into the spruces.

They had tied the corpse down to the stretcher and then fastened the stretcher to the box of the pickup with ropes. It was nearing four o'clock. Victor would be home by five and at the motel past Portage la Prairie by seven. She would not have run off; she had no money and she sounded strung out.

They passed Cuthand's tent. He should have taken a statement from Carl Cuthand. And where had the boy disappeared to? A lot of loose ends. A sickening feeling that he was letting the force down. The Force. He almost laughed aloud.

He said to McNair, "We'll have to come back."

"You," McNair said, "have to come back. I'll start the lab stuff tonight."

"Tomorrow. Yes. Me. Complete the interviews."

"And finish up tomorrow. Labour Day. It seems appropriate."

The pickup bounced over the ruts. Home by eight, maybe nine, then a good night's sleep. It seemed days ago that he had made the bologna sandwich and opened the cold beer and watched the late show. Maybe the bologna had irritated his stomach. He glanced over at McNair. His eyes were closed; in a few moments he would drift off. What Victor would give for a deep sleep.

He reached across the bench seat, opened the glove compartment, located the roll of Tums and chewed down two, then a third. Probably not the best idea. Lumps of chalky stuff formed under his tongue. He needed a drink of water. Then it came to him. "A bayonet," he said aloud, and when McNair squinted open his eyes, he said with more excitement in his voice than he could have imagined possible only a minute before, "you fix a bayonet to the barrel of a rifle with a catch spring and the catch spring pivots on this tiny brass cylinder. Yes. A bayonet of the kind you might fix to the Lee Enfield rifle, issue WW II, for example."

She was going into grade ten that fall. It was arranged that she would attend the high school in Beausejour. Classes began the day after the Labour Day holiday, but the death of LaFlamme meant she would not be starting until later in the week. She was to stay with Mrs. Samson, a widow who took in weekly boarders. Ruth had stayed there when she was in high school. It had been decided that Roger would not return to school after he'd pushed the girl and broken her arm. Decided by who? Virginia wondered. And wasn't that illegal?

Mrs. Samson was a stooped white-haired woman, who, according to Ruth, made the best roast beef and Yorkshire pudding in the district. Virginia had been to the house to visit Ruth just before she'd graduated in June. She had seen the colour TV in the living room, and the hooked rugs on the walls, and the Pomeranian with a cold black nose that leapt into her lap while they watched the local news at six o'clock. It smelled like wet socks but was warm against your thighs. It was one of those silly little dogs that snuffled rather than barked, a moist, fussy thing.

Mrs. Samson tut-tutted through the news. But she watched with intense interest the disasters occurring in other places in the world: an airline crash, the war in Vietnam, a flood in Africa. She muttered to herself and said they were lucky to live in a wonderful country. If only the taxes were not so high. She smiled at Virginia. "I'm not moving to the Bahamas, though," she said. She offered them cocoa and made herself a pot of tea, into which she poured a large quantity of cream when she brought it in from the kitchen. The tea cup was real china. Cassie used Melmac.

Mrs. Samson's was a two-storey red brick house with hardwood floors and bay windows. It was a proper house, not rooms that had been tacked on to a store as after-thoughts. Mrs. Samson's bedroom was downstairs, because of her rheumatism, she told Virginia, and the boarders' rooms were upstairs: a single bed, chest of drawers, curtains, prints of English countryside scenes on the walls. In her final year of high school, Ruth was the only boarder, and she had the upstairs bathroom to herself. Out of her hearing, she called Mrs. Samson by the name she had heard her bridge cronies call her, Meg.

"Meg gets her hair in a knot," she told Virginia, laughing, "if you mix the whites and the colours."

That seemed a very small price to pay to get away from Cassie. The hypocrisy was just one thing. She yelled at them, though not in the same tone as LaFlamme. His death did not seem to be bothering either of them much. Maybe it was something that had happened out at the rock plateau. She felt more at peace in herself, above thinking about him. There was a lot to that spirit stuff.

They had decided not to go back into the store when they returned from their afternoon with the Cloud girls. Not right away. They were sitting on the mattress in the granary, drinking warm Cokes and eating potato chips from a bag. Ruth had taken them from the store shelves and hidden them there earlier. She had taken cigarettes too, which she'd hidden in the rafters of the granary. She felt no guilt about taking stuff. They owed it to her, was her opinion. It was her way of getting back at them, of showing Cassie that there were ways of making him pay. A moot point now.

There was a hardness to Ruth that went beyond spunk. Once when she was given the job of doing the laundry, Ruth had used a pair of scissors to cut up his favourite shirt, claiming it had become entangled in the washing machine's agitator. She spit on his food in the kitchen before taking it out to him. And Roger let the air out of the tires on the tractor, just soft enough to be a nuisance but not obviously flattened. Their hatred was palpable to Virginia—and frightening. They had talked about driving the tractor over him and throwing the body in the lake. And of faking an accident with the shotgun. Virginia thought it was just talk, and little more. She thought Ruth was exaggerating to impress her. Roger did that sometimes. The truth was they all were terrified of him; had been and would continue to be, even though he was gone. Wasn't that peculiar?

She was still getting used to the idea that he would not come clumping down the hallway to her room, smelling of whiskey and horrible aftershave. She could close her eyes and see wiry hairs on the back of his hands, and then vomit rose in her gorge.

"I followed him," Ruth told her. They had left the door of the granary ajar. The cigarette smoke Ruth exhaled from her nostrils curled towards the ceiling and then picked up an air current from outside, drifting through the afternoon sunlight coming in at the door. It looked like a transparent bluish scarf floating away from them. The beams of the sun just reached their outstretched feet, warming Virginia's toes.

Virginia's mouth was dry. The chips were salty and the warm Coke did nothing to alleviate the thirst. Made it worse. But they had been hungry from the long walk, so they had eaten them, onion and garlic, Ruth's favourite, and then it was unpleasant. Virginia felt bloated. Soon she would have to go to the bathroom.

"Not the other night," Ruth went on hastily, "so don't worry. This was weeks ago that I followed him. Remember when I was limping around on this foot?"

Virginia was watching a long-legged spider making awkward progress across the rough floor boards of the granary. Ruth hated spiders. If she noticed the spider, she would squirm up on the mattress and make Virginia kill it.

He'd come into her room, Ruth explained. Virginia knew she had taken to keeping the bayonet on the floor beside her bed. She had seen it there when she was doing the vacuuming. Ruth was not to be surprised. But when he came for her and Ruth took it out, he'd laughed and struck her on the head with the back of his hand and knocked her to the floor. She had lost consciousness. When she came to her senses, she was in a rage like only Ruth could be, so she picked up the bayonet and went after him. She ran down the path toward Moose Point, the bayonet in her hands. "It was heavier than you'd think," she told Virginia. "Just being struck by the thing would do plenty of damage." And she had wanted to, badly. She nearly caught up to him.

"I was that furious," she said. "I was going to hit him in the back before he knew what was happening. As hard a blow as I could manage. I'd figured out where. At the base of the skull. One blow. Crunch right into those spiky spinal bones there. Even he would have gone down. Then I'd have stabbed him."

Virginia made a face.

"Stabbed him ten or twenty times," Ruth insisted. The idea excited her. "Until he bled like a stuck pig."

"They'd have put you in jail," Virginia said.

"You don't think of that when your blood is up."

"They'd have separated us." It was that which worried her, she realized, being separated from Ruth.

Ruth exhaled into the air stagily and shut her eyes. "I could taste it, Ginny," she went on. "I would have done it that night." She looked at Virginia. "It was not that he hit me. It was you. He said something. Ugly. That's why I was on the path running after him, the bastard." But she had tripped on a root and fallen awkwardly. "So dumb," she said, "so bloody dumb to fall." She'd tumbled face first into the thistles that grew along side the path. Her ankle had twisted. When she stood up she knew she would barely be able to limp back to her room.

"I would have done it, Ginny," she repeated. Ruth had smoked down one cigarette and was fumbling in the package for another. The muscles at the corners of her mouth had tightened. Virginia thought then that she could see the woman Ruth would one day be: she would keep her beautiful face but at the cost of becoming nervous and edgy and hard. Sharp lines would crease the skin of her face. Ruth's fingers trembled, her face was flushed. "Only now I do not have to. Someone has done it for me."

Virginia nodded.

"You don't believe me but I would have done it. You twist the blade to pull it out."

Virginia nodded. She wanted to believe her.

They listened to the squirrels chattering in the trees. Leaves had begun to fall; they floated down to the ground outside the granary and swirled about on the path. She hadn't realized it until that moment but she was still tired from missing sleep the night before. And the walking. There was an ache behind her knees. The headache was gone but she felt dizzy. She wanted to close her eyes. Her head fell forward so her chin rested on her chest. She fought off the dozy feeling, but weird thoughts danced in her brain instead, and melded with others. She couldn't help thinking that they would be burying him on a sunny autumn day. Ridiculous. It should have been raining, it should have been stinking rotten weather. And Mrs. Samson kept a square-mouthed shovel with a green handle just outside the back door, that was an eccentricity, wasn't it? Like that smelly little dog she owned. Virginia jerked awake suddenly and found she was squeezing Ruth's thigh and had made her cry out.

"Take it easy," Ruth said.

"What happened," she asked, "to the bayonet?"

Or maybe she didn't say it but only thought it, because Ruth stood up without answering and said, "Let's get some real food."

Ruth reached up and stashed the cigarette pack on the rafter. They brushed off their clothes. They put the stick through the hasp on the granary door and walked in silence back to the mud room door. The sun was shining on the lake but it was cool in the shade of the pines behind the store, autumn cool. The hawk was not in the sky. But two crows were up in the treetops near the lake shore, flapping about and making their racket. Virginia had read that in the old days people believed crows were a sign of death, they believed that if a bird flew into the house someone was going to die.

She had never seen a bird in the house, but she would ask Cassie. She said, "Where is he, do you think?"

They had paused on the steps that went up to the mud room door, Ruth above, looking down. She had lifted the gold chain to her mouth and was chewing on it as she spoke. "I saw him," she said, "that night. He packed some stuff in his knapsack and then went off with Archie Cloud. He was scared."

"Those stupid girls at school picked on him because of that stammer thing."

"It was not that. His hands were bloody."

"It doesn't mean anything. They were cut earlier, remember?—when he hit him?"

"I'm worried for him. He goes out of control sometimes."

"He's not really right in the head. Because of LaFlamme." She winced to say his name. "But to be out there by himself now, that's no good."

"I know. But he knows things about surviving in the woods."

"Cassie is worried they'll put him in a home."

Ruth dropped the chain from her teeth, and then spat past her feet into the pine needles. "You're going to be well out of all this," she said.

"And you?"

"Roger says they're taking men on at the mines at Red Rock. As soon as he gets together the money for train fare, he's going."

That was it, then, the iron mines. It meant that much to him to get away: working with his hands, grunting out a life in the underground pits. Virginia said, "He likes it here. He's the only one who does." That wasn't quite a lie. She had grown tired of the silence that she used to enjoy so much, but the lake still held her, the call of the loon at night. Crickets in the grass, which she heard through the open window when she was towelling off after showering. Country life.

"Crap," Ruth said. "It's just a pile of rocks and scrub spruce and noisy birds. And mosquitoes. God, they drive me nuts."

The crows were suddenly louder. They both looked up into the trees.

"For two cents," Ruth said, "I'd shoot them." She had cultivated a tone in the past year or so, infuriated exasperation. It went with the lipstick and the cigarette smoking. She was a grown woman, these things said. Virginia wondered if she had had sex with one of the boys in her class.

"Crows are scavengers," Virginia said. "They clean things up."

"You're starting to sound like Roger. You know where that gets you."

"And you?"

Ruth laughed. "Find me a rich older man," she said. "Isn't that supposed to be every girl's dream?"

THE FINN HAD AN EXTRA FISHING ROD and he took the boy out on the rocks directly behind the store to show him how to jig for pickerel. Not that they were likely to catch anything, he cautioned, it being the middle of the day and the wrong location for jigging. That was best done at the place where the lake narrowed just before the wild rice fields. There was a hole there, a spot where the pickerel gathered to feed. But you never knew. There were plenty of fish all over the lake, and the twin rocks was a good spot to learn and practise the art of jigging: no logs or weeds under the water to snag hooks. The Finn gave the boy a hat to keep the sun off his sensitive skin and they set off.

Mort said to Alexander, "While they fish, we'll walk around the north shore of the lake."

They were headed towards the reservation, it appeared, though no fence marked the boundary between the Indians' land from the surrounding property. Alexander asked, "They won't mind?" Mort gave him a look but did not respond. He remembered that his older brother mostly kept his own counsel, something he had learned at school where the other children laughed at him for his simple-minded ideas. He came to reading late and was never much good with sums, though he had an uncanny sense of what would work out best for him and how to get ahead. When they were young men Alexander thought that he would be the successful one, and up to the point where the hardware business failed, he'd been right. But the great wheel goes around, he reminded himself. Maria liked that idea. What had she been fond of saying: the last will be first and first made last? Where was that from?

Mort pointed out to him the place where the logging road came across the lowlands. The fresh ruts from the Mountie's pickup were evident in the otherwise tall grass. That was not where they had walked the night before, he assured Mort. They climbed up the rocks that looked down over the lake. This was familiar, though it looked different than at night and approached from the opposite direction. He remembered the lichen on the rocks crunching underfoot and the tiny spruces growing in the seams of rock. Then they rounded the point at the north end of the lake and followed the trail down off the rocks into the woods, to where the path came in from the north between tall pines. Mort dropped down to one knee. In the soft earth he pointed out a shoe print. "Yours, Dick," he said.

He pointed out the print left by Peter's shoe too, and a heel mark from someone headed in the opposite direction. "You did see someone," he said, as if he had not really believed it before. Alexander wondered how he had found out about it. He had told only the Mountie. Had someone overheard every point of their conversation? It was not a surprise, really, that things said in private got around. It was worth remembering that.

They stood up. Mort spit out the tobacco he was chewing and opened the round tin he kept in his back pocket. "My fault you got lost," he said. "The directions I gave were hopeless." Alexander considered his pipe. It was a warm and fresh day. He was enjoying the country air in his lungs. They continued down the path. "Here," Mort said, "is the reservation boundary." They left the path and climbed up rocks that suddenly opened on to the lake to the south. Mort pointed back in the direction they had come, toward a gap in the trees. "You can just see them," he said, "on that outcropping of rock." Alexander strained his eyes but could pick out only one figure. He wondered about the Finn. There was something about his supernatural white hair that bothered him. And there'd been that flare-up at the table. Could he be trusted with a boy? Europeans were more used to that sort of thing, but it gave him chills.

Mort said, "When I came here that first fall I said I'll cut the wood this winter and then I'm leaving this place. God, the bugs were awful. I had never been so lonely. I sat up listening to the crackle of the radio past midnight just to keep sane. You ever get that way—bugs in the belfry? That was six years ago, and here I still am." He laughed. He sat down on the rocks. This was as far as they were going, it seemed.

Alexander brushed away a mosquito and sat down beside him, looking at the gap where Peter and the Finn were fishing. He took out his pipe and filled it while Mort told him about the pelts. They were beaver, now, mostly, though some wolf and raccoon too. Fox. The area around the lake was already trapped out, but farther into the reservation the trapping was still good, if you knew what you were doing. You could get quality pelts, the kind they paid the best dollar for in the city. And the Natives were good at it; they'd had years of experience, centuries. Around the lakes near Kenora they used snow machines to check the trap lines, but here the bush was too dense, so they walked. They had to be careful not to get caught out in snowstorms. Every year or so someone froze to death out on the line.

"We start the wood-cutting when the ground freezes," Mort said. "It pays well. A good man can make as much sawing wood in a day as a lawyer." The logging road ran into the reservation to the north, Mort said. They pulled a wagon over the frozen ground behind the small tractor that stood in the field. They followed the old logging road to the place where the birch began, the tall pines. "That's not for a month or two." It was hard work and the chainsaws were unpredictable in the cold but Mort liked it. The days were quite short around Christmas. Cold. Cassie made them sandwiches and coffee.

"She's had a hard go of it, Dick. Her father abandoned the family when she was a teenager. She had to go to work in the same truck-stop café as the mother to pay the rent and so on. Then the mother got stomach cancer. This was in the days before Medicare. So she worked two shifts at the café for ten years while the mother slowly succumbed. She never did finish high school. Then when the mother died, she came here, to Moon Lake. The aunt and uncle needed help." Cassie was young enough to be in college but she worked a full day every day. A hard life, according to Mort.

Alexander smoked his pipe, and had a deliberately placid look on his face, as if he were taking it all in, trying to understand, but inside his stomach was in a knot. This was a trick of Mort's, playing for his sympathy by painting a picture of Cassie as the victim so he would sympathize and forgive them whatever shameful things they had been doing. And he might have, he might have forgiven, if Mort were not such a sham, if he wasn't pretending to confide in him while leaving out the most important part: the two of them in the kitchen cocooned by the golden overhead light. But was he any better? And he had lied to the Mountie for them. He asked, "Where did he come into the picture?"

Mort looked at him. He must have been thinking of something else as he was talking because he seemed puzzled. "Who?"

"The husband."

"Somewhere to the south. Little town. French Canadian."

"I meant how did she meet him?"

"Dance or something. A social in Beausejour. He was all smiles and superficial charm, you know the type. Hair slicked back, a smooth dancer, but a rotten bastard underneath. Beat her, beat the kids. The boy has some kind of brain damage. He was not born with it, though, if you know what I mean."

"She should have just got shut of him. Divorce."

"It's not that easy. Someone has to pack up and leave. That's the legal point. The old folks left them the place when they retired, so it wasn't hers, not solely. So he had a right. He arranged that, husband and wife, joint property, kind of thing. If she left, he would have screwed her out of the place. Which was really hers, her family's. Which would have left her high and dry again after all those hard years. He knew that. He took advantage of that. Rotten, that's the only word for it."

"So she stuck it out?"

"It wasn't going to be much longer now. The older girl is ready to go. A year or more and they're all gone, the kids. Then things would have changed."

There was a note of triumph in his voice. Alexander said, "Things have changed." He tapped the bowl of his pipe on the rock, knocking the ash out, and then put it back in his trouser pocket. Two ragged crows flew overhead and landed in the pines nearby, where they started cawing and flapping about in the branches. "I have an affection for those ugly buggers," he confided to Mort.

"That is not really what I wanted to tell you," Mort said.

"There's a killer on the loose," he said. "Is that it?"

"The boy is dangerous. Maybe a little deranged, you could say, from those beatings to the head. He went after LaFlamme once with a pitchfork."

"Whoever it was did a job on LaFlamme."

"Bastard deserved it."

"I'm keeping a close eye on Pete. Is that what you're saying?"

Mort gave him another look. "I'm saying this. There's a rifle hanging on the wall in back of the counter in the trading post. A friend of the family brought it back from France as a souvenir. Don't know if the rifle has been fired in years. It's polished to a gleam on the outside but the works are probably rusted solid. Still, it had a long bayonet attached. I saw the boy eyeing it one day, and now it's disappeared."

Just before they came to the twin rocks where the Finn and the boy were jigging, Mort slowed and put a hand on his arm. "I tailed him one night," he said, lowering his voice. Alexander remembered that when they were boys they had followed the old man into town once.

They lived on a farmstead close enough to walk into town. Mort thought the old man had another woman. Mort insisted they keep to the shadows of the trees and stay at a distance. The old man had gone directly to the beer parlour. They had ducked down behind the cars on the opposite side of the street and waited. He remembered Mort's heavy breathing and the way Mort held his finger over his lips. Shh. They hid behind the cars. The sun went down past the grain elevator, turning the sky orange and then purple. An hour later the old man came out of the beer parlour and walked straight home along the gravel road. He was a whistler. He whistled a popular song from the war and they heard it on the still night air as they skulked behind him.

Mort had never alluded to that night again. But skulking was in his character.

"She said he claimed he was going fishing but she didn't believe him, see?"

A spruce grouse came out of the woods directly in front of them, its one visible eye glinting the sunlight. It poked its beak into the mud of the path for a moment or two, and then turned around and disappeared into the underbrush, all without noticing them. It was no wonder they were easy prey.

Mort said, "He went down the path around the lake." He pointed in the opposite direction they had come from. "He went past Moose Point, past where they found him last night, to the spot where the lake narrows. You can see the lights of the Clouds' place across the lake. He had a canoe stashed in the underbrush and he paddled across the lake."

Mort paused. His hand was still resting on Alexander's arm, thick and heavy fingers. The thumbnail had been blackened in a work accident. He was hesitating now. His eyes flicked from Alexander's to the woods. He probably should not have begun this story, but now he was in it and there was no easy way out. Or maybe he was just trying to create that impression for effect. He was a slippery customer. He could be hesitating to gain sympathy. In a moment Mort went on: "There was a rowboat too. After he had reached the opposite side, I rowed over and stashed the boat farther along the shore. He had gone up to the house. I looked in the window. He had pinned one of the girls on the sofa. The other must have run away."

There were details Mort could not bring himself to say, apparently. His cheeks had become flushed and his speech faltered. "I got back to the rowboat before he came out. Stood in the trees and watched him paddle across to this side." Alexander glanced in the direction of the twin rocks. From time to time the voices of the Finn and Peter drifted over to them. Alexander was studying Mort's hands: he was twiddling the thumbs together over and over.

"They're just kids, Dick. I didn't know what to say to her. The thing of it is, he planned it all out, see. He waited until Cloud brought something into the store, pelts, wood, and then he gave him the groceries and whatever, plus a little extra cash, knowing he would take the wife over to Cuthand's tent come night fall, get into the hard stuff, tie one on, and then he could slip across the lake and go after the girls."

"I didn't want to know this," Alexander said.

"He got what he deserved, see."

"You're not saying those girls did it, are you?"

"They're tough kids. They're used to knives and blood."

"Jesus. What about Ruth?"

"What I'm saying is the wheel always comes round."

He asked, "Are you quoting something?"

"The Bible, Dick. Ecclesiastes. You know, the wheel within the wheel. A time for love and a time for hate. All that comes from the Good Book."

Alexander looked down at his shoes.

"The old man used to read it aloud to us. Remember?"

"Does it say anything about a time to kill?"

"That too, Dick, by gum. It's right there in the Good Book."

It was clear to Alexander then: Mort wanted his brother not to think badly of him for skulking after the man in the dark of night, for looking in the window like a peeping Tom, for not doing anything to help the girls, for not telling Cassie what he had seen.

What could he say?

V̲ictor slowed for the last exit out of the city and then speeded up again when the car passed the yield sign where the highway widened to two lanes.

The miscarriage was the big event, but the grief between them had started before that. It had started in college. Sheila had come from a small town. She had trouble fitting in. Who didn't? He had been a jock. She had majored in English, the honors course, and wore long black dresses. They drew attention to her blonde hair, the red lips with the cigarette pinched between, the slender figure, small breasts. He had met her at a frat party but had seen her lounging about the halls at University College before that, drinking coffee from plastic cups, smoking, arguing with the boys with wire-frame glasses. She was nervous in a way that made her seem aggressive. He had almost not talked to her at that frat party but something about her had intrigued him. Maybe just the way she held her cigarette, then threw back her head to exhale. An affectation.

"I'm trouble." That was the first thing she'd said to him. She had looked him up and down and said, "I'm no good for you, boy." He'd laughed.

He was a beer-drinking hockey player who had gone to college because his friends had registered and because he imagined he could make the varsity team. He knew all along he was going to be a cop. So it had started as a lark, dating the girl who read poetry and sat in the corner at parties, drinking white wine from the bottle and talking loudly about the free speech movement. Most of the crowd she hung out with smoked pot. His friends said, "Look out for that one, she takes up causes."

"It's not your fight," he told her, about the Berkeley thing.

"It's everybody's fight," she snapped back.

"It's a different country."

"It's the same as Germany in the thirties. Every voice not raised in protest is the silent voice of assent." Her eyes sparked as she spoke and a vein in her forehead throbbed with blood. He flushed with desire.

She had a room on the third floor of a house downtown. They argued after sex. "We're all connected," she insisted. "What happens to me happens to you. It's a giant web of interconnections." She linked the fingers of her hand through his to demonstrate. "They take their freedom away, they take away ours along with it."

"They're blacks in the south and you're a white girl from a dairy farm in Canada."

"There's a rally next week and I'm going."

She had attended the meetings held in lecture halls and joined the protest in the open grass court in front of University College, where she gave a speech. Engineering students (all men in those days) had come over with their own placards and confronted the protesters. The engineers wore close-cropped hair and called Sheila and her crowd *hippies*. She'd been punched in the face. It had only made her more resolute in her convictions. But she had not taken part in a massive march before. "Now they want to gag us," she said. "The cops are in on it."

She knew about his plans. He had sent away the applications and had had his first interview. If he made that stage, it was off to Regina for training.

"There is no conspiracy," he said. "The police enforce the law."

"There's buses going from all over the country to join up in a town in the south to show support for the black cause. Selma, Alabama. Six weeks, two months from now. A nation-wide demonstration. The whole country is mobilizing."

"Their country," he argued, "not yours."

"It's just like you," she said, "this cover-your-own-ass attitude."

They had been over that before, his selfishness. Her room was tiny. It had a bed, a desk squeezed into the dormer window that looked down into the busy city street below, some books on shelves made of planks and bricks, a hot plate on a tiny counter. She never cared what she ate. A ratty shag carpet. Clothes strewn about, empty wine bottles. The room smelled of cigarette smoke and stale milk. They made sandwiches from bologna. She drank Cokes and had a mickey of rum stashed under the bed that they drank with the Coke after sex. The roof was sharply sloped. If he stood up on the wrong side of the bed, he struck his head. She laughed at that and at the way he expressed himself, but she was serious about ideas.

"I'm going," she said, "to Selma," There's a bus leaving here to hook up with the students mobilizing in Chicago."

The pain in her face was real. To her the fight was personal. They were taking away her freedom, whoever *they* were. When they argued this way she chain-smoked and told him she thought they had no future. But then they went to bed again and afterwards she read to him from the Beat poets and Shakespeare. The words were more real to her than her own life. At first that astounded him, but then he came to see it was true of a lot of her friends too, arts students. She wrote poems and typed them up on an ancient Smith-Corona she lugged off the kitchen table and dumped in a corner when they ate noodles off plates. She came to see him play hockey at the Bison Gardens but she sat reading a book and then made him attend the readings of poets and playwrights.

But she didn't go to Selma.

His application to the RCMP was accepted and when he asked her to go with him to Regina, she was excited. They'd had a socialist government. She was thinking of becoming a communist. He had laughed. "A Mountie and a Commie," he said, trying to joke her out of it. But they packed up a U-Haul behind his Meteor and drove west.

Down this very highway.

He was driving the squad car with the insignia on the door. Why was he so proud of that insignia? *Maintiens le Droit.* He shouldn't have been driving the car on personal business, but he loved the Chevrolet's big engine, and in that car he could drive with his foot to the floor and no one would think of questioning it. So he was speeding along the highway, driving much too fast as the distance from the city behind him grew and the distance to Portage la Prairie diminished. From time to time he put his hand over his abdomen, trying to block out the gurgling and the pain.

They were an impossible couple, he should have realized it then.

"I'll keep out of sight," she said when he started basic training. She had an idea that that was the best way to be true to her communist leanings. Work silently from within. Erode the system like a woodworm. So they led separate lives. She hung out at the college while he was at the barracks. She distributed pamphlets on the street and helped organize the union for the postal workers. She stayed out late and slept late and cooked them Kraft dinner. Was that when she started gaining weight? She had fallen out with the socialists. They were Trotskyites, actually, by then, and they told her she was too middle class. She said they were tilting at windmills—and that the better way to bring down the system was to conform outwardly while secretly undermining it. He'd become her confidant then, against them. She quoted a poet. "Be the serpent underneath." She was always quoting poets. It was her way.

In the meantime she wanted a family and a house with a garden.

That was all right by him. He had grown tired of being alone at parties and officially not having a girl, and always being the one to answer the phone. They were stupid lucky, he realized now, to have got away with it. Didn't the RCMP check out their own recruits?

They were going to post him to northern Alberta when his training was complete, but then the corporal in Beausejour rolled his car during a high-speed chase and was near death and he was suddenly sent back to the province where he came from—not the usual practice. By then Sheila had moved on to protesting the east-coast seal hunt and the war in Vietnam. Students marched in Chicago but she was not one of them.

When he was almost to Portage la Prairie he turned on the car radio. Clear and warm weather. The ball teams were in the push to the World Series. A Bob Dylan song, one of her favourites, came on. He hummed along and then laughed aloud. How many roads did a man have to walk down?

"They're dying over there by the thousands," she had told him as they sat drinking wine after supper one night a few weeks earlier. "Boys."

"Their boys. American boys."

"In a stupid war. And we're making the chemicals for the napalm in a factory in Quebec. Dow Chemicals. God knows what else. Collaboration."

They had been living in Beausejour less than a year when she had the miscarriage. "It's that nuclear reactor," she told him.

"Pinawa is forty miles away."

"Now you have an advanced degree in nuclear fission? You know for a certainty that they're not dumping some kind of effluence into the air? Forty miles is nothing to these particles. They can dance over distances much greater than that in one afternoon. They rip open a woman's womb."

"You need to see a doctor," he said, meaning a psychiatrist. That was a mistake. She hit him over the head with a china plate. He staggered and fell to his knees. She banged the door to the bedroom shut and would not let him in for two days and screamed obscenities at him. It was a mistake he did not make again.

She said, "They're in on it too, the scientists and doctors."

Then she started going out at night and not coming home until after the dawn.

He thought she was walking the streets to settle her nerves, or for exercise. She had been putting on pounds and she was walking them off.

One morning she did not come back at all. Then came the call from a motel on the outskirts of the city. Tears, rage. He had expected remorse but what he got was anger. A month or so later, the same thing happened. And so it had gone. He had learned to nod his head and keep his mouth shut and put his arms around her in bed. He kept a bottle of scotch in the house and when she went away he watched the sun rise from the living room window as he drank himself into a stupor. He was half glad some nights when the calls came that took him away from his home and to troubles that were not his own: road accident, suicide, murder.

Victor slowed for the intersections in Portage la Prairie. The sun had dropped low the sky, swollen and orange on the horizon directly in front of him. The asphalt highway shimmered. Cars coming from the opposite direction suddenly materialized out of the orange glare and whizzed past. Then he was on the far side of the town. He was humming along to the music on the car radio and missed the motel completely, but the name she had told him on the phone registered in his policeman's brain and he pulled onto the gravel and wheeled back to the parking area out front.

He paid the bill and they sat in the motel café looking out the smeared glass window at the cars going by on the highway. It was the Sunday evening of the Labour Day weekend, the booths were crowded. He ate a cheeseburger and fries with gravy, and with his coffee, a piece of apple pie. When had he last eaten? Sheila had a cup of tea and studied him out of cold eyes. This was his fault.

He held her hand across the tabletop. Her skin was cold. The flesh of her cheeks had gone puffy, her eyes were recessed in the black sockets. The hair which had once danced with light was washed-out blonde. She wore big dresses to hide the weight she had put on. He thought of a poem she had read to him years ago: *And that same flower that blooms today, tomorrow will be dying.*

She looked terrible but he still loved her. Why was that? Another man would have chucked her over years ago, but he was still with her, and it was right, it wasn't just weakness on his part.

She said, "They're talking of bombing Hanoi."

He nodded and he tried to look as concerned as she felt, but he was thinking about how much had happened in less than two years: the physical thing was the least.

"Softening up the Viet Cong," she said. When he said nothing in response, she said, "Kennedy, the media makes such a big deal about Jack Kennedy, but he got us into Asia. He's the one responsible."

"Them," he said, "he got *them* into Vietnam."

Cars coming and going from the gas pumps and the café stirred up the dust in the lot out front. Engines roared on the highway.

"There are times, Victor," she said, "when I can't help but loathe you."

In the car on the way back to the city he drank a Coke and ate a chocolate bar and hummed again to the radio. The Stones were rumoured to be coming to the city. A few clouds in the sky. The sun had fallen right to the horizon. When he glanced back, it seemed a golden spaceship was hovering over the flat prairie to the west. Drivers coming from the east had the visors flipped down inside their cars.

The gut wasn't so bad with food in it, and if he didn't turn his head quickly he could almost believe the headache had disappeared.

Sheila had the blanket from the trunk over her legs. She drank a bottle of Orange Crush and looked out the side window at the fields going by. She said, "What we need, Vic, is space. We've been living in the bush too long." She nodded at the flat prairie. Farmers were out on their combines doing the harvesting. Chaff and dust flew in the air. Trucks with five-ton open boxes stood on the edges of the fields waiting to be filled with grain. Probably the wife behind the wheel; on the seat beside her, sandwiches and a thermos of coffee, a Mason jar filled with ice water. It was a scene he had witnessed a thousand times but it still made him feel good inside: a couple working together on their piece of land.

"The bush," she said, "is smothering me. I feel it pressing on my shoulders, on my neck. It's choking me. You dig?"

"The farm you grew up on was surrounded by the bush."

"No," she said. "There were trees, true, but it was mostly ponds, meadows, rolling hills. Pasture land. You could look out the kitchen window and watch Daddy and Brutus bringing the cows in half a mile away."

They were approaching the jail at Headingley. Black river-bottom land on one side of the highway, farm buildings on the river side. Stables and riding academies. He could sense her beside him, working up to telling him something. He ran his tongue around his lips. This is how you become old, he thought.

"I'm dying in the Beausejour bush," she said. "It's killing me, man."

That's a bit much, he thought. She had taken to expressing her unhappiness in histrionic terms. When they passed the weigh station her head fell onto her chest and then in a few minutes she slumped against the window and slept with her mouth open. He reached across her body and pushed down the lock on the passenger door. He smelled the motel on her clothes: cigarette smoke, carpet cleaner, another man.

They drove through the city in the falling light. On the outskirts to the east he looked for Egerton Street and pulled up in front of a two-storey house on the river side where the technical guy lived. He closed the car door without waking her, then went around to the trunk and got the box with the envelopes and other materials he'd collected at Moon Lake.

One of the guys from forensics met him at the door. Victor felt guilty as soon as he saw him. He'd neglected the case. He'd lost the thread. The forensics guy glanced in the box. "We'll get to that stuff first thing tomorrow," he said. "Photos, good." He waved from the door and then shouted, "Footwear—collect up all their boots."

She woke with a start, not knowing what it was that had woken her. An owl outside the window sometimes hooted. Light from the moon splashed on the quilt near her feet. She put one hand on her forehead. The headache was gone. Her brow felt cool for the first time in days. She must have woken with a start because Barker was awake too. She was lying on the throw rug that ran alongside the bed, looking up at her, two green eyes in the semi-gloom. She thumped her tail a few times then put her head down again. Virginia peered over the edge of the quilt out of the window. Something told her to do this. Two eyes stared back, two eyes that glittered in the moonlight. Abruptly she pulled the quilt over her head fast, her first instinct. Then she realized what she'd seen. Roger. She threw aside the quilt and looked again. The eyes were gone. She jumped out of bed. Barker rose to her feet awkwardly. Virginia ran to the window, and then out of the room to the mud room door. There was no one there. She heard trees sighing in the wind, and the distant shushing of lake water. She peered into the darkness, then stepped hesitantly down the stairs. The wood was cold to the touch. *Roger*, she called, but not too loud. She listened. Was that footsteps in the distance, the crunching of deadfall underfoot? She could smell the heavy scent of pine sap and the ozone coming off the lake water. After a while she heard the owl hoot. Something rustled the leaves in the undergrowth, a small nocturnal animal. Her heart was pounding. Her toes were ice. She stood a while longer, and then went back to the bedroom and pulled the quilt over her head again, and curled up into a ball to get warm. That's when she felt the tremor of fear go right up her spine. What if it was the killer? That's when she realized it might not have been Roger but him.

H<small>E WAS NOT REQUIRED TO START WORKING</small> until the next day, Tuesday, but he had sat about all Sunday festering over the business with LaFlamme and was itching to get his hands on something, so he asked Mortimer where they kept the painting things and found himself in the little shed off the side of the store. It was hidden in the low branches of a cluster of trees. He had not known it was there. Rakes, shovels, brooms, and hoes hung from hooks on one wall. Cobwebs with leaves caught in them in the dusty corners. Along the other wall were wooden shelves with cans of paint, and on nails above them, wire brushes and scrapers. The paint on the store walls was weathered, blistered and peeling, so he would have to start with the scraping. It was hard work, scraping, tedious, and you could not see that you had done much after eight hours of labour, but it paid off in the end. The fresh coat of paint took to the seasoned wood well, and it lasted longer on a fresh-cleaned surface.

He lifted the cans of paint and rotated them to read the labels. Exterior gloss, that was his ticket. White. Green for the trim. With a screwdriver he pried the tops off the tins and found in each a thick layer of hardened scum. New paint would have been better but this would do, if mixed well. He had checked for ladders outside. On the shelves he had found rags on hooks and solvent for cleaning up, as well as turpentine for thinning. Underneath the shelves sat dusty cardboard boxes with the flaps closed.

When he opened the top cardboard box, he discovered a pile of old books inside and he casually flipped open the topmost of these and was just about to close it again when his eye registered what was stuck between two pages: a snapshot staring back at him; a man in an army uniform. He lifted the black and white photo up to the light coming in at the doorway. It was of a young man in the dress of a private, no arm flashings, a soft parade cap, the heavy wool worsted shirt of the infantry with the double breast pockets. Could this be the man whose rifle was hanging in the store? He turned the photo over. On the back was written *Jim*. Jim had a pencil moustache, dark hair, beady eyes. His neck was dwarfed by the collar of the worsted shirt with the double shoulder lapels. Something told him Jim was dead.

Alexander propped the cardboard box on the edge of a shelf and riffled through the other books and papers in it, finding more black and white photos, these of groups of young men in uniform: two, three, one with half a dozen, some smiling, arms around shoulders, some grimly serious. Then more photos of the same young men with women, standing outside ramshackle buildings that might have been their quarters. Only they were not army barracks. He flipped the photos over. On the back of one was scrawled *Wainwright May 1942*, another *Terrace 1942, summer*. They were doing basic training, then, and the wives had come along with the men, wearing their floppy wide-brimmed hats and their toothy smiles. You could not miss the anxiety, though. They had followed their husbands and boyfriends from stop to stop during basic training, taking jobs in cafés and factories, and then the men had been shipped out and the women had gone back to their homes. His mother had had a term for these women who followed the soldiers, not war brides, a different name, but he could not remember.

Alexander closed his eyes and concentrated but it would not come.

How many of these men had made it back from the war? How many were now dead from whatever causes? He calculated again. If Jim had been twenty-something in 1942, he would be no more than fifty today, maybe still alive and working at a job he had come home to. Maybe he'd fathered children with one of the smiling women and was a grandfather living in Beausejour? It was eerie, this prying into the lives of other people.

Alexander pushed the photos back into the box and opened one of the books. It was a ledger, he saw: pages ruled in thin blue lines. The pages were crinkled and curled from damp. A folded blue paper fell out: the grade eight report card of Emile LaFlamme. All bad grades. At the bottom of the card were cryptic commentaries by teachers. Why would he have kept such an unpromising document? Standing: seventeen in a class of twenty. Good at gymnastics and football. *Emile could be kinder to other children.* There was a space at the bottom of the report for parents' comments but it was blank.

He put the report card aside with the photos and took up the ledger.

The book was a kind of diary. April 12 1957: 61 degrees. Cash at end of day, 43 dollars. 23 September 1958: train from Winnipeg, flour, sugar, salt, 28 dollars. The hand writing was the same each time, loops and flourishes in thick blue ink, a woman's hand, he guessed. It was the log of the trading post's receipts and debts. He flipped to the end of the calendar year, 1958. Cash on hand at year end: 3500 dollars. A good year. The entries did not fill the entire book. There were blank pages at the end, some torn out raggedly. On one was a drawing in a child's hand, two men fighting with sticks or swords. A full sun beamed down from overhead.

The pages of the ledger were thick from damp as if they were from the previous century but the writing had been done less than ten years earlier. Alexander was starting out at the Elmwood McCleod's hardware store then, he reflected, and in a few years had his own store: nails, hammers, paint, a few sporting goods. He had gone from stock boy to owner in five years. Peter was in diapers and Maria wanting a second child, a girl, but something had gone wrong inside her when Peter was born, placenta, afterbirth, it was irreversible. Their own lives had been going on promisingly in the city while someone held a pen and scratched on these pages.

Alexander sat on a paint can he had placed near the door. The morning had broken sunny. There were a few clouds high in the sky but the sun was pleasantly warm. Crows called in the trees. He sighed. The air coming in at the door was fresh while the smell coming off the pages of the book recalled old cheese and wet socks. He looked over his shoulder into the yard, feeling a twinge of guilt. You shouldn't ransack private papers.

In the grassy area out front of the store, Peter was putting up wire hoops. Mortimer had told him there was an old croquet set in the crawl space under the store and Peter had dragged it out earlier. They were to play a game when Alexander finished investigating the shed. At breakfast the boy had eaten two fried eggs and six slices of toast and then downed a couple glasses of milk. All was well.

He closed the book and folded the flaps of the cardboard box back into place. The second box was more of the same: ledgers on top and a flat tin box underneath. In the first ledger there was a clipped-out advertisement from a magazine, a woman's coat, ankle length, black. The women in those days all sported wide-brimmed hats. He remembered now looking in the sewing basket his mother kept under the treadle machine: hat pins as long as daggers. On the back side of the advertisement was faded type cut off at the edge of the clipping: *the house of the* blank blank, and then on the next line *for the woman who* blank. When he flipped through the ledger he found more such advertisements and then a letter on a single sheet of faded blue paper. It was in a man's hand in ragged and blotchy letters: most of the words were illegible, but he was able to make out a phrase or two: *excessive demands... more can be....* More what? he wondered. At the bottom signed with a flourish were the letter: *SAR*.

Alexander was intrigued but also a little anxious about snooping. Guilty.

Between two pages further back in the ledger he found the package from a condom. Empty. For what possible reason would someone have saved it? People were furtive about them, he knew that. The old man had kept them inside a cuff-link box in the sock drawer. He had been instructed never to open it but had one day. Boys of his generation carried them in their wallets until the rubber ring wore a perfect impression into the leather of their billfolds. Maria found that humorous: unused safes. She'd made a play on words about it which he no longer recalled, only the way her voice rang as she laughed about it. He wondered about sexual tools: dildos, cushions. And then as he thought how long it had been for him, he felt a flush under his collar.

The thought precipitated a feeling that had been building while he was flipping through the ledgers: sadness bordering on shame. You should not poke about in people's memories. But they had abandoned the memories, hadn't they? Pressed between the ledger's pages further on there were birthday cards and a wedding announcement: Cassandra and Emile. Who on the prairie at the end of the depression would have named their daughter after a character from classical mythology? It gave him pause. And Cassie rather than Sandra? He wondered if SAR were still living, and the mother who'd named her daughter Cassandra. It was bad form to make judgements about the names people gave their children: Peter, Alexander.

There was a yellowing index card on which was typed a recipe. The typewriter reproduced the e half a line higher than the other letters. The recipe was for potato cakes: onions, chopped; potatoes squeezed through a sieve; butter; milk. A simple meal with elementary instructions. The recipe could not have been the reason for saving the card. He flipped it over. On the reverse side in handwriting someone had inscribed the capitalized letter *J* with an arrow pointing to the capitalized letter *S* and then a second arrow pointing to the words *the Greek?* He felt again the embarrassed shame he had experienced earlier.

He went on, though, flipping the pages of the ledger. Near the back he found a telegram on faded yellow paper: *James Roby*, it read. *Killed in action.* The date was 23 June, 1944. Normandy. The beaches they showed on the TV every November. Jim. So he wasn't living and probably hadn't had children, the thin man with the pencil moustache. Alexander slipped the telegram back between the pages and closed the ledger.

At the bottom of the second box under more ledgers there was a flat tin box, blue, that once had held Danish shortbread cookies. The lid was rusted shut but he pried it open with the screwdriver. Inside he found a wad of fifty-dollar bills bound up with an elastic band. He glanced over his shoulder. There must have been a hundred or more of the bills. He fanned them. In the middle a slip of paper. He pulled it free of the elastic band. On it were written numbers and beside each number a check mark in ballpoint ink. The numbers went from 1 through 12, then started at 1 again. Months of the year? Alexander held the wad of bills a moment, feeling their weight in his palm, thinking about what they could do for him: buy a house in the city, start a new business; and then he dropped them back in the cookie tin, squeezing the lid down firmly. There were things you did not want to think about overmuch. He took one of the paint rags and carefully rubbed the surfaces of the cookie tin where he had handled it. Then he folded the flaps of the cardboard box and shoved it and the other one under the shelves, exactly where he had found them.

That much money in cash!

His mother had told him about an old man who died in the city neighbourhood where she once lived. After the funeral his two sons had come to the house with shovels and spent the afternoon digging in the ground. They had found four tins with money in them. The old man did not trust the banks. The sons were convinced there were other tins with cash but they could not find them. They had dug up more than ten thousand dollars. It was 1940, the end of the great depression. The sons lived in other cities and had to get back to their families. After a few weeks passed, they went away. When the house came up for sale, Alexander's grandfather had been tempted to buy it.

"Money is the root of all evil," his old man had said, and his mother had corrected him. "Greed," she said, "greed is the root of all evil." Were they quoting the Bible? He wondered how Mort knew about Ezekiel when he did not. Maybe Cassie had a Bible and he could look up the quotation about the first and the last. He thought maybe she did not like him, Cassie. She had given him a look over breakfast that morning when he'd praised Peter's appetite and, indirectly, her cooking. She was suspicious. Could she have seen him looking in the window?

The money, it occurred to him, was hers. She could use it now, with three kids to raise. But what could he say to her—*I was snooping around in your cardboard boxes and came across a lot of cash*? She would be suspicious of him on two counts—as well as the resentment she already felt. So he would keep his mouth shut about the money. Tip his hand to Mort later when Cassie was not holding a grudge against him. It did not make him feel good to take this course, but it did make him feel safe.

When he left the shed he stood for a moment at the door, holding the hasp in one hand and the bent spike that kept the door in place in the other. It was more money than most people saw in a lifetime and he knew that walking away from it now meant walking away forever. He heard Peter call out to him. The game was about to begin. He pushed the two parts of the hasp together, slipped the spike through, and then walked toward Peter, who was standing in the grass, plocking the wooden balls with a croquet mallet.

At first he was content to let Peter win. The sun was directly overhead, warming his neck and shoulders, a breeze was shaking leaves from the poplars along the edges of the yard. Geese flew by high in the sky on their long wing south, calling and veering about. He gripped his smouldering pipe in his teeth and bent his head to the mallet. The balls had once been coloured, red, yellow, blue, green, and there were stripes of similar shades on the heads of the mallets, but the colours had faded over the years and the balls were water-stained where they had sat in the wet grass. Peter struck his ball through hoop after hoop and called out to him to get a move on, and when he fell behind, Peter hit his ball back through the hoops and roqueted Alexander into the tall grass under the poplars.

He said, "You're good at this."

"No," the boy said, "I'm hopeless at games. Just like you, Dad."

It was said lightly enough, but Alexander recognized the hurt in his son's voice. The schoolyard had not changed much in twenty years: the highest praise went to the boy who could hit a ball hardest, even if it also meant he hit the younger kids. LaFlamme had been good at games. But could be kinder to the other children.

He brought his ball back out of the shadow of the trees and roqueted the boy's ball. "Okay," Peter said, gleefully, "now we're getting somewhere."

The object of the game changed from finishing the hoops first to hitting the opponent's ball as far into the long grass as possible. At one point he knocked Peter's ball between two spruces at the edge of the clearing and they saw it bounce off a root, and then disappear from sight in the dense undergrowth. Peter whooped and ran between the trees. Without warning a pair of grouse started up from the ground, beating their wings loudly. The boy cried out, a childish scream. He dropped his mallet and ran back several steps, then, when he realized what had happened, began to laugh. He picked up his mallet, found the ball, and tossed it near Alexander's feet. His face was flushed when he came out of the woods. The sun danced on his red hair. He looked at Alexander and said in a whisper, "Scared the shit out of me."

"See," Alexander said, "a different kind of excitement."

It was a shared moment, father and son. He let the curse go, but could not help thinking for a moment of Maria: what you missed when you missed the growing up of your child. The look in the boy's face when he'd crossed the open area after uttering the curse had been purely the look of his mother, conspiratorial, half afraid that he had gone too far. Maria had bitten her bottom lip when she thought she'd failed him somehow. The daughter of a Lutheran minister, she said bold things and then dropped her head so you saw only the crown of her skull, as if she were seeking clemency, but then her head would shoot up and she'd be laughing at you.

It was the unpredictability that attracted him.

She had green eyes as well as the red hair and when she sat at the table doing the accounts she stuck the tip of her tongue between her teeth. The set of her shoulders in those moments told you she was a serious person. But at parties she sat silently at the end of the sofa and a smile played about her full lips. He had the feeling she mocked people in her heart, though never openly.

On their honeymoon she had surprised him with her carnality. Though too, it had seemed a little forced sometimes, as if she was trying to overcome being the preacher's daughter. That was it. Most of the time she was reserved in the way of older women, but then she became a force field of energy, she threw herself into activity and he had a difficult time keeping up. Dancing, for one. He had not liked it at first but she kept at him and eventually he found it difficult for a Saturday to pass without going to the Legion to two-step and waltz. She was a small-boned woman, light on her feet; if he and another man took her for the butterfly she really did fly through the air.

In bed she liked trying new things. He said, "That doesn't matter to me."

"I know," she said, laughing. "It matters to me."

"You're a bad girl," he chided.

"I'm your girl," she said. And she had longed to have a girl.

Alexander did not want these thoughts.

He put his hand on the boy's head lightly, stroking his hair, watching the sun play in its colours. "You see," he said, "life in the country isn't so bad, it's filled with surprises."

When they sat on the steps after and shared a cold bottle of Pepsi from the store, the boy said to him, "You didn't just let me win, did you, Dad?"

That was it, then. The word had got around that they had seen someone on the path, a boy, running. The Mountie had said something, or maybe the doctor. Over supper that night Cassie gave him another look. He wanted to say to her what he had been holding back all along, that the person had appeared to be an Indian. But the thought had been distasteful from the start and he had choked back the words and now it seemed they never would get said.

Cassie had her own worries. With LaFlamme gone, the government might take the trading post from her. She'd be forced to go back to waitressing. He thought again about the money in the cookie tin, but he couldn't think how to broach the subject.

He had called the city that afternoon, when they'd finished playing croquet. A man had been killed, he told Maria's mother; they were fine; would she call his parents, whom he had been unable to reach, and Maria's sister, who would be worried about the boy. The papers were right: murdered. So far the cops had not come up with a name. They were not suspects. He lied: there was no danger, a maniac was not on the loose. About that the papers were, as usual, wrong. The Mounties might bring in reinforcements to comb the area. They were sure to turn up the killer. They were the Mounties, right?

The connection was not good. The mother's voice sounded brittle. He had never felt totally comfortable talking to her. Maria's death had not helped the situation. Blame, the sister said to him in the weeks following the funeral, has poisoned us all. The sister had volunteered to put Peter up in the city, share a room with her own boy, keep him in the same school. He did not think that was much of an idea. Not good for the boy. Now he was a suspect and they might take the boy away.

Peter was unaware of the censure they were suffering from Cassie. At supper he asked for more potatoes and gravy. Cassie was sitting at the table. Mortimer and the Finn were there too. She sighed, exasperation. The younger daughter said *mother* in the way of teenagers, exaggerated exasperation. She liked Peter. She told him about the wild flowers she'd picked: names neither of them had heard before. The older one stood at the counter, pretending to dry dishes. Her breasts bulged against her tight-fitting sweater. Alexander swallowed coffee and looked down. He'd noticed her sitting on the stoop in the afternoon when he and the boy played croquet. She smoked cigarettes. She lit them with paper matches and threw the stubs into the grass. She laughed when Peter roqueted his ball into the long grass and watched to see if she caught Alexander's eye. "You try," he called out to her, but she said with a laugh that she had work to do inside and threw a stub into the grass. He wondered if it might start the dry leaves to flame. Later he went over and looked: smears of red lipstick on the cigarette paper, a few leaves touched by the butt had turned black.

She looked over at him from time to time as she wiped the dishes. Dark eyes, black hair. She placed one hand on her hip and then tugged the sweater idly so it pulled tighter round her torso, showing off her breasts. He thought he had the measure of her then: *cock-teaser*. The term just popped into his mind. Stupid. She was a girl, no more than that, aware of her effect on men and trying it on. And why not? It should have been amusing but it troubled him. Was she too attractive?

It had been more than a year.

No, she was not a girl. A young woman, and a beautiful one at that.

Cassie told them the Mountie was coming again in the morning. When she said it, she looked at him and the corners of her mouth turned down more than usual. There were crow's feet there. She had been a handsome woman when she was younger, never pretty, he guessed, but sexy in a fleshy way. And she had a forceful personality. It made some sense from that angle. Mort was a big man.

The Mountie, Cassie said, wanted to interview some of them again. Mortimer snorted. The Finn sighed and pushed his chair back from the table. The older daughter said, "The doctor went to college in Toronto."

The boy, Cassie said, was not coming home. A hush descended over the table. No one said anything else about it and she did not volunteer further information. There was a conspiracy of silence about him. No one mentioned Archie Cloud, either, or asked about where Ruth had been on the night of the murder.

Mortimer left the table soon after that, claiming he had to check a gasket on the tractor. The Finn yawned and looked tired. He took up his soft cap and made noises about getting an early start the next day. Peter said, "Dad, they've got a Monopoly game." Ruth glanced back from the counter and he said, "Maybe one more cup of coffee while I teach this boy a few things about high finance." She laughed, and when she came over to pour into his cup he smelled the scent she used; he could not identify it but was to become familiar with it. That and the way she fluffed her shoulder-length hair off the nape of her neck, the way she rolled her eyes at Cassie, the way she said *damn*, like it was two words.

It was another bright fall day, with the sun beaming through drifting white cloud. The drive to Moon Lake was almost pleasant. There were red deer on the rutted road, and grouse flapping into the spruces when the truck bounced past. He had stopped to talk to Carl Cuthand, and though that had not turned out to be as satisfactory as he'd hoped, he was humming the tune of a song that was popular in the early sixties and feeling at ease with himself, despite the drive and the strained exchanges with Sheila the night before. He had put her behind him for the moment. His abdomen was not as tight as yesterday. He would talk to her again about visiting the doctor, see if he could arrange for McNair to prescribe sedatives. Something had to be done.

Victor pulled the old pickup up front of the trading post and shut off the engine: huff of smoke from the exhaust. The flag to the left of the front steps hung limp. He'd rolled down the window on his side of the pickup. The morning air near the lake filled his entire chest with oxygen. He felt it in his brain and sensed it in his legs as he stepped down from the pickup. Maybe that was what drew people to live in the country. The sun struck his face and he smelled pine needles and the dank odour of the earth and leaves that formed the mat of vegetation under the trees. Yes. He understood why people chose to live at the farthest reach of civilization.

The new guy, Mortimer Mann's brother, was scraping blistered paint off the walls of the store. He wore a hat, a kind of battered fedora with a feather in the band that circled its base. He had a dead pipe clenched between his front teeth and waved as Victor banged the pickup door behind him. What was his story—really? Bringing a kid to this place, the end of the line? Was he running away from his failures, or was there a darker purpose to his being there? Victor knew that Mortimer Mann was a slippery eel.

Victor did not trust the wife, either. She was bustling around with a mop and a duster when he pulled open the screen door. He had the feeling she'd been doing something else just before but had the mop handy for his arrival, wanting to create an impression of some sort. Her face was flushed red from exertion. The younger daughter was cleaning the glass countertop, the older whistling a rock tune as she swept the floor. Why did he think it was pre-arranged?

He said, "The boy has not returned, then?"

"That is not unusual," Cassie said. She was watching him open the notepad to begin writing. The ballpoint pen was clipped to the cover. She went on at once, "He goes out and stays out for days at a time. It's hunting, isn't it?"

He was aware of the younger girl nodding in agreement.

"It is not hunting season," he stated flatly.

She snorted. "The Indians do not acknowledge the arbitrary time distinctions of the white man." He was not sure if she was mocking the words as she said them.

He explained that he had to talk to the boy, and his pal, Archie Cloud. "The guys at the lab," he added, "want to see everyone's boots."

She said, "I do not wear boots."

"Every man's footwear. And boy's."

The older daughter snorted. She had liked playing the rebel with him earlier too, making fun of the cop, the fuzz. She was wearing a pair of tight jeans and a red sweater that flattered her figure. On the drive up he'd decided that the younger one, Virginia, was telling him the truth, essentially. (No one ever told the entire truth.) But Ruth was hiding something. About herself, maybe, but more likely covering for someone. The brother? She probably knew where he had gone to ground.

He had moved over to the counter to put the notepad on a flat surface. Virginia took the cloth into the kitchen. Ruth said, "There's fresh coffee." Victor held her eyes a moment before saying yes. He flipped about in the notepad. He was conscious of his heart beating irregularly. She left a scent behind her that was not coffee or cleaning products.

To Cassie he said, "You say you were here at ten o'clock?"

"In the kitchen. Mortimer had come in for a cup of coffee. He had been down to the station to meet his brother and nephew, but the train was late." She was about to say more but changed her mind.

"Yes. You're his alibi and he's yours. Let's hope you don't both have a reason for covering for each other."

"I used to make pancakes at nine o'clock. Or cookies. A snack, like. We were in the habit of sitting down and yakking until the news came on the TV."

If you let them, they led you around in circles. "He beat you," he said, "and yet you never filed a complaint."

His eyes watched hers: they did not flicker. "I worried I'd be on my own again," she answered flatly. "Have to go back to waitressing to feed my kids."

"You knew what he was. He worked here before you were married."

"My uncle wanted it. My aunt too."

"They forced you to get married?"

"He was not always a total rotter. At first he was charming. He liked to dance. There was something about him. A spark of life."

"But you did not want to marry him?"

She put the mop down and stood with her backside resting on the top of the counter, looking out the windows at the front of the store. His view of her was in profile: a short nose, pale, fleshy cheek. She would not meet his eyes. "He pushed me into it," she said, "they both did." Up to this point she had been evading his line of questions, dodging, he suspected, if not outright lying. Suddenly now she was telling him the details of her life. He thought of birds that feigned injury to draw hunters away from their nest. What was she leading him away from? He tried to remember where in their exchange they had steered in this direction. What had he been trying to get at?

"I had the clear impression," she said, lowering her voice and glancing toward the kitchen, "that he had something on my uncle, something about the war."

"That's a long time back."

"That was it, the war. My uncle and aunt would not otherwise have been keen."

"On LaFlemme?"

"On the marriage."

"You mean a secret of some sort? Skeleton in the closet?"

"My uncle worked on the railway. He had a club foot, so they would not take him in the army proper. They transported war material—not weapons but civilian stuff—supplies—between the city and Vancouver. Boxes of dry goods and foodstuffs and so on. *matériale*, they called it. Things went missing. He had a partner, maybe a couple. It was all vague to me. Once when he was drunk my uncle joked about it: Spam scam. It might have been Old Beaudry. They had these confabs in the IGA office in back of the store that they made sure no one else heard. I didn't understand. It seems it was common practice, ripping the army off. The government was paying, kind of idea, so why not take a little for yourself. Truth be told, I did not care to understand. Then."

He drew a straight line across the blank sheet and asked, "Name?"

"Sam Roby," she said. "Helen Roby. They had a son, Jim, but he died on the beaches at Normandy. *Died in action*, the telegram said, but they found out somehow—a friend of Jim's who brought his rifle back from France—drowned before setting a foot on the beach."

"Your cousin, then."

"He was ten years older. I did not know him. They always felt that if someone could just have helped him reach the beach...." She closed her eyes as if remembering something painful, and then went on, "He told me something once, LaFlamme. He knew if I left him that he would get this place. His marital right, he called it." She opened her eyes and looked around. "So he had me in a spot and knew it. Knew I was stuck with him. But he said to me once that he might just pack it in himself some day. Leave me and the kids here, he meant, and go off on his own somewhere. He said I've got it covered, I'll be all right."

She'd been looking down, but her eyes swam up to his. He was familiar with this ruse, using fake emotions to misdirect the line of questioning. He'd been taken in by it before. "He didn't, though? Leave."

"Something was going on that I never knew about. See?"

"That would be another reason for you to want him out of the way."

"That's what I'm trying to tell you. It was years ago that he challenged me that way. When we used to really go at it." She snorted. "I am not a small woman. I got in a few licks of my own sometimes." She puffed out her cheeks and added, "Anyways, that was a long time ago. I hadn't felt that way for a dog's age. Things were actually getting better around here."

She glanced about. The shelves were fully stocked, the floors clean, the overhead lights glinted on the tops of canned goods. The room smelled of lemon cleaner and wax polish. She was the proprietor now. It was up to her to call the shots and she knew it.

Ruth came in with the coffee. Had she been listening from the other room? She said, "I made a fresh pot. Milk and sugar, right?"

"Two lumps," he said.

"Anyways," Cassie said, bringing the conversation to a close, "I would not go to jail for a man like that."

He was thinking about Mortimer Mann. Victor's line of questions had been misdirected when the conversation had touched on him. And then he wondered about the way Cassie put that last statement; he was to wonder about it for a long time after.

PENNY HAD SAID THAT THEY MUST not come back but she knew even as she gave her assent that she would return. This time she had worn a light sweater and loose-fitting jeans. She carried a small jar of water in one hand and had a handkerchief in a back pocket to wipe her face. Walking through the woods, she felt uneasy. Noises in the underbrush made her heart skip, but something pulled her deeper into the woods. It was more than curiosity; it was a sense that something important was about to happen, a thing that would change her life. Or maybe that was just being a silly girl. In any case, she kept walking through the still woods. At points the road was engulfed in dark shadows, despite the sun. Twigs snapped off the path, there were skitterings in the dry leaves of the underbrush and then sudden spooky silence. She heard the thumping of her own feet and thought she heard others as well, but when she stopped, there was nothing but the twitter of birds and rustling of leaves, and the thudding of her heart in her throat. She was happy to leave the forest behind when she came to the hump of rock.

The climb up the rock face was easier this time and a relief from the forest where the shadows and the stirrings in the woods set the blood pounding in her temples. As she climbed, the sun struck her face and neck. She watched geese flying over. Half way up she stopped and had a drink from the jar of water. Below she saw the tops of the spruces; in the distance, the lake; above, the place where she had put down the wildflower bouquet and then forgotten it. Above that, the plateau rock.

It was probably the remoteness of the place, its seclusion, but she felt as if eyes were watching her from the woods. A tingle went up her neck. The woods were damn silent. That was it.

She finished drinking and kicked a stone free and watched it bounce down through the undergrowth and then disappear, listening for the sound it made striking the ground below, but she did not hear it. It was a quiet day, though: the Mountie, Cassie seemed far away. She wondered if she would feel this way about Moon Lake once she was going to school in Beausejour and watching the late news and "Bewitched" with Mrs. Samson, the life she'd led at Moon Lake receding like a dream until she could no longer recall details.

She was near the top. A few loose stones came free underfoot. She was in a kind of daze and slipped on a rock. One foot gave way and suddenly she was down on her side, sliding back down the narrow path. There seemed no way to catch a foothold. She felt rocks tearing into her flesh as she slid over them. Oh God, she thought, don't let me go over the edge. Bones would be smashed. If she went over the edge, she'd be impaled on one of the sharp spruces. It would be hours before anyone looked for her. Would Ruth know to come here? There was a killer on the loose. He would pounce on her when she was vulnerable and stick a knife in her back. She shouldn't have come. These thoughts blinked through her brain and then she came to rest as suddenly as she had fallen. She was looking down into the gorge but was resting securely on a rock ledge. The smell of mud and vegetation was piquant, the smell of nature in decay. Her wrist stung and throbbed with pain. Her shirt was dark with sweat and smears of earth. She was still holding the jar of water. She laughed. After her heart slowed she sat up and then she stood carefully. What an idiot. Her jeans were torn down one thigh. Saliva ran out of the corner of her mouth.

She rested for a moment, then took out the handkerchief and wiped her face. Below she saw the tops of trees swaying slightly and the lake off in the distance. It was odd. She had thought at one moment that she might die but then it turned out she was not hurt badly at all, and now she wanted nothing more than to continue as if nothing had happened. Did people feel this way after a car crash? She was thinking she was about to die, and now she was alive as ever. More, maybe. The smells of the woods below seemed stronger.

When she came to the place where she had left the bouquet, she picked it up. Dried plants. They would look fine in the rust vase in her bedroom. She moved along the path carefully, passing the two smooth rocks and then the sharp turn that led to the plateau at the top of the path.

She saw him first and the hat only later.

"You found your wildflowers," he said. He was sitting cross-legged in the centre of the open space, looking directly at her, hands on his knees and a calm smile on his lips. He was expecting her.

"I'll go," she said. "I know I'm not supposed to be here."

She had stopped twenty or more feet away from him, watching his deep brown eyes, the same teasing expression as in his sisters' faces. He motioned her forward with one hand. "They come here all the time, it's no big deal."

"They said it was sacred ground."

"It is." He looked around. "But not exclusive. It's a nice place to come and think on a warm afternoon. It can be both." He laughed.

"You know, then, that they come here?"

"For a long time. But we won't tell them. Let them keep their secret."

He was wearing a checked shirt, open at the neck, jeans, and a pair of Adidas sneakers. She recognized them from the store. He bought things with the money he received for helping out. She was under the impression that he always waited to make his purchases until she was alone in the store. She had noticed that other men did that with Ruth. He was the first one to make a point of doing it with her and it made her heart skip.

She asked, "Where is he?" The pain in her leg was subsiding. Her heartbeat had returned to normal. She would wait a minute and have a drink.

Instead of answering he said, "Nowadays even the old ones don't put as much store in this place as they used to. I found an empty whiskey bottle here not long ago." When he smiled she saw the tooth that was chipped at an angle. She could not feel threatened by someone who looked like Huck Finn and spoke so calmly.

He motioned for her to sit. The rock was warm. She remembered that from the other time. When she was seated beside him she put the bouquet on the rock and folded her hands in her lap. She was not flustered. He'd always put her at ease, Roger too; that was why Roger liked him so much. There was something new about him: he wore a leather thong around his neck from which hung an intricately carved bone pendant: a flying figure of some kind, not quite man but not quite bird, it appeared. She did not have the courage to ask him what it meant, and he fingered it when he spoke to her. She knew he would come to what she was interested in hearing in his own good time. "Thirsty," he said, nodding at the water bottle. She passed it over to him and he took a sip. He smiled crookedly at her again. "When you're thirsty, you sip," he said. And then he laughed and added, "You have to forgive me for talking like an Indian up here." He seemed to know more than her by instinct. It was amusing to him, her being there, his knowing she would come, his knowing she would bring water.

"You like it here," she said, and she heard herself sounding more adult than she intended. She shifted the hurt leg to a more comfortable position.

He passed the water bottle to her. "You came back," he said, as if that settled the matter. They left a silence. Up on the plateau the breeze was stronger. The tops of the trees at the edges of the opening swayed. Trunks scraped together, making a grinding sound that was as off-putting as the scraping of nails on a chalkboard. He shifted his legs around and took a packet of cigarettes out of a pocket. When he dipped his head to light one, she saw that he used something in his hair, Brylcreem, probably. Roger used it too. He exhaled stagily into the air and watched the smoke rise over their heads. When he motioned to her to take the cigarette, she took one puff. "Not quite the same," he said, laughing, "as Penny's cigs."

She watched the smoke drift upward. That's when she saw the hat. It was on the end of a branch at the edge of the plateau, hanging from the string that fit under the chin. The breeze moved it when it picked up from time to time and she knew unmistakably that it was his: worn and stained brown with fingering around the brim that was flat at the front and turned up on the sides. He had brought it back from the city, army and navy, he told them. Australian.

He followed her eyes. "In the past they brought the old ones who died here. So their spirits passed from this world in peace. I told Roger that once and he remembered it, and thought maybe the hat would work a sort of spell for him. Purge away the bad."

"He's a little strange," she said, and then she felt as if she had betrayed him. What was the point of having secrets against her brother with Archie Cloud?

"I don't reckon it will work," he said. He smiled again.

"A lot there for one soiled hat to purge away."

"He doesn't think like anyone else I know, your brother. I'll give him that."

She wondered if some of the brown stains on the hat were blood and had half a mind to go over and examine it. But instead she took another puff of the cigarette and blew smoke out her nostrils the way Ruth did, two curling plumes past her eyes. She laughed when she noticed he was watching her. "If only it could be like this all the time," she said, "if only we could just sit in the sun this way forever." She meant it. A part of her was not ready for the classes in the high school and doing homework on the table at Mrs. Samson's every night and the knowledge of the world waiting around the corner. Knowledge that would increase suffering. Who had said that?

Now that the shock of the fall on the rocks had ebbed, she felt giddy from the pain in her muscles. And the nicotine was affecting her brain. Waves of sensation swept through her body: her thoughts were becoming confused. Archie's face went in and out of focus. She felt at one moment as if she was falling forward and then it seemed as if the back of her skull was lifting off her neck. She looked at him and he smiled back like a gnome. He wasn't laughing at her, was he? His face came closer and then receded until it was nothing more than the brown orbs of his eyes. She saw again the face at the window and it frightened her to think that it might have been him. She closed her eyes. An imprint from the sun, jagged fork lightning, was seared on the insides of her eyelids. She heard crows in nearby trees, the sighing of the breeze, a mosquito buzzing nearby.

His voice entered dimly into the realm of her awareness. "He's at the throne rocks, Ginny. Waiting for you."

First he showed her an opening in the trees at the edge of the plateau on the opposite side that she had come from. He pushed the branch of a spruce to one side and stepped onto a narrow ledge. She saw they were standing on the highest point of an escarpment and that the rock face fell straight down past the toes of his sneakers into a kind of valley below. It was two hundred feet to the forest floor below. He stood to one side to let her come forward and he held his arms out at his sides, as if he meant to float off like an eagle. It took her breath away. Scrub trees stood in the muskeg in the valley below and in the distance another rock face. She did not know if she dare stand like that, with a drop of hundreds of feet beneath her and someone at her back. If it was Roger or Ruth, maybe. But there he stood, arms extended, practically dropping into the depths. He turned towards her, his brown eyes even rounder in this light. He understood what was going through her mind. He fingered the amulet around his neck. He put out one hand and motioned her forward.

She was thinking about the drop and whether she could trust her injured leg not to give way, but what registered in her brain was the feel of his hand, dry as chamois cloth. He would not use lotions, and there were calluses on his palm. She put her trust in the steadiness of his arm. The ledge was so narrow the needles of the spruce brushed the back of her neck when she stood beside him. She caught a whiff of their acrid scent. The breeze was quite strong on the ledge. It felt cool on the cheeks and teased the hairs on her brow. He pointed down. Far below on the forest floor there was an open space in the underbrush where grey rocks of the kind on the plateau, only much smaller, were visible. Strewn about the rocks was a pile of white tree branches, sticking up this way and that, and thin and oddly shaped, birch, maybe.

"Bones," he said.

She misheard him and must have had a blank look on her face.

"Animal bones, maybe human. I can't tell from here. There's thousands of them in a giant jumbled heap. I keep meaning to find a way down there to investigate but then I forget." He laughed.

She laughed too, a suppressed little wheeze forced from the front of her mouth in terror.

"It's a mystery," he went on. "The forest around"—he swept one arm from left to right in an arc that stopped at Moon Lake—"is filled with mystery. Animals we never see, spirits that stay near the water, events that occurred thousands of years ago that we don't understand. The old ones say there are paintings on rocks in a nearby cave, but no one ever goes there. Bad things happen after to people who travel there."

She felt queasy then, the sensation of the nicotine in her blood returning for a moment. Was he trying to tell her something? She looked closer but to her it was still a pile of tree branches. His eyes must have been stronger. Or was he putting her on? She looked at him. His face was difficult to read. There was a placidity in his eyes that was either indifference or guardedness, but she could not tell which. Then into his gaze stole that slight look of irony.

He shrugged. "I don't know how they got there."

That was not the question on her mind. When he had looked enough, he took her hand in his again. It was warm and firm. She looked at him, thinking he was going to kiss her, and she was not ready for that, but he stepped back instead, and drew her away from the ledge. The branches of the tree sprung into place behind them. She smelled again a whiff of spruce, but also the scent of his body, manly and dank. She thought, if you didn't know the ledge was there you would never suspect. It was their secret from the girls, she thought.

The Mountie had come out on the stoop. He had pushed his cap up on his head and was looking across the open field where Alexander and Peter had played croquet earlier: the little grey tractor, the well, the path to the deer meadow. He was wearing the uniform jacket with the shoulder patches. He took several deep breaths and tapped the notepad against one thigh and said, "They've got this device now, it burns that stuff off."

"An electrical wand," Alexander said. He was standing in front of the window to the side of the stoop, scraping under the sill, an area most people did not take the trouble to clean properly, and consequently the place where rot started. "We used to carry them at the hardware store, those wands."

The Mountie grunted but did not answer. He had one hand over his gut.

Alexander was looking at the Mountie in profile. The peak of his cap was pointed at the sky. The flag on the flagpole made a colourful background to his face, which was a little pale. Probably he hadn't slept much in the past few days. "They don't work as well as good old-fashioned elbow grease," Alexander said. "Nor do the butane torches." He shrugged. "Some jobs there's just no shortcut."

The Mountie said, "My old man bought houses in the city that were in the way of freeway routes and so on, shopping-mall construction. He moved the houses to different sites in the city, then refurbished them and sold them. Mostly it was a lot of scraping and painting and re-plastering."

"A good business. Lots of development going on now."

"I got to help, painting the walls. He did the trim himself."

"Painting trim is fussy work. Not many men are good at it."

"Patience," the Mountie said. "It pays off but it's trying on the nerves."

Alexander hesitated, wondering, not for the first time, if they were talking about something other than painting. He thought again that the Mountie was a man he could warm to easily: a good clean jaw, straightforward way of talking, homespun truths. Mortimer said that the Mountie was slippery, but that judgment, like most, cut two ways. Alexander took his pipe out of his pocket and lit up the few strands in the bottom of the bowl. The Mountie watched him. "I should quit," Alexander said, "everybody tells me so." He laughed. "I used to tell my wife I wasn't hooked, I could quit any time, but I'm beginning to think I was wrong."

"Cold turkey," the Mountie said, "is the only way. I stopped five years ago and haven't touched one since." He said it with confidence but was licking his lips as if he was craving a smoke that very moment.

Alexander had heard this many times before. "The lungs recover in six months, they tell me. Pink as a baby's bottom."

The Mountie said, "Don't let anyone tell you they don't crave them." He came down off the stoop and stood beside Alexander. "I love the smell of the pipe," he added. "Maybe when I get older, I'll take it up. Retirement. Sitting on the porch."

Alexander said, "I'm going to try my hand at poetry."

A woodpecker was hammering away at a piece of tin on the roof. The Mountie looked in that direction. "What a God-awful racket," he said. "Don't they only do that in the spring? Mating season?"

"Maybe he got to liking it. Or maybe he's deranged."

The Mountie chuckled. His eyes wandered off across the field that stretched from the area in front of the store up to the breaking. You could see the clearing in the distance, mounds of black earth, tree roots projecting sideways, stones. "He had big plans," he said.

Alexander grunted. Mort had told him about LaFlamme's ambitions; he was a man restless with desire. "We don't know what's coming, that's a fact." He was puffing on his pipe and added, "The great wheel turns."

The Mountie said, "I didn't know you were a student of philosophy."

"Everybody gets a little of the Bible as a kid."

"That's not the Bible; it's Boethius, in *The Consolation of Philosophy*." He threw his head back and said, "*What is up will be down, what is down will be up.* My wife was a lit major at college. I remember it because the book had a colour illustration on the cover, a wheel with people hanging on by these little handholds. On the side going up they were laughing, on the side going down, their faces were wrenched in pain. Like gargoyles. Tongues hanging out, teeth missing. Pitiful and ugly. They knew how to depict pain back then."

It was more surprising to Alexander that he had picked up the idea somewhere other than the Bible than that Mort had it so wrong. His cheeks flushed. The Mountie must think Alexander an idiot. He would have to get hold of a Bible. He needed now to know about Ezekiel. It was a wheel, wasn't it, that Ezekiel was spinning?

The Mountie said, "The lab boys want everybody's shoes. Anything with heels."

"I didn't think to bring anything besides these shoes." He looked down at the black tops reflecting the sun. "These brogues."

"The boy?"

"A pair of sneakers and light boots too."

"You two were with each other from the time you left the station that night, right?"

"The whole time."

"There was never a period…when you got to the bunkhouse.…"

"We went to bed. Well after ten. Exhausted."

"The boy had the impression you might have gone out later." The Mountie grunted. He licked his lips again. He was dehydrated but didn't know it. "Anyway," he added, "it will only be a day or two before you get your shoes back."

He had been waiting to make his point. "You know," he said, "Mort and me went for a walk around the lake and we came across the path we were on that night, me and the boy. He pointed out a shoe print to me and it got me to thinking about what we told you earlier. The way the boot print was at an odd angle. I mean, got me thinking. See, those paths up there are not straight cuts through the bush, are they? They don't intersect at ninety-degree angles but loop and wind and double back at points. They confuse you."

"You said that earlier."

"Yes. And I told you that when we stepped off the path we saw someone running away from the lake."

The Mountie had opened the notepad. "Yeah. Toward Cuthand's."

"But what if the path zig-zagged right there where it crossed the other, wouldn't it be possible in the dark to have been turned around almost the whole hundred and eighty degrees? Mightn't he have been running *toward* the lake?"

"But you said that you went in the opposite direction and then came to the lake."

"There's a lot of paths up there. You said so yourself."

The Mountie looked at him oddly.

Or was it Mort who had said that?

The Mountie had found his place in the notepad. He unclipped the pen and made a scribble at the top of a page which was already filled with his fine hand writing. "It's a thought," he said, "but I'm going with your original statement. Original impressions are usually more reliable than second thoughts."

Alexander puffed on his pipe. He was not used to being rebuffed, but all right, he had made his point. That's about all you could hope for with the cops, wasn't it?

While the Mountie was still scribbling in his notebook, Ruth pushed open the door and let the spring crash it shut behind her. She did not look at them, but came down the steps, banging her feet on the wood loudly. She wheeled away from them and stood in front of the flag. It hung from a thin wood flagpole, about six feet high, painted white, though the paint had yellowed near the bottom. She placed both hands on the pole, testing how well it was anchored, and then threw her weight against it. One grunt and it came loose in the ground. She jerked at it and pulled it free. The flag was small. It drooped and touched the earth as she wrestled briefly with the thin pole, pulling it free of the earth. It was the old flag, the British Ensign. She held the pole horizontal, stepped back and flung it into the bushes under the window. Then she went back up the steps and came out of the store a moment later with another pole. This one had the new flag attached, the red Maple Leaf. She jammed it into the ground, then stooped, and with a couple of rocks anchored it to her satisfaction. Stood back to admire the flag. She did it without acknowledging their presence. That's when she turned to them, her black eyes flashing. "We wanted it," she announced. She was sweating, beads of perspiration on her brow. She licked her lips and continued: "Roger and Archie got it at the ceremony in Beausejour on Dominion Day and we all wanted it to fly here at Moon Lake." She looked at the Mountie and then at Alexander. There was a mole at one corner of her mouth, a mole Alexander had not noticed before, but which he wanted to reach out and wipe away. Or lick away. Ridiculous idea. He felt the tops of his ears burning, a sensation like the flush in his cheeks earlier. Since arriving at Moon Lake he had become subject to emotions that wrenched him first this way and then that. He would have to get control of himself. "Only," Ruth continued, "he would not have the new flag. *Over my dead body*, he told us." She shook her black mane of hair dramatically, daring them to say something. He could not take his eyes off the mole, the way it leapt near her lip when the muscles of her mouth moved as she talked. Her skin was a pale white that was almost translucent. He was having trouble thinking of anything other than kissing her. "Well," she said, "well, okay, then."

W{HEN THEY REACHED THE BASE} of the rock face, she walked behind him on the trail. He was not tall, not much taller than her, but he stepped quickly and lightly along the path. She remembered Roger saying something about how Archie walked on the balls of his feet, a hunting trick. She watched the soles of his shoes rise and fall in front of her. The heels were hardly worn. Her own shoes were sloped at sharp angles from uneven wear. *Stop slouching.* That was the brassy voice of Cassie. She wanted her and Ruth to walk like ladies and to hold their little fingers out while they drank tea. Such pretensions. Cassandra.

The pain in her leg had come back when she'd had to tense the muscles on the descent from the plateau at the top of the hummock on the way down to the forest. Each step caused a little needle prick under her knee cap. Roger had some salve in his cubbyhole. And liniment. She might have to see the doctor.

She was still carrying the jar. A little water sloshed in the bottom, but it would be too warm to drink now. The sun had passed its zenith and the path was shaded by the trees. Leaves were beginning to fall. They swirled down onto the path, yellow with green veins, and crackled underfoot. Soon she would have to get home. Cassie would yell at her about setting supper on the table.

When they came to the place where the path widened, he simply put out his hand and she took it. Her heart was in her throat. They walked silently for a while and then he released her fingers from his and when he gripped her hand again, he interlaced their fingers. It was almost too much to bear. She'd been warm earlier on the rock on the plateau, but that had gone away in the shadows of the trees. Now sweat ran down the middle of her back. When they were sitting beside each other on the plateau she'd said she wished that could go on forever, but now she knew it was this she wanted to continue, the grip of his flesh on hers, the smell of his shirt, a close warm man smell.

They passed Cuthand's. Someone was splitting wood. Whack, thunk, then a long pause. Whack, thunk, pause. It went on and on. It had to be a man, a man intent on finishing the job. At the next junction they turned into the reservation. They were approaching the place the kids called King's Throne. It was a geological freak, two slabs of granite thrown up perpendicular to the ground in a clearing in the woods, the larger slab towering over the other so they resembled a chair constructed for a giant. The undergrowth they passed through was less dense now. They were close to the lake. Mallards flapped past. It was that quiet in the woods that you only really noticed it when something made a sudden noise. She felt him slow their pace. She thought maybe he would try to kiss her. She would let him do that but she would not let him touch her.

Roger was slumped against the base of the smaller rock. She thought he was sleeping or hurt, but when they stopped in front of him he opened his eyes. "Well, well, well," he said, "the belle of the ball." His speech was slurred. He had a mickey bottle in one hand. Blood was smeared across the back of his wrist.

Archie said to her, "He's been like this since yesterday. Won't eat."

"She's getting real pretty," Roger slurred. "Everybody thinks it's Ruth got the looks in the family, but you just wait." He winked at Archie and then burped loudly. "Rotgut," he said. He held the bottle out to Archie but Archie shook his head. Roger looked at it. It was nearly empty.

"That's not a good idea," she said.

"Got another," he said.

"We bought them from Cuthand," Archie explained. "He made me buy them."

Roger said to him, "You didn't argue at the time."

"Have some water," she said.

Roger waved the jar away. He was still sitting with his legs stretched out in front of him. His sneakers were caked with dried mud. The bottoms of his jeans were stiff and wrinkled. There was a streak of mud on one cheek. She felt the urge to wipe it away, the same way she wanted to wash away the pain in his eyes. "Drink the water," she repeated, more insistent.

Archie had stepped back. He sat on a smaller rock to one side with his hands on his knees. She recognized again the placidity in his eyes. It was maddening. She wanted him to say something that would make Roger snap out of the funk he was in, but he just sat there like Buddha or something, implying this is your problem.

"I'm going away," Roger said. "Tha's why I wanted to see you. Say g'bye."

She knew it was useless to argue, but someone had to. "You mustn't."

"Damn right. Train tonight."

"They'll be watching for you." She meant the RCMP. Maybe the fear of being caught escaping would keep him from going.

"Got a plan," he said, "walk down the railroad tracks."

"Not a clever plan," she said, and then wished she'd kept her mouth shut.

"We'll find a way," Archie said behind her, "to fool those idiots."

"You too?"

"Red Rock. They're hiring at the mines. Four bucks an hour."

"Elliott Lake," Roger said. "The farther away the better." He blinked and it looked as if he was going to say something, but instead he turned his attention to the bottle of whiskey. He noticed her looking at his bloody wrist.

"You have to clear your name," she said.

He laughed and Archie snorted. "Don't give a damn," he said. "Fucking RCMP."

"But you didn't do it."

"They make things up."

"They lay for you and then spring the trap," Archie said.

"He was right about that, the bastard."

Roger had pulled himself up on one elbow and was prying the stopper out of the mickey bottle. His fingers were brown with grime; there was dirt caked under his nails. The lock of hair had fallen over his eyes and he brushed it away. He was determined and foolhardy at the same time. It was a terrible combination she had witnessed in him before, a combination that led to disaster.

"This is bigger than Sarah Hooker," she said. "Murder is really bad."

"She got it wrong," he blurted out. He meant his hands, apparently. He was looking at them. Dried blood had scabbed over the scrapes. "Ruth got it wrong."

"Bear grease," Archie said, "will fix those scratches. Better than your salves."

"Tell her was'n," Roger said. She gathered he meant Ruth. "She saw me," he continued, "putting stuff in my knapsack that night. She saw blood and she got it wrong."

Archie said, "You have to get something in your belly."

"This here is perfec' for me." Roger blinked his eyes as if in pain. It was a tic that had started when he was a small boy, after one of the beatings. He took a swig and wiped his mouth with the back of his wrist.

She would remember that, the way even after he wiped his mouth there was a dribble of yellow spittle that ran out of the corner of his mouth and then fell on the front of his shirt where it slowly hardened on the cloth. She would remember too the hurt in his voice, the sadness in his eyes.

"Maybe I will," he said, "have that water," He swallowed down all the water in the jar and flipped it backwards over his head where it smashed on the rocks. "Good riddance," he said, "to that and to everything." His reckless made her stomach hurt. He could kill someone; he could be killed walking down the train tracks.

She turned to leave. Cassie would be on the warpath.

"We'll get some food," Archie said to her, "I promise."

"Come to the back steps tonight," she whispered out of Roger's hearing.

Earlier in the woods they had stopped to kiss. He had put his hands under her sweater and she'd felt her belly tighten at the same time her nipples swelled. It was the only card she had to play. She knew he would agree.

Roger was swigging from the bottle and weaving around. He lost his footing but did not fall. "Was not the bayonet," he said. "Tha' I know."

"The Mountie is looking for it."

"Was not the bayonet."

"He wants everybody's shoes, too."

Archie snorted again.

"Found it in the bush weeks ago. Rusty."

"It could clear you, then."

"Threw it in the lake. Splash. Gurgle. Good riddance."

He lurched forward and she had to step toward him and put her hands out to catch him or he would have fallen on his face. His breath smelled terrible. His clothes reeked of swamp water and smoke and spilled whiskey. She would remember that for years to come. She would remember too that he hadn't actually denied it.

T HE OLDER DAUGHTER HAD GONE INSIDE, but that damn woodpecker was still banging his beak on the tin. Victor stepped away from the store to get a better view of the roof. The sun was into its descent in the west. Yellow leaves swirled down from the poplars. But he could not see the bird, which must have been hidden by the chimney. That's probably what it was banging on, the metal flange at the base of the red bricks where the chimney stack projected out of the roof shingles. He felt his hand reaching for the back of his skull. The headache had ebbed earlier but now he felt it returning.

She was something, Ruth. A firecracker. There had been girls at college like that, girls who would smack your face if you made fun of them, and then scrape your back with their nails in bed. Wildcats. They were capable of anything. They stirred up something inside Victor. Sheila had. It was a poser how desire worked. He had seen it in Alexander Mann's eyes when the girl had gone after the flagpole. It was written all over the elder brother's face too, Mortimer. But was he a killer?

He tapped the notepad against his thigh and walked away from the trading post, towards the lake. Behind him Alexander Mann was back at his scraping. He had put his pipe away and was humming a song that had been popular a decade earlier. Victor didn't know quite what to make of the other man: quoting Boethius, but then desiring the girl so openly.

He took the path that cut between the trading post and the bunkhouse down to the wider trail that circled the lake. He would walk out past the place where the body had been found. It was too late for real police work now; he had left it too long, but he would do it anyway, if only to say he'd inspected the area and followed procedure. But his conscience would never be clear. That wasn't such a big deal, anyway, a clear conscience. It was more important to get the job done than to guarantee to some inner voice that it had been done correctly.

Sergeant Black was another matter. Dot the *tees* and cross the *eyes*.

He paused where the two paths intersected. The wider path was muddier, less rock in the composition of the soil, he noted. Was that important? Near the decline in the path where the woods to the left opened onto the lake, he stopped and spit into the thistles. The burning sensation was back, the burping. But no blood. One of his uncles had had a section of his intestines removed in an emergency operation, and then five years later had to have the operation again. It scared Victor more than he liked to admit. And things like that ran in families, he knew it.

His mind drifted when he thought of his uncle, now dead, and he realized he'd walked some distance when he felt the sun on his face, coming in through a gap in the woods.

Moose Point, that's what they called the place. A tiny creek ran across the path and into the lake. He found a handkerchief in a pocket and wiped his mouth. A mosquito buzzed around his ear and he brushed at it with his other hand. Geese high in the air were honking. Already the long flight to the south? He came to the place where they found the body and turned his attention to the vegetation along the path. You never knew when the eye might spot something. But he saw nothing, nothing. When he passed the wooden crate tucked under the bushes, he wondered again about the condoms. And where was that bayonet? He stopped again and scribbled in the notepad: a question he had to ask back at the store. He was well past where the body had lain.

This portion of the path he was not familiar with. It dropped as it neared the lake. He knew he was in the vicinity of the border between Manitoba and Ontario, a fact he registered in his policeman's mind, but not because it was an issue of jurisdiction. The Mounties had jurisdiction everywhere. No, it was just a fact to be filed away. Then he came to an opening with a shoreline, it could not be called a beach, not accurately, but a canoe was beached on the rocks and a rowboat, too, farther down where the willows started and then gave way to bulrushes and plants growing in the shallows. The canoe was pulled up beside a tree and tied with a blue nylon rope to a root protruding from the earth. There was a rusting tin can in the canoe for bailing and two paddles. Mud on the wooden seats where shoes had scraped over them. He dropped to one knee to examine the area around the canoe, but the ground was rock and sand, it hadn't retained the impressions made by footwear. He did find a butt, a tailored cigarette with a filter tip. Pretty stones, pink and agate. The stones were small and sharp. His knees hurt.

When he stood up he felt a headrush, and then the headache made up of pinpricks in the corners of his eyes. If he was not careful he would get the full-blown pounder that settled at the base of the skull. He closed his eyes, feeling with each heartbeat the nerves in his face twinging with pain. His eyes were shut but he was listening. Here was an oddity. The geese seemed much closer when you heard them but did not see them. He wondered if that was a bit of knowledge he could put to use some day. Small birds were whistling in the trees, a woodpecker rapping, a web of sounds that seemed to resonate meanings about what had happened here, but did not.

It was becoming one of those cases: deficient evidence, contrary statements.

He crossed the rocky shore to the edge of the lake, where he dipped water with one cupped hand and splashed it on his throat and neck. His brain was muzzy, no doubt about it. The investigation was beginning to slip away. There were too many dead ends in the information he had been able to gather. Everybody had a story but their different accounts did not mesh. And Cassie was right, things did not always add up. There were gaps in the way people behaved and lapses in their memories of events, and there was lying and confusion and just plain muddle-headedness. Who could remember exactly what they were doing between nine-thirty and ten-thirty when several days had passed? Or that it wasn't closer to eleven? He was surprised people furrowed their brows and tried to answer such questions. He would have been inclined to laugh in his questioner's face. The part of him that wasn't a policeman. (Must never say that to Sergeant Black.)

Most murder investigations did not come down to fitting together clues anyway. Sometimes they resolved from someone saying something stupid during an interview, true, but most often it was because someone broke down under questioning and admitted they had done the deed. You gathered facts and questioned suspects with that objective in mind: to get someone cornered so badly they had no alternative but to confess. It was ugly behaviour, but then you were dealing with ugly people. Thieves, rapists, murderers.

That didn't always happen. In this case he had been unable to get to the boy, who by now would be long gone or have cooked up a plausible story. He would be difficult to shake. And Victor was running out of time. Other crises were developing. A teenager had crashed his car into the side of the service station in Whitemouth on the night he was bringing Sheila back from Portage la Prairie. The constable had done the preliminary response but he needed to check out the scene and write out a full report. He needed to take Sheila to the city to see a doctor. Some guys had busted up the furniture at the Lakeland on Saturday night. Eddie Stenko, the proprietor, had given him their names, and he had to get around to talking to them soon. That meant further reports to fill out. Sergeant Black kept a neat desk; he liked to move things to the out basket as quickly as possible and he sometimes seemed impatient with Victor's methods: too unpredictable.

He knelt and splashed more water on his face. Tiny insects scooted across the surface of the water and algae floated near the bottom. The cool water felt good, though. He must remember not to stand too quickly or turn his head suddenly to the side. No more vomiting.

He walked over to the rowboat: peeling red paint, two oars, a tin can for bailing. It was not as high up the shore as the canoe and tied to the willows with the same blue nylon rope but was held by a loose knot. A woman? He heard the beating of duck wings and looked up in time to see two mallards low over the water. From this perspective he could see a house across the lake. Smoke curled from the chimney. A pile of firewood to one side. He had to squint to see that far. That was the reservation over there, IR39, if he recalled correctly from the map on his office wall. The Clouds' house? Something had been going on over there, something violent. Were the girls suspects? He supposed so, but this did not look like the work of girls. If he could locate them, the LaFlamme boy and Archie Cloud could clear up some tricky points in the investigation. What he'd found out from Cuthand had at least proved useful in eliminating Alexander Mann and his kid, who'd been spotted at the far side of the lake at the time of the events.

You gathered facts but did not draw conclusions. He had to keep that in mind. You did not say *it's the boy*, even in your head, because then you went about gathering facts that proved it was the boy, you made it so. You did not intend to but you bent the evidence to suit the conclusion, and then you brought the case to court and ended up looking the fool. Self-fulfilling prophecy, that's what they called it. He called it making an ass of yourself.

Then the Staff Sergeant made notes in your personnel file: *bad judgement.*

Wild rice. They were the plants growing in the shallow water.

Some of the Indians harvested wild rice on these lakes and sold it to a grocer in town. In the city they paid five bucks the pound. Sheila made a casserole with celery and mushrooms. She came home from the IGA and muttered *damn, forgot the bamboo shoots.* And then he drove back to the IGA.

He'd been standing in one spot for a while, he realized.

He turned his head slightly, registering a noise to his side. Between him and the canoe stood a buck moose, no more than twenty feet away. Its black nose quivered with each breath it took. He heard it breathing. This close he could smell its fur, which was matted and dotted with burrs and bits of yellow grass: the sour reek of rotting cheese. The antlers were massive. Victor held his breath. It had to weigh a ton or more; those antlers would rip a man's body in half before he blinked; there would be no time to even reach for the pistol. Victor felt each beat of his heart thud in his temples. He was fascinated by the fold of loose flesh hanging from the moose's lower jaw, like a turkey's. What did they call that—the beard, the bell? It was prehistoric and ugly. Victor was fascinated and repelled by it at the same time. The moose's blank brown eyes stared into his without flickering, and then the moose made a sound like a cough and backed up suddenly. It wheeled on its long and angular legs, took a couple of awkward, lurching steps sideways and away from the lake, and then it crashed into the woods on the other side of the path.

Victor exhaled. He put one hand on the butt of the pistol. Idiotic.

H<small>E WAS HUMMING A SONG</small> that was popular a decade earlier. Maria said he loved catchy tunes, but she said it in a way that made it clear she had contempt for that kind of music herself. She was a bit of a snob. She knew about wines, and the correct way to make omelets, and all of the classics. That was what had attracted him to her, probably. He wanted to know about those things but was too busy making money to investigate them for himself. She was a good teacher. She'd taken him to European films and showed him how to decant wine. Her knowledge of the Bible, though, was limited, which was unusual for a preacher's daughter. She had blocked it out.

"Little sister don't you kiss me once or twice."

He chuckled to himself. He was working along the wall next to the bunkhouse now, so he could keep an eye on the deer meadow. Earlier Peter had gone up there with the Finn. There was a vegetable garden there, and grouse came to the clearing, and later in the day, the Finn said, deer. He took them water.

Peter had been eager to see. It was early but possible to catch a sighting of the deer, the Finn said. So Peter, being Peter, had to check it out.

How much did the boy actually know? LaFlamme had been killed, he knew that. Did he know that he had been violently attacked and had died from half a dozen knife wounds? Did he understand they were suspects? The Mountie had grilled him and the doctor had examined Peter's clothes. After tagging them, the Mountie had taken their shoes. Alexander had spoken to Peter as little as possible about the events of that night. He was worried that the Mountie suspected him, and he was afraid for Mortimer. The image of him standing in that cocoon of golden light with Cassie made his mouth go dry. And the Mountie knew he knew something. *Don't take my boy.*

"Little sister don't you do what your big sister done."

He stopped scraping to smack a mosquito on his arm. It was coming on to the end of the day. The mosquitoes came out of the grass then. He would have to stop soon. But he had had a pleasant first day of work, in the final analysis. The events on the path past Moose Point were receding. It was horrible but nothing to do with them; a thing that happened to someone else; a curiosity heard on the radio news. After the funeral they would put it all behind them, he thought, make that fresh start: clean air, honest labour, a chance to live a life and not feel a knot in the gut every moment you weren't working to hang on to a business that had gone bad on you. Peter would be all right. In a year he could go to the school in Beausejour like the younger daughter was about to.

She had come out a few minutes ago to tell him supper would be ready soon, tugging the bottom of her sweater the way Ruth had done earlier. When did that start? When did you feel the first twinges of desire? Had Peter felt them yet? He looked up from his work and along the path toward the deer meadow and past the well, the grey tractor. Peter and the Finn were still up there.

The woman at the train station had simply said to him *come with me*. It was years ago, on a summer night. He worked as a porter that summer. The train had come in from Vancouver and they were both on it. She had an apartment in one of the highrises in the city centre. She smoked cigarettes while he ate a steak she had prepared. *You have your red meat*, she said, *then I'll have mine*. She had a loud laugh. She straddled him and wormed herself onto him. It hurt. He had not expected that. Or that she would want it right away again, and then in the middle of the night. No condom. She was on the pill, she told him. What a relief that was to her, the invention of the pill. Her apartment was filled with bookshelves and papers, an oak desk, a long wooden table with a typewriter. She taught at the college, she told him proudly; she would have a doctorate in philosophy soon. Her parents lived in a big stone house along the river. She liked working men, she said, men who could do things with their hands. She laughed at that. He was sixteen that summer; the younger daughter was fourteen, Ruth eighteen.

He looked up again and spotted Peter on the path near the well, the splash of his red hair reflecting sunlight. He was running. He waved when he saw that Alexander had spotted him. He had something important to tell.

Deer, Peter said, four with white tails. He and the Finn had stood on one side of the clearing and looked at them for a long time. It was so great because they didn't move but their tails flicked from side to side. They dropped their heads slightly to look at you. They had brown eyes. Alexander had to come and see. The Finn was standing behind him, smiling in a bitten way. Alexander had liked him on first impression, but he saw in the light of day that the Finn had sunken, defensive eyes. No, irritable. And his mouth was narrow, as if he were biting back on something. He had removed his cap and the breeze lifted the wispy blond hair at the back of his head. When Peter turned to him for confirmation he laughed. "You bets so," he said.

So Alexander had to put away the paint scraper and see too. Peter called *so long* to the Finn who was mounting the steps into the store, and they walked up together, father and son. Alexander had not seen the tractor up close. The grey paint had peeled off the hood. The starter motor was covered in grease. On the seat there was a yellow tattered cushion. Peter picked up a bucket beside the well and pumped into it expertly until it was filled right to the top. He insisted on carrying it. He explained that the Finn had moved a trough up on the meadow so the deer could drink. In Finland the deer were smaller but there he had fed them in the meadow behind the house.

Peter had found a pal, it appeared.

Alexander had had a conversation with Peter about the Finn. "He does sums," Peter said, "like figuring out how to spend the money if he won the lottery."

Alexander said, "He doesn't strike me as the gambling type."

"He scribbles columns on bits of paper, words and beside them, numbers, and he changes the numbers in the columns and when he's done, tears up the papers and throws them in the garbage."

Alexander remembered doing calculations on sheets of foolscap when they were in the process of losing the hardware business. All for naught.

"Sometimes," Peter continued, "in exasperation he throws the papers into the wood stove."

They passed the breaking on their left. Stumps had been pushed into a pile near the path. Heaps of stones stood on the borders of the field and here and there dottetd the roughly turned ground. Flocks of small birds swirled about, twittering as they landed and pecked in the earth for the millions of fresh insects there, exposed to the light for the first time. A feast. The land smelled of loam and decay. It had been untouched a long time. Stones similar to agate glinted in the sun. In the spring Mort would plough the land and in a couple of years they would be harvesting grain from a square of land that had never been cultivated but had lain breathing and silent since before the dinosaurs.

Peter had been telling him about the deer and the porcupine they'd seen earlier, but as they began the slight climb to the meadow, he put his finger over his lips. Now was the time of silence. Peter went ahead. When they came into the meadow, the deer had gone. Peter looked crestfallen. He crossed to the trough and poured the water in. Almost a third had slopped out on the walk from the well. His sneakers were wet, the bottoms of his jeans dotted with water. They stood beside the trough in silence.

"They'll be back," Alexander said, knowing how much it meant to Peter.

There was a large bird moving about in one of the nearby trees, a crow, maybe, or a blue jay. It flapped from one tree to another and landed on the topmost branch, bending it over so it looked as if it would break. Alexander shielded his eyes against the sun but could not make out the species. It had not called out. Peter pointed to a narrow opening in the underbrush.

"Deer trail," he said, proud of the new knowledge.

There were droppings where the animals' track met the meadow. Peter said there was another path that ran up into the woods. The Finn said if you stood there and were silent, you could spot the deer coming from the forest into the clearing. But you had to be quiet and very still.

They crossed the clearing and walked up the path a short distance. It was warmer in the woods and Alexander felt his shirt sticking to his back. Was he getting fat? He heard a noise, a twig snap. He took a breath, feeling a deep unease. They went a little farther and he heard the sound again. This time he quickly reached his hand to Peter's shoulder and they stopped moving, but all they heard was the breeze in the pines. The bird flapped over their heads, flying away from the lake toward the deep woods. They walked farther up the path and he thought he heard noises again. He leaned forward and whispered to Peter, "Step up the pace," and they walked quickly for a minute, and then he suddenly pulled the boy behind a pair of pines growing close together beside the path.

His heart was pounding. Peter was breathing hard. He had placed his hand on the boy's shoulder and felt his heart pounding in the muscle and bone. Peter looked up at him with round eyes the way he had on the path on Friday night in the woods. They waited, straining their ears to the forest, and heard the peeping of small birds, insects in the grass. He strained his eyes to the woods: shadows thrown by the trees. After a minute he relaxed his grip on the boy's shoulder and they stepped back onto the path. He could not shake off the feeling that they were being watched. But he didn't hear any more twigs snapping. Only the silence of the woods, the forest holding its breath. Leaves rattled off some trees. His heart was still pounding in his throat. *Don't take my boy. Not that too.* They walked back to the meadow in silence, hearing only the thud of their footsteps on the earth. Alexander thought: we are never going to survive in these woods. When they came to the opening, they saw two does at the water trough. They glanced about, then dipped their heads, drank quickly and then bounded into the woods silently. Peter looked up at him with a smile of triumph.

Moon Lake

THE SPRINGS OF THE TRUCK RATTLED as it bounced through the dip where the logging road from Moon Lake crossed the ditch and came up to meet the highway outside of Beausejour. Victor saw headlights approaching from the opposite direction and waited until an ancient and faded orange micro-bus rumbled past before pulling on to the asphalt. Night came on fast at this time of year. An hour ago he had been standing in sunlight outside Moon Lake Trading Post, taking his leave of Alexander Mann. With luck he'd be home in fifteen minutes. With luck she'd be there to greet him and have cooked supper. It was the season for fresh potatoes and corn. He could use a can of ale. He should have thought to call before he left. Sheila got testy about things now. She called him names. She called him a liar. She told him she couldn't trust him. There was tension now in the way they moved about in the house together.

It was not just her sickness. It was him too.

For him it started before the miscarriage. It started because of Louise.

He hated those calls that came in the middle of the night: suicide, road accident, murder. This one was a multiple murder. A trucker who lived on a dirt farm near Lac du Bonnet had come home in the early hours one morning and shot his wife and kids in their beds. There were three kids: a baby and two older boys. The trucker had been fired from his job with the trucking company, so they were losing the family farm to a mortgage, and he'd been fighting with the in-laws. After shooting the wife and the two older kids, the trucker had barred the doors and windows and holed up in the farm house. When he telephoned to bring Victor up to speed, the local cop didn't know if anyone other than the trucker was still alive in the house. Maybe the baby. The local cop was a youngish guy and he sounded scared.

Victor had stopped outside Beausejour to pick up the sister-in-law. The local cop thought she might be able to talk the guy down, save the baby, if it was still alive in the farm house. Louise Duchamps. She was waiting on the sidewalk outside the house when he drove up, smoking and fidgeting from one foot to the other. She was not the kind of woman he would have called his type: curly hair in a hennaed permanent. When she opened the squad car door and hopped in beside him, she brought with her a scent reminiscent of turpentine. She had sharp features and a slot of a mouth that constantly was working on the drive to Lac du Bonnet. She was older than him by five years, he guessed. By the time she was forty her features would be hard.

He had looked across at her and thought her legs were her best feature, but he'd also thought that everyone turns into a wreck in these moments of crisis. She must have thought the same. She kept taking out a pocket compact and studying herself in the mirror. "He hates me," she said. "This will never work."

She told him she had been against her sister's marriage—the parents too, who lived near Dauphin and were on their way by car. A brother lived in the interior of British Columbia. Victor was exhausted that morning and was not able to focus on her rambling conversation; she was recounting for him the family history: something about adoptions and a child at the Selkirk mental hospital. It was spring, a warm day, a forest fire was burning in the area and bits of tiny black matter flew above their heads in the acrid air. Louise wore a skirt and had put on nylons. She shivered inside a thin jacket. He remembered thinking she could put on ten pounds.

Her husband, she told him, had been a hydro lineman. He had died on a pole when something happened with a transformer. She didn't want to know the details. She wished she had kids but that was how things worked out. There had been an insurance payout. But she was alone and lonely. She was a waitress at the truck stop outside of Beausejour. She was getting her life back together, but she had been visiting a psychiatrist in the city.

When they arrived at the farm, they saw the local cop had pulled his car across the road in front of the house just within shouting distance. Light from the sun, obscured by the pall of smoke in the air, glinted off the hood and roof. The cop was crouched behind the car and he waved them over. "Double-barreled shotgun," he informed them.

She said, "He'll kill me if he gets the chance."

They crouched behind the car with the local cop. They convinced Louise to call out to him. "Arnie," she shouted in a quavering voice, "this is silly."

He smashed out the window in the dining room and shot at the car. The pellets hit the hood and door, rattling like a handful of stones striking tin. Louise gasped. Her eyes were round as marbles. She clutched Victor's arm in a tight grip.

"Bitch," he shouted. "All three of you."

"See," she said to Victor. "He means my mother, my sister, and me."

They convinced her to try again.

"Let the kids go, Arnie," she shouted. "The baby."

He smashed out another window. They had a fleeting glimpse of him as he withdrew the butt of the shotgun from the hole in the glass before firing at them. A menacing, block-like figure with stringy black hair and a soiled white T-shirt.

That's how it went. The local cop shouted threats and warnings. The man inside let off one barrel of the shotgun at a time. They ducked to avoid the pellets, which were coming with enough force to do damage. Victor called out to ask if there was anyone in there with him. "Come and find out," he shouted back.

After a while they stopped calling to him. The local cop kept patting the butt of his revolver as if he was itching to use it. Louise sat on the ground with her knees tucked up under her chin and smoked. She looked up at him from time to time and grimaced. Grey eyes. He got a sore back. The crouching was difficult but they wanted to keep an eye on the house. He was hungry and getting hot. The effluence from the forest fire stung the eyes. It became obvious that nothing was going to happen.

Then the special team arrived from the city: sharpshooters, with a panel truck of equipment. They parked parallel to the car on the driveway. "You have no idea what you're doing," the sergeant said to him. He was short and beefy and his face was marked by the ravages of childhood acne. "You should have kept him talking. As long as they're talking, they're not shooting. This is a job for pros. Get down and keep out of sight." He had a bullhorn. "Arnie," he called out, "this is the RCMP. We're coming in with your family."

"Got no fucking family."

"We're coming in."

"Fuck off out of it."

The sergeant spoke to Louise. He told Victor, "Get her out of here for now." He was all business. He wore tight-fitting black leather gloves and sunglasses that reflected Victor's image back at him at distorted angles.

"Arnie," the sergeant shouted, "either you come out or we come in."

The pellets hit the window of the panel truck and sprayed the special team from the city. The sergeant ducked awkwardly and his hat was knocked off, and rolled under the wheel of the car. He retrieved it with a grunt. He took off his dark glasses and examined the lenses. They were scratched. That seemed to piss him off. "Get the woman out of here now," he barked at Victor.

Victor drove her to the motel on the outskirts of town. They had a cup of coffee in the café and something to eat. She told him she had been born with one kidney but had not known until she was a teenager. It was difficult to have babies. She shouldn't smoke. Her eyes were still as large as marbles: as she talked, they jumped from his face to the window and then back again. She slopped coffee on the tabletop and dropped the cigarette she was lighting. He did it for her. She drank coffee and rambled on about the jobs she'd had in the city. She had the habit of patting the hair on the back of her head and then fluffing it up with the ends of her fingers; she tapped the tabletop with crimson-painted nails. She rubbed her eyes with the back of her hand until they became glassy. He didn't like women who wore a lot of makeup but she had a nervous energy about her that reminded him of a thoroughbred horse.

He checked her into a room. "Get some rest," he told her. He felt he should be getting back to the farmhouse to help with the show of force. Sergeants from special teams delighted in writing reports that reflected badly on the district corporal. He had developed an immediate dislike for this one. But Louise's need held him there. She sat on the edge of the bed and turned on the television. She started to cry. He stood beside her and placed his hand on her shoulder. She picked it up and held it against her cheek.

"I'm a basket case," she sniffed.

He assured her she'd be all right after a little rest. He was uncomfortable in the room. The curtains were closed. The carpet smelled of strong cleaning fluids. A spider was perched in one corner of the ceiling.

She looked up at him through eyes liquid with tears. "Make love to me," she said. Her grip on his hand was furious. She was such a small woman. He had thought then that he was stronger than everyone else when it came to temptations of the flesh.

When he went to the door she stood, and then as he was about to say good-bye she looked as if she was going to step backward but fell flat on her face on the carpet, where she grunted and rolled over. Blood seeped from her nose. He picked her up in his arms and laid her on the bed. When he was dabbing her brow with a towel he had wetted in the bathroom, she put a hand on his shoulder and drew him down to her.

What he remembered was how thin she was: fine bones, small breasts, a tiny waist, lips as dry as paper. Her hair down there was reddish in tint. It was hot in the room. They lay on the bedspread with their clothes off, and afterwards he fluffed the pillows and tucked her in. She was snoring as he closed the door.

He came back later and told her about the suicide. First the trucker had shot the baby and then put the barrel of the shotgun in his mouth. The sergeant had made a mistake in timing. The special team was just preparing to break down the door and take their chances in a firefight, but the trucker beat them to it.

"Maybe it was for the best," he told her.

She said, "I would have taken care of that baby as if it was my own."

He held her in his arms. She was dressed and had taken a shower. He liked the perfume despite the arresting tang of turpentine. They had something to eat in the café and then sat over cups of coffee until her parents arrived. Her grey eyes were awash in tears when he last saw her.

The memorable thing happened on the highway back. He was driving fast, too fast, in all likelihood. Clouds had moved into the sky about the time the sergeant said they'd rush the door, dark clouds heavy with rain. By the time he'd left the motel behind, the sun had dipped below the horizon but the sky was still light, though streaked with yellow and purple, the kind of sky he liked.

He was humming along to the radio and drinking a Coke and feeling badly about the way things had worked out at the farmhouse and guilty about Louise. He was not accustomed to failure then, to failing Sheila. He was twenty-four, strong, alert; he could eat a two-pound steak and swim a mile.

He thought he saw something fall out of the sky, a comet,

maybe, but that was probably a trick of his eyes. He was nervous and exhausted. Hours had passed since he'd eaten.

He wasn't paying much attention to the road but at a dip he slowed and when the car came over the hump he saw a gold ball floating ahead of it, just above the asphalt. He hit the brake, peering through the windshield. The ball floated ten or fifteen feet above the road and about fifty yards further up the highway. It seemed to be drifting upward. It was twenty feet across and shimmered with a golden blue light. He was not frightened, exactly, but he stopped the car and got out. The ball drifted farther away, toward the woods. It was making a low crackling sound, like intense static. His skull tingled. The golden ball drifted into the trees and flickered through them as it floated away. He ran along the side of the road, trying to keep it in sight. It disappeared.

The odd thing was the feeling. As soon as he had closed the car door, he felt the force of it. He didn't have the words to say exactly. The feeling came from inside his body. It felt as if his chest had been opened and hollowed out and was instantly full, but not in a bad way. With everything that had happened during the day he should have felt down but it was neither a bad feeling nor a good one. He felt at peace, as if he suddenly understood things he had never before even cared much about. In college he'd known a guy who meditated. *You feel empty*, the guy had said, *and yet filled at the same time*. It was that feeling. His eyes had watered with tears but he wasn't crying. It was a release of some kind, but also bewildering. He sat on the hood of the car and studied the place where the ball had disappeared. Light was draining fast out of the sky. He'd never be able to tell anyone but Sheila; people like Sergeant Black would laugh at him. He took the pack of cigarettes from his breast pocket and threw them into the ditch. He'd never needed them again.

In the months following he drove over that stretch of highway numerous times but nothing occurred. He could not recall the exact spot where he'd seen the ball but he stopped here and there and sat on the side of the road, waiting. It was ridiculous, but he wanted the feeling again. He could summon it up if he closed his eyes and blocked out other thoughts, but it was becoming like the face of someone familiar that you tried to recall, vague, dim, and somehow just out of grasp. The experience was leaking away. He wanted to feel again the full force of it but knew he would have to settle with the memory and the sense of well-being that had come over him then.

He inquired about unusual events that day at the detachment in the city, and was told that meteorologists had reported nothing about falling stars or comets.

There were books on the subject in the library. He looked through a couple. The other people reported peculiar things, things that made him chuckle; their feet swelled, someone evacuated their bowels, a man in California had an increased sexual drive, a woman stopped eating red meat. Two had died of heart attack shortly after. No one had the experience more than once. Many claimed it had changed their lives, spiritually; he was not sure that would be true of him: he felt bewildered but none the wiser because of what had happened. He was uneasy about the language they used to describe the experience: transcendent, blissful. These were not words a cop dealt with often. And it registered in his mind that much of the language had sexual overtones, and that bothered him.

It was a once-in-a-lifetime thing, the experience. For the first time he thought maybe he should not have become a cop. Was that what was called losing faith?

Sheila knew something had happened right away.

He found the house oddly silent, as if empty. She was sitting up in bed, smoking. When he came through the doorway she blew a smoke ring at the ceiling. He wanted to say, I've seen something so miraculous that I can't think of the words to capture it, but then he noticed her hands were trembling as she stubbed the cigarette out in the ashtray. A half-empty glass of milk sat on the bedside table.

She said, "Just don't tell me lies."

She was wearing a white nightdress with red flowers embroidered on the sleeves. She looked at him and he thought it would be a good time to take her. She had washed her hair. He smelt shampoo and bath oils. He came over to the bed, but she pulled the quilt up and rolled away. She was a lump under the quilt, with her back to the door and to him. He asked in a whisper if she wanted something to eat and she curled further in on herself, with just the top of her head visible on the pillow. He sat on the edge of the bed with a hand on her thigh, but she did not move. Perhaps she smelled the turpentine perfume. He should have taken her in his arms. Comforting was what she wanted. But it was guilt, wasn't it? And that strange hollow feeling that filled his chest, a feeling he wanted to talk about, but she had made it obvious she wanted nothing to do with him. How could you explain something that bizarre? He listened to her breathing, watching the hump in the quilt move up and down. He had never been good at impulsive physical gestures and he did not know how to ask her to forgive him. And they had never had a real fight.

After a while he took his hand away. He should have confessed on the spot, made a clean slate. It was the unspoken that killed. He knew that now.

He sat there a long time, so long that he might have dozed off. She was not asleep but she hadn't moved, either. He did the worst thing then; he tried to take her in his arms by force, the whole lump of quilt and all. His strong hands tried to force her body to roll over to him. He kissed her neck and then her cheek. She scrunched up against his clumsy embrace and said something that might have been *no* but it was muffled by the quilt. Maybe it was *go*. He got up and went to the kitchen to fix a sandwich.

He was very tired. The call from Lac du Bonnet had come at five in the morning and it was after ten at night when he pulled up in front of the house. The thin rain which had begun after he'd seen the golden ball ran down the windows of the house. It was the kind of rain that made you sleepy. Through the open window he heard the leaves of the trees dripping. He was exhausted in every way that he could imagine. When the sergeant had barked orders at him in the driveway that morning he'd felt he was a failure as a cop. Now he was a failure as a husband.

Still, there was the feeling. It would not replace her but it was powerful.

There was a bottle of whiskey in the cupboard under the sink. He had opened it at Christmas. He fell asleep in the chair, clutching its long thin neck in his hand.

C<small>ASSIE DID HAVE A</small> B<small>IBLE</small>.
She gave him a questioning look when she fetched it from the back bedroom but she did not say anything. Her mouth registered some unease as she passed it to him. He noticed the dark hairs on her upper lip.

The passage in Ecclesiastes read *a time to kill and a time to heal*. It was part of the text which began *to every thing there is a season*. A rock band had made a song out of it and it played on the radio from time to time. That is where Mortimer must have heard it and confused it with the quotation from Ezekiel that referred to the four wheels, and the wheels within the wheels. Like the prophecies in the Book of Revelation, the passages in Ezekiel were turgid and confusing. Alexander read the passages over a number of times. The print in Cassie's Bible was tiny and he had to squint to read the words, sometimes thinking he had them wrong because they didn't make immediate sense. Maybe the words were not to be understood in the usual way. He remembered hearing the old man muttering phrases from the Bible when things did not go well—always when things did not go well, and never when they did. He laughed aloud at that now, the old man and his curses; he felt oddly close to him. The Bible seemed to have a lot to do with suffering and endurance. Not his kind of reading.

There was an entire book, though brief, devoted to the life of Ruth. He had not known that. Ruth, a daughter of one tribe, praised for following her mother-in-law, who was from another tribe, after their husbands died. The text suggested that was unusual; Ruth was somehow a model of constancy. Nothing much was said about the deaths of the men. They died. Ruth was left alone. Her mother-in-law disappeared from the story. Ruth gleaned corn in a man's field after the young men did the harvesting proper, bits of barley, it seemed. One night she lay at the feet of the man who owned the field. He blessed her, saying, *inasmuch as thou followedst not young men, whether poor or rich*. He took her for a wife. She bore him a son, the grandfather of David, who later became the king. The story was cryptic and enigmatic. What did it mean that she lay on the man's bare feet on the floor one night? Why did the man feel compelled the next day to say *Let it not be known that a woman came into the floor*? The story seemed to suggest that was unusual and slightly wicked. The story also suggested it was common practice for the young men to rape the women who gleaned in the fields—was that so? There was also a lot of discussion of real property that had something to do with the older man's taking Ruth for a wife. Was she part of a bargain? Did the man who became her second husband cheat his neighbour to get Ruth? The word *witness* figured prominently in that part of the story. The man called the elders together to witness his actions. He was concerned about doing things according to the law—but what law?

Reading the Bible was a bewildering experience for Alexander, bewildering and upsetting. The men who wrote it expressed themselves very briefly. And yet the world they documented was filled with darkness—secrets and dangers and prohibitions and ancient and mystifying laws. People were murdered and nothing much seemed to be done about it: David and Bathsheba.

He was impressed by Ruth, though. Her loyalty to her widowed mother-in-law, recorded in the story as *whither thou goest, I will go* had become part of the common parlance. There was considerable boldness in the way she lay on the bare feet of the man, despite her outward appearance of deference. In that way she was like the Ruth at Moon Lake. Had Cassie sensed this when she named her? It mattered what you named your child, he realized. He'd begun reading the Bible to find out about the wheel within the wheel, but had become more interested in names and naming. Alexander, his mother called him, not Alex, or Alec, even around the house. And the old man had sometimes cruelly referred to him as Alexander the Great.

Names gave significance to things: Mortimer, Virginia, Moon Lake. He would have to read deeper into the Bible to know if he regretted the name Maria had insisted on giving their son.

R̲uth said she wanted to talk that night, so after they had washed up and put the dishes in the cupboard they sat on the back stoop and watched the dark descend on the lake. The mosquitoes had gone to ground. Geese flew by high in the sky, honking. Barker had come out with them and she raised her head at the sound, thumping her tail before resting her grizzled chin between her paws. Ruth smoked a cigarette.

"I've had it," she said, "with this hole. I can't go on."

"Don't say that," Virginia said.

"I'm free to go and I'm going." The Mountie had apparently questioned her and found her version of what had occurred that night credible.

There were jobs at the department stores in the city, Ruth said, and a course she could take at night school that could get her into the insurance business. She would tell Cassie after the funeral. In the dusk her profile with the cigarette in her fingers looked like a shot from a movie. Maybe that was an effect she was trying to achieve. Girls shared apartments, she said, in the downtown area of the city, and ate in the cafés along Portage Avenue, where there were clubs to go to at night, and men to meet. Rock bands like the Guess Who and the Devrons held impromptu open-air concerts in parks and played at community club dances. She made it seem that everyone in the city went to these events, but Virginia thought she exaggerated, about her enthusiasm to work in the department store too. Ruth had grown up around Moon Lake. She would miss the water and the fresh air. These were things Virginia knew. But she didn't contradict Ruth. She nodded, she grunted what could have been mistaken for assent, she listened. Ruth was the talker. The last light drained out of the sky and then the moon was hanging over the lake. Someone walked by on the lake path. Barker raised her head and sniffed the air. Virginia thought she smelled sawdust and resin. The footsteps echoed briefly and were gone. Ruth flicked the cigarette stub away expertly. It made a brief glowing pinwheel in the darkness, reminding Virginia of fireworks she'd seen in Beausejour on the Dominion Day weekend.

"Finito," Ruth said. She got up with a sigh and took Barker inside.

Virginia sat on the stoop and listened to the frogs. The woods were filled with the smells of decay: decomposing leaves, the carbolic odour of stagnant water, acidic rotting pine cones. A figure materialized in the trees just out of range of the light coming from the door and the kitchen window behind her. She stepped off the stoop. Her heart was in her stomach. She stood and went down the stairs. When she passed the spruces he stepped out from behind a tree farther along. First she smelled the stuff in his hair and then she felt his quick hands under her sweater. His tongue was flat and thick, his mouth tasted burnt amber of whiskey. They held each other a long time before he slipped his hands over her breasts. His skin felt cool against her nipples at first, and they swelled and hurt a bit. She was breathing against his neck, and he against hers. "I want to kiss them," he whispered.

"Not here," she said.

It was pitch dark in the granary but he lit a match and she glimpsed his face for a moment before it went out: chipped front tooth, round eyes. She heard his breathing and felt the warmth of his skin against hers.

"It was you, wasn't it," she said, "at the window?"

He murmured something into her neck. He took her hand in his and put it on him. Instantly he started to swell and she felt afraid: excited and frightened, both. Her cheeks were hot. The smell coming off his body seemed stronger now, a smell she associated with tents and Roger's cubbyhole, closed-in male spaces and clothes worn longer than was good.

He was kissing her neck, and then down. There was an urgency in him that she had not expected.

"That night," she said, "I'm talking about Friday night."

"Friday?" he said. "So much has happened in a couple of days."

"You came to my window."

She said it just as his lips found her nipple and she gasped in the shock of it and what she had said was lost.

"Oh," he said, "oh, my god, oh."

When she was calm again she repeated what she had said.

"Don't think about that," he said. "He's gone."

She thought then of the white skin gleaming in the moonlight, an image she knew she would never forget, however many years she lived: a crooked hand like a claw, bare mottled flesh. These were fractured images that came and went in waves: the Mountie's husky eyes, the hat hanging from a tree branch, spittle on Roger's shirt front.

"Something happened at the window," she said, "that night."

"Let it be. This is our night."

He was right, there was no point in festering about him now. She felt a tingle run up and down her spine when his hands gripped her hips. His dark head was between her thighs. He knew it could not be all the way, but he used his tongue and she felt it smooth against the roughness of her bush. She thought of the cat licking its stomach. Then she realized her heart was pounding and she felt something give way inside her. When that passed she lay looking toward the ceiling, which she could not see. Her thighs were trembling. Her fingers played in his hair. She said, "If it wasn't you, was it Roger?"

He raised his head. She sensed he was looking directly into her face but they could not see each other's eyes, only glinting in the darkness. "I told you before," he said, "we weren't there that night. Nowhere near. We ran, see, and did not come back."

That was all he offered. It was not him, not Roger. It did not matter any more. What mattered were the waves coursing through her abdomen and further down. She was a woman, now, no longer a girl. After a while she began to feel chilled and she pulled her clothes back on. A match flared and she saw him do the same. He lit another match and then they were fully clothed and sitting on the mattress with their backs against the wall drinking from the mickey bottle he had brought with him. It tasted awful and her throat felt raw, and the next day she burped and tasted the sourness of it all over again.

He parked the pickup on the street and walked across the grass to the back of the house where he could look in the window. McNair was sitting in a high-backed chair reading a book. Victor tapped on the window glass; no point disturbing Yvette. McNair glanced up from the book and Victor saw their faces in the glass for a moment, his own superimposed over McNair's. He wondered what he must look like. Peeping Tom? He knew sometimes his hair was unruly from the cap. There were days when he did not get the chance to shave.

McNair came to the back door. He was wearing a baggy green sweatshirt with a school crest on one breast. He had a glass of whiskey in his hand. "Yvette is out," he said, "playing hearts at the community club." His eyes were glassy, the flesh of his thin face drawn and pale. He worked long hours at the hospital. He motioned for Victor to come in and they sat in the living room with glasses of scotch but no ice. A tabby cat curled up on the sofa beside Victor.

McNair said, "Under the lab lights we saw that there were scratches as well as the five major wounds. The uppermost wound on the back appears to have been the first that was struck, but that's difficult to tell with the coagulation pattern. Too much time had elapsed before we got the body into the lab."

"No blow, though, to the head or anything?"

"Well, yes, actually. That matted blood in the hair came from an object with rounded edges. It left a curved indentation in the flesh and skull."

"Like the butt end of a gun?"

"Something that size."

"The butt of a bayonet?"

"Maybe. The object would have been rounded and curved."

"A knife of some kind is my bet."

"He was stabbed between the shoulders first, and then downward, having been surprised, I would guess, while bending over doing something, like tying a shoelace."

"Or fiddling with that crate containing the fishing gear."

Victor thought about the condoms. LaFlamme's own girls claimed he only pawed them, but McNair could be right about the fact they were lying to themselves.

McNair said, "The wounds were of an almost uniform length, six to six-and-one-quarter inches. Except the one that hit the lumbar verterbrae. Which was probably the last in the sequence. It was just under six inches."

"Long," Victor said. "The typical hunting knife is—what?—five, five and a bit?"

McNair took a sip of whiskey and asked, "You sleeping okay?"

"My guts. I burp and then there's a bitter taste. I've been hammering back Tums but they don't work terribly well."

"Short term they're okay. But there's a buildup and then you get a kind of rebound effect. Worse than before." McNair looked into his glass.

"I'll come in to the clinic one day soon. Get a check-up." He paused and sipped whiskey. "Sheila should too."

McNair did not look up. Of course men like him did not smirk or let on that they knew anything, even when what he *knew* was only rumours, and some of those linked to the name of LaFlamme. What would they be saying in the Lakeland—and how long would it take to get to Sergeant Black? He swirled the amber whiskey in the tumbler before taking a sip. "Something caught my eye when we first examined the body," McNair was saying. "I thought it was the pattern of the wounds. Later I realized that the residue on the shirt had an unusual tone and texture. It was not all dried blood. But it was difficult to tell because of the checkered shirt, which was green and red, remember?"

"Though it looked like dried blood?"

"In the lab it proved to be traces of oxidized iron. Rust."

"Like from an old weapon that had been hanging about unused for a long time? A bayonet from World War Two?"

"He may have wiped a rusty tool on the shirt or rubbed against a machine."

"That's my bet, the bayonet."

"Only I've been doing some reading." McNair nodded toward the book on the side table that he'd been examining when Victor knocked on the window glass. "The standard bayonet blade was—is—two-edged. Double the chance to do serious damage, like."

"And much longer than six or seven inches."

"The depth of the wound inflicted depends on the strength of the person striking the blow. So that can vary from incident to incident. With a bayonet. But a one-sided weapon cannot be two-sided."

"And the wounds in LaFlamme were."

"Bevelled, yes. A one-edged blade."

Like the gutting knife in the fishing box, which Sergeant Black had had sent to the lab in the city, to no effect.

There was a clock in the room adjoining the living room, a dining room with an oak table, and it struck the quarter hour. Westminster chimes, Victor recalled; an aunt had had a mantel clock that chimed on the quarter hour in the same way. The cat rolled over, exposing its stomach, tufts of white fur on a mottled belly, a female. The room they sat in was lined with bookcases, medical texts, outdoor books, novels. Yvette read mysteries and historical romances. She had started a book club almost as soon as she arrived and Victor had hoped that Sheila would take that up and put away the bicycle and the red Wellingtons.

Victor blinked. He'd lost the thread of the conversation and must try to keep focus. And it was inept not to have brought in the notepad. "So," he said, searching for time, "not a bayonet, then?"

McNair had risen and gone to the dining room and was pouring himself more scotch. The baggy sweatshirt was green in colour but it had grey smears of paint on one elbow. Victor recalled McNair telling him that he did home improvements to get his mind off work. That was when Victor had suggested they go fishing. When McNair brought the bottle back, he splashed a bit more into Victor's tumbler and then set it on the floor near his feet. It was a good blend, Victor thought, with a rich aroma of oak. McNair swallowed, then settled his hawk eyes on Victor. "No, not a bayonet. Thinner blade."

"But longer than a hunting knife."

"There's a bayonet in here," McNair said, nodding at the book, "that has a hacked blade. Sharp burrs like the lid of a tin can after you open it. Perfect for gouging. But I thought that went out in the medieval period."

"I've seen a knife with two points, and a blade with three sides. Right here in Canada, not in some European museum."

"*Saw blade* they call it, that hacked look. Rips the flesh and organs."

Victor ran the scotch around in his mouth. "He did not die fast."

"Whoever did it was in a kind of blind fury. Had I said that before? It seems to me we've been saying the same things and going around in circles on this one forever."

"Even though it's only been days."

"In any case, the amount of blood at the scene told us that whoever did it was crazed. Did you find the hat?"

"A jacket's missing too. It was a cool night and he wouldn't have gone out without something. The wife checked. A light windbreaker. She said he always carried a wad of bills with him, too, five hundred and more at a time. When we searched the pockets it was—what?—fifty or so."

"Surely the motive was not robbery?"

"We don't know, do we? It could be one of the Indians thought he'd been cheated in the fur business. He took advantage of people in every way, that man. Then, again, the son seems to have been planning to bolt for some time. And cash can be handy."

"Or maybe it was an incidental thing."

"Maybe. Or done to throw us off the track. Maybe, maybe, maybe."

McNair sipped at the whiskey and looked into the tumbler. He was probably thinking the same thoughts as Victor. How their best efforts at detection had been subverted by ruses and lies and just plain bad luck.

"There was a serious trace of alcohol in his stomach," McNair said.

"Drunk?"

"No, but it may explain why so much stumbling around. The amount of blood."

Victor studied his boot tops a moment. "So," he said. "I should go."

McNair did not say anything. He took another delicate sip of whiskey.

"It's all loose ends up at Moon Lake," Victor said. He figured he owed McNair that much. "It might have been anyone of a number of them. The boy and his pal have disappeared. The women had motive. It might have just been someone who stumbled across him."

"Carrying a knife?"

"Not that uncommon. Trappers, hunters, fishermen."

"Someone local then?"

"If you mean off the reservation or from the trading post, not necessarily. It's hunting season and there's the bow-and-arrow crowd who like going after deer around Moon Lake."

"No doubt LaFlamme would have crossed some of those guys."

"Cuthand says they're a mean crowd. He, by the way, is lumbering around with one foot in a cast. Looks like an amateur job to me, but unless you actually sawed the thing off his ankle to have a look, you can't tell what's under there. From the point of view of alibi, I mean."

"So you've marked an *X* beside his name?"

"And he saw Alexander and his son at just about the critical moment."

"So, then, they're off the hook too."

"Most of the Indians on the reservation wear gumboots this time of year. Cassie says she sells forty pairs a season, but also dozens of shoes and lots of sneakers. The young go for them especially. When the snow flies the men put felt liners inside the gumboots to go out on the traplines. You know the kind of thing, thick treads on the soles, heavy rubber."

"Awkward for hunting."

"For hunting they have moccasins with high lace-ups or sneakers. Point is, neither of these types leaves a nice heel imprint in soft ground."

"But that doesn't mean they don't actually own shoes with heels."

"Or that the fact we found no prints from sneakers out there indicates anything conclusive. Since they have those flat, slightly ribbed soles that don't leave marks on hard-packed ground."

"If you want an opinion," McNair offered.

"Not really."

"It's the boy," McNair went on, "the son. He had motive, a weapon, and the time necessary—and he took off."

Victor said to himself, *yes, but go easy there*. He took a deep breath.

Victor's stomach growled. He realized he had not eaten much. Cassie had given him bread when he left Moon Lake, but his stomach was burning. He stood. His legs were a bit uncertain. When he got back to the pickup he'd have to make notes on his conversation with McNair. He glanced at his watch. Just then the phone on the coffee table rang. He waved to McNair as the doc picked it up.

When he entered the house something was amiss. He sensed it before he hung his cap on the peg by the door. It was as palpable as cigarette smoke. The hall light was burning. The bathroom light was on, the medicine cabinet open. Were these signals? He stepped quickly along the hall to the bedroom. There was no point in calling out. She lay face up on the floor, mouth open as if a deep sleep had overtaken her before she could climb onto the bed. Snoring heavily, or was it a deeper slumber? He dropped to one knee and listened at her mouth, felt for the pulse at her throat. Not yet, not then.

O<small>N</small> T<small>HURSDAY MORNING</small> S<small>ERGEANT</small> B<small>LACK</small> arrived. They had heard he was in the neighbourhood. He came on a special train from Beausejour with two young officers and they walked up the path from the abandoned station in the sunshine One of the corporals carried a briefcase. Alexander was spreading a sheet on the ground in front of the store so he could mix paint without getting grass and leaves stuck to everything. He had placed his brushes with a can of exterior gloss on one corner of the sheet and was unscrewing the cap from a bottle of turpentine. He was thinking it was a pleasant day: warm sun and fresh air. His muscles were becoming accustomed to physical exertion. It was a good life, working with your hands, and breathing in the air, and listening to the sounds of the natural world. Peter was in the bunkhouse, happily engrossed in a Hardy Boys book. But who were these three crows materializing out of the forest?

When they approached the front steps the older man said, "You better join us." He had bright blue eyes and a manner that said he was not used to being contradicted. He took the briefcase from one of the young officers and said, "Round up everyone else." He looked angry when he said it. Alexander put down the bottle of turpentine, sensing the morning's work was about to slip away. He was a man who kept to schedules: start work at eight, take a coffee break at ten, and so on. And he was weary of men like this. The silver insignia on the sergeant's cap winked in the sun. He stood on the top step with his hands on his hips and studied the fields and forest around the Moon Lake Trading Post as if he intended to purchase them.

Though they'd heard he'd been at Cuthand's asking questions, his visit was a surprise. The train came Wednesday night and Saturday night. There was talk of discontinuing the Wednesday service. To get a train to run in mid-week a man had to have connections and pull strings.

Inside he told Cassie his name and said, "Corporal Boyd is taking care of personal matters." She was rubbing her hands on a tea towel and looked with large eyes into his face. She was not sleeping well, that much was obvious. Alexander felt protective toward her, though why he didn't know. She seemed suspicious of him. Maybe it was that money he couldn't bring himself to speak of. Maybe he felt sympathetic to anyone caught by surprise by a self-important cop, a bantam rooster. Alexander saw that the younger girl had come out from behind the counter in the store. Her cheeks flushed when he glanced her way. She wrung her hands together and then made a point of interlocking the fingers and keeping unnaturally motionless. He looked Ruth in the eye without speaking and she looked back at him with those intense dark eyes. He wanted to go over to her and put his hand on her arm and take in the scent of her hair and body. Dangerous emotions had come into play where she was concerned, a kind of sickness in his stomach.

Mortimer was turning over grain in the granary, the Finn was out near the breaking with a shovel. Peter was curled up with his mystery. Sergeant Black said, "We're tying up a few loose ends. Things got away on Corporal Boyd a little bit. Not his fault, really, in the circumstances." He pulled a chair up at the kitchen table without being asked and set his cap on the counter. His hair was jet black, combed straight back with hair oil. When he removed the cap the aroma drifted through the room for a moment. Cloying.

The black briefcase sat near his feet. Barker sniffed at it.

He carried a small black notepad in one breast pocket of his uniform and a gold pen in the other. Information had come to his attention, he said. He did not mention Corporal Boyd as the source. He asked them about times and he jotted things in his notepad but mostly he looked at them with those bright blue eyes. Alexander sat across from him at the table. Cassie poured out cups of coffee and fussed about. Virginia was near the sink. Ruth stood with her back against the refrigerator across from Alexander and behind Sergeant Black. It was difficult to tell from the way her dark eyes shifted from one face to another whether she was amused or frightened. Alexander was certain the sergeant had come not to tie up loose ends but to scare them. He seemed the type to bully until he got what he wanted.

Sergeant Black said, "The weapon was probably a fishing knife, a scaling knife." By then the Finn and Mortimer had come in. Silent glances all around. Grain dust stuck to Mortimer's sideburns. Sweat ran from the Finn's forehead down his cheeks.

Sergeant Black asked, "When is the funeral?"

Cassie told him Thursday and he said, "The body will arrive tomorrow."

LaFlamme had one sister alive and she lived in a remote village in Saskatchewan, so Cassie was burying him on the far field near the breaking. The Finn had been digging the plot. There was clay on his rubber boots. Alexander was wearing them too, as well as Mort. Peter had sneakers. Cassie had rummaged the rubber boots out of closets; they were a damn nuisance. Alexander's pinched the small toes of each foot.

"Time of death," Sergeant Black said, "nine-thirty."

That seemed precise to Alexander. He was watching Mort, who had unscrewed the cap from the tin of chewing tobacco and was packing strands in between his cheek and gum. His hands were outsized, like his feet. Alexander had the impression he was messing with the tobacco to keep from looking the sergeant in the eye.

"Your shoes and boots will arrive with the body," Sergeant Black said.

Peter had come into the room with the other officer. He stood behind Alexander with one hand on the back of the chair. He was breathing hard, as if he had run a long distance. Alexander smelled something on his clothes, a ripe cheese odour.

It was the heel of a certain kind of shoe they were interested in. Corporal Boyd had hinted as much to Alexander. They had found three sets of heels at the place where they found the body: the first LaFlamme's, the second the girl's. They had taken her clothes, too: jeans, sweaters, even a handful of underthings from the laundry basket. Some of the knives from the kitchen and the rifle from the store had been impounded. Cassie swore aloud when they took that, and made certain they signed a sheet of paper on which she'd listed every item removed. He saw where Ruth's inner rage came from.

Sergeant Black had lists too. He removed them from the briefcase, along with a wad of typescripts and forms. They were notes from the interviews Corporal Boyd had conducted. He told them he'd been to the reservation the day before and had cleared Carl Cuthand. He had a registry of all the people living in the area. He asked them, "You know how many men there are on that reserve?"

Cassie must have had a fair idea but she said nothing.

"We set up a check-point at the station in town," he told them, "but the boy and his Indian pal gave us the slip. It's only a matter of time until we catch up to them." He told them if they knew the whereabouts of those two to speak up. He said he would speak to each of them separately and it would not go easy if he sensed they were lying. When he finished his coffee he put the wad of papers back in the briefcase and said he wanted to speak to Cassie first.

Alexander stood with Mortimer on the canvas sheet he had spread out under the window in front of the store. The woodpecker banged on the tin. The sun was directly overhead and warming their faces. He looked up and saw fluffy white clouds in the sky. The tops of the trees swayed in a breeze he could not feel at ground level. Mortimer leaned over and spit tobacco juice into the grass. Some of the amber fluid had dried on the toe of his boot. It was Mortimer's opinion that the Mounties were going over everything because the investigation had ground to a halt. "They don't seem to have a theory," he said.

"There's three possibilities," Alexander said. "Someone followed him to the place, someone who knew his habits and watched for him to come out of the building, and then waited for the right moment, kind of thing, when his guard was down."

"He wasn't one for keeping regular habits."

"Possibility number two is this: someone arranged a meeting with him out there."

"Was laying for him."

"Someone with a distinctive heel mark, it appears."

"My feet are hot in these damn rubbers."

"My toes have blistered."

Mortimer worked on the tobacco, moving it with his tongue to where it was most comfortable. It was slightly ridiculous. He looked like a cow with its cud. Finally he said, "But it could have been a spur of the moment thing. One of the many who hated him just happened by. That's what I think it must have been."

"It's what they think that counts. The girl saw someone out there."

"You saw someone running on the lake path."

Mortimer's voice was strained. He wasn't sleeping well, either. The skin on the end of his chin was inflamed and there were dark pockets under both eyes. In the night Alexander heard him tossing and grinding his teeth.

"This new cop is pushy," Alexander said, wondering if his brother really needed to be cautioned. "He seems determined to get to the bottom of things."

"It's a front. Desperation. A final energetic effort before they collapse and give up. You see it in animals all the time."

"The other one seemed distracted. Truth be told, I kind of liked him."

"It's his wife. She ran off, then tried to kill herself. So Cuthand says."

He got around, Mortimer. During the days when Alexander scraped the walls of the store he puttered inside, helping Cassie with the stock. He brought out coffee and cinnamon buns on a tin plate. Then Alexander saw him with a shovel on his way to the granary. Then later carrying a bucket out to the well. Hours passed in the afternoons when he didn't seem to be about, but he materialized for evening meals, and then took Peter out on the rocks to fish. They had caught two pike the night before and Cassie had cooked them for breakfast. The boy was proud. He wanted a scale so he could weigh each fish he caught and keep a record.

So he was a good uncle in a way, but he was slippery, Mortimer. He had pumped Alexander about what happened to LaFlamme when it was he, not the cop, who was intent on promoting a theory. What more was he after?

"It's confusing, " Alexander conceded. "The cops don't like to decide on anything too quickly, but they've got a handful of suspects at least and lots of evidence that doesn't really add up to much, as far as I can see. The other Mountie told me as much. The problem is not just that it was night. So much time elapsed before they got to the body. The doctor was unsure when he died. Unlike this new Mountie. Did he ask you where you were at the time?"

Instead of answering, Mort said, "And they haven't located a weapon."

Alexander said, "Cassie seemed shaken about the kitchen knives."

"The Finn has a couple of scaling knives," Mort said, as if he'd half been expecting Alexander to make that point. "But I don't think I'll mention that."

To Alexander it felt like some sort of bargain had just been struck. Years ago he had learned to play chess from Maria. *Mate*, she said to him across the board, and smiled wickedly. *Checkmate*. Alexander did not quite understand what had happened in those games that put him in a position where he was cornered, and he did not understand it now, either.

The cat suddenly darted out from under the stoop with a bloody mouse in its mouth, and then, when it saw them, stopped and sidled away. It went around the corner of the building, its black and white ringed tail curling up as it disappeared from sight.

Mortimer grunted. The cat, he'd told Alexander, had taken to killing baby squirrels and bringing them into the building where they bled to death under the shelves in the store. It bothered him. It was unnatural. She had the bloodlust, he said. She was a good cat but they were going to have to put her down.

But it wasn't unnatural, was it? Just not the norm. And that's how it was with people too. They did cruel and violent things that were not the norm, but were really natural. It was not an easy idea to come to terms with. Murder. But it was part of civilization. On the grand scale too. Nigeria, the Congo, China. In nature an animal often suddenly did things that you didn't expect it to do. And humans were part of nature. They behaved erratically and could turn violent in ways you did not want to acknowledge were part of human nature. So we weren't really progressing upwards as they said on the radio and TV. Or was Alexander just being bloody-minded?

They were silent for a while. He had tried to trap his brother with that question and now he felt awful. The business was getting to all of them, but that was no reason to turn on his brother. Mort had taken beatings for him on the schoolyard. When they'd worked for the farmer in Carman as young men, Mort had used his impressive energy to make up Alexander's shortfall. When Alexander had called about the possibilities at Moon Lake Mort had sounded genuinely excited. So, if anything, he owed Mort. And who was LaFlamme anyway? By all accounts a nasty piece of business. There seemed to be some ugliness concerning the girls. He pictured Ruth yanking at the flagpole and glaring at them, daring them to say something. Such wild energy. He felt that sickness in his stomach coming on. They said that once you'd been in love, it did not happen again, but that was not his experience.

"You think it's the boy, don't you?"

"Or his pal the Indian. If it is them, there's no reason for you to worry about Peter. They're long gone."

They had arrived at a point where there seemed little more to say. "Let's put him in the ground and get on with our lives," Alexander offered.

Mort spit in the grass again. He had a strange look on his face, as if he was about to say something important, when the young officer came out to say Sergeant Black was ready for him.

To talk to him Sergeant Black came out on the stoop. Alexander checked his watch. Almost an hour had passed. He had glanced in the store window from time to time. Many of the families in the area had come in over the past two days. Some said things to Cassie, but most avoided the subject and left after purchasing bags of flour and sugar, or treats for the kids. They nodded at Alexander as they came down the steps. Some of the men offered cigarettes, which he declined with a smile. From his position at the bay window he could just make out the sergeant's back where he sat at the kitchen table. He saw the younger girl behind the cash register. Ruth flitted up and down the aisles, checking things on shelves and dusting the tops of tins.

Her fingers were often red from the work, but the bones of her cheeks were fine and the skin of her face that almost-white that is set off by black hair and scarlet lips. She scraped her feet when she walked, even in the moccasins she wore around the store, adorned with beadwork. He could not help thinking of that mole in the corner of her lip. He was crazy to have noticed so much. She was not unaware of it. She stood with her butt up against the counter at mealtimes, pretending to listen to the conversation, and lifted the hair off the nape of her neck with both hands and then shook it, like a mane.

She was ten years younger than him. What would Peter think?

When Sergeant Black came out, he had stretched his arms, then puffed out his cheeks and exhaled dramatically. "Your brother's shoes," he said, "they're size fourteen. Hard to miss out there."

"Special made, those, at a place in the city. He calls them gunboats."

"He was out there. The marks are obvious."

"But not necessarily that night."

"It looks it." He had the cap on again and pushed the peak up his head and then tugged it back down. "Corporal Boyd," he said, "thought you were telling the truth. Your story checked against your son's. Of course, you could both be lying."

"You would have caught him out. No?"

"It was your shoes, actually; they did not match the prints out at the scene. Though there were a few inconsistencies between your stories."

"Bound to be, don't you think? Dark of night, everything new to both of us. We got a little turned around on the paths."

Sergeant Black exhaled again and closed his eyes. Maybe it was all bluster, his no-nonsense attitude. "It's stuffy in there," he said. "I was starting to get a headache."

Alexander was glad he had the paint brush in his hands. It was the kind of verbal fencing that made his body tighten up. In the courtroom when the lawyers argued over the mortgages and finances of the hardware store, he sometimes felt as if he would pass out. He had spent his life working with his hands, stocking shelves with paint cans and boxes of nails. Things felt good to the touch. He disliked mental jousting. He studied the grain of the wood on the windowsill as if for the first time, and then worked the brush back and forth, applying the paint evenly. He was not bothered by silences.

The sergeant was. He cleared his throat. "Your brother was in trouble over a bit of skirt down south."

"I wouldn't know about that."

"He got into a punch-out in the local hotel and hurt a man badly. The husband. The report said forty stitches. The report said he carried a knife in those days. He left town shortly after that."

"He moved around a lot. Young men do. He was looking for the right thing to turn his hand to. He doesn't have much of an education and no head for business. He's a hard worker, though. I think he found something here." Alexander had made a pact with himself not to run off at the mouth, but there he was doing it again. They brought out something in him, cops, like the judge at the trial. He was not good with authority. He took a deep breath.

"The report said this guy's wife left town shortly after he did, your brother."

A statement, not a question, a fishing expedition. Alexander stepped back from the window. He laid the brush carefully across the open top of the paint can and took out his pipe. The sergeant's bright blue eyes watched him fill the bowl with tobacco and then tamp it down. His gaze met Alexander's and did not waver. Some years ago Alexander had driven out to Morden one afternoon and found Mortimer nursing a bruised hand and a black eye. He laughed it off. "Fellow caught me with my head down." Alexander thought it was probably something else that was down when the man caught Mortimer. It would not have been the first time. They drank beer in the local hotel and then sat in the coffee shop over burgers and fries. When he left, Alexander rolled the car window down to shake hands. "Dick," Mortimer said, "I'll be all right, Dick. There's a situation over in the Whiteshell that I've got a line on, trading post kind of thing, up near the Lake of the Woods. I've about had my fill of grubbing around in the dirt for someone else."

"He's had a few scrapes," Alexander conceded, "but he's my

brother." As if that was enough explanation. It was the sort of comment he wished Mortimer could overhear. He'd always gone in for the family solidarity stuff.

"He's violent, is what I'm saying, he has a violent streak." The sergeant tugged at his cap. "As long as you don't cover for him. That would drag you down. The boy, too."

Alexander puffed on the pipe. *Not the boy, not my son.*

"We're relentless," the sergeant said. "If not today, then tomorrow. You know what they say about the Mounties. And the file on a murder case never closes." He looked off across the field and tugged at the cap again. What was he seeing? Earlier in the afternoon geese had landed to feed on the scraps of grain the machines had missed. Flocks of small birds gathering for the flight to the south swept down near the well and then swirled back up again, making a racket that was quickly blown away by the breeze. Branches tossed, and leaves whirled about. Everything was in motion as the winter approached, hunkering down, closing off before the snow. The case was closing down too. Sergeant or no, the man standing before him knew it. There was resignation behind the roving eyes despite his outward demeanour and artfully veiled threats.

Alexander said, "It's wearing us all down, this, the questions and the constant interruption. My boy doesn't sleep well and I wake up with a gurgling gut." It was not a lie. He had woken one night with burning sensations in the stomach. Peter was edgy. But he was mostly thinking of Mortimer, a man with hands like hams who had once bent a steel bar in half, who ground his teeth while he slept now and looked down the logging road constantly as if expecting trouble to materialize from that direction.

Peter had noticed it too. "Uncle Mort has a twitch," he said. And it was true: a muscle in one shoulder flinched every minute or so. Alexander had not noticed it before the boy pointed it out. He wondered if the sergeant had.

"You're in the clear at this point," he said, "but that can change."

Alexander nodded and stared back at him. The sergeant's eyes were shadowed by the bill of his cap, his gaze intent. He did not like giving up.

The sergeant said, "It is a case of murder."

Alexander puffed at his pipe, inhaling the smoke.

He looked off across the fields again. "We'll arrest someone soon."

If only, Alexander conceded, to get the reporters off your backs.

They'd had a go at everyone during the past days, but since there was no place to stay at Moon Lake, had retreated to the city and other headlines.

Neither of them seemed to know what to do. The paint was hardening on the brush. The sergeant had had his say. Was he going to threaten him further? It seemed pointless. The sergeant must have thought so too. "Well," he said, to bring things to a close. After a while he turned and climbed the stairs back into the store. Alexander heard him saying something to the young officers in the voice of resignation.

So it was all bluster and bluff. He smoked the pipe down before dipping the brush in the pail and resuming his work. He heard the crows calling in the distance, two short squawks followed by one long. In that grainy sound he discerned a kind of longing. The night before he had kissed Peter's sleeping cheek and then wandered out toward the lake to smoke a final pipe. He had stopped near a spruce, seeing Mortimer standing down by the twin rocks, a solitary hatless figure, staring at the swatch of shimmering silver the moon painted on the lake. Alexander watched him for a few moments, the breeze tufting up his brother's hair. He read in the curve of Mort's shoulders and his quiescent stance the loneliness he felt himself. So he knew it too: the long nights, the feeling you were hurtling into the darkness alone. A wave of fellow feeling swept out from him to his brother. Then he saw him scratch his buttocks, and as Mort turned to walk back along the path, Alexander stepped behind the spruce, suddenly anxious that Mort not see him. He did not want to acknowledge the loneliness in Mort—or in himself.

The breeze grew stronger as the light drained from the sky. A flock of Canada geese, slightly off their flyway, slanted across the horizon, their honking distant and eerie. When he lowered his eyes, he saw the slice of moon just over the tops of the trees. He walked around the corner of the building and saw how its image danced on the water directly in front of the buildings. There was an unusual odour in the air, something dense and green; he thought of what it might be like to plunge your nose into a pile of soggy moss, and the thought made him laugh at his own foolish notion. He thought he could also smell winter in the air. He listened and did not hear one bird call. A branch fell in the woods nearby. A small animal rustled in the undergrowth as they had done for centuries. Then silence. Yellow and brown leaves from the nearby trees cascaded down and swirled about his feet.

PART TWO

Glendower: I can call spirits from the vasty deep.
Hotspur: And so can I, and so can any man;
But will they come when you do call for them?
—*I Henry IV*

T HE PHONE HAD ALREADY RUNG a third time when he put his hand out for the instrument. On the fourth ring the machine downstairs kicked in. He was still in the half-conscious state of coming out of sleep and had been dreaming, or rather sleeping very lightly, so that a set of impressions was crossing and re-crossing his awareness. He was entering her from behind, nudging his way into the warmth between the split moons of her backside; he could smell the herbal shampoo in her hair and her soft and amiable body, and desire radiated in his groin, but it was a diffused and distant desire, domestic rather than passionate. The bleating of the phone pulled him away from the reverie. He felt resentful and weary. Who could be calling in the middle of the night? He checked the red lights of the digital clock on the bedside table: just gone five o'clock. It was either bad news or an idiot dialing the wrong number.

"Hello, Dick?" At first he thought it was the wrong number. He blinked his eyes sleepily and was about to say so, but instead he said, "Mort?"

"Sorry to get you up. Sorry." It was Mort all right.

"One second," he whispered. He pushed the quilt to one side as gently as possible and slipped from the futon onto the hardwood floor. If she was disturbed near dawn the migraine came on. The floor was cold to the touch of his feet. He glanced over and saw her dark thatch of hair move, but she was only burrowing farther into the quilt. He closed the bedroom door and crossed to the bathroom, where he closed that door too.

"I'm sorry," Mort repeated. It was him, yes. Since the lung problems, Mort had become a worrywart about his health, but that was not all. He visited nutrition stores and subscribed to health magazines. One of the strange side effects of his concern was that he had become soft in other ways; he was always apologizing to others. His voice had taken on a wheedling quality, peculiar in such a big man and surprising to Alexander, who had known him from childhood as pushy. "It's just I've been up all night, Dick," Mort was saying. "It's Cassie. She went out last night and hasn't come back."

There was a long pause. He realized he was expected to say something and roused himself to action. He asked, "She went out? Like, to visit? Drove the car somewhere?"

"Sorry. Let me explain. It's the perfect time of the year for picking fiddleheads. Which she loves, and so do I. You only get a two-week window, she claims. So she went out last night after supper. Took a plastic pail. She's usually only gone an hour or so but when it got past dark I started to get worried."

"You called the cops?"

"I wasn't sure what to do. That's why I phoned you."

"You should have called the RCMP first."

"I did. Right before I called you. Didn't I say that?" He seemed angry on the other end of the line.

Alexander wasn't thinking clearly yet. It might have been the cold he felt throughout his body, but probably just the fact that they were talking over the telephone. "No," he said, mollifying. It was freezing in the bathroom. He had put down the toilet seat and was sitting with his feet on the braided throw rug. His toes were turning to ice. He felt the morning chill on his shoulders. He should have put on a robe. In a moment his own voice would betray his pique. "It's all right," he added—lamely, he thought. "You were confused and upset."

"Could you drive out here? I know it's a giant pain in the ass."

"I could."

"What do you think?"

It is a pain in the ass, was what he was thinking. He was thinking of climbing back under the quilt and feeling the warmth of her back against his groin. First the warmth of skin to skin and only then the other, waking her slowly, sensing her strong, thin limbs respond to his, hearing those little grunts of satisfaction she made, a gentle morning thing, both of them half asleep at first but then wakening to the urges in their bodies. But it was not to be; he knew it and he resented it. So. "Yes, I think yes, Mort," he said. "I can—we can—be there in a couple of hours."

"I hate to bother you, but it's unlike her."

He shifted the phone to the other ear. It was one of the portable types, a metal telescope of an aerial protruding from the top. He wondered where Mort was at that moment: bedroom, living room? He was probably standing in the kitchen, looking out the windows toward the lake. The ice would be off Moon Lake but the water would still be frigid. Mort would be biting his lip and worrying that the upset would take its toll on his delicate health. That was Cassie. She'd spent the past five years being his personal watchdog: can't eat this, mustn't do that. She was *domineering*, that was the word. A certain kind of man needed that, he guessed. Oafish old Mort needed a woman to lead him by the nose. No, he did not think that, not really. That was the old man talking, dead now these five years. That was the resentment talking, his selfishness. He shook his head to clear away the sleepiness and asked, "Have you called Ginny and Roger?"

"Vanora," Mort said, "is what she calls herself now. I was just about to do that."

He'd forgotten about Vanora; it was difficult to put another name to a person you'd known for so long. Little mousy Virginia lived in the city now and did massage therapy and was known in all the women's action groups as Vanora.

"All right," he said. Light was coming into the sky and was just visible through the smoked glass of the bathroom window. Where Mort was the lake would be a sheet of glass, but when the sun rose the breeze would come up and the water would ripple up to the shore. That's when Peter had liked to do his fishing, puffing ghosts of breath into the frigid air as the blue filament of line sang out of his reel and the lure at its end plopped into the dark water. Peter still liked fishing.

"I knew I could count on you, Dick."

"Two hours," Alexander said, figuring it might be closer to four. He felt the cold creeping up his legs and shivered. Though he had been naked in colder temperatures before, he didn't think he'd ever felt so chilled in his life. It was a function of age, he surmised. What wasn't a function of age? His teeth hurt now sometimes for no reason at all. And swellings developed in his feet.

Mort said, "As soon as it's light the RCMP are starting a search party."

Alexander put his hand over his abdomen. This was the thing about Moon Lake. He couldn't help feeling anxious about the place, troubled and guilty. He had seen things that first night that he had never mentioned to anyone. Mortimer and Cassie had gone on to make a life together. Was he implicated? He knew it was too late to think such things. So he said, "If she's not back by then."

He'd intended to be reassuring, but it sounded as if Mort choked on the other end of the line. Maybe he was weeping, or maybe it was just the metallic resonance of the connection, which gave a raspy quality to Mort's voice. *Hold on, old fellow.*

"Sorry," came the voice from the other end of the line.

"Try not to fret until then. These things usually just work out." It was what he always said now: things work out. They didn't always. He didn't think he believed that anymore but he still said it. What else could you say?

By the time he slipped back under the quilt his hands as well as his feet had turned to ice, and she moved away from him when he put his hand out to touch her. *Not right away*, she had hissed out at him before: *cold hands!*

Now that he was lying in bed and could think past the cold, he realized it was going to be possible, and the resentment he'd been feeling while Mort had talked, lifted. It was not only possible but likely. And so now he regretted being short with Mort. He was a selfish old goat. But then he felt the warmth of her under the quilt. So what if it was four hours, not three until they got to Moon Lake—only to discover Cassie was safe and sound, if somewhat embarrassed by the attention? He nuzzled in closer.

He'd told Mort they'd arrive in Moon Lake in a couple of hours. First he had to phone Henry, who would be happy to take charge of the shop, though the kids on the floor were not that keen on him. At the last staff meeting there had been uneasy looks when Alexander had talked about leaving Henry in charge when they went to France in July. He was pushy with the kids, Henry, but an ass-kisser when it came to the boss. He was the first person he'd ever heard mention Boss's Day. Mother's Day, Secretary's Week, Boss's Day. What next? Though it was good for business. On Father's Day they sold a lot of golf clubs, jogging shoes, polo shirts, even water bottles. What kind of cheapskate bought their dad a water bottle for Father's Day?

She wriggled back against him. It was her signal. He put one hand on her hip and shifted forward so his body nestled into the curve of her haunches. Soup spoons, Peter called it. He talked about sex the way he talked about ball scores and Bill Clinton. It was a generational thing, this ease in talking about bodily functions and sex, something he would never be able to manage—or her. He smelled her hair. It was no longer uniformly black: strands of grey folded in now. Some evenings she lay with her head in his lap watching TV and he idly counted as he played with her hair: one whitish-grey strand to every ten black. He could not see that now. Sitting in the bathroom where the window faced east he'd sensed light coming into the sky, but it was dark in the bedroom. He could just make out the outline of her head. Her hair picked up light when the morning sunshine came in the window, imbuing it with tints of red. That would be in an hour. He breathed in the bath oil scent of her body.

Her muffled voice came from under the quilt: "What?"

He nuzzled in closer and breathed onto her neck.

He should have told her but it could wait. He lifted the hair off the nape of her neck and kissed above the vertebra. She wriggled her haunches closer to his. Like him, she slept naked. He felt his penis move and he shifted slightly. There was the warm crack. He had to remind himself the way he had the first time: slow. He slipped his arm between her arm and her rib cage and his fingers cupped one breast.

She didn't seem to need an answer.

He could call Henry at seven, and be on the road by eight. So, yes, three or more hours. Maybe Mort would have called by then, apologizing. Cassie would have got turned around somehow in the woods, but knew enough not to thrash about in the bush in the dark. She would have gone to ground. That body fat finally would come to good use. She'd be hypothermic but no worse for wear in the long run.

Still, he should have told her.

Everyone was always on edge about something happening at Moon Lake. It came from that time: secrets, half-uttered accusations, suspicions, fears. They all wanted to pretend it had not happened, to scab over the wound and get on with life. He was no different. He preferred to think about business. He must not forget to call the Bauer guy and leave a message on his answering machine; they all had them now. And cellular phones. He was considering that himself. The Bauer guy would be pissed off if he arrived on a Friday morning and Alexander wasn't there. Yes, he must call the Bauer guy and the Columbia rep, who was easygoing, but what the hell, it was a trip for him too. The numbers were in the diary. Then Orin, the hot-tub guy. They'd left it too long already: the water was murky. Then too he had to check to make sure that no one had called in sick. Henry was good with the customers but got in a flap about personnel stuff.

She rolled over to him and slid one leg between his. There was a way to do this but she didn't like it. His lips were at the top of her breasts. He kissed the collarbone on the top shoulder, his lips nibbling the gold chain. Then her arms were around him. She scraped his back with her nails. He squirmed about until her fingers moved up and down the centre of his spine. It was a conviction with him now that people did not learn much in their lives, did not learn anything, really, but he had to admit you did modify some patterns of behaviour if it was insisted upon enough and you wanted a thing badly enough. You altered minor things. He waited before moving down.

That first time, yes. He and Peter had been back in the city a couple of months—because of the Department of Education, he told Mort, and that was true, but if he had wanted to, he could have fought that, other parents had. So Peter's education was the ostensible reason but not the real one. It was so quiet at Moon Lake, that was the point. Once the snow fell it was like living inside an avalanche: twenty-foot drifts outside the bunkhouse, the paths that ran into the forest piled shoulder deep. There was only the one road to where they did the woodcutting and one trail onto the path for ice fishing. The birds all went south. The lake froze solid, so the waves stopped lapping the shore Only the whistle of the Arctic wind in the barren tree branches, the Finn's soft cheesy breathing in the bunk next. And for company, old *Reader's Digest*s in the dim light and games of Scrabble at the kitchen table with Cassie and Mort barely able to contain themselves. It was he and not Peter who had almost gone stir-crazy. The whiskey began to look good.

But maybe that was not the real reason, either. Just being around Mort and Cassie, and knowing what he knew, that was unsettling. Knowing what? That something was amiss, that something bad had occurred. In any case.

Before the summer came they moved back to the city. He borrowed money from Mort and made the down payment on the first SportHut. The hockey guy who'd owned it did not have the head for business. It took Alexander weeks to untangle the books and set up a proper inventory base. They were poor. They lived in an apartment on Furby Street and ate Kraft dinner. Peter never noticed. He got a new bike and played tennis at the club in Woodydell, part of a reciprocal arrangement. And Alexander had known the sports business would take off.

Then Mort called one day. Ginny had a friend who was moving into an apartment in the west end and needed help with the one big item she owned, a trunk, but he had fallen off the roof of the granary and twisted his ankle. So on a Sunday afternoon in the fall Alexander found himself parking in front of an old decaying building on Lenore Street. The sky had been lowering since morning and it was dark but no rain had fallen. Inside, the three-storey walk-up smelled of cooked cabbage, but was surprisingly well maintained. He remembered that: six-inch oak woodwork, bannisters with ornate newel posts, the smell of cooked cabbage and a stringent lemony carpet-cleaning solution. He'd brought leather gloves but it was just the one gigantic old trunk to be shifted, labels from the Cunard Line, no less. It had a wood bottom and leather straps across the top that buckled parallel to the brass hasp. Ginny and the friend's boyfriend met him at the front door. How the trunk arrived there, he never knew. The boyfriend had a ponytail. He grabbed one end of the trunk and Alexander the other. It was not the trunk's weight that made navigating the staircase difficult but the bulk. Still, it was an easy job. At the first landing he realized he'd be home in time to catch the televised baseball game.

He heard voices inside the apartment, like a party. The door was open. The girls went in first and then he backed through the door, lugging the trunk. He was expecting it to be strangers and had his everybody's friend smile ready. When he put the trunk down he turned around and she was offering him a beer in a bottle. "Sorry," she said, "all the glasses are still in boxes."

He wouldn't have gone if he'd known she was there. Over the long and desperate winter he had put that behind him. She was a fantasy he had exorcised over those months when she was no longer there but in the city—a fantasy borne of the loneliness that had grown after Maria's death, a loneliness that moving back to the city had not dissipated, or the casual dates been able to dispel. One of the cashiers at the SportHut was recently divorced. He no longer remembered her name. They went to movies together, and the fireworks display on the long weekend. They were not really a couple, but companions. Maybe something would have happened. So meeting up that way on Lenore Street was what you called fate, her being there and him not knowing it, smiling and offering a beer with one hand. Fate. Yes. There were times now when he believed in it.

"They said you would be here," she had stated flatly that afternoon.

He had forgotten how straightforward she could be. She was wearing a yellow pullover and jeans, and sneakers, only no one called them that anymore. The scent he remembered from Moon Lake. It was the yellow pullover that got him, a turtleneck which fit snugly around the breasts. Its shade perfectly set off her black hair and red lips. When the mole registered in his mind, he felt a soft thud in his chest. Blood rose from his throat to the tips of his ears. He had not intended to but he helped unpack the cardboard boxes and put the plates and glasses on the shelves. She showed him what went where. Ginny and the two other girls were in the bedroom with the boyfriend, unpacking the trunk, laughing. Someone was smoking dope. After an hour had elapsed, she kicked a box out of the way. "We've done our bit," she said. She opened the refrigerator. "You want to share?" They'd finished their beers and she was opening another. He was studying the mole. Foam stuck to her lower lip after she drank and glistened there. She passed the bottle to him and licked her lips, and the mole jumped.

That same sickness he'd felt that fall at Moon Lake filled his stomach. It was the loneliness, he knew that now. It had always been the loneliness. A life spent trying to get past that hollow feeling. Was it the same for everyone, or just him?

As he took the bottle of beer from her hand he vowed: I'm not going to offer to drive her home, I will not beg.

There was that energy about her he had noticed immediately at Moon Lake, a kind of force field that surrounded her body and seemed to make her face glow. She energized everyone around her, that was it, including Virginia, who called herself Vanora now. When Ruth moved around a room, the eyes of everyone in it followed her. He thought of it as a kind of magnetism: sexual energy, yes, but more than that. Ruth possessed a zest for life.

She went in to talk to Virginia and when she came back she asked, "So, you going to give me a lift to my place? I'm just around the corner."

It had started to rain, giant drops that struck the roof of the car with a dull smack. When they were inside the car, she rolled down the window on her side. "I love the feel of the rain on my face," she said. Droplets ran down her cheeks. Her hair was wet. He could smell it over the scent he'd noticed earlier and he thought of wet dog fur, only it did not smell like that at all. The watery smell of water. "It's the one thing I miss about that place," she said. "The smells of nature."

She told him the address. It *was* just around the corner. He pulled the car up front of the building and she said, "Yes, you are coming up." She leapt out and left him to park the car and when he came to the door she held it open. A different smell enveloped him: dampness and decay. This was an old building too, not as well kept up as the other one. He had expected her to offer him coffee but instead they sat in a bay window so she could watch the rain. There were trees outside, tall elms and maples, and cars rushing by on the asphalt streets below. Lightning. There was one loud clap of thunder and the rain started in seriously. Ruth sat at the window with her elbows on the ledge and her chin cupped in her palms. He wished he could see her eyes.

After a while she said, "Most people get sleepy. I want to have sex."

She was still looking out the window and he was glad then that she was not looking at him. He blushed. She stood and walked into the bedroom. She had told him she had a roommate and that there were two bedrooms. He had not even touched her. But he followed her into the bedroom where she'd piled her clothes on the floor and was standing naked in front of him. That never ceased to amaze him: how casual she was about sex. "I've got an infection," she'd say sometimes when they snuggled in front of the TV, "so we can't." Or when Peter was sleeping over at a friend's: "Let's do it now on the dining-room table."

Her breasts were the breasts of a young woman, the nipples brown but the aureoles pink. When he'd taken off his clothes, he knelt in front of her and kissed her belly. She wriggled because it tickled. "Go slow," she whispered into his hair, "I've never done it." He felt the roundness of her belly, the pale skin smooth with fine hairs that ran down into the bush. Tears started in his eyes and ran down his cheeks. It had been so long, there had been so much loneliness.

He choked that back and said, "I thought you kids were all doing it now in high school."

"Not all."

He had not realized at that moment the full implications of what she was telling him. He kept thinking about the roommate. What if she came through the door and found them going at it? It was only later that she told him the roommate was out for the day. He felt the beating of her pulse in her belly. She ran her long fingers through his hair. "Let's do this," she said.

He stood up and they fell back on the bed. He rolled on top. There was fear in her, yes. Her fingers gripped his shoulders. A hot wave of rage swept through him as he thought of how deeply LaFlamme had terrified his own flesh and blood, and what effort it was taking her to overcome that fear. A serious shit, LaFlamme, who had deserved to die. If Alexander had known at the time he probably would have stuck the knife in to LaFlamme himself. But he mustn't think of that. It was his job to go slow and make it the best for her.

She looked at him with those round anxious eyes and he melted inside. He kissed the mole. He kissed her mouth and took her tongue into his mouth, and then he felt her fingers reaching for him. He was remarkably rigid. All those months of masturbating and nothing else. Thinking about her, actually. And of course he started slow, but then when he was inside her, desire took on a life of its own and he was breathing hard and thrusting in and out and grunting, and then he suddenly remembered what she had said about going slow, but it was too late, he had taken her in just the way he had meant not to. Such a klutz. "Sorry," he said.

She was wiping her thighs with a tissue. She asked, "Is there always that much?"

"I've been saving up," he said. "Three years going on a lifetime."

She laughed then, and that was when he knew it was going to be possible with a woman almost ten years younger than him. She could laugh at him. That and her casual attitude to what they did in the bedroom. But she would not come to their apartment at first. Because of Peter. "I'm his aunt," she said, which was no more true than that he was her uncle.

After she'd washed up she said, "I like it." They were lying on the bed, naked. She was running her nails over the hairs between his pectoral muscles. Her breasts lay flat on her chest, the nipples soft now. He watched the beating of her pulse in her belly. By then she'd told him the roommate would not be back until after supper. He had told her Peter was at a friend's. The rain had stopped. The bedroom window was open and a breeze fluttered the curtains.

He put his hand over one breast and looked into her calm eyes. Then he leaned forward and kissed the mole again. "I've been wanting to do that for I don't know how long," he confessed. Something had slackened in his chest. It was like an ache in him that suddenly had been released, a thaw. And tears were welling from his eyes again. It was too much.

She must have sensed he was about to utter some mawkish sentiment because she said flatly, "I like fucking you."

"Some people call it making love."

She left a long silence and then she said, as if trying it out to see how it sounded: "Fucking. Fucking."

He liked thinking about that afternoon, turning over in his mind all the details he could recall. She had longer legs than he had thought, and a wider ass. He liked that, a woman with haunches. He liked, too, the fact that she painted the nails of her toes but not her fingers. And the way she ran her hands over his chest. There were reproductions of famous paintings hanging on the walls and after they were finished they lay flat on their backs talking and looking at them through the spaces between their feet. She told him how Munsch had died and that Emily Carr was considered a fruitcake when she was alive, but now was considered the country's foremost female artist. What a shame, to be celebrated too late, without ever knowing anyone really cared.

She hated her boss at the restaurant. He grabbed her ass. But she was doing well at the insurance course and by spring she would have a job and she would tell the boss what to do with waitressing.

She had thought about things: how you picked a mate, the right kind of schooling for kids. Montessori. She did not care about china patterns and flatware but had read up on Orff music techniques. Were all women like this now? He and Maria had stumbled into marriage and had had Peter more or less as an accident. Or rather, like most men of his generation, he stumbled into marriage. Maybe women never did. She knew why she liked him. Gentle eyes, she told him, and wonderful hands. She ran her nails over the veins above his wrists. She said that a man should insist that a woman always tell him whether or not he was insensitive, but never the other way around; she said women were better at deception than men. He recalled her saying these things but could not be certain it had been on that first occasion. They'd lain there often and the conversations blurred into each other, he realized. "I'm getting fat," he confessed that first time, "fat around the middle." She pinched him there and said it was the next inch that he could not afford.

"We'll keep an eye on that."

He had been thinking that for her he was just a casual thing, someone to do it with the first time. He had only dared hope it might be different. The breeze blew over them and ruffled up the hairs on his legs. She ran her nails over his chest absently. He had his hand on the upper part of her thigh. The hairs there were a reddish tint and fine as the thatch on a baby's scalp. He asked her about a scar on her shoulder. Slipped on the rocks and fell into the lake, she told him. The doctor in Beausejour, the one before McNair, had put in seven stitches. He raised himself up on one elbow and reached his finger out to the mole. When he touched it, a thrill raced up his spine.

"What's it like," she asked, "doing it in a swimming pool?"

He did not follow the line of her thinking.

"I saw a couple doing it in the water at Moon Lake," she said. It was exciting, she confessed, and at the same time a slightly ridiculous activity, the woman's legs clenched around the man's, his hands supporting her butt, the pair of them looking like they would topple over the whole time.

It seemed so long ago, even then, the summer after the events, what had happened at Moon Lake. "The RCMP guys just gave up," she told him. They had too many other things to look after, was her take on it: fresh murders and suicides and road accidents. They were understaffed and it was a rough-and-tumble district where there was lots of petty crime. Roger was back at Moon Lake after a terrible winter in the mines at Red Rock; he had lasted there less than a year. He had a ponytail and a tattoo and had thickened through the chest but given up smoking. Archie Cloud was back too. They planned to buy a couple of small power boats and guide fishermen around Moon Lake. The tourist industry was taking off: rich men from Chicago wanted to fish the well-stocked lakes of the Shield, and there were German businessmen with fantasies about testing their mettle in the Great North. They'd drawn up an advertisement, Roger and Archie, and she had placed it in the *Free Press*. That he remembered; though much that she had told him blurred and he did not mind; it was part of a hazy and beautiful time he would never again experience.

What did she remember? He asked her once. It hurt. It had been her first time, in spite of the pawings of LaFlamme and the eager high school boys. It was something she liked. That was just the sex part. She couldn't believe it had taken him so long to come around. She had almost given up on him. When Virginia told her he was going to be at the friend's that day to help with the moving, she cancelled a date for that afternoon. He was a little chubby in those days, she recalled. She decided he needed to floss, too.

He had worried about Peter, and he was right to worry. From the start, things had not gone well between them. Peter did not remember his mother well; in fact, it was shocking to Alexander how little he did remember, so it was not that. "She had black hair, right?" Peter answered when Alexander asked what he recalled. And there was a time Maria bought him cotton floss at the Red River Exhibition. But other than that, his recall was abysmal. Alexander had snaps of the two of them. He showed them to Peter. One showed him and Maria standing beside a dinosaur they had made out of snow one winter afternoon. Remember this? Peter looked at the snapshot. Maria was wearing dark glasses, he was wearing a green toque with orange lettering. He remembered the toque. So it was not fond memories of Maria that made him hostile to Ruth; it was something more primitive, and to Alexander, more frightening. She was coming between the two males. She was the intruder. Peter referred to them as the bachelor boys. He liked it that way, just the two of them sharing the cramped apartment on Furby Street: Kraft dinner, popcorn and Cokes, and the late-night *Chiller Thriller.*

When Ruth came to dinner the first time, Peter had to be coaxed to say hello to her; he refused to answer her questions about school until Alexander prodded him with his own questions; he stood beside Alexander's chair when the meal was finished and gave his father a long hug. After she left, he said to Alexander, "I don't like her, she has thick lips." That was just what had drawn Alexander to her: her pouting, wet mouth. Somehow the boy knew it.

So it started badly between them and never really improved. Ruth tried. She bought expensive birthday presents, she got down on the floor to play games with him, something Alexander himself never did. She took Peter to see *A Clockwork Orange.* He loved the movie but refused to warm to her. When Alexander and Ruth sat on the sofa, Peter squeezed in between them. He asked one day, "She's never going to live here, is she?" Then two years after that first afternoon, she did move in.

Peter was thirteen then, a not-too-difficult teen, but that changed: door slamming, tantrums. Alexander tried reason, he tried coaxing, he tried threats, he tried nothing at all. *Hands off.* One of the cashiers at the SportHut had read a pop psychology book about troubled teens and he read it too. Ruth suggested a psychologist. But before that was arranged, Peter ran away from home. Or rather, he packed a knapsack one Friday night and went to a friend's place after school without telling them, so Alexander had to phone around: first to one parent, and then another. It was frightening and embarrassing. Alexander had always wondered what it would feel like to lose the boy and he found out that night: emotional freefall. By the time they tracked Peter down, Alexander had consumed a half a bottle of whiskey. He drove over to the friend's house in a mood of rage mixed with confusion, tempered by relief. Standing on the doorstep, he did not want to explain to the friend's mother. She was sympathetic. It was almost ten o'clock. She said Peter was welcome to stay the night and he thought that was probably the best idea: no need to exacerbate the situation. Alexander did, though, want to talk to Peter, but the boy was determined to humiliate his father, so he would not come to the door. The mother went back and forth between them. Alexander remembered that doorway clearly, though he'd only stood in it once in his life. A wooden bannister divided the foyer from the sitting room to his right; on the wall to the left hung a plaque in flecked gold lettering on a bright blue background: *Home Sweet Home.* The smell of strong cleaning products, the flicker of the television in an adjacent room. In the end, Alexander returned home without speaking to or seeing the boy, and when he telephoned the following afternoon, Peter agreed to come home on Sunday.

That was the way things went after Ruth moved in, after they married in a quiet ceremony the following summer. It was not in Ruth's temperament to take things lying down, but for his sake she suffered Peter's antics. Peter sometimes refused to talk to her or answer her questions. "I'm invisible," she told Alexander, "I'm not here. That's what he really wants." The SportHuts were doing well. Alexander considered sending Peter to a private school, day boarder, but it left him hollow inside to think of the boy sleeping under someone else's roof. Was that giving up on Peter? There were weeks in succession when he felt sick to the stomach. "You chose her over me," Peter accused. It was not true, but the boy felt it to be so. How could Alexander explain to a thirteen-year-old about loneliness: the nights spent staring blankly at the television after Peter was asleep, or drinking coffee at the kitchen table mornings with only the radio for company, or waking to a cold, empty bed. His was a world of silences, where he needed background noise. Yes, he was weak, he admitted that, a weak man who needed a woman, but he would not accept that he had betrayed the boy.

Between gritted teeth he told her, "This will pass." So they stuck it out. Once Peter called Ruth *slut*, another time *whore*. Tears came to her eyes. It was what Peter wanted: to hurt her as he felt she had wounded him by coming between the bachelor boys. She told Alexander, "This is not healthy. I have to choke back my anger. It's eating me up inside." The migraines started. First, they came at four-month intervals or so, and then more frequently: whenever Peter lashed out. He provoked her by stomping over the carpet with muddy boots, by dropping china on the floor, by forgetting phone messages. She said to Alexander, "I did not want it to happen, but day by day I'm hardening my heart against Peter." He took her in his arms. Not that, not that. He felt the beginning of disintegration: the family he had tried to build after Maria's death was pulling apart like so much wet cardboard. The next time Peter called her *whore*, Ruth lashed back and that episode ended with Ruth spending two days in the spare bedroom with the blinds drawn.

They talked about it over white wine and drank too much and she became enraged, saying hurtful things to him which he knew she didn't mean but which left a tension in the house for days. "It's not you," she said. The rage in her voice went deep.

Yes, they were caught in the soggy process of disintegration.

When he was sixteen, Peter moved into an grubby downtown apartment with the older brother of a school friend, bringing relief all around. He came home at odd times, occasionally staying a week or more, but always departing without notice, having left his old room in a mess. "Stick it out," Ruth said, and that was what they did. Alexander bought him a ticket to Paris when he graduated from high school with undistinguished Cs. But when he returned in the fall, Peter had a moustache and a new attitude. He'd been picked up hitch-hiking near Lyons by a man who made his living selling mutual funds, and Peter had decided that was what he wanted to do: make lots of money. With finagling, Alexander registered Peter in the MBA program at the university and he placed on the Dean's Honor Roll at the end of first year. He came for Sunday supper and explained about P/E ratios and stock buy-backs. He became a bore on the subject of the DOW but they feigned enthusiasm. "If you win the gold medal," Alexander told him, "I'll buy you a new Mustang," which he did anyway when Peter won the silver medal. At his graduation Peter let the photographer take a portrait with Alexander on one elbow and Ruth on the other. In ten years he had never so much as hugged her and on that day he allowed her to peck him on the cheek.

But the damage had been done. She had, as she'd said earlier, hardened her heart to Peter. "I would not knowingly hurt him," she told Alexander, "but the feelings are no longer there." He was not so sure. Feelings were there, but not the kind Ruth wanted to acknowledge. He had seen it before in her: inside she was boiling. He wished away what he knew was very possible: the grand blow-out that would make his son and his wife enemies for life.

THE WOMAN BESIDE HER, Angela, was about to nod off, so she poured more tea from the pot and silently passed it to her. She was one of the two others with them this time, Sally making four sitting in a circle around the flickering candle. It was their first time. Light was just beginning to come into the sky. It was spring, her favourite season, when the sun came back into the sky in the morning, trees budded, birds sang outside of the window, and her own body came back to life, leaving the husk of winter and death behind. Sexual desire coursed like sap in her veins. Yes, spring was her favourite season. Karrin preferred autumn: *autunno*, she called it, season of colour.

Karrin glanced over her teacup and raised her eyebrows at her in a way that suggested they move outdoors. It was time to quit. She didn't wear a watch during the sessions but she had developed an instinctive sense of time. Five-thirty, she estimated, maybe slightly earlier. They had been staring at the flickering candle for over an hour and she was beginning to get light-headed in a way that forced her to blink her eyes to maintain her focus. The muscles in her buttocks were beginning to stiffen. Angela was alert but Sally was straining to stay with it. Karrin was *dolce*.

"Good, that was excellent," she said, raising her voice slightly to let them know it was time to bring the session to a close. "Let's get some fresh air." She leaned over to blow out the candle and caught Karrin's eye again: sea-green irises, even in this light.

She hadn't realized it until that moment but a headache had developed: she felt it as a flashing ache just above the eyes. First she needed a drink of water; then the walk. If you drank eight glasses of water every day you did not get headaches. Of course, there was stress. If she let that get the best of her, she lay flat on the floor with her knees crooked over a hassock for ten minutes so the blood pooled in the belly, and then brought the legs down and did deep breathing for five. It was Karrin's suggestion: the Alexander technique. Karrin had trouble with deep breathing herself. She fancied herself an athlete because she had played field hockey in college, but she had weak lungs. Everyone had something.

There was a lot they had not known about each other two years ago: a weakness for chocolate, on the one hand; a propensity to snore on the other. She had never told Karrin about the men between the men: Gareth and Anton, Ralph and Trevor. She had never said anything about that business at Moon Lake that nearly got her brother sent to the slammer. She'd never spoken of Archie Cloud. Yes, there were secrets—no, not secrets, but twilight niches of the life she lived before Karrin came along that had not yet been exposed to full light. What hadn't Karrin told her? Vanora suspected there had been affairs with male professors, and in Karrin's photo album there were snaps of bungee jumpers and people standing at a ship's rail looking at thousands of penguins.

When they had all swallowed down a glass of water they went out the front door and crossed the street into the park. The grass was a velvety moist carpet, the trees loomed ghostly. Because of the park nearby, the house was more expensive than the same house in other neighbourhoods, but you had to have a park. You needed grass, the river, birds in the trees. The sun was just coming over the horizon. Jays were screeching. A man was jogging with his spaniel. The dog ran from the base of one tree to the next, nose low to the ground, its long shaggy tail wagging. She should get a dog like Barker: black lab with a wet snout. Symbol of potency.

"What a gorgeous morning," Angela said. She was the booster in the group, a redhead with a big laugh and a ready wit. Had she always been such a booster, or only now that she'd had a personal disaster and then the enlightenment? They grunted agreement. A breeze had come up from the south. The sky was low, with a slight yellowish tinge in the east. But it was going to be a warm day; she had listened to the weather forecast the night previous.

Karrin had placed herself on the far side of Sally and was striding along slightly ahead of them, her short legs working. She turned back toward them from time to time to catch what was being said, a quizzical look on her face. She squinted sometimes, as if she were imitating deep concentration. Her hair looked brown in the grey dawn light. Pictures from her childhood showed a mop of hair so blonde it was almost white. Who else had Vanora known with hair like that? She thought about it for a moment but it would not come.

They walked on the gravel path. Dust puffed up beneath Vanora's feet, reminding her of the puffballs they used to kick at on the trails around Moon Lake. In the cool of dawn she had come out wearing slacks and the black boots Karrin had bought her in the shop off the campo in Siena. Our city, they called it. Chianti, bruschette, crostini. When it comes to Italian restaurants, Karrin said, first you check the toilets, then the wine on offer, and only then do you talk about what's going on in the kitchen.

The grass was wet with dew. Crows called from the trees down by the river. A group of three men wearing nylon windbreakers jogged by, nodding as they passed. They were familiar. Every Friday morning they did a circuit in the neighbourhood, though she did not think they lived there. Karrin didn't like walking where groups of men jogged. They disagreed about that, as they disagreed about many things: decaf latte on the one hand, espresso on the other. You could not agree about everything. You could *disagree* about everything. The year of marriage to Darrin proved that. You could not really call that marriage, though, could you? Worse was that gutless worm Harold, who came after the men she had not told Karrin about yet, Harold the Hitter. You were best not to think about certain things: Harold's inflamed cheeks; LaFlamme's body lying on the path in the woods; Cassie holding Mortimer's hand at the graveside.

She had not been back for a long time. More than twenty years had passed. A two-lane asphalt road had been built where the old logging track had run from the trading post to the outskirts of Beausejour. She grew up with the name *Beausejour* on her lips and had never really noticed that it meant something. She did now, though. The lodge was a kind of rugged resort. Cassie and Mortimer had converted the trading post into a more conventional store and what had been their bedrooms, hers and Ruth's, into a guest suite with its own kitchen and beds. The granaries had been made into tiny cabins, and small additional cabins had been added.

Cassie wrote to her, enclosing the brochure. It was a tourist place, with horseshoe pits, a kids' play structure, and guided fishing excursions. They had formed a company and the development was a huge success, Cassie said. She was proud of what they had done. They were to share in the profits, she and Ruth. That part was Roger's idea. In the early years he had done the guided fishing tours with Archie Cloud. The mines had been as horrible as she had imagined and he had lasted only eight months before he returned to Moon Lake and was promptly arrested by the RCMP. Archie Cloud too. They were questioned. Their fingerprints were taken, their boots examined. They were questioned further, together and then separately. But after three days they were released. That was the end of it, apparently.

It was not the end of the nightmares, though. He lurched out at her from behind buildings that resembled the lodge or the granary and chased her, so that she woke with her heart pounding in her throat. Sometimes he was just a figure in the distance, closing on her, sometimes just a face or a voice. He accused her of things. He yelled at her in French and raised his arm as if to strike. Then at other times he was the body lying inert on the path, bare flesh glimmering in the moonlight. Once she picked up the body and carried it to the water and bathed its head, like a picture she had seen of John the Baptist. She had no desire to go back to Moon Lake. Bad karma.

She wondered sometimes about Penny and Lucy. Their lives had not gone well. The daughters of a trapper, they had grown up accustomed to cruelty and blood. They had skinned the animals their father brought in from the trapline, stretched and hung the pelts, gutted the fish, butchered and cut up the deer and moose and bear the family ate over the long hard winters. It was their way. They had grown up used to shooting and still-warm bodies and bloody hands, and they knew where on the body to plunge in the knife. It had not seemed so when they were kids, but she sensed it was a callousness to life that Penny and Lucy had acquired at Moon Lake, a hardness of character that went beyond passivity about violence to acceptance of its everyday occurrence. Lucy had drowned on Lake Winnipeg and Penny had several children and lived in the Core with a man rumoured to beat her. Vanora winced inside when she thought about them now. She wondered if she tensed up with Native patients, who invariably triggered memories of the Cloud girls; she wondered if she treated them less thoroughly than her other patients.

She had not kept in touch with Cassie the way she would have liked to. She did not like Mort and suspected he knew it, so he did not accompany Cassie when she came to visit in the city. It was Vanora's own fault. Ruth said in her accusing voice: "You're always so wrapped up in your man." It was a sickness, she saw that now. She needed a man, a strong masculine man, and she went from one to the next trying to find him. The Lost Father. Ruth had the same sickness, only she resolved it a different way, taking up with an older man. You could not tell her that. Everybody was sick in some way, so it didn't matter in the end, not really, that Vanora was a little twisted inside over her dead father, her murdered father. She was not a psycho and she didn't poison neighbours' cats. She was, though, afraid at times. Following her Out-of-Body Experience, she knew how fragile the thread between life and death really was.

Karrin said it's like falling off a horse. You have to get up and get back on again. Karrin meant life, the way men had wounded them both—wounded, Karrin insisted, but not damaged. She liked horses. There was a stable on the outskirts of the city where a Scandinavian woman gave riding lessons. She and Karrin had talked about giving it a try. Angela had told them about it. She rode twice a week. She had had her OBE as a result of riding in the forest, where she fell, struck her head and had to be rushed to the hospital in an ambulance. But she was living through it. That was the way. Sally lived through it by hiking with her kids in Arizona every summer. Yes, the message was simple: you got on with life.

The OBE, Karrin said, is not an end but a beginning. Like a baby.

They were not talking about the baby—they called it the baby now—but were keeping an unspoken conspiracy of silence in case the adoption fell through. Karrin had done some minor frepairs in the small bedroom: bold curtains in a crayon motif, a mobile suspended from the ceiling. They were holding their emotional breath and trying not, as Karrin put it, to ransom too many hostages to fate. In the end, who knew which way Family Services would jump? Or when? June seemed a possibility.

They had lit the candle at four that morning. This was Karrin's idea: the body needed rest but also could be stretched, like the mind, so channel before the workday began, start with a clear and calm mind. "We meditate," Karrin liked to say, "so that our minds cannot complicate our lives." She had instructed the class at the university that Vanora had attended. She had seemed young then, and still had the eagerness that went with being in her twenties. "It will work," she told the women who came to them, all wounded in some way, "the inner journey has worked for me."

Karrin herself was the proof. A year or so before she and Vanora met, she had developed melanoma in the calves of her legs. Tumors like large hives had formed on her skin one Thursday night. She was diagnosed the following morning. The physicians were preparing to do the surgery Monday morning. Karrin was admitted to hospital. She began meditating in the afternoon. By Sunday night the tumors had begun to shrink. Every passing hour saw them smaller than before. She checked out of the hospital before the surgery on Monday. By the following Friday the tumors had disappeared entirely. It was a kind of miracle and even the doctors conceded it. Experts from around the world flew in to review the case. Karrin appeared on talk shows and as a guest at meditation seminars. She had met Sri Chimoy in New York and seen him lift two thousand pounds, a slight, ageing oriental man. "Sixty-eight years old!" Karrin said, a look of exultation on her round face, "and he lifts a ton. The power of the mind." *La mente.*

So, yes, when Karrin said channel in the dawn, they did it.

That morning Angela and Sally arrived together in the darkness. At the door she asked them, "Why are you whispering?" And they laughed, but not loudly. They sat in a circle; they did a chant. AUM. Say it as if it were three syllables, Karrin instructed, prolong each sound. Karrin had made tea and they did some stretching between sips. Angela had long smooth legs and Sally a bottom perfectly suited for long spells on the floor. A legal secretary, she'd collapsed one day at her office with what the doctors called an infarction. Six weeks later she came to Vanora. She had a powerful aura and could visit dozens of previous lives in one session. Then Steve, her rotten husband, left her, just as Harold had left Vanora years ago. He'd had to have his red meat, his scotch. Die in hell, Harold and Steve.

It was not all peace and joy and good health.

"Why green tea?" Angela wanted to know.

"It's got this eleven-syllable agent in it that inhibits cancer growth." That was Karrin, eager to show off her knowledge. The Professor.

"Sulphorophane," she said, correcting too quickly. She was too hard on Karrin, snippy and critical. *You have difficulty forgiving*, Karrin had told her once, *and the person you forgive least is yourself.* She had made a paella and the rice had gone dry and she had become sulky and then bitchy to Karrin. Stupid, really. Stupid. But Karrin had coaxed her out of that mood, as she often did. Maybe this was what she was learning: not to take life so hard.

"Excuse me," Karrin said, laughing, "thirteen syllables."

"No," she said correcting herself, "Sulphorophane is in broccoli sprouts. Wait. Polyphenols. They stop the breakdown of connective tissue via collagenese."

"What's the difference," asked Sally, "between green tea and regular?"

"The Chinese have made tea for four thousand years," Karrin said. "The green is leaves that have been picked earlier than the black. They're better for you."

"It's an antioxidant," Angela said, "isn't it?"

The path descended abruptly and she glanced down to check the footing. It was right here a month ago when she was out on an early morning ramble that she had encountered a fox, a female, mangy of coat and emaciated. It had stepped toward her and then back suddenly. Its eyes were glassy and pus ran from its nose. Rabies? Her heart had skipped. Another time she'd spotted a flock of wild turkeys, nine or ten, poking through the underbrush and communicating in subdued cackles. Wild turkeys in the city? Foxes? The city was not, as Vanora had supposed on first moving from Moon Lake, a homogeneous concrete and steel mass. "Actually," she said, "it's a difference in the processing. Green leaves are steamed lightly and retain more polyphenols. Black tea is green leaves that have been air-dried rather than steamed, and hence, oxidized." And it was closer to three thousand years that the Chinese had been drinking tea but she let that ride. Karrin was an enthusiast—in and out of bed.

Karrin had drifted ahead of them. She turned her head and said, "She's impressive, no, with her facts? It boggles the brain."

"They both make me hyper," Sally said, coming back to the teas.

"The one drawback," Vanora agreed. "Caffeine."

They had completed the circuit of the park and come to the road and then the sidewalk in front of the house. Angela and Sally stopped. They looked tired but exhilarated. They would be back. Their cars were parked further down the block. It was getting warmer already. The day was beginning to look like it smelled: the greens of the leaves bright with oxygen, a yellowish tint in the sky reminiscent of Christmas oranges. They said goodbye and went up the stairs and into the house. Only when the door closed behind them with a click did she give Karrin's hand a quick squeeze. She felt guilty, though there was no reason to feel guilt.

"I've got that thesis defense at ten," Karrin said.

"And I've got six in a row starting in two hours."

"But it's cash in hand," Karrin said, laughing.

"Cash in hands, arms like mash."

"You don't mean that. You love your work. You're a healer."

"No," she said. "No, I don't mean that." And it's not Reiki, she thought to herself.

Karrin went into the bedroom and Vanora remained in the narrow foyer, with one hand clasped in the other. The oval mirror was to her side. She grimaced at herself. Her hair was salt and pepper, falling to her shoulders in long frizzy waves. The word *crone* came to her mind, a misunderstood word, an excellent word, actually. No need to worry about that any longer, about feminine wiles and keeping herself beautiful for men. She wore no makeup. Her one indulgence was silk scarves, of which she had dozens but always a favourite or two. Ruth gave them to her at Christmas and birthdays, Ruth who had kept her figure and her face and had a man and suffered from headaches. Well, she had things too: patients who called her *healer*, pairs of sensible shoes, a serviceable car, cookbooks, a medallion. Karrin. Above all, she had Karrin. She fingered the medallion around her neck. Her one-year anniversary gift. It was fashioned from pewter, the outer rim resembling the wire rim of a bicycle wheel, with a female figure standing in its centre with a snake wrapped around one arm and a tiny dog at her feet. Sirona. Karrin had explained the significance.

Karrin was whistling as she made her toilette in the bathroom. Mozart, was it? She used just the tiniest bit of gel on the comb and set the hair dryer at medium. Everything was very precise with Karrin. She was a perfectionist. She ate muesli with real yogurt, and drank echinacea or camomile or green tea. You had to vary the type, or flora built up in your intestines. On the facial skin, Karrin used only Aveeno.

As she listened to her whistling, Vanora thought about the threads that tied them together. They enjoyed reading in bed. She liked Karrin to read to her. Poetry. They were gentle with each other's bodies but they were crazy with desire too; they drove each other wild sometimes. But then a week passed when all they did was hold each other. Yes. Karrin was precise and sensible. She wore sandals, summer and winter and she liked to make plans. On her desk there were two lined notepads with columns of figures that charted expenditures and lists of chores to do. She was a planner, but a doer too. On the tackboard in the room they used as a study Karrin had hung up a whiteboard and on it she wrote messages to herself and to Vanora in dry-erase markers. She wrote phone numbers and single words that indicated chores that needed to be done: chervil, computer, salmon oil. On a smaller whiteboard stuck to the refrigerator she'd written words in Italian, which they were trying to learn for a walking trip to Lake Como. Karrin had been to Paris with one of her lovers and would not go back. Vanora liked that in her. She was single-minded, as well as thorough and reasonable. There were many ways to say what bound her to Karrin but it came down to a simple premise: she had found a place where she could shelter—though she would not put it quite that bluntly to Karrin.

Vanora had strolled along the hallway. She saw the machine blinking. The call had come while they were out walking around the park. No patient—not even the loony lady—would call that early. Who then?

He was driving between Beausejour and Whitemouth now, driving too fast, he realized. The bush on the side of the road was whipping past. A few miles back the Merc's wheels had hit the gravel shoulder. Ruth had given him a look that he ignored. They were beyond the turn-off where they came out from the Agassiz forest when they went out on their mountain bikes for a day of cycling. When was the last time? Ruth had been hot and angry that day too; it was too hot for cycling but he had insisted they get the fresh air and that brought the migraine on and then she became violent. When they'd stopped part-way along the gravel road for a drink she had lashed out at him. "You just have to get your way. You're selfish," she screamed, "a little boy." What could he say?

Now she muttered, "I'm only saying you should have told me."

The last of the paper cup of coffee from Tim Horton's was tepid, but he sipped at it before answering. "I thought you wouldn't want to do it."

"Huh."

"I can't get enough of you. See?"

"Don't start that."

"We talked about doing it last night and you said this morning."

"I've got a sore ass. From all that cycling you had us do on the weekend."

"You should get the leather seat."

"It's not the same for me as for you. They design those bicycle seats for men."

"The 02 saddle, the one with gel. That's what you need."

"I want the one specially designed for women."

"It's more expensive but all right. I'll order it in."

"Bring it home. Put it on the bike."

"You're not really angry about that."

"I'm angry about the fact that you have to have what you want. Come on babe." Her imitation of his voice, bass tones, the pitch of an over-eager twenty-year old, made them both laugh.

This was what he had grown to like about her. They could fight and it did not end in silences. Only she didn't like the word *fight*. We're not arguing, she had told him once, we're disagreeing. I'm right and you're wrong. Soon you'll be right too. She was cheeky that way, cheeky without being pushy, as her mother was. And the thing was, she was in the right most times. And he was learning. Coming to see things her way, in any case. Which was not a bad thing. He was selfish; it needed tempering. And there was the sex. That morning they'd broken one of the wooden slats of the futon frame. They had been almost there and she'd frozen a moment when the wood snapped, then laughed. For a moment they lost their rhythm and he thought maybe she would not but then she did and it was bloody marvellous as it had been for more than twenty years. He had to think hard to recall the years of loneliness. So he listened when she talked.

"Anyway," he said, "I'm sure everything's all right. You know Mort."

She was silent. She had this theory about Moon Lake that she'd picked up from Vanora: bad karma. She had tried to persuade Cassie to move into the city, to move anywhere. She had nightmares. LaFlamme chased her through the woods. She could not outrun him; she became lost in the woods. "It's an evil place," she told him as the Merc rocked through a dip in the road.

"Evil," was all he could think to respond. "That's a strong word."

She grunted. Her unhappiness, the part he saw of it, had to do with internal sufferings. He tried to know as little about that as possible. But he helped her deal with the physical manifestations, the migraines.

They crossed a bridge over a creek and two mallards flew up from the reeds. The sky was low but the weather station had said mainly sunny and no rain. That was in the city. He glanced down at the speedometer. He shouldn't drive this fast but he was trying to make up for the lost time. For staying inside her so long while Mort twiddled his thumbs and stared out the window and twitched with every sound, anticipating their arrival. They'd get to Whitemouth in five minutes and be at Moon Lake by nine o'clock. He glanced at Ruth again. It appeared that the migraine was not coming on. Though her brow was furrowed up in anger—or was it thought?

She was thinking of LaFlamme, he guessed. They never talked about him, but he had been her father. That business held a strange power over them all, even though it was twenty years ago. No, twenty-five. Probably because the issue had not been resolved. He woke sometimes in the middle of the night with the strong conviction he knew who had done it. A name would suddenly materialize out of a dream and he would wake, certain he had solved the riddle. But that was nonsense and in the morning it was obvious. Once, it was Peter's name that came to him. That time he had felt weird and sick to the stomach the entire day. Such nonsense going through a grown man's mind. He had called Peter at work and talked to him for a long time before he felt able to turn to his business affairs. There was a strange feeling in his body all that day. It was no wonder that people put stock in visions and such. Archie Cloud and Roger were both deeply into the pop-psychology.

Ruth thought Roger had brought his life together very well. The brain damage he'd suffered as a child had not made him simple, only a little erratic. He was lithe and tan and strong. For several years when he was in his thirties he had run the marathon in the city. They stood at the finish line to see him run the final metres: he wore a red and yellow braided headband and people mistook him for a Native. He ate little red meat but lots of rice and pasta. He lived in a log cabin on the Roseisle River. There had been women when he was younger, one that he lived with in the city. They bought a gigantic colour TV that took up nearly one whole wall in their house, but then the woman threw him out and kept the TV and he lived in tiny apartments that smelled of mouldy cheese. The woman had thrown Roger out over drinking. But now he was very moderate in that regard. He smoked though, pipes of a Native concoction not unlike marijuana, Ruth claimed. He'd given some to Vanora and Ruth to experiment with.

Vanora, Ruth said, had made herself into a pupa. She had gone from man to man at one point earlier in her life, sometimes within the week. Ruth feared she might lose her job at the girls' school. She was unhappy, she was searching for something, she tried whatever was going, New Wave, and so on. Maybe there were suicidal moments. Then she discovered she liked women more than men and met Karrin and started meditating and channelling. She was spinning into herself, spinning a cocoon around herself, Ruth said. She'd grown lumpy and dishevelled. Her long grey hair resembled a permanent in the process of exploding off her skull. She ate only organic foods and soups.

It was all a bit touchy-feely for Alexander, who thought New Wave just another kind of indulgence, prettied up to look deep and philosophical but basically selfish and self-centred. These navel-gazers were essentially weak, he believed, sexually-deprived types who explored the inner self as a feeble alternative to what everyone really wanted, regular and thorough boinking. Only it was all holier-than-thou with that crowd. They'd experienced a higher reality, according to them, levels of understanding beyond the common run. It was just a need, a need to be special. Alexander saw it in Vanora's eyes, a kind of inner trembling. Ruth did not agree with him. She claimed Vanora's inward journey was a genuine thing, that her sister had finally found herself.

"She's my mother," Ruth insisted now to him, "that's what I'm saying."

"All right. Okay."

"What I'm saying is next time you tell me."

He gave her the last word. That was what she really wanted. After a minute or so she sighed and shifted on the seat and took the coffee container out of his hand. "And you don't have to drive so fast," she added. "Five minutes isn't going to make a difference now."

T HE PHONE RANG WHILE SHEILA was tying the laces on her Nikes. "It's for you," she said. "It always is at this time of day." She said it in her perky voice but he heard no false tone, no effort to force gaiety.

He glanced at his watch. Seven-forty. She let him sleep late if he came on the walk around town with her in the evening. He took a quick sip of coffee and reached for the phone with the other hand. The odour of the coffee went from his nostrils to the back of his tongue. He loved the Columbian dark. Theresa sent ten pounds from Starbucks in Vancouver every Christmas. Sheila let him drink decaffeinated if he ate the boiled eggs on the banana bread and sprouts on the tuna sandwich she fixed for his lunch. And she better not call at noon and discover he had slipped out for a doughnut or a burger.

He pushed the phone's talk button. Sheila was doing stretches at the door, the early morning light playing in her hair as her head bobbed from side to side. She had a better ass than when she was thirty and had slimmed down to a hundred and twenty. She ran the middle section of the marathon, team division, every year, just weeks away now, and pinched his gut and teased him about getting fat. It was true, he could easily shed ten pounds. It was sitting behind the desk at Fingerprints in the city all those years, and then again in Beausejour: reports, paperwork.

She rattled the door knob as he was saying *Boyd* into the phone. She waved at him as she went out. Blew a kiss.

He talked to Corporal Sutton. Cassie Mann was missing. Sutton and Sawatzky would organize a search party once they got out there. Did he want to join them? He did, he didn't. Paperwork was piling up but he wondered how the fishing was out there. Pickerel season had opened. McNair had left a message on the machine at home a couple of days ago. Sheila ran past the bay window, breasts bouncing under the sweatshirt, waved again, and then turned and went down the drive, heading for the loop around town. They didn't snicker at her now. Or maybe they did. Small towns. Extremes of any kind not wanted, even the healthy ones. When he had put his name in for Staff Sergeant, head office transferred him out of Fingerprints in the city and posted him back to Beausejour. Sometimes the wheel really did come round. Staff Sergeant, though. Take that, Gerald Black.

Sutton was waiting for his answer, breathing quietly on the other end of the line. The thing was, he felt weary, and he felt guilty on a couple of accounts.

He told Sutton he'd meet him at Moon Lake. The kids at the elementary would have to wait for their annual pep talk. He sipped at the coffee, savouring the dark brown of the beans. Sheila's bright green tights flickered as she went through the birch trees at the end of the driveway, and then disappeared behind the Ansons'. He could smell the banana bread she'd put in the oven while he was making coffee. She made it with real maple syrup. It was part of the regime: no refined sugar or flour and never chocolate bars or Cokes. *Think of the liver.* She was suspicious of alcohol but let him drink a cheap Chilean red if he accompanied her on the walks.

How long had it been that they'd been eating this way? Ten years, but it seemed all their lives. Sheila and Terry had conspired together against him before Terry moved into residence at the university: pasta salads, kashi, kamut. When Sheila came back from the psych ward she could talk about nothing but her body and its functions. There were foods that gave you gas: that had been his problem all along, according to her. She had books and magazine articles and could quote statistics. Your joints became inflamed when you sat for long periods and your hair oily if you were anxious. If you sat at your desk, reading intently, you should look up every five minutes and focus your gaze in the intermediate distance for thirty seconds. Scarcity of sunshine made the skin itchy and coffee gave you hives. Almost everything upset the balance nature set in operation in your organs. You had to be vigilant. Terry did a school project on vitamin C. They were in it together. In high school Terry had become a vegetarian. She and Sheila refused to take aspirin and antibiotics. There were natural cures. They drank distilled water. If he caught pike, it had to be boiled because of the possibility of toxins in the water.

Moon Lake. He pulled on his cap and the jacket. The forecast was for sun but you never knew. He'd been fooled by those meteorological guys before and had come down with pneumonia once on a suicide past Lac du Bonnet.

Moon Lake. He had never felt good about the way that had worked out.

In the past twenty years or so more than one case had slipped away from him, but that was the one that bothered him. Maybe because he'd been taken off the case. He should have known the rumours would have flown thick in the hotel. The Mountie had every reason to drag his feet on this one, they would have said, to confuse the issues, to cover up what really happened. Gerald Black didn't believe that officers took vendettas, as the locals liked to slyly hint, but he was not immune to rumours around town either. So he'd had one of the other corporals trace Victor's movements the night of LaFlamme's murder and then calculated how long it took to drive out to Moon Lake, walk out to Moose Point, and then return to town. There was plenty of time, it appeared, for Victor to have done what some in the Lakeland were eager to pin on him. So Sergeant Black would have taken him off the case anyway. Justice had to be seen to be done.

Sheila's suicide attempt only hastened matters along.

In any case. Gerald Black had said at his retirement party that you couldn't win them all. But you wanted to. The boy had slipped through their fingers. Or maybe it really had not been him. He was living out Roseisle way now. Years earlier, he and Archie Cloud had bought those boats, and they'd done well at the guiding business before he got into the men's movement. People change. Everything changes.

The squad cars were white now. Outside of town he put the pedal down and watched the needle on the dashboard climb. There were clouds in the sky but they were thin and white and high up and it probably would not rain. It only occurred to him as he passed the Shell that it was probably a false alarm. Cassie would have returned home; they would be having coffee at the kitchen table by the time he got there and laughing about it. Mort with the gimpy leg and Cassie whose flesh sagged around her neck. He would have wasted the morning. The paperwork would have piled up. He should have waited. But the guilt he felt about Moon Lake had been behind his decision: so, no, time did not change some things.

The road to Moon Lake. He pulled the squad car off the asphalt where the road dipped and curved east, and then he stopped the car on the gravel verge. The highway was busy with cars for a Friday morning. He needed privacy. He'd been chewing gum and he wrapped it carefully in foil and poked it into the ashtray with the other wrappers.

Outside he felt the wind on his face, a breeze really, and he looked up at the sky as he walked down the hard mud trail into the forest. The milky sun of May was trying to shine past the clouds. A flock of sparrows whirled up from the grass noisily and crossed back to the other side of the road where they settled on the gravel verge. It was cool for the time of year but the birds knew the big thaw was on the way. The ground underfoot was stony and uneven, but hardy native plants grew everywhere: prairie sage, Canadian thistle, the bright yellow and ubiquitous dandelion. Marsh nettle, whose sharp burrs stuck in the cotton socks he wore to absorb the perspiration inside the heavy cop shoes. Sheila would not remove the burrs and neither would he, so he threw the socks in the trash when he got home after these outings, an extravagance he considered offensive, being the child of parents who had lived through the Great Depression and had nurtured him on its lessons, along with the oatmeal and the chicken noodle soup. He stepped off the path and pulled down the zipper on his trousers to relieve himself.

Yes, the big thaw was almost on them again, though you could be fooled this time of year and come out in a light jacket only to be returning home in a blizzard. He glanced at the sky again. You could be fooled by what you saw up there. Things were not what they seemed.

He listened to the cars whizzing past on the highway. The sound of his own body function.

Things were not what they seemed down on the ground either. Two years ago he'd been called out on a case just as he'd been sitting down to supper with Sheila's book club friends. An eight-year-old girl had not come home after school and her body had been found in a garage on the edge of town. She'd been strangled. The evidence they found over the next few days pointed to a boy one year older than her. (A hockey card, was it—a shoe lace?) In any case. He interviewed the boy, a nice kid who got good grades and played on a hockey team that Victor had helped coach one weekend when the regular coach was sick. Victor could not believe that boy had strangled the girl. He'd argued with Sutton: "This boy could not have put his hands on this girl's throat and squeezed the life out of her." But the parents put pressure on the boy and he confessed. Sutton was right. Things were not always what they seemed. It was a lesson to him. Then a month later it came out that a second boy had been in the garage, an older boy. He had actually done the strangling. So Victor was in the right after all, but it didn't matter who was right and who wrong. The girl was dead. The boys' lives ruined.

He zipped up and walked back down the path to the squad car. Things were not what they appeared. A good motto for a cop. You had to look into things, no matter what you saw first, or what you were told by witnesses or suspects.

But you could trick yourself by looking too deeply into things too. So when they seemed to be more than they were, they could not be that too. They could turn out to be less. Sometimes thinking this way made his brains hurt. He was not a terribly clever man, he had come to understand. Ambitious, yes. Impatient.

So he'd have to go slow at Moon Lake. Let Sutton and the young corporal take charge. He could adopt the role of observer, a role he'd never found satisfying.

He stood for a moment by the squad car and listened to the birds. A couple of frogs had started croaking from the ditch. Soon there would be mosquitoes and black flies. Soon the soft weather in the evenings and kids drinking beer in the gravel pits and rolling the family pickups on the back roads.

It was more fair to say she had tried to come back to Moon Lake and had been unable to. This was in the days of the men between the men, when she was still called Virginia. She felt shitty about only phoning Cassie then, and dropping cards in the mail: Happy Birthday. So one Friday after school was out, she threw a bag in the rusty Volvo and drove the miles to Beausejour. She parked in the town across from the doctors' office. It was called Clinic something then, but McNair's name was prominent on the list of doctors. The clinic was across from the liquor store. She wondered if she should bring a bottle of wine to share with Cassie and Mort, a kind of peace offering.

She had intended to drive straight out, down the logging road; the Volvo was built, the ads claimed, for just this terrain. But she was hungry when she reached Beausejour. It was past seven. Her stomach was rumbling. She'd gone into the diner across from the clinic. It was new, prefabricated and smoky inside, and filled with men wearing baseball caps and smoking roll-your-owns. Their voices ceased when the door closed behind her. Someone laughed. It was all wearyingly familiar. In the big city dailies they called these people with their wall-to-wall bigotry the salt of the earth.

She ordered a chicken salad sandwich and sat with a tepid pot of orange pekoe looking out the greasy window at the street. Wondering why she'd bothered coming. Stupid. It was a fall evening. Kids on bikes puttered along the sidewalks. Teenagers sat on a park bench smoking and flirting.

She saw a man and a woman come out of the liquor store, one after the other, but then the woman placed her hand in the crook of the man's arm. He looked down at her. They laughed. As they were about to cross the street she saw it was Mortimer and Cassie, who was wearing a pink ski jacket and too much lipstick. She was still laughing, her mouth wide open. She stood with Mortimer on the curb a moment before walking toward a pickup truck parked along the street. When they got there, Cassie looked up at him and he leaned down and kissed her once on the lips. The kiss was over in a moment, a peck really, but something went small inside Vanora's chest at that moment. The gesture was so intimate, so exclusive, that she knew she could never break into the world they had made together at Moon Lake. Cassie had written to tell her that the business at the lodge was doing great. She was watching out for her interest, she wanted her to know: hers and Ruth's and Roger's. It was touching, Cassie's concern, and Vanora had left the city to tell her mother so, and to say that she did not really need to bother, kindly as it was, to look out for the interests of her children, who were all doing well for themselves. She had wanted to say that face-to-face, to hug Cassie as a way of reciprocating her mother's concern. But when she saw them walking arm-in-arm, the way they kissed, Vanora could see that Moon Lake was really just the two of them now, her and Mortimer, however the interests of Cassie's children might stand legally. She'd felt hollow inside.

She couldn't remember whether she'd finished the sandwich. She never did buy the bottle of wine, and when she started the Volvo's engine, she knew she would not be making the drive down the old logging road that night. On the highway back to the city in the dark a deer leapt from the ditch through the headlight beams of the Volvo and most of the drive back her heart was in her throat.

This time was different. She was with Karrin, for one, and Karrin had a steadying influence on her. And she was not coming on an impulse, a whim, but to be of help, you could say: summoned.

Only it might be serious.

In the past few years Cassie sometimes drove into the city on her own. She'd put on weight and kept a cushion on the front seat of her Cavalier so she could see over the steering wheel. She tinted her hair. She wore bright lipstick and scarves that clashed with the patchwork jacket she favoured. Her clothes were not cheap and the Cavalier was new—red, with a good stereo system.

They had tea and sandwiches in the place Cassie liked in Osborne Village. Cassie seemed depressed sometimes, and on others on the verge of telling her something important, but then she always reverted to small talk. There were huge deserts of each other's life they could not cross into: Karrin and lesbianism on the one hand; Mortimer and the LaFlamme business on the other. Cassie knew more than she'd told the Mounties, but talk about those days always led to sudden silences.

They were afraid of each other and retreated into silences. Silence, Karrin said, is the absence of love. Or the absence of need, Vanora was tempted to say.

On the drive up from the city Karrin had put in a tape of the Crash Test Dummies and was singing loudly along as the car whisked over the asphalt. Low grey clouds hung above the treetops. Karrin's singing was off-key but that didn't matter to either of them. Though she wished she could be that way. *You can't let go*, Karrin had accused once, and she was right. When they came to the turn out and what was once the logging road, she looked at the dreary sky again and thought, that's the ugliness inside me up there in the sky—grey, dark, compressed. It's my refusal to let go of that life and that place. Ruth has gone on and so has Roger but I cannot get past it somehow, cannot even face up to it. How stupid. Karrin would have laughed it off, or bungee-jumpred it away.

She had run away that time when she saw Cassie and Mortimer together, but was going back now. She was about to make a fresh beginning. She geared down the Volvo to make the turn. As a child she had loved the place, and then as a young woman she had come to fear it. Now Vanora was a full-grown adult whom some of her patients called doctor and it was time for the wounds of Moon Lake to heal.

T HE SEARCH FOR CASSIE STARTED FROM Moon Lake Lodge, what had once been the trading post. Cassie and Mortimer had changed more than the name. There were still some shelves with foodstuffs, chips and crackers and so on, and a few canned goods, and sunscreen and mosquito repellent, but the dry goods were gone, as was the hardware on the shelves behind the counter at the back. Kids' treats featured prominently now: trading cards and cheap plastic toys, good for one rainy afternoon of diversion. The Lee Enfield still hung on the wall. Probably it had not been fired in forty years, or even oiled in decades. Cassie felt a sentimental attachment to it, so it had stayed.

The Mountie was waiting for them on the steps, Sergeant Boyd, now, and two of his subordinates. They were to walk in pairs, Boyd said, fanning out on the roads and trails that ran back and upward toward the reservation. Cassie had last been seen by Mort, heading that way with a white plastic pail in hand. They were to stay in pairs and shout out Cassie's name every minute or so. But nothing else. No talking. She was presumably hurt, perhaps with a broken hip or twisted ankle. By now she would be cold and exhausted so her response might be weak: they would need to be attentive to hear her. If they discovered her in a collapsed state they were not to move her but call out at once for Boyd.

There were two dogs near the steps with the Mounties, in addition to Mortimer and Roger and Archie Cloud, as well as the two kids who were to be guides that summer. Roger's hair had turned to salt and pepper. It was tied back in a ponytail. Alexander remembered that LaFlamme's hair had been jet black, and he had died in his late thirties, younger than his son's current age. So this grey must be attributable to Cassie's line. Roger had high cheekbones. Alexander had thought of him as oriental when he first encountered the boy, but he saw now that there must have been Métis blood in the LaFlamme line. Ruth's dark eyes, Vanora's olive skin. The dogs were German shepherds on leashes, giant beasts with black and brown coats. They stood silently and sniffed a garment Mort had brought out of the bedroom, which seemed somewhat foolish to Alexander. Wouldn't Cassie's scent be everywhere?

Mortimer explained again where she liked to pick fiddleheads. His anxious eyes moved from one face to another. The skin of his cheeks looked unhealthy: pasty and fallen. It was all becoming real to Alexander: his brother was frightened. Cassie was a woman of regular habits. She and Mort had lived together for twenty years. She did not make mistakes out in the woods only half a mile from the lodge. Alexander remembered that Peter had been afraid of predators on that night when they first walked to Moon Lake years ago. Jaguars, was it? Laughable. Probably his own fears on that eventful night were that insubstantial too.

Mortimer stuffed a wad of chewing tobacco under his tongue and picked up his cane in trembling fingers. He had trouble walking. Some years earlier he had fallen off the roof of the lodge and done something to his hip that the doctors could not fix. First the hip, and then the lungs. He would stay closer to the lodge and meet Vanora when she arrived, he explained. Vanora and her friend.

Victor took the middle trail, the old logging road. It was the way she had gone into the forest, according to Mort. Victor took one of the shepherds and the young corporal, Sawatzky. Victor had become a little thicker around the middle, and his hair, when he lifted his cap to scratch his scalp, had thinned to the point where a skunk's stripe of shining skull coursed down the centre of his head. He put out his hand when he recognized Alexander and nodded to Ruth, appraising them both with those husky eyes that betrayed no emotion. Athletes often had them, Alexander had come to recognize. Blank concentration masking the killer instinct.

He and Ruth took the trail closest to the lake, walking slowly and peering into the woods. In the low spots, the ground was soft. Mort had mentioned they'd had a lot of rain in April. The trunks of the birches looked black. Their boots squished through the muskeg sections. The rocks and exposed tree roots were slippery. He let Ruth do the calling: *Cass-siee*. From time to time they heard a voice in the far distance echoing her: *Cass-siee*. The hair stood up on the back of his neck.

Ruth took his hand. They had not visited for some months but she had grown fond of her mother in the past years: forgive and forget, an article of faith with her now. The grip of her hand in his told him she was frightened. He hoped she would not break down suddenly. It took so little to set her off sometimes. He took out his pipe and lit the few strands in the bottom of the bowl with a match. Puffed. He no longer inhaled. When she found his hand again she squeezed it hard.

Every few minutes they paused to look into the woods. Small creatures were rustling in the dry leaves of the previous autumn. The breeze stirred grasses along the path. A blue jay screeched in the pines. Once when they were moving he heard a twig snap behind them and he was transported suddenly back across the years to the night when LaFlamme had been killed; and he thought of Peter's round eyes peering up at him in the dark. His heart was thumping but he would not look around and frighten Ruth.

It was the time of year when the plants in the woods were bright green and giving off the heavy odour of chlorophyll. New leaves on the chokecherry bushes, willow stems with tight buds, saplings of maples bearing fresh leaves, the shepherd's crooks of ferns with their dark verdant hues. Early buttercups were out and nests of a tiny plant that grew close to the ground with delicate white flowers. Cassie had called it something—Queen Anne's Lace? No. He was no good with the names of plants and trees and did not want to ask Ruth, who gave him a look if she had told him something on a previous occasion. The Mountie had cautioned them about wood ticks. Soon the forest would be buzzing with bees and wasps and insects that flew through the air and landed on your face. The sun was over the trees and splashed down on their backs. The temperature was no more than fifteen degrees but in the shelter of the woods it felt warm and would soon be hot.

So far no bugs. It was early enough in the year for the mosquitoes not to be hatching in large numbers yet. The black flies came later, no-see-ems, they called them. And the house flies would be staying close to ground until the air became warmer, and then lazy with winter hangover when they did come out. Still, there were the ticks. He loosened the top of his windbreaker and felt the cool air strike his throat.

After a half hour of walking they came out of the woods and could see the lake on their right and the houses of the reservation ahead. Where Carl Cuthand's tent had stood years ago there was now a small building constructed of logs, a kiosk that sold Native artifacts and beadwork and the canvasses of not just the well-known Native painters but a few from the Shoal Lake Reserve. He and Ruth had talked about buying their friends moccasins for Christmas. Unique beadwork; dense, smokey odour emanating from the deerskin.

Alexander looked east toward the lake. The water sparkled in the low sun. He shaded his eyes to look back across the lake toward the wild rice fields and the narrows. In the pause he heard a hawk screeching but he could not spot it. They were in the shade of a stand of spruces. The lake looked flat, a plate of bright metal. The Natives must have had a name for the lake he did not know. How old was it? The lake had been there before anyone had thought to give it a name, and would be there when it was no longer called anything. *Lake*, even that was a recent concept for water that had pooled in a crevice finger left by a retreating glacier. In a few hundred years man would have come and gone. The hawk would float overhead, and the crows call as they always had. He shook free of such thoughts and he turned back to Ruth. When his eyes readjusted, he saw that she was trembling. Ordinarily she was strong-minded, stronger, he would have said, than him: he could not have taken those headaches. But it was difficult to read her deepest feelings. Her determination was great; she possessed tremendous stick-to-it-iveness, but then it collapsed suddenly and she became child-like dependent. It was an emotional roller coaster with her but a ride he was glad to have taken.

He wondered if Mort felt the same way about Cassie.

Cassie had gone out to pick fiddleheads. They passed great patches of them, some not where he would have expected to find them, on the higher and drier ground. Ruth claimed they grew near mossy trees. He wondered about that: she occasionally made authoritative claims about things he knew not to be factually true. He wondered about Cassie. She could not have been more than thirty minutes from home in her walk, yet Mort had waited until past ten before thinking something was amiss. Maybe they'd had a fight or something that prompted her to storm out of the house the way Ruth did when she became angry. They were women in whom emotions ran high.

Not fighting, he reminded himself, disagreeing.

He could not say he was fond of Cassie. He could not get out of his head the first image he had of her, standing with Mort in the golden light of the kitchen. A conspiracy of some sort was implied in the way they looked at each other. Or was that all in his head? Conspiracy. Ordinary people that you knew were not involved in conspiracies. Deceptions, maybe. Cassie was capable of those. And of making it clear to him that she did not really like him, despite the fact he was Mortimer's brother. They had begun openly living together the spring he and Peter moved back to the city. They were married two years later. They started to transform the trading post into a tourist lodge shortly after, and had made a go of it, you had to give them credit for that. Roger and Archie Cloud had helped, then moved on. Now there was talk that Roger was going to return for special weekend sweat-lodge sessions for German tourists, like the ones he did out at Roseisle for the men's movement. There was talk that the railroad might start up a once-a-week service to Moon Lake as a kind of nostalgia thing, catered meals in a dining car, live bands playing swing music as they had immediately after the war. Dancing. A bar. People were into that now, reliving the past as long as it was in relative luxury. So there was potential to do even better with the lodge than was already the case.

Mort was happy. Money was rolling in. He had bought a new car.

Still, Alexander felt there was something not quite right about the way they had come into possession of the business. There would always be a shadow hanging over Moon Lake and their marriage, and he sensed that Cassie felt it too. She seemed moody to the point of surliness around him. These were things he could not tell Ruth because they reflected badly on her mother. And Mort had loaned him the seed money on the sporting goods store, so that was another debt. That he could talk about with Ruth. She teased him when he was about to make decisions regarding the SportHuts: "What does your father-in-law think?"

When they approached the cluster of houses just inside the reservation—wood smoke rising from chimneys, steam shimmering on roofs—they turned back and retraced their steps. Cassie would not have ventured that far. The sun was beating down on them. Crows flapped from one tree top to another and squawked at them. A few mosquitoes buzzed about their heads. Except for the occasional shouting of Cassie's name, they walked quietly, feet crunching over the last year's fertile litter on the forest floor. A mole or black mouse scooted across the path. They heard wood frogs and the drumming of grouse in the underbrush. Then a whistle neither of them knew: Virginia, now Vanora, claimed there were snipe and woodcock in the area. Once when they were visiting and he'd gone walking on his own, he had spotted an egret and what he thought was a pair of cormorants. Farther along the path they saw in the grass on the verge the feathers of a large bird in a swirled circular pattern, as if it had taken a rough bath and left all of its protection behind: feathers, down. But it was not that, it was a kill, though there was no evidence of a struggle, no bones, no blood, no carcass. The black tail feathers and wispy grey down of a crow or raven that had been ambushed by a predator.

When he'd first come to Moon Lake Alexander had liked the noisy, scruffy buggers, but before the spring had passed he'd been tempted to take a shotgun to them. They were so irritating. He'd noticed things about the calls, though. In the morning they made a series of five squawks: three followed by a brief gap, and then two more. Toward evening the squawks numbered three or four in one string. When they were flying from treetop to treetop, they called out more than a dozen times. He had intended to look that up at the library but had forgotten. The calls must mean something: mating rituals, warnings?

Ruth pointed at the ball of feathers and asked "What is it?"

"Just a bird."

"It died violently. It scares me."

"It's just a natural thing in the bush."

"It's a sign. Something horrible has happened." She screwed up her lips and then walked on in silence.

"Just a fox," he said, "caught a bird." But he felt troubled too.

They walked a little farther. Ruth said, "Every year people die in the woods. They walk into the bush and never come out again."

Alexander said, "Strangers to an area, maybe. Tourists."

"I can feel it in my bones. A killer on the loose."

He thought that was childish talk but he did not say so.

They stopped by a bush with beautiful white flowers. "Chokecherry," Ruth said, "they would just be coming into bloom." She stopped to finger the blossoms. The hawk swooped over again. He reminded her that the Finn had made wine from the berries, the Finn who now owned a chain of Chicken Delight outlets in the region. He was a man of harder mettle and more ambition than had appeared years ago when Alexander had thought him feminine. More than one of the Chicken Delights was a business he had ruthlessly taken over from ineffective owners. He'd run as the Reform candidate for the district in the last federal election and spoken with disturbing passion about the French language and the rights of

Natives. Sometimes he came into the SportHut in the city on the pretext of buying fishing equipment, but Alexander thought he was mostly just keeping in touch. The fried chicken at his kiosks was crispy and tasty, though Vanora claimed it was pumped full of antibiotics and tenderizers, and Karrin was reported to have said the Finn was a monster with his employees.

They came to a straight stretch. Ruth pointed to a log across the path. "That wasn't there before," she said and looked up at him, wide-eyed.

"I can't say I remember it."

"It was not there."

"I can't recall it, but you know how it is in the woods. The shadows can fool you. And you see things from different angles on the walk back."

"It wasn't there, I tell you."

"It had to be."

She was worked up, so there was no point in disagreeing with her.

They came up to the log and he pushed it gently with the toe of his shoe. Where it rolled away from the ground, several large beetles and a slug could be seen against the dark earth, the beetles scuttling awkwardly away. "See," he said.

"When I was a girl," Ruth said, "I hated coming out here alone. I thought someone was following me."

"The woods make noises. Animals stirring, branches falling."

"Listen," Ruth said. They stood in silence a moment. Alexander's heart raced. Ruth's neck and cheeks were flushed. The breeze rattled leaves in the underbrush, but otherwise they heard nothing. She looked at him and he shrugged.

"*He* used to say the Indians trailed him through the bush. He said they were just waiting for him to drop his guard. Then pounce."

"That's called projection."

"Putting a fancy name to it doesn't change the feeling."

"You're going to excite yourself."

"The woods have eyes, he used to say."

"Come on," Alexander said. "You're going to scare us both." He noticed that sweat was running down his neck. Ruth and her silly talk.

When they were almost back to the lodge he spotted morels just off the path. He wondered if Ruth would think it frivolous to be picking mushrooms when her mother might be lying injured in the woods. Her lips were set in a pout that he found irresistible. It was like the migraine. Instead of making him less interested, they turned him on, these signs of frailty. There was something Victorian about his desire and he felt somewhat uneasy about it, wanting to possess a woman because she was frail and vulnerable. But Ruth did not seem to mind.

In the final minutes of the walk back to the lodge her eyes were focussed down on the path. By the time they got back to the lodge they were hot and disheartened. Vanora and her friend, Karrin, had arrived. He found the words *spouse* and *partner* difficult, and *lover* he had never liked, even for people for whom it was accurate: movie stars and other casual romancers. Vanora and Karrin—as in *car*, not *care*, he had been informed by Ruth—had made coffee and put out cinnamon buns. The smells filled the tiny kitchen where they had all gathered to confer. But no one was very interested in the food. Roger and Ruth and Vanora embraced and tried not to appear too scared. Sergeant Boyd was putting butter on a cinnamon bun and blowing steam off a cup of coffee. The two corporals had taken the dogs down to the lake front. An eerie silence hung about the room. No one said anything about Cassie. Mort was slowly rolling chewing tobacco over in his mouth.

The heating system ticked in the walls. The walls had been painted recently, a greenish yellow, and new curtains hung over the sink. Small crescent-shaped shelves had been added to the exterior of the cupboards over the sink and ceramic mugs sat on these: flower patterns in bright blues and yellows. The smell of coffee permeated the room.

No one knew exactly what they should do next. Victor said search round the other side of the lake. Maybe she had gone bush loco and walked straight by the lodge in the dark without knowing it. What else was there to do? "Our spirits are down," Victor said, "so let's refresh the body." He was the only one taking an interest in the food, but they all chewed away at the cinnamon buns and sipped the dark coffee in silence.

T HE SPIRIT WAS NOT DOWN, the spirit should never be down. She'd wanted to correct the Mountie, but years ago she had been intimidated by him and she found it difficult to speak up. Karrin, she noticed, had rattled the coffee cups when he said that, but she had not said anything, either. It was a matter of doctrine with Karrin: when you're with a new group, you listen but you keep your mouth shut. Vanora could not help but wonder what chain of experiences had informed that view—was Karrin secretly afraid of life?

The kitchen seemed foreign without Cassie bustling about in it. The tea towels had been her choice, mismatched as they were. Someone had recently dusted the plaques with their sentimental inscriptions. At Christmas she and Karrin had sent a wall calendar from one of the catalogues but it was not to be seen. Perhaps Cassie thought the sayings of famous feminists would offend Mort. Her reading glasses had been on the table when they had come in, resting on a copy of Sunday's *Sun*, screaming the headline *Election Scandal*. Vanora had hung the black frame glasses from a peg in the hallway. A whiff of Cassie's lavender scent had come off them and onto her fingers.

She whispered in a half-voice *mother*, knowing that Cassie might hear and awake from whatever funk had closed over her out in the woods the night previous. She had that power now, Vanora did, everyone said so.

She had been feeling light-headed and thought it was from the early morning meditation and the drive up to Moon Lake. But she sat suddenly at one of the kitchen tables and she knew then what it was. Fear. A terror in her bowels like what she had felt out on the path that night years ago. Yes, that same paralytic fear. She took in a deep breath and hoped Karrin was aware of her need.

Mortimer had left his baseball cap on the table, the kind with a logo on the front and a plastic mesh backing. Yellow sweat stains on the headband. She and Ruth had bought him a Tilley hat several birthdays back, but he would not wear that, would he? It hung on a peg near the door, as pristine as when it came out of the package. He was common, Mortimer, a small man spiritually, despite his once impressive physical bearing. She did not like him, that she knew. Though he was good to Cassie, and good for Cassie, who needed steadying. But he had a weaselly little mouth and he was mean. Yes, that was it. He had put Roger to work in the trading post the summer after the LaFlamme business, but at the end of August had offered the boy a single twenty-dollar bill for his troubles. *Tightness with money*, Karrin said, *is a spiritual weakness*. And he voted conservative; a character defect, Karrin claimed.

She had begun bustling about in the room as soon as they arrived. It was musty and smelled of old clothing. She opened a window and the door that opened toward the lake. A light breeze blew through, cool but not chilling. Karrin had picked up the dirty plates and cups from the table and put them in the sink. She'd found the washcloth and wiped the surface of the table and then the counter top. Was she nervous? Meeting people was difficult for her, she'd once confided to Vanora. She bit her lower lip, she developed constipation. But there was a tremendous reserve of energy in her young body. She went to Shapes twice a week and had a sleek bicycle set up on a wind trainer in the basement. Maybe it was just that: she had built up too much energy on the drive and had nowhere to focus it now that they were on the scene and everyone else was tensely silent. Or maybe death frightened Karrin more than she dared to admit.

"I'm not going to be a fat cat," Karrin had told Vanora. She was thinking of the greying men in the college faculty who sat around at Monty's drinking beer and railing against the excesses of capitalism, most of which the managers of their pension fund were taking excellent advantage of on their behalf. Karrin despised them. She called them the clowns: *i pagliaccios*. At meetings she voted against them just to watch them squirm.

She had written a thesis on the language of exploitation in governmental circulars, something so complicated that even when she explained it, Vanora did not understand, though she pretended to. Now that she had tenure, Karrin was working on a book that exposed the American Medical Association. She spent hours on the couch poring over the texts of medical journals while sipping tea. She held a purple-inked pen in one hand. From time to time she shouted, "Aha!" and underlined something Vanora had made fun of sociology before meeting her, but she no longer quoted W.H. Auden on that score: above all, do not commit a social science. It seemed to her that Karrin was comfortable with her place in the world, and that she understood it.

Vanora had had some of the coffee Karrin had put in front of her and was feeling somewhat more at ease. The fear that had washed over her minutes earlier was ebbing from her body. Her breathing had returned to normal. Voices did not sound like mechanical recordings. But she needed air, she needed wedges of bracing oxygen in her lungs.

Outside the sparrows were swirling in little flocks, pecking in the grass and then suddenly alighting into the dogwoods that grew near the steps. Milkweed grew thickly in the plot under the big window fronting the store. When she was a child it had grown in profusion near the abandoned railroad station. Monarch butterflies had hovered around the station in their mating season.

They were standing at the bottom of the stairs, she and Karrin on one side of Sergeant Boyd and his two corporals; Roger, Ruth, and Alexander on the other. The two kids who worked as guides were standing somewhat off with the Natives on the gravel of the parking lot, deferring to the family. Mort came down the steps. He was wearing a toque. He had been in the bathroom and must have wiped his face with paper: tiny flecks of tissue stuck to the bristles of his beard. He had not slept all night. He had not shaved. His eyes were red-rimmed. He was holding the cane crossways in both hands and looked like a tightrope walker who was about to fall. Vanora felt he was putting on a show for them with his cane, and a surge of resentment like the current from a battery went through her body, and she knew she would have to watch what she said.

"I guess we should get going," Mort said.

The Mountie asked, "The deer meadow is not possible?" He looked out in that direction, past what was now the soybean field. Vanora remembered when Mort and the Finn had done the breaking and clearing.

"No, no fiddleheads that way," Mort said.

"Maybe...," the Mountie started.

Ruth put one hand on Mort's shoulder. "Maybe she wasn't out for that."

"I was here," Mort said, his voice changing rapidly from wheedling to obstinate. "She took the ice cream pail."

"No," Ruth insisted. "You don't follow."

"No, no. She took the ice cream pail. If it was mushrooms she went out for, she had a special wicker basket. That's still here."

"Maybe she was angry," Ruth said pointedly.

"Maybe," Vanora chimed in, "she was depressed." The voice was hers but she hardly recognized it; it was the voice of exasperation she had been forcing back.

"That's ridiculous," Mort said. He clamped shut his thin lips. Vanora recalled that when they all lived together he'd slurped his soup and tea and that Ruth had laughed at him behind his back and called him Velcro lips.

"She had moods," Ruth said. "We know that. *Blacks*, she called them."

"You know nothing. Nothing."

"She was our mother," Vanora said, taking Ruth's side and making it obvious.

"You. You never even came to visit. At least that one—"

"Don't try to turn us against each other," Ruth said.

"I was here. I've always been here."

"Yes," Ruth said, "standing right beside the cash register."

Mortimer's jaw fell open. "You little minx," he said. "Cassie let you smart-mouth her that way, but not me."

"No, you're the tough guy."

"Spoiled brats who look down their noses at ordinary folk. She should have taken you in hand. She should have nipped that in the bud."

"The three of us are a family," Ruth hissed, "whatever you might—"

Alexander interrupted Ruth, tugging on her arm. "Don't excite yourself."

"Tell him to stop that then. Insinuations."

"You think you're better than me," Mort muttered, "because you went to college."

"We are. We're—"

"Stop," Alexander said loudly.

"We're wasting time," Mort said sharply.

"We're trying to help," Ruth answered. "She suffered from depression. It was that, not picking fiddleheads." Alexander tugged her arm again.

"Reading motives into our life," Mort said. "Criticizing."

"She was down. She could have wandered anywhere."

"We're not city folk who waste their good money going to

psychiatrists and whatnot. Telling other folks what their dreams mean and other such nonsense."

"Maybe you should." It was sharply said and slipped out, and Vanora regretted it instantly. Ruth gave her a look of one kind and Karrin a different kind and Mort spat tobacco juice into the grass at his feet.

"All right," the Mountie said. "This *is* wasting time."

"Anyway," Mort said, "I found some fiddleheads near the junction of the path that used to cross over to Cuthand's and the lake path."

"So did we," Alexander said. "A whole field of them."

"*Picked* fiddleheads," Mort said. "They must have fallen from her pail."

There was silence. They expected Mortimer to say more but he didn't. He was biting back his anger, though they could see it in his face: flushed cheeks, jaw trembling. Vanora felt that way herself: hot and edgy. Ruth took Alexander's hand in hers. The Mountie lifted his cap off his head and scratched his balding scalp. He was eating poorly, Vanora decided; he had a distracted look to his eye. Had he had the experience? If he had, he would not have told anyone, not even that absurd wife. He might have discovered the liberated soul and maybe was looking to have the experience again. With her help he could get back there again, as she had: Vanessa, Leonora, her previous selves, her soul sisters.

"All right," the Mountie repeated, and his voice fell into silence. The tension that had flared up died as suddenly as it began. "We'll wait a few minutes for Archie and the others. Then we'll find the corporals and fan through the woods going up the south side of the lake."

She wondered how many times he had led search parties like this that came to nothing. Probably that was what happened most of the time. Was he just going through the motions? She wondered if he really cared.

She was wishing they would find Cassie but for a different reason than the rest of the search party. She thought maybe Cassie had had the experience. That would bring them closer together, mother and daughter, but more than that, it would bring Cassie and Karrin together. The OBE did that.

Five years ago she had been teaching at the girls' school in the city centre, doing the baccalaureate English program. She was overworked and stressed out. The man was Harold. She thought she was happy. They lived in the Wolesley area and she walked to the IGA on the corner with the church to get groceries. One afternoon she'd just crossed the street on the way back and was looking up at the church spire, when it happened. She heard ringing in her ears, and as she turned to see what was making the sound, she felt herself falling, but as in a dream, as if she were watching her own body fall while standing outside it. Then there were bright lights all around, intense, so that she had to blink her eyes and then shut them. The ringing went away but she felt herself drifting up, only she was looking down on her body which was lying on the sidewalk. A kind of sadness came over her, but then as she kept drifting upwards, she experienced a deep peace within. It did not matter that she had left her body behind, wearing the red jacket and designer jeans. She was floating and saw below her not the city but expansive green fields, the roofs of farm buildings, and the spires of churches. When she came down she was standing next to a wood frame house. Pigs grunted somewhere. Chickens pecked at the gravel near her feet. A man and a woman were throwing grain into a pen for geese. She walked over to watch them but they did not seem to notice her. She was wearing the same kind of clothing as they were: heavy shoes, a turn-of-the-century bonnet. Her name was Vanessa, she knew that somehow. After a while the man and the woman went into the house and she stood beside the pen looking at the geese. She felt a kind of sadness. Another sound was pressing itself on her awareness. It was a blipping sound. She opened her eyes and discovered she was in a room in a hospital. The nurses said she had suffered a mild heart attack. She was at peace with herself. She did not want the sterile hospital room. She wanted to return to the farm and the person she was there: Vanessa, who wore a bonnet and leaned on a wooden fence rail and felt at home in the world.

 She recovered from the heart attack, which the doctors told her was a freak thing—there was no evidence it would occur again—and went home. But nothing was ever the same again. She had to tell someone. And she wanted the experience again.

 When she told Harold he laughed, and when she took books out of the library and then got in contact with Libby, he said, you're going weird on me, don't go weird on me, babe. Libby said it was an out-of-body experience, a foretaste of death that was really a return to lives she had lived previously. Libby understood immediately. Libby was a wonderfully soft person. She made green tea and they sat on her couch and talked for hours. Libby was from a Celtic background and she wore a pewter medallion around her neck: the cross of Malleach Mhor. She had made a spiritual quest to a sacred island off Scotland. She told Vanora these things in a hushed and breathless voice that implied they were sharing a secret. Libby's hands were large and warm. She covered Vanora's with hers as they talked about spiritual journeys. Her bright blue eyes grew round when she told Vanora about the voices she'd heard while standing in a rock cairn on the island near Scotland. Libby took as given the things that Vanora had been ashamed to tell anyone before. When she put her soft hand over Vanora's and pressed flesh to flesh it was an invitation to a secret society. Libby told her about a shaman she knew and about sacred places and told her not to fear what had happened to her. They drank tea and went on long walks. Then she started channelling with Libby's group. She learned how to go back to the farm in Vermont and then travelled forward in time to Highcliffe Castle where she was Leonora and had servants and a husband who beat her and from whom she escaped in a cart one night with a lover. She stopped making the meals for six o'clock sharp and started drinking herbal tea. A year or more passed. She was away from the house for longer and longer periods. Channelling, taking long walks down by the river. She bought meditation music and listened to tapes while she sat on the couch staring blankly out of the windows. Squirrels played in the trees; she had never noticed them before. The sun came in from the south and warmed her legs. Harold seemed to be watching her. When she told Harold she wanted to visit Emerald Lake with Libby on a spiritual quest, he hit her in the face with the flat of his hand and then he informed her that he was leaving.

 At Emerald Lake a deep peace came over her. She slept with Libby but that was less important than the spiritual transformation she had undergone, a kind of baptism in the clear waters of Emerald Lake. She felt at ease with herself. She slept better.

 After Emerald Lake she went to the class in meditation at the university. A couple of years had passed since the OBE. She met Karrin, who rode a bicycle to and from the university in those days and had tufts of orange dyed into her close-cropped hair. They meditated together for a year. Karrin bought her a pair of hiking boots and they trekked in the Pembina Hills and had picnics with red wine and panini. They made banana bread and their own teas. Karrin told her about the cancer and she told Karrin about the OBE. They did not laugh at each other's stories. They had looked death in the face and come through on the other side, knowing something most people did not. Death was the spirit's avenue to growth. Death was a door.

Perhaps Cassie had experienced a similar thing in the woods in the night. Now maybe Cassie would be her friend as well as her mother.

He had told her about what had happened on the road back from Lac du Bonnet that time. But not at first. He had waited a couple of years after she came back from the psych ward when she'd returned to normal and they had made the adoption of Theresa formal. He described the golden ball as well as he could and tried to explain the hold it had over him. He told her he had read books but he still did not know how to name the thing. Her response was not what he had expected, although he had expected objections. The books warned about that. "I don't want anything to do with other realities," she said flatly.

They were sitting out on the lawn chairs watching the sun set. He drank beer from cans then but she was into fruit juices. "This reality is difficult enough for me to get around in," she said. "It's like a field with giant craters in it, the kind you see in pictures of the Great War. I do not want to stumble and fall into a deep crater and find that I have dropped into another place suddenly with no bearings."

He told her she didn't understand. He told her that the experience had bewildered him at first, but then how he had come to see that there was more to this reality than he'd once believed. (Death, he ventured to say, was merely a parenthesis around life.)

"You're not going to make a speech about inner peace," she said ironically.

"No. I'm not a head case." The out-of-body experience hadn't changed much, he admitted that. He still got angry over minor things; still suffered from ulcer in his guts.

She told him that he was the one who did not understand. "This reality," she said, "is a foreign reality, all of it. We are dropped into it as strangers, flail about a certain number of years believing we're in control, and leave not knowing exactly what it is that happened to us." She talked that way now: like a book. "I don't mean just the big things—birth, death, fornication, and so on. I mean all the ordinary stuff, the everyday stuff. Think of how the trees know when to shed leaves, think about all the tiny creatures creeping about the earth and hiding under rocks, creatures that have their special defense mechanisms. How did porcupines develop quills? How did skunks learn that particular way of warding off enemies?"

"The dodo died of stupidity."

"What I'm saying is they belong here more than we do. We humans."

"We've done okay. We've got the big brain."

"Thirty thousand years of history, what's that?"

He put his Bud down with a slight look of distaste and not only because it had become warm in the can. Bread and beer, they went right to the butt—and the gut. Yeasts, Sheila claimed. He was going to give up the beer. "We've got the opposable thumb," he said.

"This is their reality, not ours. The dinosaurs lived for millions of years, and the cockroaches will be here long after the last human being blows away as dust. What is a paltry thirty thousand years compare to a hundred million? We don't even notice them, but they are the reality. Thousands, no millions of worms digging their way through this lawn alone. If you had the right seismograph, you could feel the ground trembling with their efforts."

She still had the tendency to become morbid. But the doctors had told him not to resist, to go with the flow, that it would burn itself out now. And they were right. Once the adoption had taken place, she was on top of things. Theresa absorbed her enormous nervous energy like an emotional sponge. Sheila was fragile when it came to that one issue, the way she had run off on him before, but otherwise strong. The failure was in him, he realized. He was too impatient, so he had to intervene. He wanted too much to protect her from herself.

"You look death in the face every day," she said to him. "Is it pretty?"

"Not every day."

"People say they want to look death in the face. They're wrong."

"They want to be strong and they imagine that will do it."

"The trick for us humans is to look life in the face. To get up every day and embrace the simple, fantastic fact that we are here."

"Something which is easier said than done."

"You have to work at it."

"You have to believe in it. And I don't."

"What's to believe in? You cultivate the senses. Smell the flowers, listen to the birds, take the time to rub a dog's nose. The eastern mystics say *this is it*. Embrace the here and now."

"That may sound goofy to most people. Self-indulgent."

"Then most people are fools. In less than a hundred years each one of us is food for those worms. No, I want to look life in the face. When I die that will be enough to have accomplished."

McNair had said something similar to him once. They were at the scene of a road accident, two teenagers dead under a pickup. There was blood all over and they found one of the kid's arms fifty metres away. McNair had said he had seen enough of death. "This is the doctor's life," he'd said, "presiding over death."

"It's a meaningful moment," Victor said. "Like birth. Doctors get to preside over the meaningful moments in people's lives. A cop presides over stupidity."

They were fishing and drinking whiskey in a boat. They laughed at that.

McNair said he wished he could spend the remainder of his life in obstetrics. He and Yvette had raised three boys who'd all moved to the city: the Pig, the Joker and the Quack, they called themselves. The one who became a doctor was the same age as Terry. Victor and McNair had stood on the sides of soccer pitches and skating rinks, growing grey together and planning increasingly less frequent fishing expeditions. McNair still acted as the medical examiner for the area. If something had happened to Cassie, he would be the one to perform the official examination. It was all wearyingly familiar.

It was the sudden scream of a blue jay that brought him back to Moon Lake and Cassie Mann.

Victor did not realize everyone was waiting for him to say something.

He was having trouble concentrating that morning. Maybe it was the bad night's sleep he'd had: a nightmare about Terry. And then earlier when he was walking through the woods calling Cassie's name, he'd felt the way he often did now in the woods: as if someone or something was watching him. He was getting too old for this job. Sheila was right about that. Take the early retirement. Only she wanted to move to the west coast and start up a gardening business. He was prepared to retire except he did not want to live in Vancouver. He loved the sun on the prairies and became depressed when the sky was overcast as it was for months at a time on the west coast. It was her opinion that they would grow to love the seaside climate.

She spoke about the prairie climate with a kind of irony. And that angered him. She talked a lot of nonsense about health and exercise, and he listened patiently because she needed reassurance, but when he said something positive about the place where they had grown up, their home, she made jokes and became ironic. He couldn't stand her irony. It was an affectation she'd acquired in college and had refined into a weapon, a defense mechanism. He wanted to give her a good shake, which, of course, he didn't, but he often retreated into a kind of stony silence.

He wondered, stupidly, what Sheila would be cooking for supper that night. Lately she'd been doing oriental things: lots of rice and vegetables. His thoughts were wandering but he brought his focus back and asked Alexander to repeat the question he had directed at him.

"What about the path that ran back toward the abandoned station?"

Before answering, Victor patted his hip reflexively. Cinnamon buns. Bread and sugar. He was going to give up all these yeast things.

Mort answered for him. "Thick with poison oak."

Ruth asked, "What if she became confused?"

"She'd never go that way," Mort insisted.

Victor looked from one to the other and saw they were waiting on him, deferential. He'd only realized in the past few years that people were afraid of him. He'd thought it was respect for the RCMP, but Sheila had used the word *intimidating* to describe him.

They were standing a little off from the stairs that led into the main building. The flag on the pole was limp. It had a cement base that looked sturdy and the pole had been recently painted bright white. He recalled how Ruth had come out of the store and ripped the pole out of the ground years ago. (It had stirred Alexander Mann sexually but Victor had seen in her action passion; it showed she was capable of murder.)

She took up the issue, persisting where Alexander did not. If Cassie had become turned around in the dark, Ruth said, she could end up anywhere.

Mort said, "I know her," his voice rising on the middle word. There were tensions among that family that twenty-five years had not diminished.

"All right," he said, trying to sound decisive, "we'll join the corporals and fan up along the far side of the lake."

So they set off on the gravelled path that ran between the lodge and the bunkhouse, where the kids who acted as fishing guides slept now. It looked pretty much as it had years ago, except that it too was painted bright white with trim in hunter green.

Suddenly she knew. She'd been listening to the birds in the trees, to the rumble of Alexander and Roger talking behind them as they walked slowly across the lawn in front of the lodge toward the lake. There was a breeze coming off the lake and she felt her nose turning cold, and probably red. She'd been thinking about that, about how the air was cooler at Moon Lake than in the city, how the woods held the snow in spring long after the melt on the plains, when suddenly she knew. Dead. They would not find Cassie alive. She'd been suppressing the knowledge and it came to her the way such thoughts come in dreams, with stunning clarity. She woke sometimes with a start, thinking *something has happened to Ruth, or to Roger*, convinced that one of them had died at that instant and that she had received some sort of psychic vibration. Only in those instances a terrible thing had not occurred and she felt like a fool after some time passed, but now the knowledge came to her and she knew it for a fact. Dead. She paused. Karrin was walking beside her and paused too. Vanora put one hand over her abdomen; she knew. She felt the sickness rising in her guts and she recalled abruptly the Labour Day weekend long ago when she'd stumbled into the water at Moose Point, sick with the knowledge of death. She felt the same way. Only it was Cassie this time. She would have Karrin and only Karrin now, and that frightened her and also freed her in a way that was as puzzling as it was enticing.

O NE OF THE CORPORALS WAS WALKING swiftly through the woods in their direction, head down, unaware at first that the group was crossing the grass toward him. When he spotted them, he slowed his pace and Sergeant Boyd stepped forward from the group as if on signal, moving quicker than Alexander anticipated he could. He met the corporal ten metres ahead of them where the lawn sloped down toward the rocks and the lakefront. They spoke with their heads down for a moment. The group had slowed their pace. Alexander felt Ruth's fingers tighten on his and his chest tightened. Vanora murmured something to Karrin. In the silence he heard the hawk screech again, and when he looked up he saw it this time, drifting above the treetops along the east side of the lake, a vee like a child's drawing of a bird on the wing.

The corporal wheeled and strode off in the direction he had come from. When the group came up to Victor, he said to them, "Just wait here a moment." He followed the corporal over the rocks toward the water, moving quickly.

They looked at each other and then away. The birds were making a racket in the trees. It was mating season, Roger said. They were building nests. Soon the frenzy and breathtaking abundance of the summer. Then they heard a beautiful whistling coming from near the lodge. "Meadowlark," Roger said. One arrived every spring and stayed a few weeks before moving on. It was not their habitat, the Shield, but this one had taken a liking to the place. Or maybe it was just instinct. Once it had stopped the first time, it had to follow that route every year. Its descendants would too. Roger blinked as he talked, the only visible residue from the beatings he'd endured as a child. He seemed happy to share his knowledge about nature. The ponytail looked good on him. Long salt and pepper hair, like Vanora's; it was thick and with his high cheekbones and dark eyes made him look wise. He wore a thick checked shirt and had an amber pendant hanging from a leather thong around his neck. His face was deeply tanned. Ruth had told him Roger had an outdoor job of some kind but he could not recall what he did.

Whatever, things had worked out for him, despite the fact that he could seem a bit simple at times, and Alexander was happy for him. As a teen Roger had seemed lost almost to the point of being desperate. That business with LaFlamme had hurt him more than the others. He was not that much older than Peter, and Alexander had developed a soft spot for him on that account and others. He cared about his sisters. He made a point of calling Cassie on the phone each Sunday, Ruth told him. Cassie wanted him to take over the lodge some day. It seemed a likely outcome: it was work he could handle and it would keep the business in the family. Neither of the girls was interested.

After his stint as a fishing guide at Moon Lake, Roger did maintenance work for the city and had become involved in the men's movement. He spent a year in Kansas and when he came back he bought a piece of land on the river near Roseisle and built a house out of logs. Alexander and Ruth visited him. It was a simple but beautiful house, in tune with Roger's life. Two other men lived there but it was not a homosexual thing. They organized sweat lodges on the property and other outdoor activities, like canoeing on the river that ran through the valley where he'd built the log house. Men from the city came for the weekend. Roger was called The Wild Man. He was a kind of leader who helped citified men get in touch with another part of themselves, the dark underside, Roger called it. They smeared soot on their faces and beat drums and chanted and did other things Alexander could not recall. According to Ruth, Roger helped the men find the male buried deep inside themselves after centuries of suppression and middle-class compromise. They chewed on hardtack and pemmican and drank a strong home brew and had visions and told each other the stories of their dreams. Alexander thought it was a lot of nonsense.

Roger had theories about things. On one occasion when they'd visited him at Roseisle he'd taken them for a walk along the river. It was a summer day, mosquitoes and big blue flies. Roger pointed to the river. Two girls drowned here, he said, in the fifties. They were on a summer holiday. Sisters who were in grade school. Their canoe capsized. The parents were devastated. But the woman who had the place across the river made them whole again. Roger pointed to the roof of a house in the distance. Mrs. Geary. She made the parents promise to come back in a month and when they did, she made them immerse themselves in the river. Not so kooky as you might think, Roger told them. The river has been here how many thousands of years? The parents were reluctant but Mrs. Geary insisted and after they'd immersed themselves she made them promise to come back in a week and do the same thing again, week after week. Places, Roger said, have auras; they heal. By the end of the summer, the parents bought a piece of land on the river, and built a wooden log house there the following spring. The land heals, Roger said. The water regenerates the human spirit. At the time Alexander thought he was talking as much about the waters of Moon Lake as those of the Roseisle River.

He was interested in what Roger said about the meadowlark. They had heard a woodpecker earlier and he wondered if it was the grandchild of the woodpecker that had banged on the tin flange of the roof years earlier when he was painting and Peter was carrying water up to the deer meadow. It seemed absurd to be thinking such thoughts at that moment. It must have seemed odd to all of them to be doing nothing at the moment of crisis, because the group edged forward and was at the place where the lawn gave way to the stones. They were slightly to the south of where Peter and the Finn had fished off the twin rocks years ago. The area had been cleared for the landing of boats, and farther up the shore in the shelter of the trees there were orange and blue tarpaulins thrown over objects, gas cans and spare motors and so on, Alexander guessed.

The Mounties were farther along the cleared area toward the southernmost edge of the clearing. The shore was rocky there too, but red-barked willows grew in thick stands that hung over the water. Red-winged blackbirds alighted on their thin branches. The Mounties were in the water up to their knees. They were stooped over a body.

When he arrived, the corporals rolled the body over. Victor had seen this face before: the skin pale almost to the point of green, the eyes staring blankly upward even though they did not see. The hair was fanned out in the slightly susurrating water, but then after the disturbance of the water subsided, the hair formed a tight helmet round the skull. Light from the sky played over the features, which shifted in hue as the body bobbed in the shadows of the willows: blue giving way to a dirty pale, like weathered white paint. Sutton pointed out what he had already noticed: a large indentation above one eye that extended sideways into the temple. A bruise that was purple at the centre and red at the edges was developing around it. Once out of the freezing spring water, it would swell to the size of a baseball. There were scrapes on the cheeks and the chin, scratch marks. She had fallen, he guessed, on the rocks and struck her head and drowned. He did not want to consider the other alternative, but he made a mental note: have McNair examine the back of the skull. He nodded at the corporals and stepped back. The water was so cold his toes felt to be burning.

A lump had formed in his throat. He swallowed it down.

Victor stepped back over the rocks, being careful not to slip. Sutton and the young corporal had positioned themselves to lift the body and were stirring up the water with their efforts. He glanced quickly at the willows: no clothes snagged on the branches or evidence of an object that might have been used to strike a blow. Farther down, though, a plastic pail bobbed in the water. He could not tell if it had once contained fiddleheads. One of the corporals would have to retrieve it. His feet were damn cold. One shin ached all the way up to the knee. He could not get away from there quickly enough.

When the corporals brought the body out of the water and onto the rocks, the group behind him moved forward. Vanora uttered a cry and fell to her knees, reaching out to the face. "It's not her," she cried, "that's not my mother." He did not want to look. Mortimer had doubled up as if struck by a blow to the stomach, and he seemed to be making noises, so Victor stepped over beside him, at the ready. Ruth dropped her head. She was weeping and holding tight to the arm of her husband. In a thin, high voice that unnerved and perturbed Victor, Vanora was saying over and over, "That's not her, that's not her." Her hand rested on the shoulder of the soggy sweater that was draped around the body and dripping water onto the rocks now that it was out of the water. The woman who had come with her knelt beside her, stroking the back of her neck. The gravel crunched under their knees as they swayed in rhythm to her keening. Vanora's voice was shrill and came in gasps. Roger seemed to be as upset by it as Mortimer was. His face had gone pale; he breathed deeply; tears coursed down his cheeks. He was looking at his feet, or maybe at Cassie's.

Victor looked down, and when he raised his head, he felt dizzy. He looked from one face to another. They all seemed to be strangers.

Even as her chest heaved with the sobs, she was conscious of her torso bent to the ground and she was not thinking *not my mother*, which was what her mouth was saying, she was thinking *this time it's me, it's me on my knees this time*.

The point was Karrin was young. They had fought one night. Karrin had spent the afternoon making timballo and was worked up from the hot effort in the kitchen and also exhilarated and pumped up with adrenaline. They had started in on the wine early. And then after the marvellous timballo, they got into an argument. It was about Karen Horney, whom Vanora believed had some good things to say but whom Karrin called a psycho-bag, a Freudian enslaver of the feminine, which was worse than the men, who at least were obviously the enemy. *The enemy!* She lashed back. *Childish thinking.* Karrin called her a menace. *Menace!* They should never drink wine and then disagree, and about such a silly thing, not even a personal thing. Vanora could hurt with her words, it was her power. *Spoiled child of the idle wealthy*, she spat out, reminding Karrin of her architect father and dentist mother and the summer trips every summer to Cornwall. It was Karrin's weak spot, and it was vile of Vanora to go after it. Tears came to Karrin's green eyes but Vanora did not stop the flow of angry words. She was the better arguer, which did not mean she was right; only that she was more skillful with words, only that she was more able to deliver pain, even as she cursed herself for it.

Karrin threw down her napkin and ran into the bathroom, and banged the door shut.

Vanora sat at the table a few moments, collecting her thoughts. Wine. It muddled her brains. She heard sounds coming from the bathroom. She pushed the door open. Karrin was down on her knees, banging her forehead on the floor. Vanora wanted to shout: *Stop!* Stop this childishness. But Karrin was in a trance. She kept striking her forehead on the floor. The skin above her eyes broke. Blood trickled past the corners of her eyes and dropped onto the floor. Vanora put her hand on Karrin's shoulder and felt the muscles tense and rigid under her hand. Karrin winced; she was cold but her breathing was hard and hot and noisy. Rasping, because Karrin had weak lungs. Karrin pushed her hand away. *Go*, she cried out.

But Vanora did not leave. She sat on the edge of the tub. Karrin banged her forehead on the floor and began moaning, a sound that was more choking than sighing. Vanora wanted to put her hands on her but that was just the wrong thing, the thing that Karrin hated most. A horrible conundrum, she called it. The men who had forced her and then beat her had put their hands on her, and the ones who came later, the college boys, had condescended to her. Karrin hated them all, all men. So Vanora sat on the edge of the tub and studied the linoleum on which Karrin was striking her forehead every few seconds: a pattern of black and red diamonds on a white background, now dotted with spots of Karrin's blood. After a while Vanora got up and left the room. Her own breathing was not normal. She sat at the kitchen table. That did not stop the thumping in the bathroom. It seemed louder than when she had been in the room and she could hear moaning too, and sobbing. Karrin liked to cry: cleanses the soul, she claimed. She screamed too, sometimes, and beart the pillows with both fists. She'd said one time I have to kill the pain or it kills me. Vanora did not understand that; she did not understand many things about Karrin, who at first she'd thought was a bit of a cliche. Vanora pushed away her plate and put her head on the cool surface of the wooden table top. She wept.

He had an arm around Ruth's waist and was holding her up as they walked across the rocks and up the slope of the lawn. She wanted to get away from there, from it, and from her sister's wailing. But she stumbled after a few steps and he saw that her face had gone completely white. A clicking sound was coming from her throat. His arm around her waist supported her trembling body, though it was awkward walking that way. The grass was wet, and when they reached it, the mud on the path circling the lodge, slick.

Behind them the dogs were whimpering. They had stood unmoving on the ends of their leashes when the Mounties brought the body up from the water. Sniffing the air and twitching their heads this way and that. Vanora was still weeping behind them, though the sounds were barely audible. The others had remained in a clutch near the body.

Ruth suddenly said, "She meant it was not *like* her." And when he did not answer, she continued, "Ginny meant it was not like her to go out on her own like that." She'd stopped walking and wiped first her eyes and then her mouth with the sleeve of her coat.

Alexander wondered how Vanora would react to being called Ginny, but what he said was, "Mort said she went out all the time."

"She was afraid of him."

"Cassie was afraid of no one, least of all Mort."

"She told me."

"She meant something different. She said she was afraid *for* him."

"He was not the man she had married."

"Age. It corrupts the hormones as well as the organs."

"Not that. He'd become secretive."

"He went to see a lawyer, that's all." They were walking again, separate now. "He went to discuss estate stuff."

"He was trying to wheedle the lodge out of her hands. Out of our hands."

"Exactly the opposite. He was making sure it went to you, despite his legal right as husband."

"He was visiting lawyers as if he was planning something. Plotting behind our backs."

"It was her."

"He scared her."

"Not him, something else. And that scared him."

"He's your brother. You're protecting him."

They'd come up to the pines that bordered the lodge. Birds twittered in the branches. He smelled the rich decay of leaf mould. A tiny black mole darted across the path suddenly. It disappeared under a pile of sticks at the base of a pine. When they got to where the path curved to circle the lodge he put his hand on her elbow but she shook it off wordlessly. A crow was croaking in the trees. He looked up. It was sitting at the topmost height of the tallest pine, swaying the thin branch. They were marvellous creatures, he thought: prehistoric, their beady eyes frightening.

"Mort's sneaky," Ruth said. "When I was a girl he gave me the creeps. I had a feeling he followed me into the woods one day." He wanted to protest, but recalled how Mort had talked him into shadowing the old man into town that time, skulking behind cars parked on Main Street so they could spy on him. So he did not say anything. He fumbled for her arm again.

"She suspected him."

"Why would she be suspicious of Mort?"

"You figure it out."

She went on like this now sometimes, watched the late news and saw conspiracies at city hall and in Ottawa. The multinationals. It was his job to calm her. He talked reason to her but what worked best was gifts: he brought home gifts in bright-coloured wrapping. She liked getting things from J. Crew and Land's End. The closets were full of jackets and fleece wear. She didn't really dislike Mort, she just had to find blame, and this time Mort was the handy person to point the finger at. Another day it would be Peter. Or himself.

She was impulsive and could turn violent. He remembered how she had come out of the trading post and pulled down the old flagpole. That was twenty-five years ago, around the time that LaFlamme, whom he'd never met, had been killed. Now Cassie was dead. For a beautiful place, Moon Lake was a dark one.

"He's sneaky, your brother," she repeated. "He gets what he wants."

He grunted. It was better not to say anything that could be contradicted. All that did was add fuel to the fire. Besides, he felt a headache starting at the base of his skull. Up too early, worrying about the stores. Stress. Maybe there was Tylenol in the kitchen. He'd sit her down and fix a cup of tea and she'd be calm by the time Mort and the others came up to the lodge. He took a deep breath. The smell of decaying leaf mould bothered him.

They walked around the lodge and up the stairs and into the building. She was weeping now, quietly, and soon she would regain her composure.

Leaf mould and sewage. The smells came back to him. Autumn a number of years ago. The pathway through the park near the hospital where they walked that day.

In the first few years they were together they'd talked about having a child. Five years, Ruth insisted. Her career. By then the SportHuts would be on a sound financial footing. So they waited, using the pill, and in the seventh year found themselves in a cubicle of the obstetrics ward of the hospital—examination table, weigh scales, two chairs, a curtain, antiseptic odours.

"You bastard," Ruth screamed at the doctor. "You lied to me, you told me it would work." He was a man in his sixties, white hair, glasses and when she screamed, he stepped backward. His colleague, a woman, came into the room just then. "Bitch," Ruth screamed.

The woman doctor said, "We told you the odds were eighty per cent in your favour." She had come directly from obstetrics. She wore a rubber apron smeared with blood and was wearing Wellingtons. "Eighty is not one hundred."

"Bullshit," Ruth screamed. She slammed one hand on the gurney that stood between her and the doctor. The implements on the gurney jumped and rattled: syringes, examining instruments, gauze, tongue depressors. The doctors looked at each other.

"Easy," the woman doctor started to say.

"Fuck you," Ruth screamed. She suddenly pushed the tray of implements of the gurney and onto the floor, where they clattered noisily across the linoleum.

Alexander was sweating.

Two burly orderlies arrived at the door and looked in, the kind of men who worked out regularly, their T-shirts under their white lab coats indicated. The woman doctor held up one hand, keeping them at bay. Alexander knew it was futile, but he placed one hand on Ruth's shoulder, hoping the warmth of contact would distract her. She brushed his hand away. "Son of a bitch," Ruth screamed, "son of a bitching pack of liars, all of you."

At that the doctors stepped back and two orderlies moved forward. But suddenly Ruth's energy just drained away. She sat heavily in the chair behind her. The nurse who'd been lurking in the doorway for some moments with a syringe jabbed it into the fleshy part of her arm. Ruth's head slumped forward onto her chest. She breathed easy. After a while the doctors went down the corridor, the woman's boots squelching as if she'd just come in from milking cows. In a few minutes Ruth looked up and him and said, "I'm a menace, a fucking hagbag menace."

"No such thing," he said. He put his hands under her elbows and raised her gently, embracing for only a tick of the clock.

"I lose my head sometimes."

"You're entitled."

"I'm going to do myself an injury," she said, weeping into his shoulder. "Myself or someone else in this family."

"Come away from that talk," he said. They wound their way through the hospital corridors and out into the park across from the main entrance.

"Hold me," Ruth murmured, "take care of me." She was weeping copiously and he remembered the smell of her as leaf mould overlaid with a slight pungency of sewage. "I'm a bloody menace," she repeated, "to myself and to everyone around me." And then they walked in silence to the car parked on a nearby street.

T̲HE BODY WAS LYING in what had been her bedroom, now the bedroom of the guest suite in the lodge. It was a good thing, Roger said, that the fishing season had not started yet. No one was about. Once the body had been brought inside, Roger and Karrin had made coffee. Mortimer sat at the table looking at his large creased hands. The Mountie had sat across from him for a while, making notes in a notepad, and then he got up and went outside with the other two and they talked in subdued voices. The dogs were tied by their leashes to the door handle of one squad car. They did not bark. Vanora felt Alexander beside her, sipping coffee. She watched Ruth, who stood leaning against the refrigerator the way she had years ago, biting her lower lip and running one hand back through her hair. She must tint it. Roger had said once that it was she, not Ruth, who would maintain her looks, but he was wrong. Ruth was beautiful; fragile but beautiful. There was a kind of tremor about her body, like an aura. She was probably a bit daft and not just with grief. It would not take much to set her off. But that was, no doubt, unkind. Judgements. She shouldn't make judgements. But she wondered how Ruth felt about Cassie; not now, but when Cassie was still living. They had not talked much in the past few years, she and Ruth. She was occupied with Karrin and Ruth and Alex were busy running their business. They had become mid-life yuppies: travelling, eating at tony restaurants, driving swish cars. She had the feeling that Ruth objected to the channelling—and to Karrin.

Ruth had suppressed what had happened to her at Moon Lake. Which was another way of saying she had not embraced death.

That was not surprising. What had surprised her was how readily the children had. She'd been teaching at the girls' school for a decade when she made the discovery. That ten years had gone well. She was doing the Honours class in grades eleven and twelve. The principal sent her on a course to New York to learn about the AP program. On Parents' Day and Grandparents' Day her classes were jammed; she received high praise. The girls who graduated brought bouquets at the end of the term. She was happy in the way people approaching middle age can be, comfortable with themselves, at the height of their professional competence. Things could have gone on for years that way. She'd travelled to the Lake District at spring break; she had seen Wordsworth's daffodils in a meadow near Ambleside and the tombstone in the churchyard at Grasmere.

She had had the experience, but she did not talk about it at school. To her, dying was a passage, little more, the beginning of a journey and not something to be frightened of. She saw that Death, the event, scared people, and it frightened her, too, the ultimate moment of pain and anguish. But she did not agonize over the steps following the event of dying. For like dying, as opposed to death, they were part of the process of being-in-the-universe. These were not things she talked about with people ordinarily.

But then she made the discovery. Or rather, the girls made one.

The discovery came by accident, as they often do. Every student in the Eleven Honours class had to memorize a long poem and then recite it before the class. A shy girl with big glasses did *The Raven*. Then she said before sitting down, "If I have a girl I'm going to name it Lenore." One of the other girls protested: "That's morbid." The first girl was insistent. "There's nothing after death," she insisted. That sparked a debate that took them to the class bell: what about the soul, and God, and what about reincarnation? Their faces were flushed. After months of plod, the class had come alive. The next day they wanted to know what she thought about death. She had never realized before how fascinated they were by mortality. She talked in generalities, which she hoped would fob them off, but they were persistent. So she suggested they do a project: they were to locate the most interesting statements about death, make posters with illustrations, posters that featured the statements, and she would have the maintenance guys build a display board that, when completed, hung at the front of the room over the blackboard; each day a new poster was displayed.

The project was a great success. The posters were beautiful and brilliant. But that was not enough. Someone suggested they each write an essay on funeral procedures in different cultures. They read them aloud to the class and answered questions. They had heard about Auschwitz but not about Babi Yar. One of the girls researched the massacres and exterminations in the Old Testament. Vanora was aghast. They wanted to go on a field trip to a local cemetery. She hesitated there, taking them into her confidence. The school authorities might think that weird. She would arrange for a walk around a local park that abutted a cemetery; and then they would visit it by seeming accident. When they did, the girls went from headstone to headstone, writing down memorable facts and epitaphs. It was an eye-opening experience, and not just for the girls. The students were astounded by how many girls had died as teenagers. Was it suicide? they wanted to know.

They finished the required course but now the girls had a mission. They wrote journal entries about their own experiences of death—grandparents who had passed away, pets, a classmate struck down crossing a highway. Each of them memorized another poem, a poem about death. She could hardly get them off the subject. One part of her was exultant; they had discovered the great secret of her life. But another part was fearful. This kind of thing plunged teachers into trouble. They developed reputations among their colleagues. She did not want to acquire the nickname "Nevermore." She did not want one of those visits from the principal. But the girls' energy carried her forward: they filled journals with entries and they wrote dozens of their own poems. Many were in the yearbook. Vanora had never been such a successful teacher. She arrived at school each day full of energy. Her colleagues commented on it. Not good, she thought; mustn't give the business away. Colleagues wandered into her classroom and noticed the posters. "The girls have caught millennium fever early," she joked. She did not say that to the girls.

On one occasion they viewed Zefferelli's *Romeo and Juliet* and one girl claimed boldly that the great poets only wrote about two subjects, sex and death. There was some oohing and ahing, which Vanora dismissed by saying the girl had a point. The most clever girl in the class said they were really the same thing, sex and death, seemingly separate events but actually the same act in nature viewed from different angles. Vanora called this muddled thinking but praised the girl for making a daring imaginative leap.

One of the girls asked, "Is sex a trap?"

"A delicious one," she averred, and tried to laugh the question off.

The girls wanted to know: "Is death a trap?"

"Dying is a natural process; a kind of growing down that follows our growing up. Nothing to be afraid of."

"To be welcomed, then?"

She knew the teenage fascination with suicide; had read that seventeen per cent of teens attempted suicide. "Not to be embraced," she stated. "To be taken when it came."

That was the first class. In the year following, the girls in the grade below had caught the fever: they wanted to stage famous death scenes and record them on video tape. Vanora felt giddy with excitement and apprehension. The classes were slipping out of her control, a good thing in one way, but frightening too. She insisted the curriculum come first and was astounded how quickly it could be completed: the required essays poured in; novels were read over weekends. Then it was back to the projects on death and dying. They were fascinated by reincarnation. She knew the inevitable was coming. When they asked her about OBEs, she tried skirting the subject but they sensed duplicity in her answers and forced her to talk about what had happened to her. "I'm embarrassed by the whole thing," she told them, lying. "Please don't tell anyone outside the class." It was insanity to imagine that could happen. She made a mark on the calendar that day.

It took exactly a year less a month. First the principal said to her, "Your girls are skipping through the curriculum again this year." The principal wore her hair in a severe bun. She wore wire-frame glasses. She was not a joker. It was a warning. Then she called Vanora into her office. They were sitting in the Principal's office on either side of her gleaming oak desk. "I've had complaints," she said. Vanora wanted to know: who? Parents. Vanora had been a favourite but she had crossed a line. Vanora wanted to know: how many parents had complained? The principal looked over the tops of her glasses. "Well, only one," she said. That was apparently not the issue. The issue was that the vice-principal claimed it was unseemly, all the focus on death in Vanora's classes. That was it, then, the vice-principal, a former English teacher who had been booted up the administration ladder so Vanora could teach the Honours classes in the top grades. It probably was not a parent who had complained at all. The vice-principal was vindictive.

The principal said, "Take a year off. We'll arrange a sabbatical. Make it an educational thing. Travel in England, walk the country lanes, visit the houses of the famous authors you love so much, come back to the school with a clear head."

She had a clear head; and she did not want a sabbatical; she wanted to continue teaching the girls. The lawyer she contacted said the school's position was not wholly unreasonable. Of course, the lawyer could proceed on an action—they might even prevail—but Vanora was better off taking the sabbatical. By then Vanora was adamant. The core of her existence was in question. She had met Karrin by then and Karrin said: "They want to deny your essence; they are small people who are determined to negate the reality of anything larger than themselves. So you must fight." She talked this way: the professor; she used words like *compromise* and *bourgeois*. Vanora went to the principal's office. She stiffened her back and said in the voice Karrin had used: "I cannot renounce who I am."

"You're a frightened woman with a tendency toward dramatics."

"You are trying to deny the Liberated Soul."

"That gibberish may go over in your classroom but not in this office."

"You and your kind would have been at the right hand of Pontius Pilate."

The principal was not to be baited. "Someone said you were a suspect in the murder of your father. The vice-principal has spent some considerable effort…"

These were insane words. She could hardly believe the principal had uttered them. "That's absurd. It was twenty-five years ago and I was not a suspect."

"Is that where this obsession with death began?"

"It is not an obsession. The girls suggested every project. The whole point is to understand death so as to embrace life. A positive thing."

"Dragging children around cemeteries. It's ridiculous."

"They were looking for epitaphs. Things fascinate them that adults do not want to acknowledge—or that adults try to deny the reality of."

"Death is not a resting place, whatever you may say in your classes."

"Dying is a physical event; Death comes to tell us to reinvent ourselves."

"Nonsense. It frightens the girls."

"It frightens you."

"It has to stop. People talk."

"They call you The Hag. Does that mean you meet secretly with covens when you go on summer vacations? Do you drink goat's blood and whisper 666 to each other? Should the vice-principal hire detectives to check out your grandparents and your obsession with traveling to Romania?"

"I will not mention what they call you—and your girl friend."

"At least there is someone in my life. I am not a dried-up old prune."

"You're becoming irrational."

"And you're telling me the interests of my girls have no validity."

"*Your* girls."

The principal's face had flushed. There was a wooden ruler on her desk and she picked it up and revolved it slowly in her hands. "Little educational validity," she said. "This morbid fascination with death has little educational validity. It's like rap music and video games. Okay, if the students must do it on their own time. But you must stick to the curriculum."

"We've covered the bloody curriculum."

"Skipped quickly through it, you mean."

"You prefer busy work to real thought?"

"I prefer you to be a professional."

Vanora had not realized how much she hated the principal. For years she had heard rumours, which she refused to believe, that the principal laughed at her behind her back because she could not hold a man. So she was only tolerated, it appeared, because she secured such good results with the girls: their AP scores were all in the top quartile. In the end she was offered a severance package on the condition she not reveal to the students why she was retiring. The lawyers drew up the papers. She went to an office in a glass tower downtown and signed. She released the school from further legal action. The girls in the graduating class took her to La Gare for dinner. Bouquets of flowers, poems, tears. At a small reception with teacakes her colleagues pretended to be upset that she was not returning the following term, but secretly, she knew, they were relieved.

"Piss on them," Karrin had said, "you're better shut of that pack of hypocrites."

"Worse. They hurt people. Ruin careers."

"Small-minded cowards, piss on them. Their intentions are good but what is that? The measure is what you do, not how noble your intentions."

This was one of Karrin's theories. Words did not matter—only actions. An odd position for someone who made a living by speaking and writing words. But then, like most, Karrin was a bundle of contradictions: she loved Thai food but refused to eat sushi or sushimi; she was a good researcher, but not a great teacher, according to her student assessments.

Vanora had been a good teacher. It was not something she said to others but teaching the girls had made her life worthwhile. What was she to do?

Karrin said, "Pay off the mortgage with the lump sum severance. You've often talked about doing physio or massage therapy. You have beautiful strong hands. You can be a healer. Heal yourself, heal others."

Karrin was like that: sensible, practical, visionary. Vanora talked to the banker and paid off the mortgage. They burnt the papers over the garbage can, drank too much red wine, poured Cointreau on each other's bellies and licked it off. The massage therapy course took the last three thousand dollars of her severance package. But in six months she was an RMT. Karrin bought her a massage table. In the first year only a few patients came; but then the word spread among the women's groups, and now her appointment book filled up months in advance. She scheduled eight sessions a day, as much as she could physically handle. Her forearms grew strong. She played tapes of new wave music while she worked on backs and shoulders and legs. The women groaned and wept and called her *healer*. At the end of the day she was not a bundle of nerves as she had been most days at the school. Sometimes she wondered why she had ever gone into teaching.

But she had learned a lesson there: most people are timid and frightened mice. They are afraid of ideas and even more important, totally lacking strength of character when challenged by anyone in authority . They will not stand up for a colleague. Karrin said: perfido; no guts. They do not want to know about death, and parents in particular do not want you to talk about it publicly, especially with their children. They want to keep it a secret through a collective act of denial, and they want you to conspire with them in their deceit. *Perfido.*

H<small>E LEFT</small> S<small>UTTON TO TAKE CARE OF THE DOGS</small> and walked down to the lake to make sure he had not overlooked anything when emotions were running high. He saw where their shoes had left smears of mud on the rocks and where clumps of matted leaves had fallen off their soles. He saw two cigarette butts in the rocks, as if someone had stood there smoking and contemplating the lake. When he picked them up, he saw the brand name. He saw fiddleheads floating on the water. The little white pail had been retrieved by Sutton and put in the trunk of the squad car. He looked along the willows and studied the rocks. No blood, no bits of clothing. A clean site. He put his hands on his hips and studied the water, turning his back on the woods. Leaves and twigs floated on the water's surface, dancing in toward the willows, then bobbing back out. At the lake's edge, one season was much like another. With your back to the trees and viewing only the water, you could not tell from the lake or the sky whether it was spring or fall: the same chill air, the same dull grey sky. The willows were not yet in leaf. There was that. In the reflected light something drew his eyes at the water line some metres farther along. He was about to check it out when he heard a crash behind him, like someone stumbling in the undergrowth. He wheeled abruptly, heart pounding in his chest. Only the silent trees. His eyes scanned the underbrush, alert to movements. He stepped over the rocks, back toward where the sound had come from. He put one hand on the butt of his pistol. Then he saw it. The orange tarpaulin had become water-stained and dirty over the years. It covered a forty-five gallon oil drum and a stack of cedar slats. On top of the tarpaulin lay a dead tree branch, teetering this way and that. It had fallen and clattered on the oil drum. He stepped over and stilled the rocking movement of the branch, as if reassuring himself this really was the explanation. Then he glanced into the poplars above him. Idiotic. He put his hand over his chest. He should be getting back to the lodge.

It was days later before he thought: *what was that down along the willows that glinted in the light and arrested my eye?*

SHE TOOK CASSIE'S HAND and held it in her own, then moved them both up to her face and pressed them to her cheek. Victor looked away.

Over the years he had seen many dead people and had seen relatives react to death in all sorts of ways. A few went off the deep end and wailed or pulled their hair, but most were prepared and knew themselves and stood silently in a sort of frozen decorum for a few moments before turning away.

The one who called herself Vanora now had fallen on her knees when they brought the body up from the water. She had wailed and blubbered something that he did not quite catch. He thought that if there were to be histrionics, it would have been from the older one, from Ruth, who had destroyed the flagpole that time. But people change.

When they'd made their preliminary examination of the body, he told Sutton to fetch a blanket from the lodge. They waited silently until Roger, the last to leave, had made his way over the rocks behind the others. The breeze off the water was cool. Victor felt his ears tingling. He motioned to Sutton and Sawatzky to proceed. They carried the body up to the lodge where he had them lay the body out in the bedroom and wipe the face clean before he let the family in. They came in as a group. Roger stood at the foot of the bed, fingers gripping the wooden frame, eyes closed. It looked as if he was praying. Vanora stood on one side and studied Cassie's face as if she was locking this final image in her mind. She did not appear to be praying. Mort was shaken; he had said he would sit in the kitchen a while longer. Ruth came in ahead of Alexander and went immediately to the bedside. Her eyes were bloodshot and her cheeks whiter than the pillowcase Cassie's head lay on. She was biting her lower lip. She fumbled under the grey army blanket Sutton had placed over the body and seized Cassie's hand and drew it out from under the blanket. It was the left hand. Cassie's wedding ring glinted briefly in the light. Rigor mortis had set in and the arm and fingers were stiff. Ruth held the hand awkwardly in her own.

To his right Victor felt Vanora take a deep breath.

He found he was staring at the carpet at his feet, a dirtyish off-white broadloom that had worn and greyed in a rectangle around the bed. There was an odour in the room, must and damp, like athletic socks. Someone should open a window.

He had wanted them to come in and out quickly for their one last look. He wished for calm and dignity. But Ruth had brought a whiff of desperation into the room. He sensed something dramatic was about to happen. She seized the hand in her own and raised them both, forcing the stiff muscles to bend in angle they resisted. She pressed both hands to her cheek. Vanora inhaled a deep breath. Roger's fingers tightened on the wood frame of the bed. The floor creaked under Alexander; he had his hand on Ruth's elbow; he seemed to be holding her back.

Victor thought, how can people do this, look on their dead, and then he realized it was a foolish thought. We do what we have to do and that is all.

Boxes and garbage, that's what a life amounted to. It was three days later. They had been home to fetch clothes and cancel appointments and make excuses. While they were at Moon Lake the alarm system had gone off by accident and the security company had been to the house, leaving a note saying they would have to visit again to do a servicing. Alexander had talked to Peter. He and Nancy were driving up in the evening. They might not make the funeral but they would make it to the lodge later. Alexander had talked to Henry, who sounded more like the manager when he picked up the phone at the store than Alexander liked. They had driven back in a thin rain.

While they were in the city making phone calls and packing fresh clothes in over-night bags, Ruth had developed a headache, which she had almost been able to head off with acetaminophen with codeine. She'd spent the day in the city biting her lip and looking strung out. Alexander tried to keep her off coffee; he chatted mindlessly about goings-on at the stores. On the drive back to Moon Lake he'd stopped the car and rubbed the knots in her neck. He felt the tightness in her shoulders and smelled the rinse she used in her hair. "Drive on," she had told him irritably. He sensed a migraine like storm clouds on the horizon.

It was the day of the funeral. Wreaths of flowers filled the rooms. They gave off a sickening scent. For a while Alexander sat with Mort at the kitchen table over cups of coffee. Mortimer had said to the girls, "Take whatever you want, because the rest goes as garbage." He meant Cassie's stuff. There were dozens of blouses and pairs of slacks that neither Ruth nor Vanora liked or had any desire to take as keepsakes. There were rings, three, which they did want: a wedding band, a set of garnets, a diamond. In strained voices they discussed who should get which. One of them would say something, and then there would be a long pause. They didn't want to fight on the day of the funeral. Neither wanted to appear petty or just out to get the best for themselves. They kept saying, "What would she have wanted?" In the end Ruth took the diamond and Vanora the garnets and Roger was left the gold band. There were brooches with stones and earrings in gold and silver and bracelets and chains and pendants and watches and costume jewelry. Alexander wandered into the bedroom as they were sorting through the scarves.

There were ornaments and nicknacks on the dressers. Ruth

picked up a china figurine, white with daubs of yellow and blue, turned it over in her hand and put it back without comment. She held a round object up to the light. A coin or medal. It was bronze. "Look," she said to Vanora. "There's lettering but I can't puzzle it out. It hurts my head to focus."

Vanora took the medal and turned it to the light. The head embossed in the centre was that of a woman; the letters around the outer rim were worn and faded. "Could be Cyrillic script," she offered, "or Greek." She passed it back to Ruth who placed it absently beside the china figurine. They went back to sorting the scarves. Ruth liked this, Vanora preferred that. What they did not want went into cardboard boxes. In two hours there were four boxes at the foot of the bed. Alexander poked into one of them.

That is what a life came down to: cardboard boxes of junk. Combs and brushes with hair still in them. Envelopes with photographs. A large packet of colour photographs and a small packet with black and whites. Photographic negatives. Lockets of hair: Ruth's? Virginia's? Nail brushes, nail files, nail clippers, nail scissors, nail polish, nail polish remover. Medicine bottles, sunglasses, hair pins. Packets of letters tied up with string; and then a packet of greeting cards of every imaginable type, some going back to Cassie's marriage to LaFlamme and even earlier: her eighteenth birthday, anniversaries, the births of her children, Christmas.

"It's a collection," Ruth said.

"It's a historical record," Vanora said with enthusiasm. "A life history."

"It has sentimental value," Ruth said, "we have to keep it."

"It's a document of one woman's life," Vanora said. "My goodness. It could be donated to the university and become an exhibit." She was exhilarated by the idea and was flipping through the cards one by one. "It's a book," she said to Ruth, "we could publish it and Karrin could write an introduction."

Ruth pursed her lips but did not say anything.

On an upper shelf in the bedroom closet there were sun hats and a hat box containing three fancy hats. Alexander remembered Cassie wearing one of them at their wedding. Ruth put it on and stood in front of a mirror: it had a wide brim, pink and white flowers. She laughed and Vanora said, "It was right for mother but you look ridiculous." They laughed. The tension in the air earlier when they had sorted through the rings dissipated. They began to reminisce about the trips into town they had made with Cassie when they were girls: doctors' appointments, school visits, haircuts. Cassie had smoked in those days: Cameos. Alexander wandered back into the kitchen where Mort was sitting with his cup of coffee. When someone died some people threw themselves into busy work. That was the girls: organize the funeral service, throw out the accumulations of a lifetime. Action. Mortimer slumped in the chair at the kitchen table. He looked like a cow that has been struck a blow to the head. His eyes swam up to Alexander's.

Alexander placed one hand on Mort's shoulder. "It's tough," he said.

"Something's missing," Mort said to him.

Alexander took the chair opposite Mort at the table and reached for the coffee pot. He asked, "Something's missing from Cassie's stuff?"

"I don't know, but when I went into the bedroom I knew it as certainly as I smelt her scent in the room."

"Stress. We get these presentiments. Déjà vu experiences."

"Papers in a manila envelope. She had them on the top of the dresser and now they're gone."

"They'll turn up."

"They were important and now they're gone."

"You should tell the Mountie, then."

Mort grunted, and the look that passed between them was not so much one of conspiracy as resignation. Mort said, "Her ring was there, her wallet, but not the manila envelope. You know, like comes from the lawyer."

"Maybe the lawyer knows."

They sipped coffee silently.

"The Mountie said death by misadventure," Mort said.

"The wound on her skull was consistent with a fall on the rocks, yes."

"She said she had found something out."

Alexander stood and poured himself more coffee. There was a microwave oven on the counter now and he heated milk in it. There were sweet buns in cello packages and pans of baked goods on the counter too, presumably for after the funeral service. He resisted the temptation. He sat across from Mortimer. "What are you saying?"

"She had been digging around in the past again. That business with her uncle and LaFlamme ate away at her; she could never let it be."

Alexander sighed. "Yes," he said, "LaFlamme. It's an irony how he has haunted this family. I never met the man but he's an eternal presence, a dark angel we live with. Devil, more like."

"She went to visit an old codger in the seniors' home in Beausejour. I drove her but went for a walk while they talked. Old Beaudry, they call him. You know the kind of person, filmy eyes, unruly hair, brown spots on the skin of his face and hands. He was a crony of her uncle's back when. During the war."

"And what did she say?"

"She told me she had to puzzle over what he'd told her. I don't think she believed him entirely. You know how those old people get. Muddle things up, confuse what they know occurred with what they imagine might have occurred. Or wished had occurred. It had something to do with a lot of money they made during the war. Illegal."

"Her uncle and someone else?"

"It was all vague. She didn't want to tell me until she was certain of the facts."

"Why?"

"She had this idea that I thought her family was weird."

"These guys in cahoots with the uncle," he said, "maybe they're still living?"

"She said something about a Greek family that runs a diner on the edge of the city." Mort gazed at him blankly. It was not sinking in.

"They have names? They keep in touch with Cassie?"

"She had some photos. Nice-looking family. Greeks."

"What I'm saying is there's a lot at stake. Blackmail, maybe. Maybe someone had a lot to lose if things from the past came out—too much to lose."

Mort had blinked his eyes. "No. It was a kind of scam. The uncle was a railway guy during the war. Things went missing, if you know what I mean. They made money selling stuff on the black market."

"I thought that was in Europe, black market."

"Here too. Everywhere. Sticky fingers, you know."

"But somebody found out what they had been up to. That's what I was getting at when I called it blackmail. LaFlamme, maybe, found out."

"He came along a lot later. It was all over by then."

"Yes. But if he knew, if he could get them in trouble if he told what he knew to the authorities. Prison, maybe."

"She said nothing about that, but now that you mention it, it could be."

"He was the type who made enemies."

Mort laughed. "And the type who made money—legal or not."

Alexander hesitated. It had been more than twenty years since he had opened the cardboard boxes in the shed and found the folding money. Cassie was out of the picture. Mort deserved some consideration. It had been bothering him for years, that money; it should have been Cassie's when it would have done her some good. He didn't understand why he hadn't said anything. "There was a lot of cash," he said finally, "in a cookie tin in a cardboard box stashed under the paint cans in that old shed."

The information did not seem to register. Mort sipped at his coffee and stared off out the window that looked toward the lake. The sky was clouding over. A spring breeze had come up. The branches of the trees, just coming into bud, shook. Now that the entire area in front of the buildings had been cleared, you could see all the way down to the lake. The water glinted in the sunshine. The quiet he had hated that winter he and Peter had lived at Moon Lake was as palpable as rain. Your heart slowed out here. It had something to do with the water: its presence, its suppurations, the gases that rose off the surface in the morning mist. The water exhaled a kind of drug to the soul. He had not liked it out here on the edge of civilization, away from the things that made life busy, but he recognized its attraction, its almost fatal allure for the troubled spirit. Nature's simple rhythms and motions. A balm.

"I always hated painting," Mort said finally, breaking in on his thoughts. "Gets on your hands, in your hair. The old man liked to paint, remember?"

"It was a kind of therapy for him."

"You, too." Mort cleared his throat.

Alexander nodded silently in agreement. During that fall he and Peter had spent there he had painted the trading post and the bunkhouse and the shed and both the granaries. He'd done such a good job that repainting hadn't been necessary until a few years ago. The work had been good for him.

Mort said, "A lot of cash, you say?"

"I did not count it. To tell you the truth, it frightened me, that money."

"So much money sets a scare in a man."

"Too much to be in a cookie tin. There had to be something wrong."

"LaFlamme, yes. There was something screwy if he had something to do with it."

"I thought you knew about that money. It was old bills, the ones from the fifties, maybe. Remember that picture of the Queen's head on the notes that everyone laughed at until the government withdrew them and then came out with a more flattering picture? There were a hundred bills in largish denominations, maybe more."

"She looked like the devil, everyone said." Mort laughed and then added, "I'd no idea about any money. I never looked in those cardboard boxes. They belonged to LaFlamme, I thought, and Cassie. It was their business."

"I assumed that was the money you loaned me to start up the SportHuts."

"No, that was my ill-gotten gambling winnings." Mort looked up and laughed, snorted, really. "I could not tell Cassie about it. How I got it. She would have flipped out. So I was happy to lend it to you. Get it out of the house. See, when I worked in Cartwright I got into a poker game that went on for a couple of months. Friday and Saturday nights. I've never been a gambler so it was a once-in-a-lifetime type of thing. But I hit a streak of luck. When I look back on it I was lucky to get out of that place alive. The whole town must have thought I was cheating. Five thousand was a lot of money in those days and farmers are close to their money."

"Plus the interest that I gave you."

"Exactly. It set us up here." Mort snorted again. "If Cassie had ever known about how I came into it she would have sold up the place or booted me out. She was an old-fashioned Catholic in many ways. But I told her it was from an uncle in Alberta who died and that you received both our portions from a lawyer."

"So what happened to it, then, the cash I stumbled across?"

Mort shrugged. "Cassie must not have known because she never said a word about it. We had a joint account in Beausejour, which we'd had for years. So there's no stash of money in a Swiss bank account or something like that."

"Maybe she had an idea where the money went."

"She never told me, Dick."

"Or maybe she figured that someone else had laid their sticky fingers on it."

"Who?—these mystery partners of her uncle's?"

"And you say the shed is gone?"

"When we converted to the lodge. There were bugs coming in and the builder thought maybe it was from there. I don't know what happened to the stuff in that old shed. It was Cassie's business, I thought, those cardboard boxes, from her time with LaFlamme, which I always felt uneasy about. You think we should look around? You think the money is maybe still here somewhere?"

"Where?"

"I can't think," Mort said, shrugging. "I know what's in the closets and the storage rooms and there's just no way." He shrugged again and sat silently looking at his hands. For a moment Alexander thought he would get up and search for the money, which was to him an exciting prospect. But he did not. Maybe the money didn't matter. Not now, and maybe not ever. Cassie might have kept something from him but now she was gone and that was far more important than a roll of bills.

Alexander looked at his watch. The funeral was in three hours. The sisters needed help shifting the remaining cardboard boxes. He had been sitting about most of the morning and he was feeling edgy and anxious; he needed something to occupy his hands.

O{FFICIALLY HE DID NOT NEED} to be there and he should not have been for other reasons, but it was guilt, wasn't it? He'd never quite put the Moon Lake business behind him. Probably because he'd been taken off the case and Gerald Black had muscled in the way he had. *Thoroughness*, was that the word he'd used? They had not done a bad job out there twenty some years ago, but it had not been resolved, and Gerald Black thought it should have been. Sheila's suicide attempt had muddied everything up. Victor had spent two days away from the case while she recovered in the Beausejour hospital and by then he'd lost the thread of the murder completely. After that it was a month in the psych ward for her and constant visits for him. The recovery had been slow. But while she was in the psych ward Sheila had seized on exercise and diet as the tools to recovery, and they had worked. Sheila was as normal as she had ever been. A little fanatical about jogging every day, but what the hell, who wasn't going a little nutty with Y2K approaching? And she was sexy again, no doubt about that. So there were compensations for banana bread and herbal teas.

He had asked her if she'd wanted to come with him. "To Moon Lake?" She rolled her eyes. "It's been nothing out of your mouth for thirty years but Moon Lake." An exaggeration on two counts, but she had a point. Maybe Cassie's funeral would put the business to rest. He had driven up alone. It was a Monday. A good day for a funeral: quiet, warm, not too hot. The sky to the north looked threatening but the rain would probably pass.

The tires of the squad car hummed on the asphalt. He felt expectant and hopeful, a diluted but nonetheless real memory trace from that event on the road years ago.

He unwrapped a stick of gum and put the crushed foil in the ashtray. It was better than chocolate bars, Sheila said. Not that his gut was totally cured. He woke when the blue jays began screaming and tossed from side to side with a gurgling gut until it was time to rise. Not pain exactly. McNair had tried him on Losec for a while. They had moved on to Previcid. He thought it was gall bladder but McNair said no, gall bladder pain came as sharp attacks. Sheila had found a home remedy: cleanse the intestines with Fleet soda, and then lie on your right side for six hours after drinking a half litre of olive oil. It had cleaned out his intestines. A lot of green stuff like algae came out in his stool. He felt mildly nauseous for a week. But the damn gurgling continued. It was not a lot to complain about and it could be minimized if he stayed away from the red wine. Gerald Black's pancreatic cancer took him off in three months. McNair himself had developed a heart condition which prevented him from trekking over rough terrain or doing more than operating the trailer crank when they took the boat out trolling. Past fifty everyone was inflicted with something.

McNair had said, "There's no reason to believe this death was anything but what it looked like, an accident."

He'd been down to the morgue on Saturday afternoon. He disliked the smell of the place. It made him nauseous. After their years together, he did not want to tell McNair that he required absolute certainty, but McNair had a sense for what was going on in his brain. "You can't let it go," he said, "that death up at Moon Lake."

"You see things. As a cop. You put things together."

"You develop a paranoia about people, and a suspicious mind."

"They've all got secrets, that Moon Lake bunch."

"Everybody's got secrets."

"That girl, for instance, the one who married Alexander. Just after LaFlamme's death I saw her in town with Billy Cuthand, sneaking out of the theater and into his car."

"Teenagers."

"Laughing like they'd pulled the wool over someone's eyes."

"It was twenty years ago and more. She was a kid."

"She looked guilty."

"It was you, the RCMP, that she was afraid of. She knew what you thought of white girls going with Indians—Natives. You'd arrested him, remember?"

"She was hiding something."

"A little teenage lust."

"This was just weeks after LaFlamme was murdered. Billy Cuthand."

"A little groping and fumbling in the back seat of a car. She was a kid."

"She was a grown woman. All the men in town could see that plain enough. And she knew what had gone on that Labour Day weekend."

"She had every reason to be wary of you. You were after her brother."

"They say he's simple but he's cunning."

"Maybe you have to develop cunning when you're simple."

"And Cassie was hiding something too. She went to her grave with it."

"Probably just the obvious. Married to Mort so soon after the other's murder."

"Shacked up with him before that. And that was suspicious."

McNair screwed up his lips. "I've never liked that expression, *shacked up*." He wiped his fingers on a towel. "And there was no evidence of that—only gossip."

"She wouldn't look me directly in the eye, Cassie. Not since."

"We've been all over this. You've got boxes of notes."

"She knew something and did not want it to come out. You heard about her going to visit Old Beaudry recently? Paid him off to keep his mouth shut, is my bet."

"You're jumping to conclusions."

"It was not a social visit. Mortimer sat in the car while she went into the old folks' home carrying a manila envelope."

"With pictures in it, the nurses there told me. Old black and white snaps."

"Ho. That's what she wanted them to see. But she was there for something else."

"The photos were of a family from the city, just outside the city."

"Cassie's aunts live on the west coast. If they're still alive."

"Not *her* family. Relatives of the old Greek codger who retired from the CP ten years ago, remember? They threw a big party at the Lakeland. Beaudry went."

"We're getting off track here. You have that habit."

McNair laughed. "And you're getting yourself in a nice little lather."

"Yeah. And then the goddamn guts start up."

"Have you been taking that stuff every morning?"

Black and purple pills. He hadn't because the specialist in the city said they were for a stomach problem and his was in the guts, a blockage of some kind. He still kept the Tums on the bedside table and the Maalox in the bathroom. Sheila said no junk food after nine o'clock, no fats, no sugars, no yeasts. That regime worked better than McNair's pills but he did not tell him that. He said, "She was always lying to protect that Roger. He had the eyes of a killer when he was a kid, like his old man. Now he's gone all touchy-feely."

"You were wrong about him."

"People go touchy-feely because they've got something on their conscience."

"He was a kid. He was not a killer."

"Mortimer wasn't a kid, and he's always had his eye on the main chance."

"Oh, God," McNair said. "We have been all over this."

"I hate to see someone get away with murder."

"Well, it wasn't murder this time, though I know you want to tie the two together."

"It makes sense that way to me."

McNair paused. "You remember, don't you, someone telling us years ago that not everything has an explanation. It's two violent deaths separated by twenty years of time."

"Two suspicious deaths occurring within a stone's throw of each other."

McNair drew a deep breath and paused a moment before saying, "There were green stains on the fingers, from fiddleheads. There were no signs of a struggle; one contusion on the skull and water in the lungs. So. She slipped on the rocks, struck her head and drowned. Those are the forensic facts."

Victor had told McNair only the scantiest of details so that his own account did not influence the official verdict. "What was she doing down there?"

At one time McNair would have shrugged, implying that's your area, not mine, but he said authoritatively, "Washing the fiddleheads. A few bits of stem and whatnot stuck to her skin and snagged on her clothes. I found leaf meal under the nails."

"And Sutton and Sawatsky located fiddleheads floating in the willows when they recovered the pail."

"So there you go."

He was tempted to disagree, but there was no point. He recalled the look on Mortimer Mann's face after they found the body. The girls had wept. The one who called herself Vanora now had bruised her knees and legs on the rocks. Her girlfriend had had to bandage the bleeding skin when they went back to the lodge. They would all be relieved to hear the official verdict, as relieved as he was. Relieved but not pleased.

"It was Cassie told us once," Victor said finally, "that things don't always add up."

"But this adds up."

"Yes. But I don't feel particularly great about it."

McNair busied himself with drying his hands on a towel. "You can take them the news at Moon Lake without hesitation."

But not a clear conscience, he thought. Never that.

It was a short ride from Beausejour now that the paved road ran through to the lodge. He had liked it better in the old days: grouse fluttering up from the logging road, deer with white tails bouncing into the bush. The trees were pretty but the asphalt road meant civilization. The creatures had moved back another mile or so. In fifty, a hundred years, there would be cottages around Moon Lake and tiny strip malls with kiosks selling junk food and videos or whatever. Service stations, a liquor outlet. The animals that survived would have retreated north. Years ago when he'd spent some time in the library looking at books about out-of-body experiences, he'd picked up a volume about the Shield that someone had left on a table. It was filled with scientific words and tiny but elaborate notes at the foots of the pages. According to the author, the Shield looked impressive— massive rock formations, forests that stretched for hundreds of miles, strings of lakes. But it was actually a delicate ecosystem: sensitive lichens that one or two degrees of temperature change would kill, tiny plants that grew on the forest floor, moths and insects that relied on only one or two species for sustenance. If the temperature were to rise as little as five degrees, the lakes could dry up. For every thousand pine cones that fell, only a few took root. The Natives had understood this intuitively. But then the Europeans came, intent on progress. He wasn't one of those Greenpeacers, but the trade-off seemed hardly worth it.

Victor pulled the squad car onto the gravel lot in front of the lodge. Alexander Mann's grey Mercedes was parked beside Mortimer's Buick. The red Saab belonged to the Finn, who must have come up for the funeral. Odd how everyone who was connected with Moon Lake had done well for themselves. He wondered about that. But then again that's what happened with the passage of time: despite his roiling gut, he was Staff Sergeant Boyd, detachment honcho for the Oakbank RCMP. He had done okay too.

S HE HATED FUNERALS. It was a fine thing to celebrate someone's passage to another self, and you were able to do that privately, but that never happened at the public event. The age-old Christian terrors asserted themselves at gravesides, ashes to ashes, and a bitter taste that said it really was all over, dead meat chucked in the earth, even though the words of the service suggested a new possibility for the self. While the priest talked she had to keep reminding herself that Cassie had taken an important step towards realizing the Liberated Soul. Not a release, as the Christian service had it, but a voyage of discovery. She closed her eyes and sent out mental messages, images Cassie might be able to receive. When the service was over she stood by the grave longer than she intended. She felt hollow inside, not triumphant, as Libby had indicated she should. Karrin was at her side. It was a warm day but she was trembling. Roger knelt for a moment and tossed a handful of dirt on to the casket. His grey hair bobbed slightly when he stood and his eyes were red-rimmed, so he did not hold her gaze long. Tears streamed down Mortimer's face. The Finn and the other non-family members had moved off. Ruth was clinging to Alexander's arm. On the surface she looked composed but she was deeply agitated. Her brow was furrowed. Earlier she'd been wearing sunglasses. Maybe she had a migraine.

Were Ruth's headaches worse in the bright sunshine? She seemed to recall Ruth telling her that. When Vanora looked at her, squinting behind the dark glasses, she could tell she was wound up like a clock. It was hot too, hot for spring.

At least there were no mosquitoes yet. During the service a blue-bottle fly had buzzed around her head. Cassie was a fanatic about killing them. She kept several swatters in the kitchen. Disease, she claimed; but it was probably nothing more than irritation. She was fussy: cellophane over the bedroom lampshades. Still, mid-May and no mosquitoes. In a week or ten days Cassie would have planted the garden in the deer meadow. She'd put out her tools and bought packets of zucchini and carrot seeds and onion pods. Between the beets and bell peppers she'd plant zinnias and marigolds. She claimed the bright flowers kept the crows away, but Vanora knew it was Barkette, the granddaughter of their childhood pet, who prowled the yard just enough to keep them in the trees. Cassie had tried to grow tomatoes but the soil around Moon Lake was not right. What a pity. Cassie loved tomato sandwiches: toasted bread, mayonnaise, the thinnest slices of tomato. She had been fussy about that too: the thinnest slices of cucumber to make cucumber salad.

There was no headstone. That seemed more important than it should have. Roger was going to arrange for one. Vanora would drive up in the summer and see what it looked like. Ruth too, maybe. A family ritual. It was peculiar but they never spoke about LaFlamme's death. In one way they had never really buried him: and they were all edgy because of it. It was a terrible mistake not to bury someone. His grave was over on the far side of the oats field that the Finn and Mortimer had been breaking the fall that he was murdered. She should at least stand by the spot for a moment. She remembered that at the funeral years ago she had stayed behind at the graveside with Ruth after the others had gone, and Ruth had looked around, assuring herself that they were alone. "Good," Ruth had finally said. And she kicked loose dirt onto the casket—once, twice, with the toe of polished black shoe. *Good.* Vanora recalled, too, that she'd dreamt once that LaFlamme came back from the dead, pointing at her and accusing her of killing him. *No, no,* she had shouted in the dream, *not me, Roger.* But LaFlamme had laughed.

These were thoughts she did not want. Her stomach hurt just to turn his name over in her mind. But she recalled, too, that years ago when they were terrorized kids, Roger and Ruth had talked about killing LaFlamme. It was only the talk of frightened kids, she realized now.

A decade ago she and Ruth had fought about that. One time, in a joking way she had mentioned Roger's fantasy about driving the tractor over LaFlamme. She thought Ruth felt the same way as her: that it had been just kid's talk, a memory they could laugh over now. "You must never tell a soul," Ruth whispered harshly. She had been very agitated then, biting her lower lip, and she was agitated now. Most likely she had TAS. She put so much emphasis on going forward that she got herself bound up and could not unlock. Karrin said there were few things worse and none more difficult to undo than tight ass syndrome.

Karrin said that Vanora must listen to the shaman. And the shaman told her this is the time to focus on the future. You've confronted the past, Vanora, and now it is time to heal. To look forward, not backward.

She whispered to Karrin, "Cassie had placed a new pair of gardening gloves in the basket of tools she'd used for thirty years." She was weeping; the words choked out of her dry mouth.

Karrin gave her arm a gentle squeeze. "Some things," she whispered, "remain a mystery. We do not know why they happen; they do not obey logic."

Vanora did not remember walking back to the lodge. She did not remember sitting at the table. As he sipped coffee, the Mountie looked at her and Karrin the way some people just had to look. Washed-out blue eyes that still unnerved her. All her men had had brown or hazel eyes, her own colour, LaFlamme's, now that she thought about it. But she did not want to think about it, did not want to recover the lost father. Even though Roger was now making a vocation of it.

The Wild Man. It suited him. Ever since Ruth had hissed at her *tell no one*, Vanora had wondered if Roger really could have killed LaFlamme. He was a gentle and good man now, but a lot of time had passed since that event. Roger had been an angry boy—and an erratic one, psychologically. He'd killed small animals with zeal. She couldn't help wonder if Roger's enthusiasm for the men's movement wasn't a form of beating his chest, and in more ways than the most obvious one. Maybe his pursuit of the father was a kind of compensation. Over-compensation. She studied him as he moved about the kitchen: the high cheekbones, the round eyes. There was Métis blood in them. Years ago Roger had confided to her that as a child he was convinced he had been adopted after being abandoned by a Native mother. And then later he believed that he was LaFlamme's but not Cassie's child, offspring of a drunken liaison between LaFlamme and a Native woman he'd had in the bush behind Cuthand's tent. When she was in high school Vanora had proudly declared herself French Canadian, on the few occasions when the subject arose. But in his thirties, Roger had done some digging around in the public records; at the turn of the century the family had lived along the LaSalle River near St Norbert, Louis Riel territory. She was proud of her heritage now. The thong Roger wore around his neck showed that he was too: he wanted to re-establish contact with his primitive self. The Wild Man, she could not help reflecting, was not far removed from the medicine man, also known as the crazy one.

Roger was an example of how sometimes the good and bad fitted together, how they needed each other, as visionary thinkers were fond of saying. Yin and Yang. She had explained this to her high school students when they read the proverbs of the wild English poet, William Blake. In needs out; white needs black. Roger was living in that dangerous territory, where impulse and vision were as important as science and thought, but she could not believe he was a killer.

Karrin had brought herbal tea and she poured boiling water into Cassie's old ceramic tea pot. Did Mortimer drink tea? He was in the room they used to entertain guests, sitting between Alexander and Ruth, who bit her lower lip and nodded as Mortimer talked. He'd recovered his composure. He was telling a lengthy story about two brothers he had worked with on a farm near Vida: one stuttered, the other wheezed. If you got them both excited, as Mort apparently had taken pleasure in doing, it could be quite amusing to get them stuttering and wheezing in unison. Sergeant Boyd was standing near the door, smiling as he listened to Mort's story. Archie Cloud was talking with the Finn, heads bowed together like conspirators. Roger was moving between the kitchen and the sitting area, carrying plates of cold meat sandwiches and baked goods. Everyone was sipping coffee. The Finn, Roger whispered to her, had chokecherry wine in the trunk of his car, but he was waiting until the Mountie left before he brought it out, at which time the wake proper would begin.

The rear wheels of the squad car spit a little gravel when Sergeant Boyd shifted from reverse to forward. He waved at them through the window one last time and the car glided off in the direction of Beausejour. "That guy has always got under my skin," the Finn said. "Ticks me right off."

"There was talk years ago," Archie said, "that he muddled the evidence so as to cover up his own involvement."

Alexander asked, "In the death of LaFlamme?"

"His wife," Archie said, "and Roger's old man we're going at it, folks said."

"Ridiculous," Alexander said. "The Mountie's a man of integrity and good sense."

"Sure," Archie said. "You go on believing that until he throws you into the clink."

Alexander said, "You boys are talking nonsense."

"He's talking more sense than you," the Finn said. "You know from nothing."

"When I was a kid," Roger said, "he scared the hell out of me. But now I see he was just another Old Man Down Under. To find yourself, to actualize your true self, you have to make the descent to him, you have to wrestle him to find the real man inside."

"Stick the knife in his heart," Archie said, striking his own chest with a fist.

Roger snorted. "The Old Man," he said, "not Dracula."

"That reminds me," Archie said. "Old Beaudry has a theory about what's been going on out here."

They were sitting on the stoop, the Finn and Alexander on the top step and Roger and Archie Cloud below them. Alexander had taken out his pipe; the Finn dug around in a back pocket and produced a tin of chewing tobacco. They were all still wearing the sport jackets they had worn at the graveside. The sun was low on the horizon, its last rays turning the lawn on the far side of the parking lot yellowish green, but the air retained the afternoon heat. Alexander was wondering when Peter would arrive, Peter of the Tag Huer watch and downy chin. Alexander worried about road accidents. He saw again Cassie's pale face staring back up at him when the Mounties had laid her out on the gravel and realized he had known she would be dead as soon as he put down the phone on Friday morning.

The Finn stuck a wad of tobacco under his tongue. "A habit I picked up here," he said, "working with Mort those many years ago. A bad habit." He chuckled the way old men do, mostly to himself.

"They're secretive, the cops, is the thing of it," Archie was saying.

"They cover their own asses. Look how they locked up Billy Cuthand."

"That was just to get the press out of their faces," the Finn said. "They let him go as soon as the hubbub died down in the papers."

They were talking about LaFlamme, but no one said his name. The front pages had been filled with Billy Cuthand's face when he was arrested years ago, but there wasn't even back-page coverage of his release.

"The cops question you," Archie was saying, "as if it's a God-given right, but they won't tell you anything."

"Or do anything. First the old man is murdered and now my mother."

"You ask them something," Archie insisted, "and they look down their nose at you and tell you to keep your mouth shut."

Roger said, "You know about the stone came down near Lac du Bonnet?"

The Finn said, "That giant field stone near Jessica Lake?"

Alexander added, "Left by the glaciers, wasn't it?"

"That's what they want you to believe," Roger said. From his position below them it was awkward to converse without turning his whole body around on the step. He moved over to the edge of the step and turned to look up. "It was a meteorite. Big as this building. It came down in 1965 and it was hush-hush for twenty years. At first the cops refused to say anything at all. But lots of folks had had these experiences, eh? Out-of-body events. Like they'd died or something. The cops hoped people would lose interest. Then they said it was a field stone, it had been there for centuries."

"They think people will believe whatever crap they tell them," Archie said. "And "white people do for the most part."

"They still won't admit it's a meteorite, but now they will tell you where it is, but they will not show you or explain how to get there."

"It gives off an aura," Archie said. "Powerful manitou."

"When it came down," Roger said, "people for miles around had experiences. You know, sensations and premonitions. Out-of-body stuff. Folks driving down the highway claimed they'd seen a big blue ball in the sky. A man out Whitemouth way drove off the road and nearly killed himself."

The Finn said, "I've seen the crop circles near Portage la Prairie."

"This is not a crop circle," Archie said. "Way more powerful than that."

"An aura," Alexander said, quizzically. "You can see something?"

"And feel it."

The Finn asked, "You've been?"

"We both have," Archie said. "It gives off a kind of golden blue aura for about a ten-foot radius. There's a kind of static in the air. You feel you're in the presence of something bigger than man."

"Up close, you kind of tingle," Roger said.

"In the presence of something from the spirit world."

"Your hairs stand up."

"Huh," Alexander said. He did not believe a word of it. From the time Archie was a kid, he'd been a fruitcake, and now Roger was into this male bonding stuff. It was all a bit goofy. Grown men going touchy-feely. He'd heard that in the sweat lodges the men shed their clothes, danced naked, and lay prostrate on the mud floor for hours at a time. They ate dirt. Going down into the ashes, Roger called it. Nonsense in his view. And now they were on about auras emanating from rocks.

"Meteorites come down but they won't admit it," Archie went on.

Roger banged his fist on the wooden steps. "Your old man is murdered and they accuse you."

Archie said, "Falsely. They throw you in the lockup with no explanation."

"No explanation when they release you two days later."

"No apology."

Roger banged his fist on the step again. "People die at Moon Lake but there's no explanation."

"You're not saying there's a connection?" Alexander felt himself flush. He meant between the meteorite and the deaths of LaFlamme and Cassie.

"Damn right," the Finn said.

But before he could go on Roger continued, "I'm saying people who live in a place all their lives, who have a feel for the landscape, who know trees and rocks like the backs of their hands do not slip on the stones near shore and bash in their heads."

Archie said, "People are pushed."

"But then comes the official pronouncement: misadventure."

"Close the case," Archie said. "No more to see here, folks."

Alexander felt himself becoming warm with irritation. "But there was an investigation. And there was no evidence of foul play."

"Evidence," Archie said, "can be made to suit."

"Or made up," Roger said.

"Or left out."

"Cops," the Finn said. "You have no idea."

Alexander felt this last comment was directed at him. The Finn thought him weak and naïve, and Alexander felt resentment surge through him suddenly.

"The point is," Roger said, "she'd done this thing with the fiddleheads in the springtime one way for dozens of years; then one day she suddenly decides to wash the fiddleheads in the lake, not at the kitchen sink. Doesn't that seem unusual? And it's on that very same day that she slips on the rocks and conks her head?"

"It doesn't add up," Archie said.

Roger butted his fists together. "Cops," he sniffed.

Archie said, "There's a killer on the loose and—"

Ruth had come out on the landing. She hissed at them, "Why are you talking this way?" Tears flowed down her cheeks, turning them red again. Her fists were clenched and she butted them together. "You know what happened but you're talking idiotic crap. All of you!"

Alexander was suddenly embarrassed. He stood. He said, "Stop it, now, honey. The boys were just talking."

"They are not boys. And they're talking stupid shit."

Alexander felt a deep flush of shame spread though him, hot and sudden in his bowels. He reached out for her but she pushed her fists against his chest, a blow that caught him off guard. He staggered backwards, stepping awkwardly off the landing into the grass. The flush raced to his face. "Easy," he managed to say to Ruth.

"Everybody's talking shit," she hissed at them.

The Finn stood suddenly and seized Ruth's arm.

She wrenched away from him. "Old Beaudry says it's Mortimer."

"Ridiculous," Alexander said.

"First he kills off LaFlamme, Old Beaudry is apparently telling everyone in town, and then he goes after Cassie." She choked on the words. "He says it's all to get his hands on this place. He says the Mann family is money-hungry."

"Old Beaudry," Alexander said looking up at her from the grass, "should be locked up in Selkirk. He's a menace to the town and to himself."

"And you're bloody crazy," she went on, "all of you, to be talking this way with mother just gone."

"Easy, now," Alexander said.

"Crazy," Ruth screeched, "crazy, fucking bloody crazy."

The Finn's hand came out of nowhere. It struck Ruth flat in the face with a smack.

Ruth screamed and staggered backward against the screen door.

Alexander leapt back on the landing. He grabbed the Finn's arms. The Finn tried to break free but ended up grabbing Alexander's arms. They were in a clench like prize fighters in a ring, lurching and swaying about in a bizarre dance.

"Damn you," Alexander managed to breathe out through gritted teeth. "Strike a woman, my wife."

"A wife who needs a husband, a strong man," the Finn hissed back.

"Fuck you," Alexander said.

He felt Archie's strong hand on his shoulder and realized he'd pushed his way in between them. Roger had stepped past them and had his arms around Ruth, opening the screen door and easing Ruth through it. Alexander smelled the cologne Archie used and the Finn's foul breath, a mixture of wine and onion and what might have been shellfish. "Okay, now," Archie said, forcing the Finn and Alexander apart. Alexander felt the blood pounding in his temples. He was conscious of Roger and Ruth at the door, and Vanora behind them, looking distressed and frightened. He looked the Finn directly in the eye. "All right," he breathed to Archie. But when the Finn stepped back, Alexander added, "I'm not done with that bastard."

"Fuck you too," the Finn hissed.

"All right," Archie repeated. His voice was loud and authoritative. He had one hand on the Finn's shoulder, holding him at bay. To Alexander he said, "You cool down. Take a walk down to the lake. Get hold of yourself."

Alexander thought: *this is unseemly, on the night of the funeral.* Before he could say anything, Archie nudged him with his free hand.

"I'll take care of this one," he said flatly, meaning the Finn, "talk him down." He nudged Alexander in the chest again. "Go," he said, "do the same."

Alexander stepped off the landing. The grass felt spongy underfoot. His mind was reeling. He glanced in the window and saw Roger and Vanora with their hands on Ruth's shoulders. He drew a deep breath and forced his feet to move away.

He passed the twin rocks, where the Finn had shown Peter how to fish years ago, the goddamn meddling Finn. There was a straight drop off to the lake from the granite hummock: a good place to throw a line into water. The lake was bright that evening, the shores outwards to either side reflected in the water, blue-black, the details of the jagged spruces and firs as clear as in the original. It no longer looked like a reflection in the water, but like another dimension, with depths continuing downward in wooded slopes toward a bottom he could not see. He continued walking across the lawn and down the sand and gravel toward the place where the willows grew along the shore. Here the lake and the terrain blended easier, the trees were part of the lake. The rocks at the edge of the water varied in size: at places he had to jump from one to another, being careful to keep his footing. But the rocks were dry. The danger was not that you would slip so much as misjudge your footing and tumble. That did not sound like Cassie, but she was getting on in years—and carried a bit of weight. But it would have been a place to wash fiddleheads, an opening of sorts where the lake was shallow and you could dip your hands into the water. He stopped where the larger rocks gave way to stones not much larger than coarse gravel. When they had first come to Moon Lake, this was a tricky bit to negotiate: the willows were at your back and the uneven stones beneath your feet; but now the area was more open and navigable. He was breathing hard, it occurred to him. Adrenaline raced through his veins; his heart thudded in his chest. He had remembered something, though, and was focussing on it so as to stop obsessing about the Finn. He was looking where the willows stood almost in the water. When the Mounties had been occupied lifting the body he had seen a glint coming from the base of one of the willows. Probably nothing: a foil gum wrapper.

But maybe it had drawn her too.

There was a smell down by the water he hadn't noticed three days ago: a whiff of rotting fish. The birds sometimes brought them up on the rocks to feed. He recalled Peter telling him that certain birds were the closest living ancestors to the dinosaurs, a subject he had never tired of, as a boy.

Alexander looked over his shoulder. He was wearing an alpaca jacket and it bound slightly in one armpit when he turned his head. The shoreline up to the lodge was deserted. The sun had almost set, though there was still quite a good light over the lake. A light breeze. You could smell the acidic pungency of pine cones and the brown decay of the previous fall's leaves coming from the forest bed. A blue jay was screeching in the spruces. Noisy. He'd been tempted the fall that he and Peter had lived in the bunkhouse to shoot one that woke him every morning at five, but he hadn't and was glad of it now. A mosquito buzzed past his face. The water lapped at the feet of the willows. Yes, there it was again: glint of metal in the dark water.

The air down by the lake was cold. He took it in in large gulps. It cleared his eyes and slowed the exaggerated thudding of his heart.

He made his way carefully over the stones. Attached to the base of one of the willows was a fish stringer. He lifted it slowly out of the water, dripping water on the tops of his black shoes. The stringer was a style they did not manufacture any longer: metal clips. The sections that had been exposed to the air had rusted badly; those that had lain in the water still shone dully despite a buildup of mineral deposits. At the end of the stringer hung a knife. A hole had been drilled through its wooden handle and the last clip of the stringer was clipped through this aperture. It was an old knife, crusted in places on the blade with mineral deposits, though not much deteriorated from oxidation. Alexander held it up in the light. The blade had been sharpened many times with a file or by machine. It was worn thin. There had once been a name etched in the metal but it was no longer legible. He revolved it slowly in his hand. The blade glinted the sunlight back at him. Why did he think the knife looked European? Then he understood something he'd seen all those years ago. He said aloud: *and a fucking Catholic.* He detached the shaft from the stringer clip. It was not easy. Bits of minerals crumbled into the water as he twisted the clip this way and that to free the knife from the stringer. With his finger he tested the edge of the blade. Dull. But the point was sharp. He was about to test the point of the blade when he heard something behind him: crunch. He turned his head abruptly, one foot slipping awkwardly on the rocks, half expecting it to be the Finn, bent on revenge. Ridiculous. The woods were in shadow now. Depths the eye could not penetrate. Darkness. But the woods had their own noises. He knew that. Small animals rustled around in the deadfall. Pine cones dropped. Night birds flitted from branch to branch. Ruth's silly talk had put him on edge. The bush was the bush: filled with its own life and indifferent to the cares of humans. He could see nothing. He took a deep breath. He slipped the knife into the inside pocket of his jacket, feeling uneasy about taking it but not looking back toward the buildings. If he fell now, he realized as he made his way across the stones and rocks, the long, thin blade would slit right through his shirt and puncture his heart.

T̲hey did not drink much as a rule but after the pushing and shoving on the stoop Karrin said everyone should take a stiff belt of wine to calm down, so they did. The wine was good. It had been made by the Finn. It had a peppery taste and the essence of the chokecherries from which he had made it—and an odd taste: sausages? When Vanora took her first sips she murmured appreciation. The Finn was very proud of his product. He had explained the whole process earlier: he froze the berries, that made it easier to crush them. He strained the pulp through cheesecloth. Pure, cold well water was added to the juices. Some kind of pectin went in, and a commercial concentrate that gave the wine its spicy taste. Vanora did not get the bit about the carboys and the air locks and how many weeks elapsed between each stage. She was watching the Finn's face, more animated than when he had been a young man, but lined with creases, too. She recalled that she had thought him attractive when they were young. But he was all eyes for Ruth in those days. She wondered if anything had ever happened between them. Such an intense time when you're young and coming into sex.

He was out on the stoop now with Archie who'd stayed with him and was speaking to him softly, talking him down. The Finn was a man of passion, clearly, despite the fact that he had never married. Alexander said that after he bought the first chicken place the Finn had thrown himself into his work. There had been rumours of a woman coming from Finland. He lived a bachelor life: small house on the edge of town, a few beers in the hotel on Saturday nights; Sunday afternoons in the coffee shop with the other bachelors wearing black shirts and polished loafers. If he'd been Italian, he would have taken up *bocce*, if he were German, he'd have joined a right-wing political party.

Alexander had been dispatched by Archie on a walk, it appeared, and told to cool down. He was defensive about Ruth, a man, Vanora realized, whose surface intelligence masked a lot of bottled-up anger. Ruth was lying down, nursing her migraine. When she'd come in from the stoop after yelling at the men, her face had been flushed. She'd stood in the kitchen for a while, trembling and trying to regain her composure. She drank a glass of water. Vanora thought it was silly of her to have shouted at the men. But then everyone was on edge; emotions ran high at funerals.

Vanora herself had felt little since they found the body other than confusion that amounted to a kind of numbness. Why had her mother been taken from her in that way? In her mind she knew Cassie's death was a passage to another life, a good thing; but in her heart it was difficult to feel that Cassie had left behind the travails of the earthly body and ascended into the etheric plane, yet perhaps she had. Death was nature's way of taking the body back to itself. Vanora understood that. Dying freed the soul to reach the planes of being it could not while trapped in the body. Still, it was a good thing Karrin was at Vanora's side. If Vanora was coping reasonably well, it was because Karrin gave her strength. It may have caused the Mountie to smirk in his condescending way, but Karrin had taken Vanora's hand at the graveside and steadied her through the heart-numbing ceremony. She'd felt the thick band of Karrin's sapphire ring pressing into her own flesh and that had comforted her.

She felt numb, yes, but somewhat distracted, too. Earlier in the day she and Ruth had been in the kitchen together and she had told Ruth about the Native woman who came to her for massages. Her husband was a medicine man. They made herb teas out of local berries and leaves. Vanora had asked the woman, "Which berries and leaves were good for making herb tea?" She and Karrin liked to experiment with the plants in their her garden, and she hoped to accumulate some Native wisdom. The woman said, "George doesn't like to talk about that. He likes to keep that sort of thing to ourselves." When Vanora had finished telling Ruth the story, she had the feeling it should have a point; there was a point when she'd begun it. Something to do with Ruth's headaches?

Vanora had been prone to babble on that way for the past few days, to talk as if to no point at all. Was that a form of denial? Was she still resisting death? Then she saw the rigid, swollen and pale face looking up at her again, the face that was not her mother's but had been her mother; and she went silent.

In any case, because of Karrin, Vanora had been able to weep. A kind of clarity had come when the tears passed. Dying was inevitable. That was the point. It was how that knowledge affected you that mattered. Did you live better because of it? Did you prepare yourself for the next moment in this one? We were here but a blip of time, then this earthly body and its accoutrements were gone. She recalled a few weeks ago going past the army barracks in the south of the city.

One of the crests on the fencing read: "Princess Patricia's Light Infantry." Obviously important in her time—one hundred, as little as fifty years ago?—no one any longer knew who Princess Patricia had been. Or King George, for that matter. His face had graced the coins when Vanora was in school, but gradually they had been replaced by others, bearing the likeness of Queen Elizabeth. In less than fifty years King George and Princess Patricia were forgotten—and they were royalty. No, surely, the point about death was that it reminded us how insignificant was this life we led. She had learned much from Karrin and Libby. She believed herself content in her knowledge and hoped the same had occurred for her brother and sister.

Roger was sitting cross-legged on the floor. A bottle sat on the floor between his legs. From time to time Vanora caught his eye. He had an amused look on his face, a look she remembered Archie had often had on his face as a boy. She had not seen Archie since he and Roger set out to work at the mines after LaFlamme's death. Like Roger, he'd aged well. His skin was smooth and nut brown, his hair long, but well-groomed. There was a twinkle in his eye. From time to time over the past days, it looked as if he wanted to say something to Vanora, but Karrin was always at her side, and she imagined that was holding him back. He wore the same amulet around his neck as he had years ago: the flying man. Perhaps he had noticed her medallion.

They had both travelled a long distance since that night in the granary. Cassie had told her that Archie had spent some time in the states, working with the American Indian Movement. He'd lived with numerous women, Native and non-Native, but never married. He had children. He worked for the government in some capacity, but Cassie had been unclear about what he actually did. Vanora wanted to tell him how sorry she was about his sisters. Their lives had unravelled. She wondered if he had reached the same stage in life as Roger: not happy, exactly, but content as long as the anger did not boil over. As kids they had both been treated badly over the LaFlamme business—it had hurt them and they had never quite put it to bed. But on the night of Cassie's funeral they looked to be in good spirits. They were smiling and laughing as they had done as boys. And exchanging anecdotes—about fishing, she guessed—man stuff.

Car headlights splashed on the bay window. Mortimer stood. He was expecting Peter. Alexander had said earlier that he worried about car crashes. He worried that there would be a flare-up between Ruth and Peter. Vanora knew that things had gone badly between them when Peter was a teenager and she did not think they had improved much since. The young were so unforgiving. Though she'd loved teaching while doing it, Vanora was glad she no longer was stuck in a classroom with teenagers, straining to empathize with their galvanic moods.

Peter came in wearing a polo shirt and pressed trousers. His hair was slicked back. A pleasant, slightly overweight man now, he was a stockbroker and he went to a stylist for a trim every Friday, Alexander had told her. Alexander was very proud of what Peter had achieved: mid-thirties and already he was wealthier than any of them would ever be. Ruth was proud too, despite their difficulties. Cassie had felt that Peter made too much money too fast. He was cocky, she thought, and brash. But Cassie had had a soft spot for him. Grandchild, almost.

Vanora thought he was too focussed and too worldly. Money, money, money. He owned three vehicles—one of those Jeep things, a fancy sedan, and a Boxter, whatever that was. He and Nancy went to Martinique for the month of February every winter. New this, renovation that. Probably a Rolex watch, if that was still the kind to own. But what about the spirit? He would live the high life but die never having known the inner self. Well, Vanora couldn't rescue everyone.

He seemed a kind enough young man.

After Peter had shaken Mortimer's hand and nodded at everyone else, he spoke briefly to his uncle and then went out of the door he'd come in. "I told him his father was down by the water and he just had to see the lake," Mortimer explained. "He hasn't been back over all these years, so he just had to walk out to the twin rocks and have a look at his old fishing haunt."

Vanora had the impression that it was immediately after Peter left the room that Roger stood up and stretched and said, "I need to pee like ten men."

"All that wine," Mortimer said, "it will come out blood red. You'll need the rag."

Vanora looked at Karrin: crude male joking.

Roger started towards the door that led out from the kitchen.

"There's an indoor now," Mortimer said. "A facility."

"A facility," Roger said in a mocking tone. He paused, as if righting his balance, then continued moving. "In the bush," he said, "you gotta avail yourself of the outdoor crapper."

Mortimer laughed. He was standing near the door that opened on to the parking lot, presumably watching for the return of Peter or Alexander. "So," Mortimer said, "avail yourself to your heart's content."

Roger said, "It ain't my heart that needs contenting."

Mortimer found that rejoinder witty. He slapped his hand on his knee. Vanora looked at Karrin again and shrugged. In any case, Roger left by the kitchen door with his own laughter rippling around him, heading for the outhouse that stood at the edge of the woods in back of the tourist cabins. He was a little tipsy; as he got to the door he had to steady himself by putting one hand on the frame.

Vanora thought he went out just after Peter but at the inquest it came out that several minutes had elapsed.

Alexander wandered along the rocks and found himself directly east of what had once been the bunkhouse. He had put his troubled thoughts about the knife he had found behind him and was thinking about how enraged he and the Finn had been at each other. Their eyes had gone as blank as fighting dogs'. He had been prepared to rip out the Finn's throat. To kill. The Finn had said he was not a good husband, implying that Alexander should move aside. But Ruth was his wife. That had enraged him, but the Finn had not given ground. Something territorial was going on, like antelope crashing antlers to decide who got the females. Did the Finn believe they were fighting over Ruth? It was primitive and sickening and deeply disturbing, the equivalent of bloodlust.

Alexander found himself walking slowly up the path that looped around the far side of the bunkhouse. The ground was soft underfoot. He smelled the wet grass and the odours coming off the leaves. Archie had been right about the walk down to the lake. He was calm now and could think. Archie had an inner strength that few men possessed. He seemed to sense what was good for a person before the person sensed it themselves. Alexander was just beginning to wonder what had brought Archie to the wisdom he had when he saw headlights splash into the parking lot in front of the lodge. Peter. He was too far away to call out when Peter got out of the car alone, so he stood and watched his son mount the steps, nodding at Archie and the Finn as he dodged past them and went into the lodge. Alexander still felt awkward about approaching. He would take a few more minutes and then join Peter inside. He stepped back into the shadows and looked up at the sky. Bright moon, distant stars. He wished he'd learned the names of all the constellations and not just the dippers and the bear.

He heard the door of the lodge open and close. When he looked, he saw the Finn and Archie were still sitting on the stoop. Alexander took a deep breath. It was time.

He came out of the shadows and they saw him as he saw them. With his tweed jacket on, the Finn was sweating and his body gave off a peculiar tang. Maybe it was true that bachelors showered less often than any other demographic group. They were close to their money, Alexander knew that. They came into the SportHut looking for bargains. They seemed to be happy with inferior quality as long as they didn't pay a high price. They were secretive about their fishing holes—maybe not secretive so much as not used to sharing confidences. They loved to chew the fat, discussing the weather or automobiles, but shied away from real conversation. Then they suddenly blurted out the most private things.

Alexander stopped at the foot of the steps, wary. Archie said, "You two need a glass of wine." When he stood and went inside, Alexander studied the Finn's unblinking eyes. The Finn drew his wrist across his mouth.

"I was out of line there," the Finn said.

"You were," Alexander said. He came closer to the steps, moving into the light from the bulb hanging over the lodge door. He sensed he had not spoken in a forgiving spirit. He was still deeply angry. He was giving no ground.

The Finn looked away. "The thing is, I done that for her own—"

"Don't say that," Alexander said. He felt his blood boil up again.

"She needed that. Ruth needs a strong hand, a man who—"

They'd been speaking in low voices but now Alexander found himself shout: "How dare you, how dare you instruct me about how to treat my own wife?"

Archie came through the door. He had a bottle of wine in one hand. "Stop it!" he shouted. "The both of you, right now." He sat abruptly beside the Finn. "What did I say?" he asked, his temper obvious. There was silence as the Finn looked into Archie's face and then exhaled deeply. The Finn looked down. "All right," Archie said. "Say it."

"I apologize," the Finn said. "It was not my place."

"All right," Archie said. He looked at Alexander.

"Okay," Alexander said, more to Archie than the Finn, still not giving ground.

"I have apologized," the Finn said, wheedling. "I am apologizing, Christ's sake."

"Okay," Alexander said. "It's been a long day. Everyone's stressed out."

Archie sighed and said, "I forgot the glasses." He stood. "Hold your peace," he said, "until I get back. We're going to have a drink together and behave like gentlemen."

When he popped back through the door a moment later with

three water tumblers, he poured each of them some wine. "All right," he said, "drink."

"Okay," Alexander said.

"Drink and be whole again beyond confusion." Archie laughed. "That's from a poem I learned in school. I don't think the poet was talking about wine."

Alexander had taken a seat on the bottom step where he could look up at the other two. They sat silently for a while, sipping and letting calm descend. The breeze whipped up from time to time. The sky was mostly clear. Rain seemed in the air. Archie poured more wine in their tumblers. "This is good stuff," he said. The Finn grunted.

In a few minutes Alexander said, "We're okay now. No more shouting."

Archie nodded his head and sipped and breathed through his nose. After a while he told them that Peter had arrived but gone to the lake. Nancy had been unable to make it, a crisis in the dialysis unit. That's why Peter had arrived late: hanging on until the last minute, hoping a replacement could be found for her. But no replacement was available. In any case, Nancy had never met Cassie, so it didn't matter much that way, but Peter wanted her to see Moon Lake, the place where he caught his first fish. He called it his magical place. "Should be back soon," Archie concluded.

That pleased Alexander, the prospect of seeing his son. But he said to Archie, "Leave us alone. We're quiet now. It's over but there's something we have to talk about. Private like."

Archie stood. He took a long swallow of wine. "I'll check back," he said. "Okay?"

When the door closed behind Archie, Alexander said, "The wine's good."

"You don't got to say that."

Alexander realized the Finn had consumed a lot of wine. Alexander had seen six bottles come in the front door. They were drowning their sorrow inside the lodge too. When he looked at the sky again, Alexander saw a full moon. That's why it felt cool on the stoop, despite the alpaca jacket. Beads of moisture dotted the Finn's chin. When Alexander touched his own brow, his fingers came away damp. The Finn had his chin raised, a pantomime of someone listening intently to the sounds of the night. "Crickets," he said, "you can hear them moving through the grass and breeding."

Alexander heard a loon on the lake and somewhere in the far distance a dog barking. From across the lake at the reservation? Sound did carry long distances over water. He'd been surprised years ago while he was walking out near Moose Point to hear distinctly the tune Peter whistled as he fished at the twin rocks.

The Finn said, "It's a good thing dying that way, going fast, like." It was a form of small talk and Alexander recognized it was also a form of rapprochement.

Alexander said, "The shock is traumatic."

"Not hanging on like a vegetable. Becoming a burden, like."

"It's painful though. Rips your guts out."

"Even," the Finn said, "when it's not your direct family."

"Yes, even then."

"Ya," the Finn said, taking up the thread gamely. "In Sweden years ago the King was assassinated. It was the whole country in mourning. In Finland we abolish all that long ago. Royal families and such." Still, he'd made a sign of the cross when he spoke of the King and it twigged a memory in Alexander for the second time that day.

"Sometimes it's kind of nice to have a Queen. This one has lingered a bit."

"Why not give Charles a shot at it? That's what everyone says."

Alexander realized the wine was making them both maudlin. "She's turning a bit sour, the Queen," he said.

The Finn laughed. "Remember when they called her the devil?"

The Finn's comment caught Alexander off guard, and when he looked at the Finn quizzically, the Finn added, "On the old bank notes, the folding money, ya? They said her picture looked like the devil."

"Right," Alexander said. "The pattern in the wave of her hair. The devil's face, people said. Satan. There were pictures on the front pages of the papers and editorials and letters to the editor, and finally the Canadian Mint officially withdrew those notes. What a to-do. Re-issuing the bank notes cost the taxpayers millions."

"Ya, Satan's face."

"I'd forgotten about that."

"A long time ago."

Alexander sipped his wine. He was counting years back and forth, calculating, but his brain was clouded with wine and exhaustion. After a while he asked, "You arrived in this country when?"

The Finn said, not having to think a moment, "On Air Iceland in 1966. The year before the centennial. Many goings-on. My plane landed in Montreal and I took a taxi out to the Expo site even before it was opened. My first looks at my new country. Very impressive. Habitat village or city or something or other. The new flag flying."

Alexander was doing mental calculations as he sipped at his wine and was not following all the other man's words. He had the feeling the Finn was going to treat him to reminiscences of Expo but instead the Finn said, "Any case, that's how I want to go—out like a light." He snapped his fingers. "No pain, no lingering, no burden to others." The Finn pulled down his lower lip and spat out a wad of tobacco.

It was at moments like this that Alexander realized Ruth had kept him young. He was almost ten years older than the Finn, but it was Finn who weaselled his mouth around like a pensioner and gave all the appearance of being the older man. "You'll probably get your wish," he said. "It's freaky, but people do."

"LaFlamme, he told me once he wanted to go to the grave with his boots on."

Alexander snorted. "You see what I mean about getting your wish." They were a long way from the conversation Alexander wanted to have. He sipped at his wine. He leaned forward, cradling his wine glass in his hands. The back of his neck was warm with sweat. He reached up and loosened the top button of his shirt. "You were the one," he said, "did that thing to LaFlamme."

The Finn studied him a moment with his bright blue eyes. "No," he said.

"And I know why," Alexander said. He felt the blood rising to his face again and he drew a deep breath. He had to go slow.

"I done nothing that night," the Finn said, "but Mort did and now Mort's in danger. Real danger of his life."

Alexander glanced over his shoulder.

The Finn whispered, "Not at this moment. But someone got Cassie and now they will be after him. They'll kill him too."

Alexander had imagined himself as the leader in this conversation but the Finn had turned the tables on him by attacking Mortimer. He said, "You've had too much to drink. That wine addles the brain."

"No, listen," the Finn said, gripping Alexander's elbow

suddenly. The odour of chokecherries and onion hit Alexander in the face. "Mort done that thing long ago and now someone's out to get him, same as Cassie."

"You mean the LaFlamme thing? You mean killed him?"

"Ya."

"No," Alexander insisted, raising his voice. "It was you. That night you were scratched up like you'd been in a fight, your shoes squished with water."

The Finn snorted. "You noticed all that?"

"Everything here was new. It made a lasting impression. Mostly I noticed that you were agitated. You'd just done something terrible. Killed a man."

"I was there, ya. I climbed a tree out there and waited for him to come. He was supposed to meet someone, I'd seen a note he was looking at earlier in the day."

Alexander nodded. "The Mountie let it slip that there was a map."

"Ya. That too. Drawn in pencil and showing Moose Point."

"So you waited and ambushed LaFlamme out there. It was you."

"No. I saw him come down the path. He goes to the wooden crate he keeps hidden in the bushes. He was bent over going through the box. His hat hooked on a branch and came off. He was a little confused for a moment, fumbling for it. Just then Mort comes along the path, running. Carrying something in one hand, like scissors, only bigger. He strikes LaFlamme before LaFlamme knows he's there. Thunk down on the ground. Stabs him, once, twice, three times in the back with the scissors thing. Then he run away. LaFlamme was bleeding and dying, crawling along the path, moaning and kind of calling out for help. He was weak. No one heard. It was awful. But he deserved it. I waited until I couldn't hear him calling any more and I climbed down the tree and got the hell out of there."

"You weren't afraid Mort would come after you too?"

"I knew how to get across the lake to where the Clouds lived. I got wet getting into the canoe and slipped and twisted my ankle in panics on the other side."

Alexander said, "Which was why the bottoms of your pants were wet and you were limping when you came around the corner of the bunkhouse later."

"I forgot you were arriving that night. Panics, ya."

"And he bled to death out there on the path, you say, from those three wounds."

"Your brother Mortimer, see, was the one. Now someone's got it in for him."

Alexander sipped the last of his wine. The Finn was lying, he knew that much. Alexander had overheard conversations between McNair and Boyd when they thought no one was listening: LaFlamme was not killed with scissors. There had been five wounds on the body. Also, he did not think Mortimer was a killer, but there was also a ring of truth to the Finn's story. Alexander was wrestling with the idea that his brother was basically a good man. He was wrestling with what the Finn had said about Mort being in danger. The Finn was sweating profusely. Wet patches had formed on the underarms of his jacket. He took a big swallow of wine and his eyes glinted in the light coming from the building behind them. "Tell him," he said, "Tell Mort he has to get out of this place."

The Finn rose to his feet suddenly. Alexander was formulating an answer but saw the Finn stagger sideways, throwing out one hand toward the flagpole. He had had a lot to drink. He regained his footing, then said, "This talk makes a man thirsty." Apparently he intended to fetch another bottle of wine; he weaved to the foot of the stairs and then started up. Alexander thought what the hell. If offered, he'd have another drink himself. He didn't believe a great deal of what the Finn had told him, but he was curious to find out if any more revelations were at hand. He glanced over his shoulder as the Finn went through the screen door. He saw the Finn and what he thought was a figure moving down the aisles of fishing tackle and light snacks in the direction of the stoop, but before he could confirm that impression, Alexander heard the crunch of gravel underfoot and then Peter came around the corner of the lodge. He was walking fast. He had his head down and his arms pumped at his sides, reminding Alexander of the way Peter went after soccer balls when he was a teen. That determination had won him the silver medal when he graduated as an MBA. It had helped him found his own brokerage firm at the age of twenty-seven, and to make his first million by thirty. Peter came up to the stoop fast, looking out of breath.

Alexander said, standing, "So how was the lake? Everything you recalled?"

"Forget about that." Peter was breathing hard. "I saw him," Peter blurted out, "I saw the guy we saw on the path."

At first Alexander had no idea what he was talking about. But Peter was intent on his story. "That night," he insisted. "When we stepped off the path. I saw the guy who came running through the woods that Labour Day weekend."

"You're mistaken. It was twenty-five years ago. A fleeting glimpse." And the memory plays tricks, he was about to add. We see what we want to see.

"It was him. I forgot at the time when the Mountie was grilling us and it has never occurred to me since, but that guy we saw had a distinctive way of moving, as if he were doing something halfway between walking and running."

"Like he had an injured leg?"

"No. Not halting, but sort of bouncing along—"

"A lope?"

"That's it exactly. Loping."

It occurred to Alexander that the loping walk accounted for the fact that he had thought through the years that it was a Native they had seen. This was not information that made him feel better.

"Indians walk that way," he said. "Natives."

"This was not a Native, but I can tell you who it is. His loping walk is not the only thing distinctive about him. He wears his hair in a ponytail."

Alexander put his hands on his hips. "You're sure?"

"I'm positive."

Alexander thought Peter was mistaken. Peter had left the city in a state of agitation about his wife, was upset about missing the funeral, and suddenly, thrown into environs he had not visited in a long time, had made a wild leap of imagination between that long-ago set of perturbing events and the current ones.

"You were just a child," he said. "Your memory is bad."

"I remember more than you do. The loping walk, for one. I remember that he was carrying something in his hand also, a knife maybe, something anyway that glinted in the moonlight. I've thought a lot about it since. It was in his hand and it reflected light."

"You're so damn sure of yourself."

"I remember uncle Mort had a gun in his hand that night."

"You were mistaken then and you're on the wrong track now."

"I remember that when we came up to the window of the kitchen after we saw the boy on the path that we saw uncle Mort and her together. They were hugging. You tried to hustle me away from there, but I saw it."

"You saw that?"

"You were embarrassed for uncle Mort then and later you lied to the Mountie about what we'd seen."

"You told him?"

"I was a kid and he was a Mountie," Peter said. "Anyway, that doesn't matter any more. What does matter is that you know who it is, don't you?"

"I have an idea. But you're wrong about him doing it."

"I'm not wrong."

"You jump to conclusions and make mistakes."

"You make mistakes. Those birds you've been calling crows all these years are really ravens."

"Crows, ravens, whatever. What's the point?"

"The point is I'm an adult. I run a corporation. I do not fly off the handle and chase phantoms and apparitions."

"You were scared that night and the mind plays tricks."

"You were scared too. I was just a kid. But what were you afraid of?"

"Lots of things. That everything would just go bad. It was just a feeling, really. That things would go bad for us. That we'd be separated."

"So you lied to me."

"Correction. Your father did not tell you everything he feared."

"To protect me?"

"To protect us both from what I thought I'd seen."

"As you're trying to protect me now. But I didn't need it then and I don't need it now. I'm a grown man, I make important decisions and judgements."

"I know all that," Alexander said more testily than he'd intended. There was this friction between them now. The boy was headstrong. He wanted to be in charge. A decade ago he'd told Alexander on the quiet, "Invest in rubber gloves. Buy stock in one of the big drug companies. The AIDS panic is spreading and soon anyone who touches anyone will have to wear rubber gloves for protection." He was right about that. But Alexander had not made the investment. And Peter had said *see*. So at Christmas Peter told him, "Buy an Internet mutual fund. In ten years half of America will be buying books and CDs and

309

clothing off the Net. It's the biggest thing to hit retail since catalogue shopping." To please him Alexander invested ten thousand dollars, and in six months it had grown to thirty. Peter was right again. But it was not entirely a good thing. Peter had done so well in the financial markets that he assumed it carried over into every sphere of life. He was The Man. The young. So headstrong, so determined they were right. So insistent. Peter had inherited many winning characteristics from his mother and himself, but this one came from neither of them. Pushiness.

Peter was bouncing from one foot to the other. "I should call the cops," he said breathlessly. "Jesus, the Mounties should know this."

"That can wait."

"So at least tell me, then."

The Finn had come through the screen door. He was holding a bottle of wine by the neck and two fresh glasses. He asked, "What's that? Tell what?"

Alexander made a hand signal to Peter. "He wants to know where they found the body."

"That's easy. Down along the stones to the east of the twin rocks."

"Where you and me used to keep our secret stringer? For the giant pike we never caught?" Peter laughed at the memory, an affectionate laugh that the Finn did not return.

The Finn stepped off the landing and weaved down the steps until he was in front of Peter. He said, "You need a glass, Peter. I bring an extra."

Peter said, "I shouldn't. It alters my blood sugar. I'll have to shoot up. But what the hell."

When Peter stretched forward to take the glass, the Finn said, "Now this you will like. Not your fancy Beaujolais nouveau, but good because it comes right from the soil under your feet. So, better, in my opinion."

Peter's eyes followed the progress of the pouring: the Finn was unsteady and some wine splashed over the lip of the glass. "That's okay," the Finn said, "a few drops for the gods of the earth. They make a good harvest for us this coming fall." He laughed and asked Alexander, "More?"

Peter had raised his head to drink. When he had tasted the wine, he said, "Good."

The Finn said proudly, "No chemicals, this here."

Peter swallowed and asked, "Was that Ruth at the door a moment ago?"

Alexander turned to look.

The Finn said, "Ya. Ruth. I offered her wine but with her brains so bad these days, she does not want it."

Alexander said, "I should see how she's making out." His own brains were a little muddled. It was a cool night but his cheeks were flushed and hot.

"I should go in and say hello," Peter said. "I missed her before."

"Stay for a glass," the Finn said, "one glass of wine with your old fishing pal."

Peter took a hasty swallow. "This is good," he said. He sipped more.

Alexander knew Peter was trying to finish the wine so he could move on. He was agitated, he was on the verge of something big.

The Finn said, "Now suddenly I got to pee." He glanced back at the door and then dropped his voice to a conspiratorial whisper. "So I go just around the corner of the building. The natural way. Won't be a minute."

"The mosquitoes might be bad," Alexander said.

"Not now. They're asleep." He put the bottle and his glass down on the steps and performed an exaggerated tiptoe. "I will not wake the little buggers up. Don't want them all over my dick, eh?" He said over his shoulder, "Don't run away now, Peter."

When the Finn had disappeared around the corner, Peter whispered to Alexander, "You have to tell me."

He was impatient. When he was a teen and in school, he snarled the mathematics problems up because he rushed to be the first finished. Alexander drew a deep breath.

"You must promise not to go off half-cocked."

"Dad, for Christ's sake!"

"You saw Roger," he said as calmly as possible. "Tonight you did."

He was standing on the top step and Peter looked up at him, his eyes hooded by the shadows from the lodge. He ran one hand through his hair.

"Shit. But we have to tell the cops, dad."

"That can wait. We need time to think."

"No. It's been thirty years of thinking and waiting. It bothers me."

"Twenty-five. Not quite. Twenty-five this fall."

"Whatever. I don't know about that, but I do know about this: I'm not standing around with my finger in my ass."

He had been annoyed at Peter's impatience but that annoyance turned suddenly to anger. He did not like this kind of talk. It was part of the surliness Peter had developed as a teen and that flared up from time to time still. Alexander felt his comfortable life was on the verge of disintegrating even further. He drew a breath. "We'll go in the morning. When we've got clear heads. We've all been drinking."

"I have not been drinking."

"We don't want to do or say something hasty, something that cannot be undone."

"No. I'm going to shoot up and then I'm going to town."

Peter wheeled suddenly and walked swiftly away in the direction of the far cabin. He had been diagnosed the year before with diabetes and had to give himself an injection if he drank alcohol. Alexander heard Peter's shoes crunch over the gravel. When he came back, he would try once more to dissuade him from driving to Beausejour. It was not far but it was an unnecessary drive, foolish even. The young could be so infuriatingly single-minded. Alexander felt dizzy and blinked several times, trying to clear his mind. The Finn's wine had a greater alcohol content than the store-bought vintages. The Finn had explained that earlier. Alexander saw the light go on in Peter's cabin and then in moment go off again.

He heard a noise at his side. The Finn came up beside him, tugging at his trouser belt. "Always in a hurry," he said, nodding in the direction of the cabins, "chasing after something, always, the young." He picked up his wine glass before adding, "What's got his shoes on fire this time?"

"He's got it in his mind he knows who did in LaFlamme."

"Now? After all these years pass?"

"So he has to drive to Beausejour and tell the Mounties."

"No ways."

"There's no point in arguing once he's made up his mind."

The Finn was silent. He lifted his glass to his lips to drink and when he did, wine dribbled past the corner of his mouth and down the front of his shirt and jacket. He did not notice. At the time Alexander recalled thinking *slob*; he thought it unbecoming for someone to drink to the point of being drunk at a funeral.

After taking a second glass of wine, Vanora felt queasy in the stomach and light-headed. She had never been a good drinker and it annoyed her that she was not thinking as clearly as usual. She liked being in control. Her gaze wandered around the room. On the sideboard near the whiskey bottle there were two potted impatiens plants, drooping and looking sick. Cassie had them there for transplanting once the risk of frost had passed later in the month, but no one had been watering them and the pink flowers were curled in on themselves, the stems turning brown. She felt annoyed about that too, annoyed that Mortimer had fallen into a funk from which he seemed unable to rouse himself to do anything except pour a glass of whiskey every half hour or so before slumping back into a chair again. The impatiens would expire from neglect. She had decided years ago that he was one of those conventional men, strong on the outside but weak inside, and nothing she had witnessed over his years of marriage to Cassie and on that weekend in particular had changed her opinion. What had Cassie seen in him? A place of shelter? She wondered if after LaFlamme any man at all looked attractive to her mother. But Vanora thought Cassie had made two bad choices in one lifetime. She had not done much better herself.

And look at Ruth. A man ten years older than her, probably did push-ups every day to keep his ass firm; probably huffed and puffed to keep her happy in bed.

She didn't like turning bitchy like this. Cassie had said to her once, "You decided on a certain course, okay; but stick to it, girl, and stick to it with good humour." That comment had touched the morass she felt inside herself. That day she had almost cried. Cassie had that kind of common sense about her when it came to her children. But not about washing fiddleheads, apparently.

Vanora reached out her hand and put it over Karrin's, who had been speaking with Archie Cloud about the amulet he wore on the leather thong around his neck. He had come in from the stoop, where, according to him, Alexander and the Finn were patching things up. Vanora had heard Archie say that the amulet he wore was a carved piece of bone in the shape of a flying man. *Pagouk*, he said, was the man's name. That was the name he had been given as a child by his people. Pagouk was a bird-man, symbol of the energy in nature and of man's desire to transcend his state, to transform himself. When Archie was a child he'd loved to run around with his arms stretched out from his sides, as if he were a bird soaring in the sky. He was always, he laughed, telling Karrin, looking for ledges to jump off. Vanora remembered that suddenly: how he had stood right at the edge of the escarpment years ago with his arms extended and she had been terrified.

Archie turned his brown eyes to her. "Sirona," he said, nodding at the pewter medallion hanging from the chain around her neck. She had not taken it off since Karrin gave it to her.

"God of transformation," Vanora said softly, "a very spiritual talisman."

"Yes," Archie said, "I know. We lust for the spirit world." He smiled at her in the way she remembered, half mocking, and for a moment it felt as if they had flashed back over those many years and were looking into each other's beings again, her not-quite-woman to his not-quite-man. Over those years she had dreamt about him often: she always seemed to be searching for him but could not find him. He was as elusive as his namesake. It pained her to recall those dreams.

She smiled back and squeezed Karrin's hand to compose herself. The room had become warm from their bodies. The wine had a potent scent: dark and cloying. It was not entirely pleasing, but the taste was, and she took another sip.

She wanted to ask Archie why he did not call himself Pagouk, but Ruth appeared briefly in the archway between the part of the lodge that functioned as a store and the kitchen. Apparently she no longer needed to lie down. She was holding one hand to the back of her neck. Vanora hadn't seen her go the other way. Her head was bent down; she was hurrying it seemed. Or perhaps in pain. To Vanora, Ruth's distress seemed affected, as if she were playing for sympathy. She knew that was not how it was, but these thoughts crept into her mind when she was tired or on edge. The wine had turned her sour. She would not drink again.

It was all confusing and worrisome to Vanora. When had Ruth come out of the back bedroom? Vanora had gone in earlier to ask her how she was feeling. Ruth was lying flat on her back with an ice pack on her forehead. Her elbow was crooked to hold it there, and for a moment she looked to Vanora like a picture she had seen of a Victorian courtesan, swooning on a couch. She had almost laughed.

Instead she had put her hand over Ruth's. "It's crazy," Ruth had said, "I can't even talk. I open my mouth to speak and pain shoots up my jaw."

Vanora said, "You rest."

"At moments like this I realize I'm not my mother's daughter."

"She only pretended to be tough."

"Did she tell you about finding the knife?"

Neither of them acknowledged who they were talking about but Ruth went on: "She came across it when she had to move the refrigerator for the repairman last month. It was a paring knife that went missing when he—LaFlamme—was killed. A little paring knife with a yellow handle."

"But I was here, right in this room that day. She told the Mountie all the knives were accounted for."

"She lied. She knew right away that little paring knife was missing and she feared the worst."

"She thought Mortimer took it."

"No, she was actually with him all that evening."

"So that was not a lie."

"She feared one of us had done it. So she covered. She was always covering in those days. Lying for him, lying because of Mortimer, lying to us."

"She was afraid they would put Roger in a home."

"So suddenly she moves the refrigerator and after all these years, there's the knife. No bloodstains, nothing. As harmless as worms. She sat down on the kitchen floor and cried. She had no idea what about exactly. But you're right. Cassie only pretended to be tough. She phoned me that night and blubbed to me." Ruth sniffed and closed her eyes and appeared to drop off.

Vanora stood at the bedside a moment in silence. This had been Cassie's room. Alexander had cleared away the boxes earlier. The air was stuffy and redolent of the lavender Cassie had liked. If she lay there long enough, Ruth's clothes would take on the scent. Vanora realized that bothered her. On the day they had walked through the woods calling Cassie's name Roger had said, *you look more and more like her.* At one point she had called out, *watch out for the poison ivy,* and he had called back, *yes, mom.* She glanced in the mirror attached to the dresser but all she could see in the dim light was a large shape. Maybe that was the most telling detail: as a girl she'd thought of

Cassie as little more than a large shape hovering about the kitchen and their lives. And now that's what she had become: a shape with fallen breasts under a head topped by wild and unruly grey hair. It was not Ruth, but she, who had become Cassie. So she had no need to feel bitchy about Ruth; no need to envy Ruth on that score.

She patted Karrin's hand and stood. Something told her to do this. She wanted to take some fresh air. Alexander and the Finn were still out on the stoop. She had heard their voices, Peter's too. The spring air would be cool. Maybe there would be a moon; maybe if she walked out to the twin rocks she would see the moonlight dance on the water as it had when she was a girl. Why wouldn't it? The moon had shone on the lake for centuries before mankind had come along and would be shining that way centuries after humans disappeared. The thought was comforting, in a way. One part of her was emotionally attached to Moon Lake: it was the place where she had grown to womanhood, and a place where mother earth was potent. But another part of her believed Moon Lake was a place of bad karma: both her parents had died violently here. Thousands of animals had been killed and skinned and brought to the trading post over the years and then swapped for food and for money that was sometimes used to buy alcohol at Carl Cuthand's. These forces were at odds with each other in her soul, but she knew that when she stood by the lake and heard the water, a peace would come to her, a wisdom larger than the human heart but which contained it. She bent to whisper in Karrin's ear that she was just going to step out for some fresh air. That's when they heard what she thought sounded like a massive plate of flat steel falling *whap* on a hard surface.

"Two," she shouted at the portable telephone in her shaking hand, and in saying it Vanora realized there really might be a curse on the place. Two more.

"Listen carefully," the woman on the other end of the line said. Vanora heard the woman speak past the machine to someone else in the room miles away in Beausejour. The woman barked two quick phrases and then she was on the line again. "Listen," she repeated, "if the victims are supine, do not move them. Got it?" There was a pause. "Are you still there?"

"Yes," she said. She had been looking at Karrin, hovering over the bodies with Alexander and Mortimer. Archie Cloud had run back into the lodge for blankets.

"Do not move them," the woman repeated. "If there are blankets handy, cover them, keep them warm. The important thing is to stop the blood. Can someone there apply a tourniquet?"

"We know that stuff. CPR."

"Tourniquets are only useful if there's lots of blood from a limb. Tie above the wound. Between the wound and the heart."

"We're not idiots here."

"More people die from loss of blood than from injury to organs. Listen. Applying compresses to wounds is usually good enough. You have to stop the bleeding."

"Yes, stabilize."

"Stabilize is the point exactly. Stanch the blood. Do not move the bodies. Do not give them water or try to force anything down the mouth. The paramedics are on the road now. They will be there in ten minutes. They have equipment and know what to do."

There was some breakup on the portable phone but she thought she got everything the woman said. She watched Karrin moving from one body to the other, placing two fingers against the artery in first one throat and then the other.

"They don't look too terribly bad," Vanora shouted over the crackling on the line.

"You can take their pulse now and have the numbers for the paramedics when they arrive. It may help."

"They're unconscious," she shouted into the phone inanely. Archie had come back with the blankets and was helping Alexander put them over the bodies. Alexander's face was grey. His hands shook with every movement. It looked as if he might pass out.

She shouted, "I have to go."

"Ten minutes," the woman repeated.

"I have to go," she shouted into the machine.

"Stop the blood."

T HEY STOOD WATCHING THE TAIL LIGHTS of the ambulance disappear into the woods in the direction of Beausejour. The siren was on. Red lights flashed on the dome and the hood of the ambulance. Vanora heard Archie breathing to one side of her and smelled the scent of Karrin's clothes on the other. While everyone else had stood aside to let them do their work, Karrin had bustled around with the paramedics, securing straps on stretchers, tucking in blankets. The paramedics had not minded. Karrin said now, "I'm going inside to check on Roger." He had collapsed on a chair inside. The Finn had passed out on the sofa in the sitting room. Mortimer was sitting at the kitchen table with a cup of coffee and a bottle of rye whiskey.

Archie said, "I should have gone with them."

"There was no space in the ambulance."

"I should have taken the pickup."

"It will be all right," Vanora said. "They know what they're doing."

When he looked down at her, Archie's eyes seemed sunken. Everyone was worn out. The funeral, the fighting on the stoop, the shooting, the ambulance. "You handled yourself well there," she said.

"Lots of practice. In the city I work with emotionally-disturbed teens."

She had half expected it. "Native kids?"

"We help them heal the child in themselves." Archie sighed. "They're all fucked up, you know? We sit around in circles talking and playing games that help them reach a point where they can laugh, then let go. Break down and cry. That's stage one."

"Liberation of the soul?"

"Emotional release. Stage two is the getting out the anger."

"They beat pillows and stuff?"

"Scream therapies. Discharge of anger. My people are burning with rage and they don't even know it."

Vanora had stepped back from him. There was a thickness in his torso and in his upper arms that she had not noticed before. He worked out. She had noticed the scent coming off his body, though: a musky cologne. "You seemed angry yourself on the stoop earlier tonight. When you and Roger were going on about the cops and so on."

"That was stupid, eh?" Archie ran his hand through his hair. She remembered that when he was young he had used Brylcreem to hold it in place. It was a smell she never came across without recalling him. "It's a constant struggle," he added, "not to give in to the demons of rage. They get the better of me. I'm not always successful."

"But you encourage the kids you work with to express rage, to let it all out."

"They need to once they see how—and who—hurt them. That's the only way they can get to stage three: expulsion of demons. But I am an adult. I do not need to shoot off my mouth about the police and every other dumb thing that crosses my pea brain."

"And Roger?"

"We do not agree about everything. He wants to be the Wild Man, but he does not acknowledge that first he must heal the child inside himself."

Vanora wondered if after the kind of therapy Archie was involved in the wounded child died and that led to the discovery of a new self, a transmutation. She felt that she and Archie would get along if they were to spend time together, though not for the same reasons they had when they were young. She said, "You have children yourself?"

"Two. But I was not ready to be a parent when I had them. You cannot be a good parent until you have healed the child in yourself." Archie sighed again. "I'm starting to sound like a recording. Forgive me. My two girls are in the States," he said, "living with their mothers. Healthy, happy. We talk on the phone every week or so."

It crossed Vanora's mind that Archie's concern for Native children was probably a displacement of his need to be a good father, a compensation, but she said nothing about that. Instead she said, "Roger's father—our father—damaged us in ways that can never be healed."

"I don't believe that and you don't either. Not really. And neither does he, in his heart of hearts. He made that gesture, remember, going back that night to get the hat."

"It was him—not you?"

"It was Roger who fetched his father's hat."

"But you were out there when it happened—you and him?"

"I had nothing to do with the death. And Roger neither." Archie waved his hands in the air, dismissing the subject. "The important thing is he saw the magic in the hat and was ready to use it to address the wound. He was open to healing. Then."

"And it's not too late, you say?"

"He was open then, he can be open now. It's all we have."

Vanora said, "You're becoming wise."

Archie laughed and patted his abdomen. "I'm becoming fat." He paused to study the sky, which was dotted with stars. "I drink too much and I'm becoming chubby."

"But your people need you."

Archie turned his eyes to hers, searching her face, she guessed, to ascertain if she was mocking him. "I care about the children," he said, finally, "and they about me."

"That's a noble thing," Vanora said. "The most noble thing we humans do is bring children into this world."

Archie was about to respond when they heard footsteps behind them. Karrin had come out onto the stoop. Roger, she told them, had roused himself and was restless. He wanted to drive into town. He was insisting on leaving alone.

He sat in the hospital waiting room alone. There had only been space in the ambulance for the two of them and him. On the drive to town the attendant hovered over Ruth and Peter, adjusting the IVs and checking pulses. He'd assured Alexander that they both would be all right, but Alexander had felt on the verge of vomiting the entire drive from Moon Lake. Archie and Roger and Mort were at the lodge. Vanora said she and Karrin would come in after an hour or so. They would bring in the Finn, who was in no condition to drive. He'd drunk too much wine and had fallen asleep on the sofa while they were waiting for the ambulance to arrive from Beausejour.

Alexander had prayed on the drive into town: folded his hands and prayed silently but fervently. He recalled the night Maria had died. He had thought then that he would come apart, but he had gone on for Peter's sake. The death of his son or wife he would not be able to bear. But that was ridiculous, wasn't it, an expression but not a fact of people's lives. Because people did go on even when their children and wives died. They got up for work every day, they ate toast, they paid bills, they plodded onward.

The hospital smelled of antiseptics and carbolic. Awful. He glanced at the covers of the magazines—coiffed starlets and other idiots—and after a while went to the machine in the hall and got a cup of coffee. He knew it would be bitter and he'd been resisting the temptation, but then he suddenly gave in.

The doctor on duty was a young woman. She did the suturing on Peter's wounds as soon as he was wheeled in, and then she came out to tell him that Peter would probably be released in the morning. He'd suffered superficial lacerations on the back and legs. The barrel of the ancient gun exploded as the bullet jammed in the corroded barrel, misdirecting it away from his body. It was the metal fragments from the barrel that struck Peter in the back. Ruth's hands were singed and had been bandaged. The fire from the explosion had run up her wrists, burning the material on the sleeves of her blouse. She was lucky not to have been badly injured. McNair had come in minutes after the ambulance arrived. His hair was grey at the temples and thinning on top. If anything he'd become more gaunt over the years. He had checked that Ruth was properly sedated. He'd called Victor. He'd sat with Alexander for a while and then had gone into the side room with the young doctor to talk with her about Peter's condition in detail.

Alexander drank the coffee, as bitter as he'd anticipated, and then looked at the notices on the bulletin board in the hall. The hospital staff were having a golf tournament in July; the nurses' association had a meeting on Tuesday; farewell party for Frances Turk. Children were born, old people expired, but ordinary life went on. A hospital was a place of crises for those who came through its door twice a year, but a place where the people who worked there engaged in a complex social life. It was as difficult for him to get his head around the idea as it had been seeing the undertaker wearing brightly-striped jammers at the beach one summer afternoon. He glanced down at his feet. There were bloodstains on his Italian shoes that he knew would not come clean. At Moon Lake he had helped lift Peter into the ambulance. He had been breathing heavily but he was conscious; he'd smiled wanly at Alexander. It was Ruth who had passed out. It was Ruth who had vomited. In the bathroom down the hallway earlier he had washed the traces of vomit and blood off his hands. Despite the strong hospital soap, he could smell vestiges of the odours.

When he burped he tasted chokecherry wine and coffee. Sergeant Boyd came in as Alexander was taking a second cup out of the machine.

"That stuff is awful," Victor said.

"I have to keep my hands busy."

"I know what you mean, but I hate bitter coffee." Victor pursed his lips and looked down at the floor, as if reluctant to begin questioning him. There was between them an unspoken understanding that bordered on affection. Alexander remembered that years ago he had admired Victor's tact and laconic manner.

Victor walked with him back to the sofas in the waiting room. They were the only people there. It was past one o'clock. From time to time a nurse went by on squeaky shoes but otherwise the hospital was silent. Overhead the fluorescent tubes hummed and flickered.

Victor pushed his cap back on his head. "You know something."

Alexander considered his answer. He was glad he had the paper cup of coffee in his hands. "I know she was out of her head with migraine," he said.

"That's not quite what I meant."

"They won't put her in jail, surely? Not a woman who suffers from such severe headaches she cannot see straight."

"It depends on the judge."

"Peter is okay. And you can't jail people for their intentions."

"In the circumstances, it's more likely to be a suspended sentence."

"What? One, maybe two years?"

"Yes. Peter seems not to have been hurt." Victor's fingers tapped the arm of the sofa. He looked at Alexander out of tired but bright blue eyes and added, "Not badly."

"It amounts to a kind of mischief, then?"

"More serious than mischief. Endangering public safety."

Alexander shifted on the sofa. The jacket he was wearing was starting to bind under the armpits. He was glad that in the confusion at the entrance to the hospital he'd put the knife in an empty metal locker standing in a bank along one wall. He cleared his throat. There was no point in making Victor force the issue. He said, "She overheard Peter say something. She misunderstood what he said."

Victor grunted. He shifted around on the sofa and then reached his hand under his leather jacket. Alexander thought he was going to take out a notepad but instead he scratched his side and then sighed with relief and said, "Mosquito bite."

Alexander said, "You're better off not to scratch."

Victor grunted again. In the silence Alexander heard the soda machine in the hallway whir into operation. He said, "It was about LaFlamme."

Victor sighed. "It would be, wouldn't it?"

"She was listening at the screen door and misunderstood what he said. Peter thought he recognized the man—the boy—we saw on the path that night."

"So she was going after this other guy and shot Peter by mistake?"

"No. It was Peter she was after."

Victor blinked quizzically and waited for him to continue.

"She was protecting Roger. All these years she thought—she feared—it was her brother who killed LaFlamme. She never said that to me, not exactly, but I knew it the way you do when you spend your life with someone. In the first years it ate away at her, so much so that she muttered his name in dreams and so on, but then it faded for the most part. She rarely thought about it or spoke about it. It was a wound that had scabbed over. She did not want the knowledge but knew to her own satisfaction that he had done it, but believed Roger was in the clear now because so much time had passed. See? Then tonight Peter told me the man we saw on the path that night was Roger. He said he recognized the way he walked."

Victor sat forward and looked Alexander directly in the eye. "After twenty-some years elapse, he suddenly recognizes him?"

"He'd never seen Roger. Years ago he and Archie Cloud disappeared on the night LaFlamme was murdered, the night Peter and I arrived at Moon Lake. And we were gone in the following summer by the time they returned to Moon Lake. It only occurred to me on the drive over here. I've been back a number of times visiting, I've seen both Archie and Roger since, but Peter has never once been back to Moon Lake. Their paths never crossed."

"Until tonight."

"Peter's probably mistaken about it being Roger. I told him that."

"Your wife didn't think so."

"She overheard us talking; she heard Peter say he was coming in to see you and tell you it was Roger. She was out of her mind with migraine; she's spent her adult life feeling sorry for Roger—and guilty about Roger."

"Guilty?"

"He took those beatings from LaFlamme—for her and Ginny. The way she saw it, he killed that bastard for what he was doing to them."

Victor said nothing. He scratched under his armpit again.

"She grabbed the old Lee Enfield rifle," Alexander explained, "in a state of panic because Peter was determined to see you tonight. He's like that: impulsive. And she's like that. Unpredictable. She had no idea what she was doing. She ran out into the night to threaten him, to scare him off, and just when she got near to him she tripped on a tree root and the gun went off."

There was a silence. They heard the sound of feet moving down corridors, doors they couldn't see opening and closing. "At the time I thought it was him," Victor finally said. "Years ago."

Alexander sipped from the paper cup. By morning his stomach would be acting up. "And now?"

"Roger came back. That seemed out of character for a killer. Despite what they say in the movies, murderers are not drawn back to the scene of the crime. They put as much distance between their despicable deeds and themselves as possible." Victor paused and then added, "And something about his personality. Roger is really a gentle soul."

"It was to protect Roger," Alexander insisted. "She was going to tell Peter to keep his mouth shut and she thought the gun would show she was serious. She's never had a gun in her hands in her life."

"Or a knife?"

"Oh, don't start on that. Back then she was just a kid."

"With a temper. Then and now."

"He's her brother and she had to protect him."

"And back then, who was she protecting? Her sister? Herself? You?"

"I know you," he said. "You can't believe her capable of that."

"You'd be surprised at what I'm capable of believing."

"She has never done anything remotely violent in her adult life."

He did not know whether Victor believed him. He did not know if the Mountie was guessing that he was insisting on this line because he was trying to hide what he did know. He watched the watery blue eyes take in what he had said without blinking. It was the second time he had lied to the Mountie about the LaFlamme business—or rather, the second time he had not told the entire truth.

L̲ies, lies, I can't believe a word you say." It was a poem Sheila had read to him. Or maybe a popular song he'd heard on the radio.

In any case, that was his life, listening to lies. Criminals told the cops none of the truth; while good witnesses, such as old people, did their confused best to tell the truth; and everyone else told the cops part of the truth. He was used to it. It didn't grate the way it had when he was younger and believed that getting to the bottom of things was a matter of asking the right questions and being persistent. In those days he took failure to close a file personally. That was the influence of Gerald Black—and look where Black's persistence had landed him. Being a cop was only a job, Victor had come to accept, not a religious calling. (No point in strapping yourself to the heart-attack machine.) In any case, sometimes there simply was no bottom to get to, persistence or not.

Victor stood out on the concrete pad in front of the hospital and looked at the sky: clouds were obscuring the moon and stars. When the call came in past midnight he was asleep and Sheila too. Sutton was off. Sawatzky was out in the squad car half way to Lac du Bonnet. Kids had rolled a SUV in the ditch; it looked as if there might only be bumps and bruises. Victor wondered: was there a full moon? They did not usually get two calls on a weeknight. The full moon would explain the calls. The full moon affected women, he knew that; a gland the size of a large pea that sat at the base of the neck reacted to the magnetic pull of the distant planet. Roger LaFlamme and his crowd howled at the moon. What next?

He unwrapped a stick of gum and popped it into his mouth. Across the street the lights were still on at the Giant Hardware: glowing fluorescent lighting, which was less expensive to run all night than to switch off and on. And a security measure, in addition. The hardware store was part of the new mall. Developers had paid Young Beaudry fifty grand to stop farming that twenty acres. There was talk that lawyers were offering him twice that for the acreage next to it to put in a mega car dealership. In ten years the town would have doubled in size. He was glad he was retiring soon; let Sutton and Sawatzky fight with the mayor about hiring proper town cops to look after the town and leave the RCMP to do their specified job properly, which was to patrol the outlying areas.

He had been surprised at how much development had occurred at Moon Lake. There were plans for further expansion, he understood. They would push the forest back farther. Before you knew it, developers would be subdividing and putting up ticky-tacky cottages. The tourist industry. There was talk that the Finn was going to put in a takeout chicken kiosk. Next they'd be applying for a liquor licence. Carl Cuthand would have a laugh over that. What it amounted to from the RCMP perspective was extra terrain for the detachment to cover. Progress, they called it, but he wasn't sure. The deer and the small birds had moved farther back into the woods. Only the crows and magpies seemed more plentiful. Development and scavengers. That's where they were headed.

Yes, Vancouver was looking attractive. At least Sheila would be happy. And they would see Terry more than once a year. He loved hugging his tiny daughter to his chest, though soon another man would be doing that: Tim something or other, a geologist she'd met backpacking on a glacier tongue.

He heard an owl hoot and then another. Odd, he did not hear them at Moon Lake but in town they were becoming more plentiful. Fewer natural predators? Better pickings around the garbage cans of the citizens? He looked around, cocking his ear to the resonant hoot that came every minute or so. In her last year of high school Terry had worked on a project in Riding Mountain National Park that involved the tracking of owls. A biologist from the college made a tape of owl calls in mating season and then spent nights playing it to attract the owls in the area for the purposes of estimating their density in the region. Terry had put in many long, chilly nights, and she came home with a sniffle. But the project had led her to a vocation: she tracked heron in the remoter lakes of British Columbia's interior. She spent her days in heavy hiking boots with a pack on her back and binoculars around her neck. She ate a lot of muesli and yogurt and she did volunteer canvassing for Greenpeace. His kid, a nature nut. She used the phrase *mother earth* the way Natives did on TV.

Victor ran his eyes through the trees near the hospital, hoping to spot the owls. The breeze that had come up earlier when the clouds moved in had died. The leaves on the trees were hardly moving. He glanced across toward the mall and spotted first one and then two baby owls sitting on the lip of the roof of the Pharmasave. They fluttered about from one perch to another, hooting from time to time and ruffling their feathers. Practising to become adults. Then they flew off into the bluff of trees behind the mall where the car dealership would soon be going. If the baby owls looked for those trees next spring, they would not find them. It annoyed him to see the birds pushed back, but his anger was pointless. He did not believe, as Terry did, that you could stop the march of progress. Bully for her, though, she stuck to her principles and waved her placard to demonstrate her dissension. Like her mother had done when they were in college.

Behind him he heard the automatic door of the hospital open with a pneumatic whoosh. It was one of the young nurses going off duty. Victor had half expected it to be Alexander Mann—who wasn't lying, exactly, but he hadn't told Victor everything. Maybe if he pressed him in the morning; maybe if he took a statement from the Finn. This was something else Victor had learned. In the city, perhaps, it was important to track things down without delay, to knock on doors in the middle of the night, to rush from place to place with SWAT teams and search warrants. In his territory, no. He would take statements in the morning: Ruth, Peter, everyone at Moon Lake. If he was lucky, he would learn what had happened between Ruth and Peter; if he was really lucky, the business of twenty-five years ago would be part of what he cleared up. He would close the file. Too bad Gerald Black was not there to see it.

He was just about feeling smug about that when he saw headlights approach and then a car turn into the parking lot and drive up directly in front of him. The car was a rusting Volvo station wagon and the driver who got out was Roger LaFlamme. He said as if by way of apology, "I just had to see for myself."

"It's late," Victor said, "and they're sleeping. There's nothing anyone can do."

Roger ran one hand back through his hair. "I get twitchy," he said. "It's like when you get a stone in your shoe and you have to remove it, only this is more like an itch in my soul." He was breathing hard, Victor noticed and blinked his eyes when he spoke.

"You all were drinking out there, right?" Victor said. "You shouldn't be driving."

Instead of answering, Roger turned on his heel and looked across toward the roof of the pharmacy. "Owls," he said. "See them?"

"I was listening to them hooting. They're babies who are learning how."

"That sound they make isn't so much a hoot as a screech."

"It's a shame: the animals are being driven back into the forest."

Roger grunted. He was standing a few feet in front of Victor and Victor smelled an odour coming off his clothing, something like incense. Roger said, "Did you know that the crow is one of the few animals who plays?"

"Squirrels play," Victor said, "and kittens and puppies."

"Youngsters of most species play," Roger said, "to learn certain survival tricks—hunting. But the crow plays only to amuse itself. Lies on its back and juggles objects between its feet and its beak. Totally frivolous. An acrobatic routine where they tip backward from an aerial perch dizzily, then daringly let go with one foot and then the other, switching, like, in mid-routine. They're the hot-dogs of the animal kingdom."

"Sounds like they're too smart, like they've got too much brain for the simple life they've been allotted, pecking seeds and whatnot."

They stood in silence and listened to the owls. Victor felt tired, as exhausted as he'd felt in his life. He needed something to eat, something with sugar to jump-start the system. He needed a cup of coffee, preferably with cream, but he would not drink that swill in the hospital machines. He felt sorry for Alexander Mann: reduced to drinking that crap. And with his wife and son both lying wounded in hospital beds. Finally Victor said, "She thought it was you killed LaFlamme. All these years Ruth thought it was you."

"I should have." Roger was silent a moment and then added, "In African tribes they know the Old Man must die, so when it's time, the sons kill him. It's just part of the way they do things. We have not learned that yet."

"We've unlearned it," Victor said. "It's against the law."

Roger grunted. "We should not have buried him either. When you bury the Old Man, you put him underground but you have not rid yourself of his spirit. He haunts you, waking and sleeping. The people of the Amazon understand this: they burn the Old Man so his spirit can fly free to the spirit world where it belongs—not trapped underground."

Victor had heard people talking like this on television. It was all the rage among the academics and intellectuals now, rediscovering the primitive. Soon somebody would have a theory about leeches. People would be smoking peace pipes to cure Alzheimer's and cancer. Maybe that was what he'd smelled on Roger's clothing before: exotic Indian tobacco. He said, "Cassie thought it was you did it, too."

Roger was silent a moment, and Victor wondered if he was trying to buy time, but then Roger said, "At one time maybe. She'd discovered something, though, a few years ago or so that showed he had a dark past, that LaFlamme had a secret in his past."

Victor moved a little closer. "Murder?"

"Extortion, maybe. Something to do with a lot of money—which she never found."

"She worried that he'd be sent to prison over this money?"

"No. This was after he was dead. She was worried one of us—us kids—had taken the money from him."

"You mean killed LaFlamme to get the money?"

"It happens. Kids kill parents. Anyway, Cassie was always covering for us, so it was just a reflex for her to cover for us about that too." He gestured with both hands, lifting them up like a preacher giving a benediction. Victor saw how the muscles bulged under his shirt. He worked out, it seemed. His shoulders were square and enhanced the solidity of his lower back. Probably he canoed on the Roseisle River as well as chopping his own firewood.

"What did she find?"

"Something that put us in the clear. Notes or something, it seemed, writing in a book or a diary. It put us in the clear. She'd secretly obsessed about it being one of us for almost thirty years, see? So she was major relieved."

"She was trolling around town with a manila envelope."

"I'd heard about that."

"There were people she talked to, cronies of her aunt and uncle."

"She'd obsessed about it a long time. Then she thought she'd discovered evidence that put us all in the clear. But she needed confirmation. She needed one of LaFlamme's old cronies to confirm what had really happened, that we were innocent."

"She told you this?"

"She hinted at it. Called me on the phone not long ago and blabbered. She must have been drinking—which was not like her. I sensed that Mort was not there. It was all kind of vague. She didn't want to say anything until she was certain." Roger sighed. In the past few moments his shoulders had slumped and Victor could tell that he had closed his eyes and was breathing deeply.

"You seem relieved," Victor said.

"It feels good to get it out. We've all been keeping it locked in a long time. You can actually feel your chest hurting sometimes. It's not just an expression, locking things up in your heart. We've been evading you and lying to you too long."

"Covering for each other."

Roger shifted from one foot to the other. He was not afraid of anything, Victor guessed, just tired with the lateness of the night and weary of going over old ground. He sighed and ran his hand back through his hair again. "We did not set out to hate you."

H E'D NEVER VISITED the house but he knew where it was located and what it looked like. Who had told him? Ruth? Vanora? He was looking for a two-bedroom clapboard bungalow, in any case, with a collapsing picket fence and a lilac hedge. It was on the far side of town where the asphalt road gave way to gravel. He crossed the street from the hospital and he walked past the mall. Ruth and Peter were both sleeping quietly. McNair said it would be best to let them alone until morning. The lights were blazing in the Giant Hardware. That's what it was nowadays: Home Depot, Office Depot, Costco. The megastores were squeezing family businesses out. He had learned from Henry that an outfit called SportChek was going to put up a place in the strip on Pembina Highway. It was only a matter of time before he felt the squeeze himself. Was it better to sell out now, as Beaver Lumber had done, or hang on, relying on elusive customer loyalty? Alexander knew the answer. In any case, he had made his million. Maybe the thing to do was move his SportHuts out of the city proper and into towns like Beausejour. He did not think so. He wondered what Peter would say. *Invest in the market.*

A car went by on Main Street, teenagers with the music up so loud the car shook. In the city Ruth always wisecracked: "Isn't that nice of them, they want to share their music with us." When they drove up at the streetlight in the city, he was tempted to crank up the volume on the Merc. Blow them away. Childish, really. The car's tail lights blinked twice in the distance as the driver braked at a dip where the road crossed a culvert out of town. Alexander was headed there. His head was still muzzy from the wine, and the coffee had upset his stomach, but he was feeling better than an hour ago: his wife and his son were going to be okay. "This too will pass," he thought. A good motto for life.

He was breathing heavily, he realized, but a certain resolution energized his steps. His muscles were fatigued and his brain cloudy, but determination was knit on his face as tight as a sock.

Alexander thought briefly of Peter's twisted face when he'd lain on the stretcher in the ambulance. And of Ruth's collapsed one: her cheeks puffing out as she breathed on the edge of consciousness. It was time this nonsense ended. He had set his jaw to it and was determined to see it through. He knew men like that often kept guns but he was not afraid. Once his feet were moving over the asphalt they developed a momentum of their own. He heard the soles of his shoes falling in turn to meet the cement of the sidewalk, which was covered with thin sand that crunched underfoot. He felt the cool night air on his hot cheeks and smelled the sap the trees gave off in spring.

The caffeine pounded in his temples. He was full of energy.

Past the Shell station the sidewalk ended and he crossed the street to face on-coming traffic, a habit he had learned from his father, he realized. Here the trees were thicker, spruces and pines as well as elms and maples. Garbage cans sat at the ends of driveways. Tuesdays must be garbage pickup day. There were almost no lights on in the houses. From the window of one place across the street the blue flicker of a television. Frogs chirring in the ditch. When he came to the collapsing picket fence, he went up the gravel drive, and then crossed the lawn to look in the window. A light was on in back, probably the kitchen. He could just make out a figure slumped in an armchair in the living room, still in tie and jacket. The smell of lilacs wafted over Alexander. He stood for a moment, sniffing. A rare spring evening, calm and quiet. A night bird was rattling in the trees.

Alexander walked around to the back door and banged on it until he heard feet crossing the floor. The Finn opened it and squinted into the dark at him. He did not say anything but stepped back and Alexander followed him into the kitchen. A teapot sat on the oilcloth-covered table, a half-empty mug of brown liquid in front of one of the chairs. The Finn noticed him studying it. He reached up into a cupboard and brought another mug to the table. The Finn took off his jacket and draped it over the back of one chair and then sat at another. Alexander pulled up the chair opposite.

He had passed an open closet as he crossed from the Finn's mud room into the kitchen and he'd seen a shotgun propped against an inside wall of the closet, a clumsy old twelve-gauge with a long barrel. He wondered if the Finn knew the government had requested citizens to turn in all firearms. He tried not to look at it.

In this light the Finn looked pale and exhausted, an old man, Alexander thought, though he was not yet fifty. But old in other ways. His hair on top had thinned and there were lines and creases around his eyes and mouth. His teeth were stained. The eyes that had once been bright blue were milky, or maybe that was just the effect of alcohol and the poor lighting in the kitchen. Alexander hadn't noticed it out at Moon Lake, but the Finn was fleshy. With the jacket off he had a noticeable pot belly and his forearms were flabby. He was a man without a woman, a man growing old alone.

The Finn did not say anything as he poured a mug of tea for Alexander and grunted as he pushed it across the table to him. Alexander recalled that years ago he had had suspicions about the Finn's sexuality when he had taken an interest in Peter and was always suggesting the boy join him to go fishing. Alexander had thought of him as a nice young man then, harmless, but he had heard things since that made him wonder about the Finn's character. He resisted unionization among his employees at the chicken places. The business people in town did not really trust him: he was a sharp and unscrupulous negotiator. There had been some shouting and pushing in the Lakeland once between the Finn and a man whose diner the Finn had bought in a bankruptcy sale. Then there were the women. When he was younger, the Finn got drunk and propositioned married women at wedding dances and socials. A waitress from the truck stop had been on the point of bringing charges for assault some years back, but then the charges were dropped when the Finn bought her a new car and she moved to Whitemouth.

He was a lonely man as well as old. The people in the town all recognized him when they saw him on the street, but what did they know of his life? What did they care to know? He was an oddity, a bachelor, a man who lived alone, not even a dog or a cat, an immigrant who would die with a million in the bank that would be scooped up by Revenue Canada. No, Vanora said it was going to long-unseen relatives in Finland. Though he had never been back, the Finn still harboured a deep sentimental attachment to his home country and the people who lived there. So be it.

They drank in silence. Alexander heard the refrigerator humming and the ticking of an old-fashioned clock. He imagined it sitting in a corner of the living room, like the one in the song "My Grandfather's Clock," which he had learned as a child and taught Peter when he was a boy. He glanced around the room: finger marks and smears around the handles of the cupboards, smudges on the refrigerator, the smell of something going bad, like cabbage or fruit. He was thankful he had been spared the bachelor life. It was not just the loneliness, though that was the worst. There was a kind of disintegration in progress.

The Finn said, "They're okay? Your boy, Ruth?"

"Sleeping. Nothing too serious."

They looked directly into each other's eyes. The Finn breathed heavily through his nose. He raised the cup to his mouth. There was a cut on the inside of one of his wrists that had not been evident before. A red stain from the wine he'd spilled at Moon Lake ran down the front of his white shirt; it resembled the country of Argentina in outline.

"This has got to end," Alexander said.

The Finn snorted and looked toward the window.

"Tonight," Alexander said.

"Don't bully."

"You lied to me," Alexander said.

"Everyone lies. I have learned this doing business in Canada. The real estate agents lie, the suppliers lie, employees, even the little kids who come in and break stuff or steal stuff at my businesses. Everyone the same in this country."

"This country has done well by you."

"I done well by it. I worked very hard. I earn everything."

"Only you started with money you stole."

The Finn grunted. "Alexander Mann," he said, "one sharp cookie."

"You stole that money, that roll of bills in the little shed."

"I should have guessed it would be you that figured it out."

The Finn stood and opened the refrigerator and brought back a plastic jug of maple syrup, a dollop of which he poured into his tea. He plunked the jug on the table between them. "LaFlamme," he said snorting, "he owed me, that bastard. When I first come to Moon Lake he takes me aside and tells me that in this country it is the practice for immigrants to pay employers a fee to hire them on. A thousand dollars, he take from me. He said he'd report me to some government agency if I did not pay him. I was a kid, nineteen years old, alone in a foreign country where I hardly speak the language, what did I know of a bastard like that? I had to sell some of the keepsakes I'd brought over with me: my father's signet ring, a diamond brooch from my mother. They both drowned while boating on a lake in Lapland when I was a child. So I was raised by an older aunt and an uncle who was a butcher. That's how I know when these bastards here cheat me by leaving a pound of extra fat on each fryer. Another type of lying, see? Any case, I give LaFlamme the thousand dollars, so when I learn later I needn't have, I don't ask it back, but in my heart I am always after that holding a grudge against him."

"It was stealing, whatever you call it now."

The Finn laughed but without smiling. "Hoh. Easy to say when everything falls into your lap—or is given to you. With that money I bought my first chicken place. It was a failing business. That Dawes, that drunkard who sold it to me, he had no head for business. You Canadians, you're either dabblers or softies. I put that money to work, see. I made something of the business and then when it became a big success, I started new businesses in two other towns. The people of Beausejour should be grateful to me. I done economic good here." He paused. "You got to seize the opportunity."

"You lied to me about Mortimer. Earlier tonight."

"He wanted LaFlamme dead so he could steal his wife. He may as well have stuck him with the knife out there in the bush that night. He done it in his heart already."

"But the point is he did not. You lied to me."

"You never understand that, see. It's what I mean by soft. You're trusting and blind, you Canadians. I hate Mortimer because he comes to Moon Lake and right away he looks around and thinks I can be the boss here, I can have the woman and the money. He's devious, your brother. Not so soft as you. Not so much smart as cunning. He would have killed LaFlamme eventually."

"But he didn't."

The Finn seemed not be listening to him. "Then when the bastard is gone, he lords it over me. We slept beside each other in that stinking bunkhouse, we ploughed those rocky fields of LaFlamme's together, we picked stones side by side. It was him and me against LaFlamme. Like brothers. Then LaFlamme is gone and suddenly he's the big boss man, the big muckity-muck. Bedding the wife, giving orders, taking the more softer jobs for himself. Bringing his brother in to do the more softer jobs too. Hoh."

"So you wanted to hurt me with that story. Up the tree and so on."

"I hate you too. From the first day I come to Moon Lake, I am in love with Ruth. Such a beautiful girl, yes? Dark eyes, a way of walking makes a man's throat hurt. She was meant for me. I am her age. She likes me. I can tell. She laughs at my jokes and comes out to the deer meadow when she knows I'm there alone so we can talk together away from Cassie. I am a good-looking young man, yes? A hard worker. Strong."

"Girls that age flirt with men. It doesn't mean anything."

"No, she would have married me. We would have been happy together. Ya. Children, all my hard work going to blood of my own instead of nieces in Finland I've never even seen." The Finn banged one fist on the table and the mugs rattled.

Alexander stared at the floor. It was a white-flecked linoleum, turning yellow and worn into black streaks where chairs had been dragged over it. The smell he'd noticed earlier was onion. A small piece of brown skin had settled on the floor near the refrigerator. The room was grubby and cramped. The Finn was living a small, pinched life. The furniture was old, the decoration tawdry. Did the man own anything that was new? Maybe the Saab. But everywhere Alexander read the signs of resentment and denial. The Finn's mouth pinched down at the corners in a permanent pout. Bitterness was growing in him like a fetus.

Alexander said unexpectedly, "Have you been sleeping okay?"

"The last week not so good. I have a bottle of wine with my dinner to help me along but then I wake in the middle of the night with a headache. It's never happened before like this. I've been drinking my wine for thirty years."

"The body changes. Develops allergies. Weak spots."

"My body is strong. I can out-work these kids today without hardly lifting my little finger. Hoh."

"You're angry at them, you're angry at me. You're an angry man."

"You cannot blame me. Ruth loved me, but then you come along, Alex Mann, with your sad eyes and your ridiculous pipe and your bumbling son who cannot even tie a fishing line. You cannot blame me when you stole away the girl who was meant to be my wife, the mother of my children."

"You wanted to kill me for doing that?"

"Ya, at times. I lay in that bunkhouse some nights and heard you snore and knew I could strangle you in the bed before Mort or Peter even woke up."

"So you tell me this story about Mort twenty-five years later to get back at me? To hurt me."

"And your brother. To hurt you both, yes, as you have hurt me. She was my age and you were an old man. What makes a beautiful young woman like that go for an old man? So. I want you to think the worst thing possible about your brother. You stole my bride and my children. Stole my future. My beautiful Ruth. And I knew you suspected him. Hoh."

"The Mountie told you something?"

"Peter told me you saw them in the kitchen that night." The Finn looked up from his tea mug and smiled a crooked smile that revealed his brown teeth. "We had many good talks out on those rocks, your son and me. He was an innocent child."

A shiver ran down Alexander's spine. He had always suspected the Finn took advantage of the boy, but never guessed the form it took was pumping Peter for information. "You're a dangerous man. I thought that because you appeared to be shy that you were meek and humble, but you're neither. You're a snake in the grass."

"I am quiet but I am not shy. That's a weakness. It's you Canadians who are weak. You trust everybody. You're afraid of your own shadows and you assume everyone else is too. You got this from your Indians, who talk a big story, but turn into scared rabbits when you wave a hand in their face. At least LaFlamme got that right, the bastard." His eyes glinted. He wanted Alexander to see that he not only thought these things but enjoyed throwing them up in Alexander's face. It was the moment the Finn had waited years for and he was revelling in it.

Alexander stood. He went to the window over the sink and looked out toward the sagging garage where a yard light burned. A plot of vegetable garden grew down one side of the property, and along side it a high lilac hedge. At the far end of the yard grew chokecherry bushes, their long white blossoms drooping at this time of year. A collapsing shed stood in a far corner. The handle of a gas lawn mower poked out from under a tarpaulin. Alexander ran a glass of water and took a long drink. When he turned to look at the Finn he saw again the shotgun propped in the corner of the closet. "You're not going to use that, are you?"

The Finn glanced at it and snorted. "My safety blanket. Bought it at an auction years ago. Didn't notice the barrel was warped. I suppose I could scare off intruders by waving it at them, but a baseball bat would work better in an actual confrontation."

"That isn't quite what I meant."

The Finn didn't seem to hear him. "In all the years I've lived here, I've never once had anyone threaten me. No one has come to the door in the night who I did not know. Kids do not throw tomatoes at my house or ring the bell and run away. Nothing. No matter what I done. Canadians think they're nice people but I think it's something else. Neglect. They don't know I'm here."

"They know you own the chicken places."

"That they know, and how to cheat me. But they don't know my name." He raised his eyes to Alexander's and asked, "Do you?"

"Saul something, is it not?"

"Sauli, not Saul. See, not even you. Sauli Affenimi."

"It's not an easy name to get."

"They know Sergio Momesso and Bramwell Tovey and Boris Yeltsin, but me, a man who makes money for their town, a pillar of the community, they can do no better than the *Finn*. I'm a nobody. A piece of shit."

"You sound like a man who might do something rash."

"I will not turn the gun on myself."

"Men who live alone do. Women, too. I won't bore you with statistics."

"Mo Lonergan done it. I know. We were sitting in the beer parlour Friday night, telling jokes and watching the young women play snooker and then he goes home and puts the barrel of a shotgun in his mouth. And for why? Because schoolgirls with little breasts play snooker and he does not have a woman. He was fifty-one. He ran a good hardware business. Last year he drove up the Alaska Highway and came back with wonderful pictures. Have you seen those snaps? No, Mo Lonergan was a weak Irish. I am a Finn. I will not give in to that. We Finns are proud people; we fought back the Russians. No one else done that. No one else had the strengths of character to push the Commies back."

It was an odd outburst of false pride but perhaps the only thing that had kept the man going for nearly thirty years. When they had first met at Moon Lake, Alexander had liked him. He'd had a twinkle in his eye, life lay before him like a promise. He'd been good to Peter. Maybe that was what had blinded Alexander to the change that had come over the Finn. Twenty-five years of bitterness and resentment. They had eaten a hole in his heart. He was not the happy boy Alexander had encountered at Moon Lake.

Alexander sat at the table. He was exhausted. His throat was burning, a sign that his resistance was running down and that he could be feverish by morning. When he moved his head from side to side, a murky wave clouded his brain. He was thinking of the bed in the motel but there was one more thing to do. He reached into the inside pocket of his jacket, and when he withdrew it, he placed the knife on the table between them.

"You did it, didn't you—killed LaFlamme?"

The Finn picked the knife up. "*Puukko*," he whispered. His hands trembled. "It belonged," he said, "to my father. The one souvenir from the old country I was able to keep when I sold everything to get LaFlamme his thousand dollars. We'd used this knife to gut fish, my father and I, on the shores of the lakes back home. He had a grinding stone and with it he sharpened mower blades and kitchen knives and so on. My first pocket knife he sharpened with that stone. And this knife. See where he gouged into the metal as he sharpened this fishing knife? I can feel my father's big hands right there." His voice choked. He said something else in what must have been Finnish. Tears welled in the man's eyes and Alexander looked away.

"There's a moment I've thought about many times now," Alexander said. "You remember what you were doing when Kennedy was shot? Maybe for you it was a different event. I remember what happened on the night Peter and I arrived at Moon Lake. After Peter had fallen asleep I awoke and stepped out to look at the lake. I was standing in the trees and saw a man down at the water. I was going to say hello to him. It was a peaceful night, serene. I saw the man stoop to the water and when he stood up he crossed himself and it made the serenity of the moment deeper. Then we found out LaFlamme had been murdered and everything changed for everyone, Peter and me too."

They were silent. The Finn's eyes were dry now but the corners of his mouth moved, as if he were chewing the lips from inside.

"It was only today I realized what I'd seen. That man crossing himself was you and you were seeking absolution for having done a terrible thing. You ambushed and killed LaFlamme that night—with this very knife."

"No. Like I said before. I happened to get a look at the note and went out there to see what was going to happen."

"Just curiosity?"

"I want to see him get his comeuppance, ya. After what he'd done to Ruth."

"But you carried a sharp knife with you?"

The Finn shook his head. "No, no. Listen."

"He spotted you in the trees? You had to come down and fight and somehow you got the better of him and killed him?"

"No. He was occupied with that crate of fishing gear, dragging it out from under the bushes. About the time his hat falls off, along comes Roger, running. He's carrying something that reflects the moonlight. A knife."

"But not a pair of hedge clippers, or scissors, or whatever?"

"Roger struck LaFlamme in the back of the head with the knife handle."

"It was Roger who stabbed him, not Mort?"

"No. He did not stab him, he struck him and knocked LaFlamme down. His legs went spastic, his arms. He was out cold. Roger stood over him for a moment, deciding whether or not to finish him off. But he was weak. He was a kid. He'd said in moments of rage that he would kill LaFlamme but he could not bring himself to do it. So, he did what a kid does, he run away. Down the path toward the canoe and the rowboat. Only he drops the knife."

"Then you came down the tree and finished him off?"

"Almost at once someone else materializes out of the trees. At first I cannot tell who. But a man. By that time LaFlamme had recovered a little of his senses. The blow to the back of the head did something to his brains, though. He could not stand and he could not speak. He gurgled incoherently, and then with his hands he started scrabbling forward on the path. He was a strong son-of-a-bitch. There was in him a terrible will to survive. He might have got away."

"This is bull," Alexander said. "More lies." Alexander's eyes were burning. He was exhausted. He drank some of the bitter tea. "And this," he said, "tastes foul." He was not fond of tea, anyway, a sissy drink, a drink for women.

The Finn stared up at him and blinked. He asked, "Where was I?"

Alexander felt the rage he had experienced when the Finn had slapped Ruth returning: a hot wave that ran from his gut to his cheeks. But he said between gritted teeth, "Another man, you say, came out of woods."

"The man who'd come out of the woods was carrying a gun, a little pistol—you've seen maybe those one-shot .25s they made during the war—painted silver. He was going to use it but he spotted the knife and put the gun away. What luck, a knife right there."

Alexander shook his head. "No, no," he said. "You hated him. Hated how he'd forced himself on his daughters. You thought he was a bastard who deserved this and more, and you had the chance to do something about it and did."

"No. It was Young Beaudry stabbed him with this gutting knife."

"This knife?"

"Roger must have got it out of my tackle box."

Alexander heard himself breathing heavily out of his mouth. "You're lying again. Young Beaudry? That makes no sense. There's no—"

"Something was going on there. Old Beaudry and Sam Roby, there was some connection that went back to the war. Cassie let something slip once."

Alexander wondered how much he should say. He was feeling a little woozy, but finally he said, "LaFlamme blackmailed Sam Roby and forced him to give up the trading post, yes. That money in the cookie tin was dirty blackmail too. That money which you stole."

"Ya. LaFlamme, the bastard, was blackmailing Sam Roby and the Beaudrys. He'd punched out Young Beaudry in the Lakeland a month or so before he was killed and the rumour around town was it had something to do with money."

Something had been bothering Alexander about the Finn's story and suddenly he knew what it was. "Wait a minute," he said. "You told me earlier that it was Mort that killed LaFlamme, but now you also expect me to believe you're telling me this new pack of lies to protect Mort."

"Ya. Long time ago I hated him and you and I want to see you both squirm, but I do not want someone to kill Mort. He is not LaFlamme. He does not deserve to die of knife wounds in the back— or from someone knocking him into the lake and drowning him."

Alexander said, "And you're saying you were up the tree all that time?"

"When Young Beaudry was going through LaFlamme's pockets looking for the note he'd sent to arrange the meeting, I made a noise in the tree and he rushed off the way he'd come."

"Leaving the knife behind."

The Finn shifted a little in his chair. "I was flabbergasted when I saw it was mine. I realized how much trouble I was in. An immigrant, and my knife the murder weapon. The Mounties would pin it on me, for sure."

"But you went through his pockets and stole that money too."

"He was a fool, LaFlamme, a fool who carried a roll of bills in his wallet even when we were working in the fields."

"Five hundred, Cassie said. So you took it."

"No. That must have been Beaudry. Taking back what he'd given LaFlamme to entice him to come out to Moose Point. A kind of teaser to lure him out there."

"But you did take the knife?"

"He was wearing a windbreaker. I pulled it off the body and used it to wipe off the blade. I'd got my shoes bloody too, I saw. I took them off and put them in the jacket and threw the parcel into the lake at Moose Point."

"You chucked the jacket and the shoes, but you kept the knife?"

"I liked those shoes. I brought them with me from Finland but the next three years I wore nothing in the summers but the striped blue Adidas."

"Yes. Cassie made a joke about sneakers and sneaks, which I recall you did not find very funny."

The Finn was looking off past his tea cup, reconstructing the events of years ago. "My father's knife," he said, finally, "*puukko*, we call it in Finnish. I felt I had to keep it. Ridiculous now I think of it. But not then. It was my one tie to his life, to our time and life together in Finland. It had a hole through the handle and I fixed a stringer through and attached it to the base of a willow far down in the stones past the twin rocks. I was going to come back for it some day when the business blew itself out. Where I hid it was a more remote spot in those days. No one ever ventured that far along the willows. The knife was a keepsake, something my father had held in his own hands. It was a ridiculous sentimental attachment. But I was a kid. He was my dead dad and I had no one."

"But you didn't go back for it later?"

"No. I didn't dare right away, and then as time passed it seemed bad luck to go down there and mess with it. Then as the months passed, I sort of forgot about it being there. I should have just chucked the damn thing in the lake to begin with and been done with it. But something held me back from that too."

Alexander took a deep breath. In his mind's eye he saw a form bending low to the water and then raising itself and making a sign of the cross. He said, "Your feet squished when you came up to the bunkhouse that night."

"I kept an old pair of sneakers in the granary for when we had to work in there. When I washed my hands by the lake I tried to roll up my trousers but they got wet and were still soggy and water from the cuffs ran into my sneakers. You cannot believe the state of panics a man gets in after something like that. My heart was as big as a blimp."

Alexander stared into his mug of tea as if there were something there to see other than the brown liquid. Something was amiss in the Finn's story but his brain was too muddled to figure out what. He took a sip of tea. It had gone cold and tasted bitter. It would coat his teeth and by morning his mouth would be foul. He said finally, "And Cassie? You found out recently that she was poking around down at the water's edge and you went after her? So she couldn't discover your secret?"

"No. She knew nothing about the stringer. But whoever killed her figured that she knew too much. She was dangerous."

"She could have seen the stringer glinting in the water the way I did."

"No, it was Beaudry again, protecting the family secret."

"Young Beaudry's got a terminal cancer. It doesn't make sense for him to kill somebody in his condition."

"It makes more sense. He has less to lose if he's going to die soon anyway."

"No, you've seen him. He's pale and weak from chemo. Feeble."

The Finn shrugged. "But it has to be him."

"You, on the other hand, are strong and angry and…."

"Who else had a reason?"

Alexander suddenly knew what had been bothering him. "The thing is, what happened to the hat? You say nothing about that. You say you put your shoes into the jacket before chucking them in the lake, but you say nothing about the hat. That tells me you're lying. That among other things."

The Finn shrugged. "A detail. There were hours of time unaccounted for."

Alexander shook his head and then rubbed his eyes to clear them. "You lie to me earlier but now want me to believe this Beaudry stuff."

"Then I am making up a story."

"And now too?"

"I'm confessing. I'm a Catholic, see."

"You're slippery is what I see."

The Finn swallowed, his Adam's apple bobbing visibly. "I am a Finn. I face up."

Alexander said, "You'll have to go to the Mounties. Make a statement."

"It's twenty-five years have passed."

"They don't close these cases."

The Finn held his wrists out in front of him and laughed sheepishly.

"Not me," Alexander said, "I'm not taking you in. But you think it over. Give yourself a day or two. Talk to a lawyer. If you haven't turned yourself in by the end of the week, I will speak to Victor. I have to."

"The important thing is to get Mort away from here." The Finn made a quick sign of the cross over his heart, then put his index finger on his lower lip a moment.

"The important thing is this: you go to the Mounties."

"I'll go."

"Tell your story to Boyd."

"I am a Finn. We are a strong people. We drive out the Commies when no one else dared. We are not weak. We face up."

Alexander wasn't sure he believed him, but as he pushed the door shut behind him and walked across the lawn with dense scent of lilac in his nostrils, he thought a thought which had occurred to him more frequently in the past months: you're lucky to be alive, Alex, you're always just damn lucky to be alive.

When he arrived back at the room he realized he'd come away with the Finn's fishing knife and he was glad then that he had not encountered any of the motel's other guests on his return—or someone from the management. It was getting late. Alexander was exhausted but he lay the knife on the bedside table and flicked on the TV while he brushed his teeth and then removed his clothes. The markets had fallen dramatically. *Pullback*, one commentator said. *Sell-off* another. A train carrying toxic chemicals had derailed west of Toronto. The weather was predicted to be unseasonably warm for the coming week—and the remainder of the summer. Mosquito infestations, the risk of hepatitis. Alexander pulled off his shoes and socks while he sat on the edge of the bed and watched the numbers from the stock markets scroll across the TV screen. He wondered how much of a hit Peter's finances would take. When he'd left Peter in the hospital, Alexander had been reminded of how he'd looked as a child, sheet pulled up to his chin, cheeks slightly flushed in sleep, a knot of red hair sticking up on the crown of his head. Alexander had leaned over and kissed one hot cheek and heard Peter's breath rattling in his throat. How long had it been since he'd done that, kissed his son? How long since he'd seen Peter asleep in bed? Something gave way in Alexander's chest and he found tears leaking from his eyes. They had hugged each other every day when Peter was ten and twelve, and he'd never shied away from telling the boy *I love you*. But not much since. Alexander found a tissue in the bathroom and blew his nose noisily. He glanced at his watch. He'd go back to the hospital at six. He'd been unable to reach Nancy in the dialysis unit but had left a message on the machine. He'd be there when she arrived from the city. Holding Peter's hand. Or stroking Ruth's forehead. As a family they'd reached the critical mass of disintegration and had passed it. He lay back on the bed with his shirt and underwear on, listening to the low burble of voices from the TV and breathing deeply through his nose. He wished Ruth was there lying next to him, warm breath on his neck, one thin arm flung across his chest. It had been a wild ride with her, but a good one. He started to think how complicated the thing with LaFlamme and the Finn and Mort and Cassie was, and then he muttered some words to the silent and dark night, and then he gave himself over to sleep.

When Alexander Mann called to ask him if the Finn had come in to make a statement, Victor told him the Finn had suddenly packed a case and gone to Finland, leaving the chicken places in the hands of their managers. Leaving a postal address to which to mail cheques but not even a phone number.

Victor asked, "You say the Finn was coming in to make a statement?"

Instead of answering directly, Alexander said, "Some remote village on the edge of Lapland, I bet."

It was late in the day. Victor's guts were acting up, a sensation like he was full of gas that had to be expelled before he would feel better. "Yes. I have called there. Have you ever heard the Finnish language spoken? It's like nothing else you'll ever hear on this earth."

"So he's effectively out of your grasp. Slipped away on you."

Victor was not used to being addressed in a censorious tone, so he responded sharply, "Oh, we can track him down through Interpol or whatever."

"You may want to do that."

"I think he was scared of something. He left in an awful hurry."

There was a long silence on the line. Victor thought Alexander was waiting for him to say something—or reconsidering the intent of his call. Alexander finally said, "He had the idea someone had killed Cassie and would come after him."

"I've been thinking in that direction myself lately."

"Someone who was desperate."

"Yes, and the Finn was desperate, too, it appears. He didn't even do up the dishes. Or turn the thermostat down."

"So you were over to his place?"

"There was a bank book on the kitchen table. He'd done well for himself with those chicken places."

"He seemed to think that Mort was in danger too."

Victor paused. He'd been eating a doughnut when the phone rang. He put it down on the paper in the middle of his desk. "I think maybe you had better come in and make a statement," he said. "You and your brother both."

MORTIMER ARRIVED AT noon the following day, a blazing hot late June day. Mirage ripples were coming off the asphalt of the parking lot. Mort extricated himself from his Buick and hobbled up the sidewalk, leaning on a cane. Victor was watching from the window of his office. He wondered if this charade was for his benefit.

When he sat down, Mortimer rested the cane against one knee and removed his baseball cap. His forehead above the mark from the rim of the cap was white. He sighed loudly. Victor wondered what Mortimer was thinking. There were many who thought he was a madman—had thought that for twenty-five years and were likely never change their minds. He'd knifed a man in the back, they said in the Lakeland, and then married the man's wife. And now that wife was dead.

"Yes," he said wearily, "we'd had a fight. Words." Victor had poured them each a coffee in a paper cup. "It was a stupid thing, about family. She wanted to have a reunion this summer and I said it was a lot of people to put up, a lot of expense and why didn't we just make it Roger and Vanora and what's-her-name and Ruth and Alex and Peter and his wife. She took that as a slight. Her cousins were as important to her as my family—even though they were only second and third cousins. She screamed at me. She was like that: when she was angry she twisted things. I pointed out to her that her children were not my family, but hers, but that I was happy to have them and always would be. She broke a dish."

"She hit you?"

"Smashed it on the floor."

Victor thought he was listening to a rehearsed speech. "That's when she decided to go pick fiddleheads?"

"She was going to do that anyway. This gave her an excuse to bang the door on the way out. You may not have known she had a temper."

"I'd heard something from Young Beaudry at the IGA."

"Yes. She broke something of his over a stupid argument."

"Cracked the glass in the front door, actually."

"She was like that. Stormed out of the house, stayed outside doing this or that, ripping out thistles with her bare hands, sulking is what it amounted to. You couldn't go near her in that mood. I tried to stop her once and she punched me in the face. Bloody nose. She was a hefty and powerful woman. After an hour or so, she would come back in and sit at my feet, weeping and saying she was just a basket case, an unworthy person."

"Up and down? Hot and cold? A roller coaster temperament."

"None of that psychiatrist crap." Mortimer sipped coffee, studying Victor over the rim of the cup. "It was just her way. She had a fiery temper. So this time was just like a lot of others. She needed time, she needed space."

"You were on top of each other out there. Things had a way of becoming tense."

"We managed good. She just needed to cool off sometimes. So that night I did not think to do anything until it was past ten. I walked down the path, calling her name but that was useless. It was dark by then and there was a strong wind. Blew the words back in my face."

Almost a month had passed but tears welled up in Mortimer's eyes as he recalled. What he would give to take that disagreement back. Victor wondered if he would end up being one of those rheumy old men in the beer parlour, resting his folded hands on the top of his cane and gazing off into space with glazed eyes. Get into the sauce in a big way.

When Mortimer had come in Victor had been eating a doughnut. Victor eyed it now and then said, "What no one seems to understand about Cassie's behaviour that night is why go down by the willows to wash the fiddleheads?"

"That was just like her. She bumbled around in those fits of sulk, feeling sorry for herself. She sort of lost it some times. She probably decided on a whim that she would wash the fiddleheads down there. Or that it was a way of getting back at me somehow. Maybe she'd planned on doing that all along, or maybe she didn't even think about it, but just found herself there and thought, here's an idea. Who knows?"

They left a silence. That was the usual with Mortimer. He looked up at the ceiling and then tapped the tip of the cane on the floor. He would rather be anywhere but in Victor's office, Victor thought, this heavy man whose hand swallowed the knob of the cane as if it was a chopstick.

Victor said, "This is all a pile of old crap. I know that."

"She had a terrible temper. And you saw the fiddleheads."

"What I saw was a little pile of manila envelopes on the kitchen table at the Finn's place. And a booklet of stamps. He'd written an address on the topmost one, is my guess, using the others as a kind of pad underneath. When I examined the upper one of the little pile that was left I could just about make out the address: each of the two names he'd written began with an M. Just like Mortimer Mann begins with two Ms."

"Maybe," Mort sniffed, "or maybe not. That could have been any two words."

"But I did a little sniffing around at the post office and Elsie tells me you were sent an envelope just like that the day before yesterday."

"So what?"

"You've had the car tuned up at the Shell."

"Jesus. You get around."

"People around town say you've sold the lodge and you're leaving."

Mortimer's head was bowed. He breathed heavily. "It's nobody's business but mine."

"We could be calling Cassie's death a murder."

"Jesus. McNair has been telling me for years to move to Calgary."

"So all of a sudden you're taking his advice? Why now?"

"It's this lung condition. The air is dry out there, I'll be able to breathe."

"You're scared, is what."

"It's time for a change, what with Cassie gone. Time for a fresh start."

"You and the Finn both. Scared out of your trees."

Mortimer studied him a moment and then said, "I offered the place to Roger but he wasn't interested. He thought it should go back to the Indians—the Natives."

"I hear the tribal council has made you a generous offer."

"Enough for me to buy a little place in Calgary. If it's any of your business." His voice had turned thin. "And I'll leave it to the kids when I pass away, so the three of them can split up the proceeds."

"Did the Finn tell you why you had to get out?"

Mortimer either didn't hear him or chose to disregard the question. "They each get an equal share of the proceeds. It's all above board."

Victor said, "He figured it out, is my guess. The Finn figured out that Cassie met someone that night—or was ambushed by someone."

"That's ridiculous. No one was out there but me."

"Someone who smoked du Maurier and dropped the butts on the rocks."

"The only person who'd been out in weeks was this guy, Spanos, who came to look at the cabins with an eye to renting the whole lot. He was organizing a family reunion kind of thing. We talked about how many cabins and so on and walked about the site a little. I haven't heard from him since."

"And this Spanos, he left a business card or a phone number?"

"No, people come and have a look. Sometimes you hear back, sometimes not. It's part of the business. You can't count on people to follow through."

"In my experience, you can count on them to act badly. Your wife's uncle, for instance. You know about him?"

"I know he made Cassie marry that bastard, LaFlamme."

"He was involved with two other men during the war. They operated some kind of scam. I found this out from an army lawyer years ago, after LaFlamme was killed. Long afterwards, actually. I did a little sniffing around when I was working at fingerprints in the city. The scam involved Sam Roby and Old Beaudry and somebody known as the Greek. They ripped off whole carloads of war matériel, eggs, butter, rubber, things that fetched high prices in those days. The army couldn't figure out how they were scamming the stuff or what they did with it. The stuff must have gone to the States and been sold for huge profits. The Greeks in Chicago are as organized as the Italians and know how to dispose of contraband. Did the Finn tell you that?"

"He didn't know any of that. It sounds like a made-up story."

"Maybe so. Only each of those three guys came out of the war with a nice little pile of cash. Beaudry bought the IGA in town. Roby renovated the trading post at Moon Lake. The Greek opened a diner on the edge of the city. Those three crooks made a lot of money and by the time LaFlamme came along their families had grown comfortable with the good life. There was a lot at stake."

"You're saying if the army found out they'd take everything back?"

Victor sipped from his cup of coffee. Someone was walking down the hall in heavy boots. They thudded on the carpeted floor dully. In his head he felt that way himself: clunking along. "I don't think they can now. Too much time has passed. It's almost fifty years since they ran the scam. But at the time LaFlamme was murdered, it would have meant not just losing the profits of their thievery but prison too."

"For Old Beaudry, you mean, and this Greek character. They would lose out if someone squealed to the army, someone like LaFlamme."

"Yes, for both of them, since Sam Roby died in the sixties."

"They're vindictive, those army types. I'm glad I sold the place, so they can't come after me."

"The Finn figured out, see, that LaFlamme was tangled up in that scam somehow—blackmail, is my guess. LaFlamme and Young Beaudry lit into each other in the Lakeland just before LaFlamme was murdered. An argument over money, people said."

"He was milking them."

"Maybe the Beaudrys had had enough."

Mortimer said nothing, just sat there with his eyes blinking and breathing heavily. "But then it all just died away after LaFlamme was gone?"

"Until recently. No one would have wanted to stir that stuff around. But Cassie must have stumbled across something."

"She was digging around in the family history. I told her it was nutsy to dig up the past. But she'd been to visit Old Beaudry a couple of times. I thought she just wanted him to see some old photos." Mortimer leaned back in the chair and closed his eyes. There was tension in his face. The past few days had taken a lot out of him. Victor could well imagine him out at Moon Lake that morning, combing his hair, dressing with care to make a good show in town.

"Cassie's visit might have been that innocent." Victor said, but he didn't believe it.

"You're saying she was getting too close."

"She may have smelled the rat."

"So it was Beaudry," Mort said. "Young Beaudry who went after Cassie?"

"That's what the Finn believed. And what he wrote to you and posted you in that manila envelope. But no, it was not Beaudry who did in Cassie. It was the son of the Greek—or maybe his son-in-law. The detachment in the city has had an eye on them for years."

"You tipped them off?"

"It's always stuck under my skin, the LaFlamme thing. Like a burr. And they're into other things—shady dealings at the track."

Mortimer's eyes shifted from Victor's to something over Victor's head, out of the window. There was relief in his eyes, Victor saw, the same relief he'd recognized in Roger's voice on the parking lot of the hospital. It was finally over, the LaFlamme thing. They might stop talking in the Lakeland now, accusing with their eyes and tongues. And anyway, he would be gone, living in the shadow of the mountains, far from the scrub bush and the lakes of the Shield, breathing the dry air he claimed would rejuvenate his lungs. Mortimer shifted his eyes back to Victor's. "So the RCMP are going to pick them up, these Greeks?"

"Soon, yes. We're finally going to put the LaFlamme business to rest."

Mortimer said, "I'm glad the place is going back to the Indians—the Natives."

Victor looked at the doughnut on the table. Fats, yeasts. He considered it a small triumph that he had been able to push it away. He said, "The net is closing in on them as we speak. We've been holding back, but we're about to make a move on them."

"I'm glad I'm getting out. Twenty-five years at Moon Lake is enough. It's starting to weigh on me." He pursed his lips together, as if he intended to be silent now for good. Victor remembered how angry he had been that day when they were searching for Cassie out at Moon Lake. His narrow mouth, his tightly-closed lips. His wife was dead, his stepchildren had gone their own ways, but he would go on, too, breathing heavily, turning grey, remembering fondly a time when he was young and powerful, as men do.

The silence they left this time was broken only by the ticking in the radiators. "That's why I wanted to have you in here," Victor said. "Go to Calgary, yes, get out, but do not stop in the city, do not make any contact with the Beaudrys or the Greeks."

"No fear there," Mortimer said, tapping his cane. He was anxious to go.

"I hope not. They're dangerous and their backs are to the wall. But it's just a matter of days now. Hours maybe. We nab them and we put the business to rest."

AND Victor recalled an exchange that made sense to him now. He had visited the psych ward in the city. The psychiatrist in charge had invited him to join the group Sheila went to on Friday afternoons for therapy. The psychiatrist talked a little at first. Two sisters in a farm community near the American border had cut off one of their husband's balls and penis. He'd been cheating on his wife. She and her sister laid for him, tipped him upside down in a rain barrel and cut off his parts with the jagged top of a juice tin. It was a Mennonite community. The sisters were ordinary women: they bowled on Tuesday nights and sang in the church choir on Sundays. The whole town was in shock. As the psychiatrist talked, he edged forward on his chair. They were sitting in a circle, eight or so patients and the psychiatrist and Victor. The chairs were stacking chairs and not comfortable but no one seemed to notice except Victor. The psychiatrist was a man in his sixties. The hair on top of his head was white. He wore a sweater but as he told them the story he pulled the sweater over his head and threw it onto the floor at his feet. Sweat was running down his cheeks. Victor remembered being warm himself.

Family members hurt each other, the psychiatrist was telling them. That was the point of the story. Or they did cruel things to others to protect each other. It was all part of the same web of feelings: a kind of territory business, only in blood. Think of the Irish troubles, think of the Mafia.

"I could have did that," one woman in the circle said. She had frizzy red hair and she smoked and fidgeted as she talked.

The psychiatrist nodded.

Someone else said, "Smack the cheating bastard, yes, hit him with a baseball bat, but slice into his scrotum?"

They talked about that, agreeing that things were bad when little boys murdered little girls: television, the influence of pop stars, corruption in high places. They were drinking coffee. Victor remembered that it was strong coffee. His heart was racing throughout the conversation. The psychiatrist sipped from his coffee mug and looked around the circle. He raised his eyebrows, which were black and bushy, at Victor. The patients were all waiting for the psychiatrist to speak. Sheila had told Victor how much she and the others admired him. "I have no doubt," the psychiatrist said, "that I could do that. Tear the clothes off and slash into the flesh with the jagged tin."

Someone said, "Your own wife?"

The woman with red hair said, "The wife or husband most of all. There's that kind of wild love, so there's that kind of wild hate. It cuts both ways."

The psychiatrist said, "Families. The emotions are that intense."

Sheila told them about what had happened at Moon Lake.

"Stabbing someone in the back," said a woman who had spoken before. "No."

"You stick the knife in," the woman with red hair said, "then you stick it in again and again. It's something about the blood. You can't help yourself."

"I don't believe in that," Victor said. "Blood lust."

"We're killers," the red-head said. "We kill animals to eat. But more important, we kill out of hate. Sometimes in moments of passion, but others with cold calculation."

"Yes," the psychiatrist said, "families do that." He stared out the bank of windows that looked down on a quadrangle of grass in front of the hospital. The windows were open. Sounds came up from the street: car motors, voices of hospital workers going off shift for the day. The room was silent and then the psychiatrist simply nodded and sipped from his coffee mug. He was inviting them to look into themselves, to the black holes at their centres of their being, places that were difficult to imagine and even harder to acknowledge as part of ordinary human life. The meeting broke up shortly after that.

In the hallway Victor said to Sheila, "I'm glad that's over."

Sheila said, "You don't like him, do you? You don't like the fact he tells the truth about all our weaknesses."

"He's sick. He's supposed to be helping you get better, and he's the sick one."

"You're afraid, Vic," she said. "You're a frightened little man who cannot face the blackness inside himself."

"I wrestle evil every day."

"The evil in others. You became a cop so you could fight the darkness in others, which is one way to avoid it in yourself."

They had gone for a walk around the hospital grounds before he left, walking in silence. Then he left Sheila at the hospital and drove back to Beausejour alone. They had never spoken about the therapy session again. He did not want to think about the darkness inside himself. He believed that if you entertained the idea of evil, then you as good as embraced it in your heart.

EARLIER WHEN IT HAD been touching the horizon the moon was a blood orange, splashing golden light over the length of the lake, from the narrows to where she was sitting on the twin rocks. It was higher now and turning bright white as it climbed the sky. She looked for the dippers. The north star was so bright it seemed to be blazing. A moment ago a loon had called and just before that two mallards had started up from the bulrushes and beat their way noisily along the edge of the willows. A soft and warm summer breeze, water lapping gently against the stones and rocks below her. As a girl she had sat here for hours, thinking what tomorrow held, what shape her future would take once she left Moon Lake. She had imagined lovers but not Karrin; she'd imagined teaching but not massage therapy; she'd imagined frightening moments but not one that led her on a spiritual journey to her liberated self.

She had not imagined Vanessa, Leonora, Vanora.

Just last weekend she had channelled into the eighteenth century to Corfe Castle, where she was Deirdre, sister to the lady of the castle. They sat on an expansive lawn, drinking lemonade and watching two boys in blue short pants and wool sweaters play croquet, the sons of Mara. Someone said *lovely*, and she saw there were English tea biscuits on a plate. The boys were playing at a distance. In the falling sunshine, the lawn was such a brilliant green that it hurt the eyes to stare at it. There were no other sounds on the lawn. Somehow she knew things were not that well between Mara and her husband, the Lord of Corfe Castle. She reached out and touched Mara's small and delicate hand. A voice told her to do this. Mara looked up and smiled and seemed about to say something, but then Vanora found herself falling through the clouds and back to the room where she and Angela and Sally were holding hands on the new carpet Karrin had bought. Her head had hurt slightly, as it did now.

Vanora closed her eyes and inhaled from the pipe she held in one hand. It had a long thin stem and a tiny bowl at the end. Earlier she had tamped in the leaves Roger had given her when he'd made her a gift of the pipe: crushed foxglove mixed with milk thistle; Indian tobacco, they'd called it as kids. You puffed at it but did not inhale. It tickled the back of your nose the way Gareth's marijuana had done in the seventies, but it did not burn the throat and you did not have to choke the smoke back into your lungs, as they'd had to with the marijuana. With this it was a simple formula: hold in the mouth cavity a minute, then exhale through the nose. You felt sleepy, dreamy. Roger said the leaves contained an element that elevated basal metabolism. The Natives had known this for centuries. The mixture gave you a pleasant buzz, but also a mild drug that boosted the immune system. She puffed at the pipe. Even if the mixture wasn't as effective as Roger claimed, it felt good to hold the pipe and to puff the thin smoke into the air.

She closed her eyes again and when she opened them she heard an owl in the distance. She'd never asked Cassie about whether a bird had flown into the house before LaFlamme was murdered, and she never would now. She glanced over at Karrin, who was sitting cross-legged on a rock higher up, meditating. Her eyes were closed. She sat motionless sometimes for almost an hour. Then when she was finished, she blinked her eyes open as if she had been sleeping. Sometimes tears ran down her cheeks. Karrin said that the water from tear ducts is a release. Vanora was getting better at meditating. She liked the flickering candle, though not the music Karrin sometimes played. She preferred channeling, transforming into a new self rather than exploring the old one.

Earlier in the afternoon she had walked around the property and visited the deer meadow and the breaking. The deer meadow was overgrown with grasses that came up to the thigh: daisies, brown-eyed Susans, sedges of various kinds, thistles. The rich odour of pollens that gave people with allergies asthma and skin rashes. The deer no longer fed there. They had moved deeper into the forest. From the highest point of the meadow she saw the collapsed railroad station house, a pile of wooden rubble now. Mortimer had tended to the breaking and the oats field through the seventies but then prices fell and the plot was too small to bother cultivating. Maples had sprouted in the breaking. The poplars stood twenty feet high. And stumps of firs that had been left on the edges of the fields had restarted themselves and towered over her head. Nature was taking her own back. In twenty years it would be impossible to tell that the grey Fordson tractor had once dragged a plough across the land and that Mortimer had seeded spring crops for cash. The ground was thick with rough grass again and plants that snagged your clothing when you walked too deep in. The oat seed, the cultivated fields, the fallow were now lying in the shadow of time. She wondered, not for the first time, what it would be like to live there, out on the edge of everything that was not human. To live with the seasons and nature's brutal round, season after season—rocks, water, trees, birds—into oblivion. Did you turn a little dopey yourself?

It was July already, two days after Canada Day, silly celebrations, but kids liked them. They would have to get used to that now. They had hoped the baby would be processed for them by the end of June, but they both realized it might never happen, the official world being what it was. There were other ways, and she had a candidate picked out, if it came to that. Karrin agreed with her about the mixing of races. They thought June was a good name, a name connected to the seasonal round, though not a name that the baby's ancestors would have chosen. Maybe they could consult with Archie Cloud and pick out a Native name. In any case, it would not be long now before a child was with them. They would bring her up to the sacred rock plateau deep in the forest and sit cross-legged in the sun. Roger could teach her bush lore and Archie could explain about mother earth and the spirit world. They could learn the names of the native plants and wildflowers, learn the cycles of nature, the round of germination, growth, and decay. She would get Archie to explain about the powwow and the magic of circles. There was a lot for her to learn too. She wondered if the pile of white bones Archie had shown her at the lip of the escarpment still was visible from the ledge. Had it been something like a buffalo jump? Yes, at the very least they would ask Archie to be the girl's godfather and to help them choose a Native name.

It would have been fitting for Cassie to have seen the baby. Would Cassie have approved? Vanora had the feeling Mortimer did not, but he had said only encouraging words. What would LaFlamme have thought? In a way it was an expiation of a kind, the baby, a personal undoing of his vile treatment of the Natives over all those years, and an absolution for the family in general. She'd heard Alexander telling someone once years ago about how everything comes round to whoever has patience. The Wheel of Fortune. She did not exactly believe in that but it gave her some comfort. So much of life was circling back to where we'd started to begin all over again: Moon Lake, Emerald Lake, Moon Lake. The circular medallion between her breasts glinting moonlight: Sirona.

She could not remember the first time she had come to the twin rocks to watch the moon over the lake but she knew it had become the habit of her girlhood, especially when things were going badly with her parents and she needed to get away. She knew every crack and cranny on the rocks, had run her fingers raw on them some nights. She had picked clean of lichen several spots on the round hummock of granite. She knew the contours of the terrain like those of her own body. In the curve of the tiny bay the trees formed a shelter and the wind did not blow as strongly there. Every night after the moon was high overhead, an owl fluttered down from the trees and sat watching the lake. They did not usually do that, expose themselves. She had hugged her arms round her knees and studied its hooked beak, the little twitches in its body, and the tiny tufts of feathers that stuck out where its head and neck met. She hardly dare breathe. Minutes passed and the owl suddenly took flight into the trees again. It did not hoot. It did not seem to be hunting. Like her it watched the water for a period, then, refreshed, left.

That was a long time ago.

Yes, it was a beautiful place, once a magical place, but it could not be that for her now. Too much darkness, too much death. In that way it was not like Emerald Lake, which was a deeply spiritual place where you sensed the astral plane and the possibilities of psychokinesis. It was an odd thought, but Vanora believed now that the lake did not want them there, perhaps it never had. It had pushed them away—her and Cassie and Ruth and Roger, as well as LaFlamme and the Robys, who came before them. White people who exploited the lake and the forest but did not understand the spiritual aspect of mother earth. It was the Native's place. Roger was right about that.

Something moved to her left. She looked over and saw that Karrin had come to the end of her meditation. Her eyes were bright and she smiled before slowly uncrossing her legs and standing. Vanora stood too. She was feeling a little bloated. One of her patients had told her last week about a diet of whole grains immersed in chicken broth and steamed in a steamer. Good for the bowels. Vanora had rummaged in Cassie's cupboards earlier that day and had found wheat, which she'd mixed with a pinch of saffron. Mortimer hadn't complained but he hadn't eaten more than a few forkfuls. Karrin had pronounced it delicious. "Add a little chili sauce," she said, "and perfecto."

When they got back to the city, she would try barley, perhaps with the sorrel soup Karrin liked: garlic, ginger, parsley. Vanora glanced at the lake. One last look. It was a beautiful place, and they would come out with Roger to visit, the child and Roger and Pagouk, but it was not a place she could ever think of as home again. Bad karma. She almost laughed aloud, but she knew that it was true. She brushed away a mosquito that had been buzzing around her head for a few seconds and then stepped up to where Karrin was standing studying the lake. She took her hand and stood in silence beside her. The moon glistened on the rippling water. The waves striking the stones shushed as they had for centuries. Yes. They would bring the child to visit.

When the moon was high overhead, the wind which had been agitating the lake into small choppy whitecaps earlier in the day died to a breeze and then the breeze fell off to barely more than a whisper of breath over the water's rippling surface. A flock of small birds that had been stirred up near the barley field flew over the lodge and dipped sharply at the shore, then wheeled and settled in the willows well down from the twin rocks, chittering a few times before falling silent. A tree crashed in the woods. Two crows fluttered down from the pines. One snapped at something lodged between a nest of white rocks, a cigarette butt, and the other flapped its wings and beat them about and then the first crow flipped the butt out of its beak and the other one hopped over to it and stabbed it up, but in a moment lost interest and also flipped it away. A meadowlark called from near the lodge. The crows tilted their glossy heads in that direction, their beady eyes picking up reflected light from the lake's surface. They opened their wings and rose as one and flew off in the opposite direction, toward the narrows. Water dripped off the willows and plocked on the rocks. The water coming ashore was little more than a susurration. What might have been a beaver smacked the lake's surface, the hollow sound travelling a great distance over still air, like an echo. Then followed a deep silence that might have been the silence of the centuries before mankind. Clouds obscured the moon for a while and then a kind of thin mist began to rise off the lake. It was difficult to tell but it looked as if something was floating on the surface of the water a considerable distance out; it looked like flotsam from a fishing expedition, or a large dead fish, or a long piece of driftwood, or maybe just the shadow of a high cloud caught in the beams of the moon hanging now directly over the lake.